Praise for *The Shadow Cabinet*

"The brilliant and fast-paced second contemporary political fantasy in Dawson's HMRC trilogy (after *Her Majesty's Royal Coven*) takes the series to new heights. . . . Dawson handles the tricky middle book with aplomb, raising the stakes and deepening the rich worldbuilding without losing sight of the pathos that makes her characters shine. Magic seamlessly weaves with pop culture references, fun soap-operatic twists, and an incisive look at the psychology of violent misogyny. This is the work of a master storyteller." —*Publishers Weekly* (starred review)

"The fast pace keeps the many stories moving as the points of view shift, and once again Dawson places a bombshell at the end to surprise readers. The second book of the series, after *Her Majesty's Royal Coven*, is filled with witty dialogue, pop culture references, and features the bonds of childhood, sisterhood, and fighting for what one believes in." —*Library Journal*

Praise for *Her Majesty's Royal Coven*

"There's so much humor and sadness here, so much tenderness and compassion and a deep love of women. The book draws a gentle thread through the visions we have for ourselves, the memories from which we build our relationships, and the ways in which we comprehend the present, and then it pulls that thread taut. Superb and almost unbearably charming, *Her Majesty's Royal Coven* is a beautiful exploration of how foundational friendships age, and it expertly launches an exciting new trilogy." —*The N*

D1432046

"*Her Majesty's Royal Coven* is a shimmering, irresistible cauldron's brew of my favorite things: a thrilling, witchy plot; a diverse, compelling, and beautifully drawn cast; complex relationships with real heart; laugh-out-loud banter; and the kind of dazzling magic I wish existed. You won't be able to put it down."

—Lana Harper, *New York Times* bestselling author of
Payback's a Witch

"Juno Dawson is at the top of her game in this vibrant and meticulous take on witchcraft. Her characteristic wit and grit shine through *Her Majesty's Royal Coven*, which paints a convincing picture of how magic might converge with the modern world."

—Samantha Shannon, *New York Times* bestselling author of
The Bone Season and *The Priory of the Orange Tree*

"Talk about a gut punch of a novel. *Her Majesty's Royal Coven* is sure to have readers who love witchy stories—and the queerer, the better—salivating from the very first page. . . . This book has more twists, betrayals, and drama than a *Desperate Housewives* episode, and I lived for that. . . . A provocative exploration of intersectional feminism, loyalty, gender, and transphobia, Dawson's *Her Majesty's Royal Coven* is an immersive story about what it means to be a woman—and a witch—and invites readers into an intricately woven web of magic, friendship, and power."

—The Nerd Daily

"Dawson, in an impressive flex, uses the rules of the fantasy genre to make a statement about people of color and LGBTQ individuals and how organizations can exclude and ignore them. Readers who enjoy witches and watching change ripple through a culture will enjoy this series." —*Booklist* (starred review)

"A femme-forward story of power, morality, and fate that is not shy about its politics. . . . Beyond its politics, what especially makes *Her Majesty's Royal Coven* shine is its impeccable voice. Dawson's conversational, matter-of-fact tone calls to mind writers like Neil Gaiman and Diana Wynne Jones; it's at times funny, at others heartbreaking, but always perfectly calibrated. . . . A thoughtful entry into the witch canon that intrigues and challenges as much as it delights."

—*BookPage*

"Juno Dawson has created your new obsession. *Her Majesty's Royal Coven* is full of her trademark heart and humor, with a delicious slick of darkness. I fell in love with her coven—and I need the next installment now!"

—Kiran Millwood Hargrave, author of *The Mercies*

"Such a joy to read—the world-building is incredible, the writing sophisticated, and the exploration of gender and identity is done with nuance and care. Utterly compelling."

—Louise O'Neill, author of *Asking for It* and *The Surface Breaks*

"The funniest paranormal epic I've ever had the pleasure to read."
—Nicole Galland, bestselling author of *Master of the Revels*

"Look, if the idea of a story about a group of girls living in an alternate England and working for a centuries-old secret government bureau of witches doesn't grab you immediately, I don't know what to tell you. Except that there's also a witch civil war, an oracle that prophecies a young warlock will bring about genocide, and a group of friends torn about how to stop it."

—*Paste*

"Cleverly constructed . . . A gradually building layer of political commentary ultimately reveals a complex metaphor for the UK's sociopolitical climate and mainstream transphobia. . . . An exciting new direction for Dawson. Readers will be eager for the next installment." —*Publishers Weekly*

"This first adult novel by YA author Dawson (*Clean*; *Meat Market*) is a story of feminism, matriarchy, gender roles, and tradition. . . . Readers who love a big fight between good and evil, who enjoy seeing magic in the everyday world, and those who like their heroine's journeys to include all facets of heartbreak will savor the cut and thrust of this battle." —*Library Journal*

EIVIND HANSEN

PENGUIN BOOKS

THE SHADOW CABINET

Juno Dawson is the #1 *Sunday Times* bestselling novelist, screen-writer, journalist, and a columnist for *Attitude* magazine. Juno's books include *Her Majesty's Royal Coven* as well as the global bestsellers *This Book Is Gay* and *Clean*. She also writes for television and created the official Doctor Who audio drama *Doctor Who: Redacted*. An occasional actress and model, Juno appeared in the BBC's *I May Destroy You* (2020). *The Shadow Cabinet* is the second book in the HMRC trilogy. She lives in Brighton, UK, with her husband and chihuahua.

JUNO DAWSON

THE SHADOW CABINET

★ A NOVEL ★

BOOK 2 IN THE HMRC TRILOGY

PENGUIN
BOOKS

PENGUIN BOOKS
An imprint of Penguin Random House LLC
penguinrandomhouse.com

First published in Great Britain by HarperVoyager,
an imprint of HarperCollins*Publishers* Ltd, 2023
Published in Penguin Books 2023

LIBRARY OF CONGRESS CATALOGING-IN-PUBLICATION DATA
Names: Dawson, Juno, author.
Title: The shadow cabinet / Juno Dawson.
Description: First edition. | New York : Penguin Books, [2023] |
Ahead of title: HMRC.
Identifiers: LCCN 2023007439 (print) | LCCN 2023007440 (ebook) |
ISBN 9780143137153 (paperback) | ISBN 9780593511145 (ebook)
Subjects: LCGFT: Fantasy fiction. | Novels.
Classification: LCC PR6104.A8868 S53 2023 (print) |
LCC PR6104.A8868 (ebook) | DDC 823/.92—dc23/eng/20220215
LC record available at https://lccn.loc.gov/2023007439
LC ebook record available at https://lccn.loc.gov/2023007440

Printed in the United States of America
1   3   5   7   9   10   8   6   4   2

Set in Sabon LT Std

Dedicated to anyone who ever felt
that they were second best

The devil doth generally mark them with a private mark, by reason the witches have confessed themselves, that the devil doth lick them with his tongue in some privy part of their body, before he doth receive them to be his servants, which mark commonly is given them under the hair in some part of their body, whereby it may not easily be found out or seen, although they be searched.

From *Daemonologie* by King James I, 1597

Grab 'em by the pussy.

Donald Trump, 2005

WHO'S WHO

Hebden Bridge

Niamh Kelly – Level 5 Adept
Last seen visiting her comatose sister, Ciara, at a coven safehouse in Manchester. Romantically involved with Luke Watts, Niamh lost her fiancé, Conrad Chen, during Dabney Hale's warlock uprising a decade ago. Niamh is presently fostering orphaned teenager, Theo Wells.

Ciara Kelly – Level 5 Adept
Ciara lost a vicious fight with her twin sister during the uprising, and has been in a coma for almost a decade. During the civil unrest, she supported renegade warlock Dabney Hale.

Elle Pearson – Level 4 Healer
Community Nurse Elle recently told her non-magical husband, Jez, that she is a witch.

Theodora 'Theo' Wells – Adept (Level TBC)
While already identifying as female, Theo underwent a physical transformation by combining her powers with her adoptive guardian, Niamh. Theo was previously thought to be the legendary 'Sullied Child' a harbinger of the demon, Leviathan.

Holly Pearson – Sentient (Level TBC)
Elle's youngest child recently discovered she is a witch, and previously had a crush on Theo.

Helena Vance (deceased)
Formerly High Priestess of Her Majesty's Royal Coven, Helena betrayed her sisters by invoking the demon Belial in a bid to kill Theo, and thwart the Sullied Child prophecy.

Snow Vance-Morrill – Elemental (Level TBC)
Helena's teenage daughter was taken away from Hebden Bridge by her grandparents to escape the shame of her mother's actions.

Luke Watts – Mundane
Luke runs a grocery service, and is currently dating Niamh.

Jeremy 'Jez' Pearson – Mundane
Elle's husband, a mechanic, is – unbeknownst to his wife – having an affair with a local hotel receptionist called Jessica.

Milo Pearson – Mundane
Elle and Jez's eldest child has no magical ability but attends the same school as Theo and Holly.

Rev. Sheila Henry – Level 3 Sentient
The reverend founded Coven Pride and sits on the board of HMRC.

Annie Device (deceased)
Helena murdered Elle's grandmother to cover up her secret alliance with the demon Belial.

London

Leonie Jackman – Level 6 Sentient

Founder of Diaspora, an independent coven for witches and warlocks of colour. Her brother, Radley, is currently AWOL, hunting the disgraced warlock Dabney Hale.

Chinara Okafor – Level 6 Elemental

Leonie's long-time girlfriend is an immigration lawyer at a non-profit. She is keen to start a family with Leonie.

Her Majesty's Royal Coven (HMRC) – Manchester

Moira Roberts – Level 5 Sentient

The Chief Cailleach of Scotland is Acting High Priestess following Helena's execution.

Irina Konvalinka – Level 6 Oracle

The Lead Oracle foresaw the arrival of the 'Sullied Child' and heralds the eventual rise of Leviathan.

Sandhya Kaur – Level 3 Sentient

Executive Assistant to the High Priestess.

The Warlock's Cabal – Manchester

Radley Jackman – Level 3 Healer

The High Priest, Leonie's brother, embarked on a mission to apprehend Dabney Hale after he absconded from Grierlings, the coven prison.

Dabney Hale – Level 6 Adept

The renegade warlock attempted a coup on the

basis of magical supremacy. He tricked Helena into aiding his escape from Grierlings, and he remains at large.

Celestial Beings

Gaia – The term, used by many witches in the west, to describe a divine feminine creator goddess. Witches believe they are Gaia's emissaries on earth.

Satanis – The most powerful of the demons trapped within Gaia's reality. Centuries ago, early witches split this entity into three weaker parts: Belial, Lucifer and Leviathan.

Belial – the Demon King of Hate.

Lucifer – the Demon King of Want.

Leviathan – the Demon King of Fear.

THE SHADOW CABINET

35 YEARS AGO . . .

Galway, Ireland

To this day, people talk about the storm that hit Ireland when Miranda Kelly went to Inishmaan. They say the sea and the sky and the cliffs were a single grey mass, and if the sun had bothered to rise at all, no one would know it.

Squeaky wipers moved water back and forth over the windscreen, and Miranda hunched over the steering wheel, squinting at the road ahead. She had a nine-hour window to get out to the island and home again before Brendan returned from Dublin. Today was her one chance. She knew she ought to be glad of his attentiveness, but their quaint fisherman's cottage in Galway was starting to feel like a prison.

The signage for Rossaveel Port was illuminated, and she turned off the main road, the car almost drifting over surface water like a pond skater. The ferry port was well-lit and she slowed into the car park. Her stomach sank as she saw the ticket office was shut. A man in a hi-vis jacket waved her down. She lowered the window an inch or two.

He said something in Irish, gesturing at the turbulent skies.

'I must get to the island,' Miranda said in English, her Irish not nearly good enough.

'Won't be happening today, darlin'. You go on home.' He looked at her like she was mad and hurried out of the storm.

Turning back wasn't an option. Miranda parked the Escort and grabbed her raincoat from the passenger seat, tucking her red hair under the collar of her jumper. She stepped out into an onslaught of wind and rain. The familiar old Aran Island ferry swayed and tilted in port, a dog on a leash. Clutching her hood over her face, Miranda ran past the ferry terminal to the small marina where the fishing boats were docked, clinking and clanging in their moorings. Someone *had* to be on one of them.

Sure enough, there was a thin light glowing inside one of the cockpits, the silhouette of a man moving within. Miranda ran alongside the tugboat, waving frantically. The fisherman wiped condensation from the window, perhaps checking he wasn't imagining the strange woman. 'Hello?' she called.

The fisherman, his white beard yellowed with nicotine, emerged from the cabin. 'You all right there, love?'

'I need to get to Inishmaan!' Miranda shouted against the wind. 'Are you sailing today?'

'In this?' He looked at her as if she was crazed. 'You out of your mind?'

Miranda wanted to shake him, to scream in his face, make him understand. Instead, she fought to keep her tone even. 'I *have* to.'

'You're on your own there, love.' With a patronising shake of his head, he ducked back inside the cabin.

He wasn't wrong. She *couldn't* do this on her own. Miranda wasn't a powerful enough witch to make the crossing by flight. At least not *yet*. As the babies grew, so did her abilities.

She had *hoped* it wouldn't come to this. 'You will take me to the island.'

He stopped dead in his tracks and turned to face her. Rain ran off his bulbous nose, cherry red from cold, or drink, or both. He looked blankly at her, almost comically vacant. 'I will take you to the island.'

Miranda stepped, cautiously, onto the boat, cradling her swollen belly as she went. She read him. He was called Seamus. 'Seamus, we will be safe. This I promise you. Now, go. Quick as you can.'

With a morning sickness that lasted well into most afternoons, she was used to feeling nauseous. The boat was tossed over surging, murky waters. With raw, pink hands, Miranda gripped a rail inside the cab, doing everything she could to keep the ship steady. Since she'd become pregnant, her powers had increased. Never before would she have been able to steady the vessel in such turbulent waters. It scared her. Her little coven in Galway were stumped, and even Brendan's contacts at the Cailleacha had told her there was absolutely no evidence that unborn children harbour supernormal abilities.

So how are they doing this? What is growing inside of me?

Another wave reared over the bow and she focused her mind. If this trip became suicide, what would Brendan think of her? She had left no note, no word with the coven. No one, not even her friends, knew of her plans.

Perhaps Aoife, or Laura, would figure it out. Why else would a witch be travelling to Inishmaan, least of all one in her condition?

As her concentration slipped, poor Seamus seemed to become more aware of his surroundings. 'Keep going!' Miranda demanded, hardly recognising the mettle in her own voice.

Away from the port, the waves seemed to calm themselves, the sea instead swelling like the belly of a great beast, breathing in and out, out and in. The little tugboat did the best it could to vault these peaks.

When the lights of the coastline became hazily visible through the spray, Miranda dropped to her knees, spent. They had *almost* made it. Seamus still had to steer them into harbour. Once more, Miranda used her gift to stabilise the boat, drive through the waves. The hull creaked and strained. She should have brought an elemental, let them in on her plans.

On seeing the vessel approach, a pair of men raced down from the lifeboat station, steering them into dock. One grizzled, silver-haired man threw him a line and reeled them in. 'Seamus, man! Are you feckin' deranged?'

Miranda pushed past Seamus on deck. 'Leave us,' she told the newcomer. He obeyed, both men mindlessly heading to the cottage. She turned to Seamus. 'You will wait for me here.' She wiped rain from her face and stepped onto the jetty, a single long strip of concrete jutting into the sea. Waves battered the port, sloshing over the gangplank. Miranda strode towards land with purpose.

In much better weather, Brendan had once brought her to the Aran Islands as a tourist. It had been many years ago, after she finally made the move to Galway, and they'd come to see the Céad on St Patrick's Day. The islands were remote, beautiful, a taste of what Ireland was, and in places still is, hundreds of years earlier. Brendan told her they'd only got electricity here in the seventies.

The islands had an innate power of their own, a Level 1 would sense it. The millennia in the limestone sang their ancient aria as she reached the road – if you could call it that. There was a desolate taxi rank – a corrugated iron shack really – just outside the marina, and there was a light on. Thank the goddess. Inishmaan was the least populated of the islands, and she'd feared a lengthy walk.

She found the office locked, but banged on the door until a red-faced woman peered through a gap. 'What do you want?' she said. 'Port's closed today.'

'I need to get to Doolin Cottage,' Miranda shouted over the wind.

The woman's face twisted in barely concealed disgust. 'You girls comin' from the mainland. Oh aye, we know what you're after. Yer a disgrace; think about that poor wee child.'

Miranda's hands flew to her bump. It wasn't an abortion she was after. 'It's not what you think.'

Recognition, and then fear, flickered on the woman's face. 'You've no business here. There's no one on this whole island who'll take you there, witch.'

Miranda braced herself. 'You *will* take me to Doolin Cottage.'

She repeated the regrettable process all the way across the island, controlling the sour woman, Gráinne, from the backseat of her taxi. Women, in general, were more wilful than men, harder to direct.

In the hills, the roads were little more than lanes, drystone walls dividing them from endless pastures, silver grasses rippling in the gales. Gráinne brought the car to a halt, rain tapping like nuts and bolts on the roof. 'What are you doing? Keep going.'

'It's up there,' she replied, her voice leaden. 'You have to walk from here. No roads to where you're going.'

'Very well. Wait here.' The command would ruminate in the woman's mind for an hour or so at least. It bought her some time.

Miranda fastened her soggy coat once more, and stepped into the endless weather. Lashed by wind, she shouldered her way uphill, following a well-trodden, muddy track. She was almost over the hump before she saw first a ramshackle stone wall, and then the half-ruined cottage beyond it. It squatted, a thatched gargoyle on the hill, overlooking the cliffs in the distance. No one would come here by happenstance, and perhaps that was the point.

A rusted gate hung off its hinges, and Miranda took care not to rip it off entirely. There was no garden as such, only a handful of spindle trees with few leaves to show for themselves. Dim paraffin light hummed from inside the cottage. *Someone* was home. Miranda knocked on the rickety front door and waited, her throat tight.

Old Biddy Needles. There wasn't a witch in Ireland who didn't know the name, and there's not much scares witches, but they knew not to darken her door. When there was no reply, Miranda knocked once more. 'Mrs Cleary? Are you there?' She heard footsteps from within. 'My name is Miranda Kelly. I'm a sister. Galway coven.'

A floorboard creaked on the other side of the door. 'What brings you here, sister?' The voice was old, tremulous.

Miranda almost wept with relief. 'I need you. I didn't know where else to go.'

The door opened and the heat of a fire greeted her,

followed by a tinge of sage, and rabbit meat. 'You better come in, then,' Biddy said, stepping aside.

The old woman was now *very* old, hunched and unsteady on her feet. Her whole head was concealed by a thick, black lace veil through which Miranda could only make out the faintest suggestion of a face. A veil of mourning, it was said, for her former husband's betrayal. She had worn it for almost a hundred years if rumours were to be believed.

'Sit, child. Warm yourself by the fire. The ash went before the oak, and now comes the soak . . .'

'Thank you,' Miranda said. The cottage was tiny, two small rooms divided by a single wall. She didn't like to think where the bathroom was. Dead rabbits and pheasants hung in the kitchen area, and there was a hunk of soda bread on the side. At least the room was warm. That was welcome. She took a stiff wooden chair instead of the well-dented, threadbare armchair.

Biddy returned to the fireplace with her sewing kit; a tidy, leather-bound case. 'You are with child?'

'Twins,' Miranda said. Biddy waited for her to continue. 'Something isn't right.' It came out as a breathless sob, a mixture of unburdened, blessed relief and exasperation. 'They all say I'm mad; my husband, the doctors, my friends. They tell me to relax; they tell me that the babies are fine, but I swear to Gaia, *something* is wrong. I just know it.'

'A mother always does,' Biddy said, opening her case. 'Lay by the fire. Take off your blouse.'

The old woman rested a woollen blanket on the hearth, and Miranda did as instructed, neatly folding her soaked blouse on the chair. 'Will this hurt?'

'No more than not knowing,' Biddy said.

Miranda lay flat on her back, looking up at the gaps in the thatched roof. With papery fingers, Biddy ran a gentle hand over her bump. 'How far gone?'

'Four months.'

'Not too late then,' she said, and Miranda knew exactly what she meant. It wasn't just witches who sought Biddy's services. Women of all ages came from all over Ireland if they were in trouble. The Gardaí knew, no doubt, but wouldn't *dare* tackle Biddy Cleary.

She found herself unable to look away as Biddy withdrew the longest sewing needle from the kit. Unlike anything else in the cottage, it gleamed. The witch held it over the flames a second and then, with the speed of a far younger woman, pricked the flesh of her abdomen and removed it. It was over in the blink of an eye.

Biddy then lifted her veil, just enough for Miranda to see the taut, burned skin of her chin. With a pointed tongue, she licked the blood off the needle's tip. Miranda heard her breath falter, tremble. Biddy passed the needle through the flame again and struck once more. She repeated the tasting.

And then she said nothing.

'Well?' Miranda asked when she could bear the silence no longer. Biddy used the armchair to rise to her feet. Miranda too sat up. 'Tell me! What do you see?'

Biddy dropped her needle in a bowl of boiled water and set it aside. 'You will have twins, girls, identical in appearance, but you knew this.'

'Yes.' Miranda sat by the fire, but was frozen, arms wrapped around her body. 'Are they healthy, though?'

'Oh yes,' Biddy said without hesitation.

Miranda clutched her stomach. 'Oh bless the goddess,' she breathed.

Biddy Needles sat in her armchair. 'They will be as beautiful as they are powerful, both. Immensely so. Adepts.'

Miranda's spirits lifted for a brief, glorious moment – the first second of peace in weeks. Perhaps Brendan was right and she was simply a first-time mother, anxious and paranoid. In a year or so, she'd look back on this day and laugh, even telling her friends about her flit to Aran. Only then Biddy went on.

'But I'm very sorry to say, Miranda, beauty and power is all your daughters will have in common. For while one will be kind, generous and loving, the other will consort with the devils.'

Miranda's eyes widened. 'What?'

'I'll say it plain. One will be good, and the other evil.'

Roberts, Moira

To me; Kaur, Sandhya

Morning Niamh

Just to say I'm thinking of you today. I do hope we get a moment after the ceremony to talk about your inauguration. We really must get a date in the diary, I insist. The Shadow Cabinet down in London are getting very twitchy, and the Americans are interfering. After everything that happened with Helena, I think there are somewhat understandable worries about our authority. Crowning a new HP is the fastest way to show them it's very much business as usual.

There's nothing official set for Samhain? How's your diary looking?

See you this afternoon,

M

Oh and sorry to be a pest but pls give Sandhya access to your diary so she can organise your schedule asap.

Moira Roberts
Chief Cailleach of Scotland
Interim High Priestess – Her Majesty's Royal Coven

Chapter One

REMEMBRANCE

Ciara – Hebden Bridge, UK

Ding dong, the witch is dead.

She could not rid her head of the tune as the casket vanished into the earth. It was driving her spare.

Petty, certainly, but Ciara couldn't help but be a tad disappointed at the turnout. There would have been scores of mourners if people knew who was *really* in the coffin. As it was, it was a pathetic affair; only a handful of faces from her past gathered around the open grave in a clearing in an autumnal Bluebell Meadow. That's what they, and they alone, had called it as children. The leaves were on the turn, a reminder – as if one were needed – that all life is temporal. Ciara chose this glade because this is where she *would* want to be buried if she had a say in it. One of the more unusual perks of burying your own corpse, she supposed.

Despite a sullen grey sky, the clearing, miles deep inside the woods of Hardcastle Crags, was as beautiful now as it was then, if smaller than her vague memories of it. It had rained yesterday, and her nose was full of mulch, moss and damp bark, of spiderwebs and nettles. The forest was beginning its yearly compost.

The clump of mourners wore black, which didn't feel right. The times they'd played here were happy ones. Hide and seek and fairy wars when they were younger, and later a place to flex their powers in private. Those long, long school holidays; Calippo lollies and daisy chains. Making dams in the beck. Learning all the B*Witched dance routines on MTV Hits. Those days.

She was glad to have them; the memories, that was. She had so few.

It made little sense that such vintage recollections remained intact, while the final years before her coma were blank. It was as if Niamh had demolished them from most recent backwards. Everything was black: endless, yawning black. Ciara remembered nothing of her adult life, except what she'd gleaned from other people once she'd got to Hebden Bridge, and it was terrifying. Unsettling that she could almost taste those ice lollies on her tongue, but couldn't fully remember how she'd wound up in that hospital.

Ciara, awake now. Darling, it's me. It's time to wake up at long last. You must awaken. Kill her, kill her now, and find me at once.

Ciara flinched. She remembered that part vividly. She remembered suddenly looming over her sister in that hospital, and—
Everything that followed.
She remembered Hale's voice, as clear as Hebden Beck in her mind.

Find me at once.

She knew one thing: she had to find Dabney Hale. But how? And where? So, she'd come here, to the only place she remembered. Hebden fucking Bridge. Her sister's home. And now, her sister's resting place.

Fuckin' Niamh, eh? She'd really done a number on her. Ciara knew that much. As such, she would *not* feel a second's guilt over what had happened at the safehouse. She would not.

Ciara drew a deep breath in and timed it out. *Pull your shit together*. She couldn't risk a meltdown. Not here, not now. Sheila Henry took her place at the head of the grave. A grave containing *her* body. Her old body. She'd traded it in.

'We return our sister Ciara Kelly to the earth.' Sheila – unchanged since they were kids – started the service. As much a part of town life as the bridge itself, Ciara could well believe the vicar had looked like a fifty-year-old butch since she was born. 'There, she will live again in Gaia, one with her great creation. Her sister, Niamh, has asked to say a few words . . .'

It took Ciara a second to remember she was Niamh now. She sprang into action. 'Yes! Sorry, miles away.'

'Quite all right, deary, you take your time.' She joined Sheila at the head of the grave, milking the procession. Funerals are inherently camp, such morbid theatre. She wished she'd had time to source a hat with a veil attached. Below, in the hole in the ground, was a simple wooden box. Witches didn't bother with expensive lacquered coffins that would only slow their inevitable return to the earth.

Sheila stood aside to allow Ciara, or *Niamh*, her big moment. Where to start? *I can't deny I have some lingering regrets about smothering my twin sister after appropriating her body, but it was chiefly unavoidable.*

The white-hot, blinding, rage she had felt in that moment. The vector stone. *She hadn't had a choice.* She felt for the ruby in her coat pocket now, rolling it between her thumb and forefinger. It was hardly bigger than a grain of sand but had contained a supernova. Now that the curse had played out, it was just a pretty gemstone, harmless. But, fuck; the charge it had given her, the *fury*. The spell that caused the soul transfer was *immense*. Ciara had felt it course through her like a million volts, giving her the strength to—

In the crowd, Leonie Jackman frowned, and Ciara buried the sour feeling as deeply as she could. She must remain impenetrable.

She tried to pass off her hesitation as a moment of fey sorrow. They *all* looked to her now, their eyes full of, not grief, but *pity* for Niamh. They didn't mourn wayward Ciara Kelly, but rather the toll it would take on poor, dear, love-sponge Niamh. Everyone loves Niamh Kelly, she's a fucking basket of kittens and puppies, that one. Leonie and Elle looked on with sympathy, side by side with her sister, even now. If only they knew the *real* Niamh.

'My sister was far from perfect.' An understatement. 'But she was my sister all the same. We shared a womb, and a home, and a childhood. I have no memories in my head that don't have my sister in them.' And it was true. Niamh had always been there. Ciara had thought her a constant.

Elle started to cry noisily. At her side, a teenage girl with pastel pink hair handed her a tissue. Holly: Elle's daughter. A child Ciara had no memory of whatsoever.

In the fortnight since she'd escaped her prison, she'd urgently tried to fill some gaps; reading minds where she could, gleaning facts and figures. She'd started in haste at the hospital, right after she'd . . . well.

With the ruby's curse still lava in her veins, Ciara had been disoriented, almost drunk, in the giddy moments after. She sat a while in the visitor armchair, staring at the lifeless body on the bed. Pale. Eyes vacant. There was a single strand of hair stuck to its lip.

Gaia only knows how long she sat for. Could have been minutes, could have been hours. All she knew was Dabney's message, replaying over and over in her reverie. *Find me.*

Why? What for? Why now? *What have I done?*

When her heart rate felt human again, Ciara had left the attic cell.

It was then she had read the elderly nurse who'd been caring for her at the safehouse. Mildred, a woman who smelled of Germolene, had been changing the bed sheets in another bedroom when Ciara encountered her on her way downstairs. She saw the opportunity and took it. Sneaking up on her from behind, she clamped her right hand down onto her frizzy grey head. Poor Mildred had let out only the briefest cry before flopping onto the bed, out cold. Ciara rinsed the old woman's mind, looking for any clues as to who, where, why, when.

The fact she'd been in that bed for NINE FUCKING YEARS had been a shock to say the naked minimum. Niamh fucking owed her a thirtieth, the cunt. The blanks the nurse filled in had somewhat helped, but it was less fruitful when it came to what had happened to Ciara personally because Mildred only knew hearsay about her past: *Devious, murderous, demonic.* Other people's memories of your life are unreliable narration at best.

The nurse remembered none of their meeting, naturally. Ciara had wiped her, and left her with an instruction to discover the body an hour later once she was long, long gone. Now, Mildred respectfully stood on the other side of the burial site alongside some of her colleagues.

Ciara waited for Elle to blow her nose before continuing her eulogy. 'It's fair to say Ciara and I had a complicated relationship at times . . .' The wry, knowing chuckle from the congregation made her want to punch someone. 'But what I am feeling now is . . . *guilt* mostly, to tell you the truth. Let's not forget it was I who obliterated Ciara's mind and left her for dead in a hospital bed for the best part of a decade.'

Leonie's eyes widened. Whoops. Perhaps that was over-egging the pudding. It was only through Leonie that Ciara had been able to ascertain what had led to her catatonia. Another brutal shock. It was a wonder she'd survived, and yet they all still worshipped Good Kind Niamh.

A striking woman called Chinara held Leonie's hand. Next to her was Niamh's newest groupie: the girl, Theo. She also looked taken aback. Ciara thought to rein it in a touch. 'Well, that was no life at all, was it? Maybe it's a mercy that she can be free now. We all can.'

Theo regarded her with concern. Unprompted, she came to her side and took her hand. *It's OK*, she told only Ciara. *You don't have to do this.*

What was it her dearly departed sister did to inspire such devotion? All these strays that flocked to her like bluebirds on Snow White's fucking finger. Theo was the latest in a long line, but there had *always* been a poorly hedgehog in a shoebox; or a new girl at school who needed showing around, ever since Niamh was a little girl. At the edge of the clearing, watching from afar, was another deer nibbling from her orchard: the man. The handsome lump who pined at her fjord. *Luke.*

The mundane was undeniably useful to have around. She could read him unhindered. Her sister's memories had lingered only as long as cigarette smoke, and now nothing remained. She really was a hermit crab moving into a new shell.

She'd missed so much. A lot can happen in nine years, and much of it had happened in the last couple of months. The war was long over; Helena Vance was dead – executed no less; her sister was shagging the local grocer and had, by all accounts, adopted a transgender teenager. And the fucking queen died. What a ride, honestly.

After leaving the safehouse in Manchester, and still a little high on the ruby's juice, she'd flown to Hebden at once. Hale had given her nothing to go on. He hadn't left a forwarding address. She'd assumed her sister's besties – *her* friends, once – would know where he was. What she'd instead walked into was carnage: the fallout from Helena's ill-advised trip to the Dark Side, and the news that Niamh was High Priestess apparent. This meant no one had let her out of their sight for more than five minutes. She was fucking trapped here. For now.

Ciara felt her aura turning red and swallowed it down. Leonie was more powerful than she was, and if she saw anything besides grief, Ciara would be shafted. It burned at her though. *Nine years.* She was almost *thirty-five* years old. At school, she and a boy called Kirk Gilhooly had made a vow to get married if they were single at thirty. She'd looked him up. He was gay now. Fuck.

Enough. She'd come this far. She'd kept the sentients out of her head for two weeks now, and was confident she could keep it up for the foreseeable. The best part was no one questioned why her reverie was so dour; with the funeral, the almost briny tang of sadness was understandable. Such maudlin content was of no interest to snoopers anyway, but she could seal off her inner musings while still participating in telepathy. She wasn't like Theo or Holly, their shrill adolescent anxieties exposed for all to see.

Focusing on the task at hand, she offered Theo a warm smile, and allowed herself to be led to the other mourners. As was the way with witch's graves, there would be only a nameless boulder to mark Niamh's resting place. Once more, Ciara felt suddenly nauseous, a panicky skitter in her ribcage. No. She would not entertain guilt. Niamh *owed her*. She owed her precisely nine years. She owed her a lot more than that.

Ciara would not feel pity for the woman who had left her mind in tatters. No healer on earth could put this Humpty back together again.

Anyway, regret doesn't get the bloodstains out. Once she'd calmed down, in the days after . . . it happened, Ciara had reasoned she *had* to kill Niamh. The ruby was old, dark and powerful. But even old, dark and powerful things can't deny the flow of nature. With her old body still living and breathing, her soul would have been irresistibly drawn to its rightful host. Similarly, Niamh would have soon reclaimed control of her own body.

For posterity's sake, did she really *want* to kill her sister? No, of course not, she wasn't a fucking sociopath, whatever anyone said. Ciara would have preferred to leave Niamh in that hospital bed for nine years, *that* would have been poetic justice, but, in that moment, she hadn't been thinking at all. All she had known was a hunger to kill. All instinct, devoid of reason.

It was the gem, not her.

The devil made me do it.

Which led her once more to the question of how the fuck Helena Vance, of all people, ended up with that stone. She was so *vanilla*. She'd put a towel down to fuck.

With the service drawing to a close, the elementals and healers stepped forward. Hands aloft, they moved the earth to fill the grave. Leonie looped her arm through hers, and rested her head against Ciara's. Ciara let her. She was warm, and her perfume smelled like Parma Violets. Ciara watched as the coffin vanished, covered by soil. As soon as the ground was flat, green tips poked through the mud, sprouting into fountains of shimmering foxtail grasses. No one would ever know she was there.

This wasn't Sheila's first funeral, and she knew exactly what tone to strike. 'The coven invites you all to the Lion and Lamb in town for a celebration of Ciara's return to Gaia. I hope to see you there.'

Ciara shot a final glance at the grave. *Goodbye, sister, I wish things were different.*

Chapter Two

WAKE

Leonie – Hebden Bridge, UK

They didn't make them like this in London. The Lamb and Lion, just up from the river in Hebden Bridge town, was comfortingly familiar: the low wooden beams and sticky carpets; the beery towels on the bar; the wall of heat coming from the open fire in the den.

Leonie could remember being fourteen or so. Big Boots in Leeds stocked 17 foundation in her shade, at *last*, and she'd got ready in Helena's bedroom, battling for mirror space with the others with Brandy and Monica on repeat. She'd worn a crop top, pedal-pushers and heels in the hope they'd get served Bacardi Breezers at this grotty pub. Leonie smiled to herself – gods, it was *so* dodgy looking back. Dodgier still were the men who had served *clearly* underage girls.

Holly and Theo were sat by the fireplace with an ill-at-ease Jez. Leonie wondered if Elle's husband had taken her *gentle* advice from solstice about breaking off his extra-marital dalliance. She was about to read him when Elle thrust a tray of food under her nose.

'You should eat something,' Elle told her. 'Cheesy puff? They're vegan.' She held aloft an anaemic-looking pastry.

Leonie smiled. 'I'm all set for cheesy puffs.' She mostly wanted a vodka tonic, for which Chinara was queuing at the bar. The landlady had closed to the public for the wake, but it was still busy with well-wishers. It was mostly HMRC people; the nurses who'd cared for Ciara at the safehouse.

Gods it was sad, man. She thought she'd mourned Ciara after what had happened during the war, but it seemed that there was some part of Leonie that had harboured *hope* that she'd get more time with Ciara Kelly. Hope is so tricksy, so addictive. She was high on it right now. And that reminded her that she urgently needed to talk to Niamh about her brother. It couldn't wait, funeral or no.

Elle had rallied round to put all this together, and Leonie felt bad for not doing more. Her pal did seem to be enjoying her pivotal role as Angel of Death, however. Some people are life's little organisers, and Elle was the best of them. If she enjoyed all this shit, if it was her way of processing grief, leave her to it.

Leonie located Niamh: beside the towering buffet, alone. 'Do you think she's happy with everything?' Elle asked.

Leonie raised a brow. 'Her sister just died.'

She gestured at the buffet. 'I meant about this!'

'Elle, there's enough food to feed a small country. It's great.' The histrionic arrangements of white lilies were also very camp. Leonie approved.

'She's been so quiet. Can you read her?'

Leonie shook her head and lowered her voice. 'She doesn't want me in her head, Elle. She's . . . she's mourning. We're gonna need to give her time.' She keenly felt Elle's juvenile urge to make everything OK as fast as possible.

Understandable, and born out of kindness, but naïve. 'Come on,' she told Elle. 'Let's just be there for her.'

They headed to Niamh's quiet corner. 'You OK, babe?' Leonie asked.

'Yes,' Niamh said, hardly able to look her in the eye. 'No. I wish people would stop asking.' She seemed frayed.

'I hear that.' Leonie shook her head, feeling the topknot of braids shift. 'This is bullshit. I always thought there'd be an epilogue, you know? Some sort of goodbye? It doesn't feel right that she's just . . . gone. Like, I wanna hear Ciara's last monologue, that shit would have been . . .' she performed a chef's kiss and Niamh grinned, despite herself.

'It really would,' Niamh muttered.

'Have you had anything to eat?' Elle asked Niamh, offering a platter of mini samosas.

'I'm fine,' Niamh said, weary. 'But thanks for all this, Ellie. It's so kind.'

Elle frowned. 'What are you talking about, of course. It's the least I could do. You were so good when Grandma . . .'

Leonie felt a dreadful hollow beneath her ribs. They all shared it. Even Elle couldn't hide that pain behind perkiness. They'd feel the loss of Annie for a long time. And then Helena, which was a whole other headfuck. And now Ciara.

And Radley.

No more. She couldn't lose her brother too. Leonie was desperate to bring him up. It was all she wanted to talk about.

'Radley?' Niamh said suddenly. Apparently Leonie wasn't as good at shielding her thoughts as her friend was. 'Any news?'

Leonie fought the urge to scream and smash every last

leaded window out of the pub's walls. No. No, there was not any news. Not a fucking crumb. The polite inertia from both the Warlock's Cabal and the coven was infuriating. Why weren't they tearing the world apart to find him? 'Nothing,' she said tersely, watching her tone. 'Still no contact at all.' It had been over three months since anyone had heard from her little brother.

'What about Hale?' Niamh asked.

Leonie shook her head. 'Nope.' Neither Dabney Hale nor her brother had been seen since the day the latter broke out of the prison. If they were in the country, they were being shielded by very powerful magic. 'I spoke to Moira.' The Acting High Priestess was chatting to Chinara, now being served at the bar. 'She said you were going to HMRC tomorrow?'

Niamh didn't look thrilled at the prospect. She sipped a black coffee, and Leonie wondered why she wasn't on the lash; if she was her, she'd want to be obliterated. Niamh nodded. 'It would seem so. I've put it off for as long as possible.'

'Can I come with you? I have some of Radley's personal things which might help the oracles—'

Niamh cut her off before she could finish the sentence. 'Of course. We'll do whatever it takes.' And then she added. 'I want Dabney Hale found more than anyone.'

Chapter Three

COTTAGING

Ciara – Hebden Bridge, UK

If finding Lee's brother meant finding Dabney Hale, Ciara was glad to help. It was the only thing she knew for certain.

Find me.

In all the world, she could only think of Dab, who'd know exactly *why* this was happening, why Helena (or the forces *inside* Helena, to be more specific) had gone to such lengths to revive her. There *had* to be a reason. And why *now*? Nine years ago would've been nice.

This echoing cavern of a mind. She knew, or she assumed in any case, that she'd spent her final years with Hale. He could help her. He could make her whole again.

Chinara, Leonie's partner, joined them, two vodka sodas in hand. She was a strong one, Ciara could sense it from across the pub. She nodded at Ciara's cup. 'Sorry, Niamh, can I get you a proper drink?'

Absolutely not. Alcohol would lower her defences in a room full of sentients. 'No. No, thank you. I think it'd make me pure morose.'

Ciara saw Luke lingering at a respectful distance on the other side of the bar, talking to Elle's husband. She couldn't remember him. They were talking about Annie.

Ciara had been upset, truly, to learn of Annie's passing. She remembered her, from long ago. That woman was a fucking diamond. She'd always had this knowing glance, a glint of genius. Whenever Helena was being a little dictator back in the day, she'd give Ciara this split-second side-eye that said *I know*.

Unlike a lot of people, Annie had always given her the benefit of the doubt, believing nothing about the future was set in stone—

Annie, in a conference room, surrounded by witches . . .

Ciara almost dropped her coffee.

'Are you OK?' Leonie asked.

Ciara assured her she was. Fuck. A clip of her past *almost* formed in her mind. She pushed, pushed to tease the image out again.

The memory was grey, granular and blurred. She was at HMRC – a committee room of some sort: lots of stern women sat around a long table, disapproving eyes, all on her. Her grandma was there, and so was Annie, sticking up for her.

And that was it. Nothing more. A room and some grim faces.

Why? That kept happening. So fucking frustrating! Worse than almost sneezing but not being able to.

Dizzy, Ciara leaned against the buffet trestle table. Leonie frowned. 'Hey, steady.'

'Are you OK?' Theo mouthed from across the pub function room, and Ciara nodded. Luke too looked concerned for his poor, swooning, Brontë heroine Niamh. Her sister always did have great taste in—

Ciara's heart suddenly felt too low in her gut, and her head swam – worse this time. *There was something she had to do.* This breathless, panicked feeling had plagued her since she left the safehouse. That awful sensation of leaving hair straighteners on or the car unlocked. There was, though, a sense of unfinished business on the tip of her tongue, and it troubled her. She could only hope it was a side-effect of the soul spell, and it would abate as she continued to fill these redacted spaces.

'You sure you're OK?' Elle asked.

'I'm fine,' she lied. 'Just tired. I haven't been sleeping.' Her friends were full of sympathy. Where was the sentiment for Ciara? The *dead* sister as far as they were concerned.

'We can reschedule tomorrow . . . ?' Leonie offered.

'No. Honestly. I'll be fine.'

'First day as High Priestess, exciting stuff,' Chinara said, trying to steer the conversation to a topic less heavy perhaps.

'Not quite,' Ciara told her. She nibbled the corner off an onion bhaji and it helped ground her a little. Maybe some food would help.

'You don't seem hugely enamoured.'

That wasn't wholly true. On one hand, her new appointment meant she wouldn't have to pretend to be a vet. That would have turned very messy very quickly. Between Luke and Theo, she'd gained a solid understanding of the woman she was supposed to be now. When she'd offered her resignation to Niamh's partner at the surgery, he'd been unsurprised – the exertions of the last few months had taken her away from the day job. But on the other hand . . . 'Do I look like a High Priestess to you?'

Leonie flashed a sly grin. 'Well, you're white and you inherited property so . . .'

Despite the surroundings, Ciara snorted. 'I'm Irish! Like, we always knew Helena was going to be HP right?'

'Turns out she would literally kill for the job, yes,' Leonie said, keeping her voice conspiratorially low.

'I didn't see it for myself,' said Ciara, sealing the deal on the understatement of the century. 'I don't.' The difference between the Kelly twins: both Ciara and Niamh had applied to be Year 6 Library Prefects. Niamh wanted to help the librarian; Ciara just wanted the shiny gold badge.

Perhaps it was being near Leonie, but another stray memory, tatty flotsam, returned to Ciara. *Their* HP, Julia Collins, in Hebden Bridge Market Square. The old crone had seized her elbow, dragging the sixteen-year-old Ciara away from a young Leonie and a group of Kappa-clad lads, one of which she'd just hexed.

Just what on EARTH do you think you're playing at, Ciara Kelly?

They're perverts. They tried to feel up Lee.

She remembered the little crowd gathering around the hexed boy, now writhing around on the pavement outside the butcher's, like he was having a seizure. It'd pass in a minute or two and he had more than deserved it. He'd groped Leonie. She remembered now.

You are a liability, young woman, and I shall be having words with your grandmother.

And now she was about to *be* High Priestess, strictly temporarily. For one thing, HMRC was inexorably tied to the crown, to colonial rule, gross enough in itself, but for a second thing, authority figures simply aren't chic. Why Niamh, an *Irish* witch, got to be High Priestess was even more perplexing. 'His Majesty' wasn't *their* majesty.

It was the *Republic* of Ireland with good reason. When the coven was officially started, yes, Ireland was still part of the union. These days, Irish witches got to be British when it suited the coven. When their parents died, the coven couldn't get the prodigious wee adepts to the UK fast enough.

'Niamh, I say this as someone who quit HMRC in spectacular fashion . . . there's no one I'd rather take over.' Leonie took hold of her cheeks and gave her a kiss on the lips.

Chinara agreed. 'Take that rusty old machine, polish it down, and make it new. Make it *good*. I mean that, and wish you well.'

Ciara smiled tersely. 'Thank you.'

She had no intention of fulfilling the role in any meaningful sense. It was a means to an end, the most efficient way to track down Dabney. The only question was how long it would take to locate him and get some answers.

As nice as it was to be vertical, Ciara couldn't relax. Not only was the world very different to the one she'd left (*Donald Trump* had been president of the United States, what the actual fuck? And which idiot fucking thought up 'Brexit'?) but it was beyond disconcerting to have holes in her history *and* questions about her future. Someone had stage-managed her comeback. She couldn't enjoy this return when she wasn't in on the joke. It felt like Dab had designs for her. She didn't like not knowing what they were.

Having HMRC resources at her disposal could only help speed that process, so for now she'd play along. He wouldn't stay low-key for long; she knew enough to know that wasn't his style.

As for the man himself, she was torn. An oily sensation

swilled around her abdomen. *That* feeling. Both wanting and not wanting to see him. Equal parts desire and revulsion. Knowing it would be dreadful and exquisite. Ciara didn't know what had played out between them, but disembodied feelings endured. She remembered meeting him as teenagers; first at a festival somewhere, and then, she believed, at university. The feeling, though, the *feeling* spoke volumes. Love and hate are just different words for obsession.

Across the pub, Ciara observed Moira making a move in their direction. No way. 'Will you all excuse me a minute?' she told her former friends. Ciara swivelled in the direction of the toilet only to walk directly into Luke's beefy chest face-first. 'Ow!'

'Fuck, I'm sorry.'

'It's OK.' Her hand reached for her nose and Luke handed her a napkin to get the coffee she'd sloshed down her blouse. 'Thanks.'

Luke was certainly handsome, although very different to . . . *Conrad*. Yes, that was his name, Conrad Chen. That nugget had been driving her insane. She had seen Niamh's old partner in Elle's mind, and he had been muscular, athletic. She wouldn't have pictured her sister with someone so, well, hairy. 'Is it OK that I'm here?' he said. 'I sensed that, um, maybe you needed some space?'

Ciara fought to keep mild disgust off her face. Men are usually awful, a fact she'd established as a teenager. Being sexually attracted to them, truly, was a curse. And while Luke was a tasty fuckin' lumberjack, a steak of a man, as if she'd go anywhere near Niamh's sloppy seconds. She had often been accused of being unhinged, but she had some standards.

'Niamh?' Luke pressed.

What did he want from her? 'I . . . she was my sister,' Ciara said, hoping that encapsulated it all.

'I understand,' Luke replied. *Well of course he does. Don't they always?* 'When my mum passed away . . . well it took me years to feel like myself again.' He took hold of her arms and she instinctively recoiled from his touch. He could not look more disappointed, but what did he expect? *I'm in mourning, you sicko. Also, you're a perfect stranger.* 'Whatever you need from me, I'm *here*, OK. It can be at a distance, but I'm yours.'

She hugged him tight so he wouldn't see her face. 'Great, Luke. Thanks.' She let go of him and scanned the room. There was no one to run to. She wished Annie was here, she really did. 'You know what? I feel overcome with emotion. I might tap out.'

Luke looked surprised for a second. 'Um, yeah, whatever you need. You want me to drive you up to the cottage?'

'No, I'll fly.' Oops, needle scratch. He looked at her blankly. 'Walk. I will walk, obviously. Because it's broad daylight.'

Niamh, for some unfathomable reason, kept entrusting mundane men with the truth about witchkind. On her head be it. Although that head was now hers.

'OK,' Luke said. 'You want me to get Theo?'

Theo was chatting with Holly near the fireplace. 'No, leave her here.' He frowned again. Why was everyone so weirdly protective of the girl? She was an *adept*, for crying out loud, but you'd think she was a delicate orchid the way people went on. She remembered the way people used to fuss around her and Niamh, even as children. Possessing multiple gifts was rare indeed. It was like they were being groomed for some ghastly pageant: *Britain's Next Top Witches*.

'I need to be alone a while,' said Ciara, her skin crawling slightly. She needed freedom, needed to let her psychic guard down. 'I'll ask Elle to drop her home.'

Elle, of course, agreed heartily, and Ciara stalked out of the pub without saying any goodbyes. Why do they call it a French Exit? Evening was setting in, the clocks almost ready to go back.

Hebden Fuckin' Bridge. How was she here again? Another memory: her and Leonie screaming SHITTY TOWN to that tune from *Beauty and the Beast*. 'Provincial' hardly began to describe how she saw this place. Stifling, claustrophobic, did the trick too.

Not for the first time, Ciara wondered why she hadn't simply fled after . . . after leaving the safehouse. That had been her first instinct: to ignore Hale's memo and find a fucking beach somewhere. But, she hadn't. She didn't even fully understand it herself. When she took flight from Manchester, it was *here* she had flown to.

She idled through the largely deserted village. Tourist season was over. The bridge part of Hebden Bridge was gone, thanks to Leonie, replaced with a temporary metal one for the time being. It was an ugly thing, like braces on bad teeth. She wandered down the high street past the model village buildings, mostly gift shops and bakeries, and wondered why her sister had come here after college. Was this twee toytown truly the limit of her ambition?

Hebden Bridge was just so . . . smug. It was so fucking pleased with itself. *Ooh we're dead Yorkshire, but also super gay and arty and vegan, bet you weren't expecting that. I wasn't born, I was knitted out of oat milk.* Theo had pointed out someone had spray-painted a trans pride flag onto one of the limestone walls on the other side of the river, and that said it all.

She started up the hill to Heptonstall village, instantly regretting turning down Luke's offer of a lift. She'd definitely forgotten how steep this motherfucker was. Niamh's body *hadn't* been laid flat for nine years, and it still needed a rest halfway up. Ciara took in the view of the valley. She wouldn't deny, ever, that Hebden Bridge was breathtaking, the trees like crushed green velvet on both sides. There had been further showers during the wake, and everything felt cleansed and crisp, earthy. It was so small though. In the years she'd been here, even as a girl, she felt pincered on all sides. She was bigger than this box.

She'd pieced together a rough timeline using some old school records she'd found in the attic, and she'd fled town the second she could – for Durham University. So had Niamh, for that matter, but she'd evidently chosen to return.

The doleful church bell rang out 6 p.m. as she arrived at Heptonstall – the historic village overlooking Hebden Bridge. It started to rain the exact moment she pushed through the gate outside her grandma's old cottage. Well, now it was *hers*. Hers and Niamh's; apparently they'd inherited it.

Ciara didn't know how, or when, Grandma Hobbs had died. Their mother's mother was a stiff, insular woman, almost paralysed by a clutch of anxieties. She'd taken them in out of obligation, not love. Even as ten-year-olds, they'd known that much. They'd been shipped from Galway to be closer to HMRC. At least they'd had each other.

At least.

Unlocking the back door into the kitchen, Niamh's dog growled at her. 'I thought we had a deal,' Ciara said aloud, fetching him a treat from a jar on the windowsill over the sink. 'You keep your mouth shut and I'll provide the Smackos.' Tiger, a Border Terrier, accepted the stinky stick and retreated to the den.

How could the cottage *possibly* still smell of her grand-mother's rose perfume after all these years and, moreover, how could she remember her scent so solidly when massive chunks of her past were lost to her?

She folded her coat on a kitchen chair and headed upstairs to what *used* to be their grandma's bedroom. Ciara kicked off Niamh's fugly, Amish-looking shoes and sat on the bed. She caught her own – her old – eyes staring up at her from the bedside table. She'd found the photo tucked at the bottom of Niamh's knicker drawer. A faded, framed photo of them both as children, not long after they'd relocated from Galway. Both wore spandex cycling shorts, Spice Girls crop tops in contrasting acid neons and denim bucket hats. It could not be more nineties.

Niamh had hidden the photo, buried it beneath under-wear, but kept it.

She shuddered; a chill clawed at her spine. *Why am I back? Why now?* And, *What did I do?* She had read Leonie, and she had read Elle, and no one seemed to know where Ciara Kelly had been for the best part of the decade after school. Apparently she had murdered Conrad Chen.

She did not know why, or how. She squirmed and sprung off the bed, unable to be still. She paced the boxy room, exhausted but wired.

Ciara flinched at the sight of Niamh's body in the mirror.

It was so strange. No matter how much people fell over themselves to stress *how* identical they were, they weren't. No twins are, least of all to the twins themselves. Ciara crawled to the free-standing mirror and examined her new face up close. Niamh had a barely visible scar on her bottom lip where one of Annie Device's cats had scratched her. Ciara traced it with her fingertip. Everyone always said Ciara's eyes were more 'feline'. Ciara couldn't see it, personally; it was probably just different eyeliner technique. She stroked her jawline, no longer feeling the mole that nestled under the curve of her chin.

A fresh, powerful, wave of nausea hit. Ciara dizzily stumbled into the bathroom off the landing and steadied herself against the sink. She inhaled deeply, telling herself she wouldn't vomit. As she leaned over it, the ends of her hair trailed into the basin. She tutted. Niamh always favoured endless Ariel hair. Ciara, in contrast, found it borderline repulsive that her mane skimmed the fucking toilet seat when she sat down to shit. Just fuckin' unhygienic.

Well, this was *her* body now. From here on in, it was *hers*. And she'd do as she pleased. She reached into the medicine cabinet over the sink and pushed aside old bottles of potions, both high street and self-made, until she found a pair of delicate scissors.

They'd do the trick.

She grasped an endless auburn lock, pulled it taut, and started to cut away at it. It didn't need to be *neat*, that would be too similar to her old trademark bob. She hacked and hacked, pulling hair around from her nape. She kept going until every hippy mermaid strand was cropped to a far more sensible shoulder length. The sink was soon full of coiled, ratty hair.

Ciara gave her head, so much freer, a shake. 'There. That's better.'

Downstairs, she heard the door slam and Tiger's nails clip over the tiles as he went to investigate. 'Niamh?' It was Theo, home from the wake. Oh shit. At second glance, it looked remarkably like she'd hacked at her hair with nail scissors. Nothing screams unhinged like a self-haircut. Fuck, fuck, fuck.

Ciara scooped matted handfuls of hair out of the sink, transferring them to the little bathroom bin. Shit. She'd made a mess. Already.

Theo's footsteps trotted upstairs. 'Niamh?' She stopped in the bathroom doorway and flinched. 'Oh.'

'I . . . um . . . decided to give myself a haircut. On reflection, it might not have been the best idea. Will you maybe tidy it up for me?'

'Of course.' Theo looked *concerned* not scared. *Poor grieving Niamh cut off her hair.* That was acceptable, but Ciara vowed to get a grip. All she had to do was keep it together for a few more weeks max.

They returned to the kitchen, where they had more room to manoeuvre. Ciara sat on a wooden chair, a towel around her shoulders as Theo more carefully trimmed the ends. 'I think it's looking less wonky . . . ?' the girl said uncertainly.

Theo was among the less irritating teenagers Ciara had known. Of an evening, she was content to read – absorbing old grimoires and diaries like a sponge – or watching television peacefully. A couple of evenings a week, she attended after-school dance classes.

Ciara had danced once. She been good too, far better than her sister. Ballet, jazz and contemporary. At one point, she'd been destined for the Bethesda School of Dance – the Welsh academy for young witches. It was a small school, only twelve students a year are admitted. She wondered why she'd turned down the offer.

Her first ballet slippers. Dusky pink, rock-hard at the toes. Christmas Day 1995. She could *smell* the box-fresh satin and leather. She so vividly remembered securing the ribbons around her ankles, pushing herself *en pointe* and ignoring the pain. She wallowed a while in what warm memories she had.

'Niamh?' Theo prompted her.

'Looks good,' she said, snapping out of it. 'Sorry. I don't know what's up with me tonight.'

'I think you're doing amazingly, all things considered,' Theo said. 'You, um, had a complicated relationship, right?'

Ciara smirked. 'There's an understatement.'

'I have a question,' Theo said, combing the knots out of her hair with a cheap tortoiseshell comb.

'Fire away.'

'You know how Elle revived Luke?'

That sounded plausible. 'Yes . . .'

Theo went on, her voice low. 'Could . . . could, potentially, a healer bring someone back from . . .'

Ciara twisted on the chair to look at her. 'I'll stop you right there,' she said. 'Are we done?'

'I think so.'

Ciara thanked her and shook the towel onto the tiles before reaching for the broom. 'Look, Theo, every teenage witch goes through the eyeliner and blood magic phase, it's a rite of passage, but necromancy isn't to be messed with.'

Theo blushed and stared at the floor. 'I just meant . . .'

Ciara continued to sweep. 'You know what? It's like *heroin*. Because it's there, there's always some arsehole who thinks they're being dead tough by skipping over a bit of weed and molly, and going for the top-shelf stuff. It's the same with necromancy. Just because we theoretically *could* doesn't mean we *should*. And it never ends well. You end up with fucking zombies or worse.'

'Worse?' Theo asked, eyes wide. She was ever so pretty, this little Snow White, with her ebony hair and cherry lips.

Ciara nodded. 'Witches are agents of nature. Death is natural. To fuck with it is unnatural. End of.'

Theo nodded, seemingly satisfied. *Got it*.

Ciara didn't want to encourage telepathy around the house. She wanted sentients in her head as little as possible, even if it was only to transmit words or thoughts.

'What about speaking to the dead?'

'Also a no-no, I'm afraid.' Ciara read her and saw a familiar melancholy in the girl. 'Is this about your parents? You want to find your real parents?' Ciara asked aloud, surface-skimming her mind. She wore her worries deep, but Ciara sometimes got a sense of them early in the morning or late at night.

Theo slotted the chair under the kitchen table. 'Maybe a little. If they're even dead, I guess.'

While it had been utterly baffling to find a teenager living in the cottage, Ciara had been able to get up to speed. She quickly established Niamh and Theo had been doing guided meditations to try to tease out details of Theo's cloudy past. Even now, a wooden bowl with azurite, diaspore and hematite rested on the coffee table in the lounge – among the best crystals for recall.

'It just feels like if I knew where I came from, I might know where I was headed,' she said thoughtfully.

Same, same. 'Don't worry. We'll keep on trying.'

'I wish,' Theo mused, putting some dry mugs away in the cupboard. 'I wish the oracles would drop the whole Sullied Child thing; you know?'

Ciara's past was shot to shit, but she remembered that story well enough: *One day a boy child will take Leviathan by the hand, and walk the Beast from the darkness into the world of man. On that cursed day, every witch will perish* blah, blah, blah. 'Look,' Ciara said. 'Oracles are full of shit, OK. They used to say all kinds of crap about m-my sister, and she turned out just fine.'

Theo blinked, unsure if she was kidding. 'Did she?'

She had her there. She crossed to the mirror in the lounge and tousled her hair. It looked less demented now. In fact, it looked rather good.

Theo said, 'Didn't she . . . kill your fiancé?'

The words were a fist. She almost physically ducked them. Ciara turned away from the mirror and looked right at her. *This little cunt knew nothing.* Only then she saw Theo staring directly at her, puzzlement all over her face. 'Theo?' A creeping feeling rose in her stomach.

Theo's eyes narrowed. Her face was pale. Ciara took a step back instinctively. *Bitch, get the fuck out of my head.* 'You're not Niamh,' she said, very quietly. 'You're *her.*'

Chapter Four

THE GROUP CHAT

Elle – Hebden Bridge, UK

No one could bring themselves to remove Helena from the group chat.

Elle sat upright in bed, propped up by a pillow. She'd been staring at the group info page for about five minutes. Four participants: herself, Niamh, Leonie and Helena. The picture, still, was all of them together at Secret Santa Night 2019.

She scrolled back and back and back. The last message Helena had sent was the night of those fucking ill-fated drinks at the very same pub they'd just left. *See you all shortly. PS what are you wearing?* Elle was almost home-sick for the trivial. When was the last time they'd talked about clothes, or food, holidays, or *Love Island*?

'What's up?' Jez said, scrolling through his personal trainer's Instagram account next to her. It was all a bit homoerotic for Elle. Why did he do all his workouts shirtless when his clients were mostly men?

'Do you think I should remove Helena from the group chat?'

He looked over. 'Well she's not gonna mind, seeing as she's dead, is she?'

Very true. But it did feel disrespectful. Her social media accounts were still online too, gathering days since their last posts. What they did to Helena was unforgiveable, and that was coming from her victim's granddaughter. Killing Helena hadn't brought Annie back, or made her any less sad. If anything, she was doubly sad. Elle did what she always did with ugly grey thoughts, and pushed them to the dark airing closet of her mind.

'Do you think I should add Chinara in?' she asked.

'Leonie's missus? Could do.'

Hmmm. Leonie did sometimes use HEBDEN GIRLIES to sound off about minor frustrations in her relationship – just as she did about Jez. God, the thought of adding Jez to the sanctum of the chat was mortifying. Perhaps she shouldn't assume Leonie would want her partner included just because she was a girly.

Instead, Elle tapped out a message to the three live members: *Hey girls, hope you both got home OK??? Lovely to see you all. Can we hang out when someone hasn't died, please?*

'Do you think today went OK?' Elle asked.

'Is this cos Niamh chipped off early?'

Well, yes. 'I don't know . . .'

Jez now set his phone aside. 'Everything was boss. I dunno, maybe she was just upset and needed some quiet time. I know I did.'

And Jez didn't know the half of it when it came to Niamh and Ciara. It was so silly, but Elle was having flashbacks to Amy Winehouse of all people. She'd loved her – she saw her on tour at the Apollo in 2007 – and, like all the fans, had been rooting for her to make a triumphant comeback, to prove all the haters wrong. And then, one morning, she was gone.

And now history repeated with Ciara. She wouldn't ever speak of this publicly for fear of being, as Holly would say, 'cancelled', but Elle had always hoped that – in time – Ciara would be on her feet and able to find some sort of resolution. Don't misunderstand; Elle wanted her to accomplish that in the confines of Grierlings, where she belonged, but there wasn't even to be justice, it seemed.

'They have so much history,' Elle said, putting the phone down. 'We were about, I don't know, maybe thirteen when Ciara started to go off the rails. It was so weird how they could look so similar but be such different personalities. Can you remember her?'

Jez frowned. 'A bit. I think I met her once or twice down the pub. And she was at the wedding, weren't she?'

Elle nodded. Jez was so shit-faced at the wedding; she was surprised he remembered they were married. 'By the time you and I got together, she was already up to no good: invoking demons and hanging out with dark warlocks . . .' Jez shifted uncomfortably. No one else would have even noticed, but she knew what every imperceptible tic, every clenched buttock, meant. Being able to discuss this side of her life was such a novelty, she sometimes got swept away with herself. 'Sorry,' she said quickly.

'It's all right.' His face said otherwise.

'No.' Elle held up a well-manicured hand in surrender. 'I said I wouldn't go on about it, so I won't.'

'I'm *fine*.' That sounded like a strain, but he went on. 'It's just in front of Milo I'd rather you didn't. It's bad enough with Holly rabbiting on about it the whole friggin' time.'

'Jez, I have told her more than once . . .'

'I know, I know.' He lay down, sliding under the duvet and resting his head on the pillow. 'It's just a big deal, Elle. Imagine how you'd feel if it were the other way round, if I were like, *oh guess what, I'm a fuckin' part-time werewolf* or something.'

Elle lay down too, facing him from her own pillow. 'Holly will get bored, I promise. It's all exciting to begin with and then it's just part of who you are, like having blue eyes.'

Jez said nothing for a second and then muttered. 'Is she still banging on about joining HMRC or whatever it's called?'

Elle shook her head. 'She's fourteen. She doesn't know how she'll feel at eighteen. *I* wanted to work for the coven when I was her age.'

It wasn't wholly accurate to say meeting Jez when she was sixteen changed her mind on that, although it certainly sealed the deal. By that point, her heritage was so far down her priority list it barely registered. Being a witch was super exciting until she realised the world was full of boys. After that, all she wanted to do was to go out on a Friday night, get served in the pubs, and meet them. It was such a fun hobby: who'd date who; who liked who; trying to pin down where a boy would be and then 'accidentally' run into them. She half missed it.

Of course, she'd met Jez well ahead of dating apps, but Elle was fascinated by them. From what she could tell it was like collecting men and putting them in a sticker album in order of preference. She'd always liked collecting things.

Jez continued to whine. 'I don't want her fillin' Milo's head with ideas.'

'Love, it doesn't work like that. Milo isn't a warlock. We'd know by now.'

'Well that's better than nothing I suppose.' Jez rolled over, no doubt ready to sleep.

That stung, and Elle couldn't pretend it didn't. She'd been hiding this side of herself since she was a kid. It had always baffled her that none of her friends, or grandmother, had cared what mundanes thought of them. Couldn't they hear the way people spoke about Annie? A *freak*, a *witch*, a *whore*, a *hag*? When Jez hadn't immediately freaked out after Fight Night, she'd thought she'd got away with it. Seemed it was more a case of delayed reaction. It had been naïve of her to think that Jez would accept impossible things without questions or concerns. Worse still, *fears*.

'I'll talk to Holly again,' Elle told Jez's shoulders. 'This house is a witch-free zone. OK?'

He turned to face her. 'Thanks, babe.' He leaned in for a goodnight kiss.

Elle did not want her husband to fear her. She guessed it was back to pretending she was just Elle Pearson, wife and mum.

Her phone buzzed; Leonie replying to the group: *Yes please. Once Rad is home we party.*

Oh *shit*. She'd forgotten about Rad. Would Lee think she was insensitive to suggest drinks while he was missing? Should she apologise? Oh God. Now she wouldn't sleep a wink.

Chapter Five

GUILT IS A BASTARD

Leonie – Hebden Bridge, UK

As ever, they stayed in Mike's Airbnb in Heptonstall, down the street from Niamh's. It was a bijou conversion in the wine cellar of a tall terrace; large enough for a kitchenette, a small table and a king-sized bed. It was more than sufficient for the two of them.

Leonie took an extra-long, extra-hot shower, rinsing the funeral off her skin. She shut off the jet and wrapped a towel around her chest before joining Chinara in the studio room. Her girlfriend was lying on the bed, ankles crossed, channel-hopping. 'That better?'

'Much,' Leonie said, carefully removing her shower cap and unfurling her new, waist-length braids. 'Do you think I should pop over to Niamh's before it gets late? She seemed weird, and then she ducked out early . . .'

Chinara frowned, settling for repeats of *Bake Off* on some digital channel. 'Grief is complicated. I never met Ciara, but it sounds like this one is extra tricky.'

Leonie cast off the damp towel and flopped onto the

bed. Chinara tutted at her dripping on the duvet. 'God, I wish you'd known her.'

'Wasn't she, by all accounts, evil?'

'Chi . . . there's no such thing as good and—' And then she saw her girlfriend's smirk. She was being teased. 'She was . . . fucked up the way the rest of us are fucked up. She just . . . acted out.'

'Acted out!' The conversation was very at odds with Mary Berry pecking at a cinnamon bun on TV. 'She killed Conrad Chen. She crossed uncrossable lines.'

Leonie nodded, suddenly feeling very sober. How to argue with that? Leonie wasn't sure even the 'uncrossable lines' couldn't be crossed back over, but she sure as shit wasn't going to argue about justice with a lawyer. *Fuck, Ciara, why did you have to do that to Con?* It made no sense. That being said, they'd all done fucked-up things under the banner of war. She didn't remind Chinara that they'd both crossed that same 'uncrossable' line.

She sometimes forgot it was the war that had brought them together in the first place. Without it, they might never have met. Chinara had only ever seen the consequences of Ciara's latter-day handiwork, nothing from her earlier, playful, oeuvre. 'I know. But I liked her. I did. I know I shouldn't, but I did. Can't help it. I knew her before she went over the line. She was fun. She was ferocious too. I remember this one time she hexed this little twat in Market Square because he grabbed my tits.'

'She hexed mundanes?'

'Yeah! In broad daylight. I know! I was there, mouthing off at them, thinking I was dead hard and Ciara just . . .' Leonie waved a hand.

Chinara raised a single brow. 'She sounds unhinged.'

'She was.' With hindsight it wasn't hard to see why Hale's notions of witch supremacy appealed to her, but then her actions had just seemed badass. 'We were kids.' While she remembered, she set an alarm on her phone for the following morning. 'I need to be up at six, OK?'

Chinara's mood darkened further. You wouldn't need to be a sentient to recognise it. 'You're going to HMRC?'

'Bri can't find Radley by herself so what other choice do I have?' Bri, Diaspora's sole oracle, had done little else except look for where her brother would next appear, but had little to report. He had left the country in search of Hale after he fled Grierlings last June from Heathrow airport. And that was all. Hale had left even less of a trace. They could be anywhere in the world.

Chinara said nothing for a moment. Leonie didn't read her. Wouldn't be fair. 'Can one dip in and out of HMRC as they wish?'

Leonie gave her The Look.

'You know what I mean, though, Lee. You either agree with their methods or you don't. Three months ago, you had me working all the hours in the day to stop them executing Helena. You wanted the whole coven abolished, and now you're asking them for favours.'

Leonie shook her head sadly. 'That's not fair. This is an emergency. And anyway, under Niamh it'll be different.' Or, at the very least, more inclusive. Trans witches now welcome. 'He's my *brother*, Chinara.' No one else would have caught the crack in her voice, no one but Chinara.

Chinara softened and pulled her into an embrace. Leonie rested her head on Chinara's breast. 'Give him more credit. He's a grown-up.'

That was true, but Leonie would always be his big sister. Radley had been a funny-looking kid – tall and skinny even then, with disproportionately large ears he hadn't grown into. And, of course, they looked different to everyone else. He stuck out like a sore thumb on the mostly white Belle Isle estate. It was only later that Leonie learned what Belle Isle meant and it was funny because that part of Leeds was neither beautiful nor an island.

No one could have known that the Jackman children were supernormal – not even their parents who were both mundanes. All the same, difference shone from them, the way it does with some kids. Radley got more grief than she did. She mostly suffered girls who wanted to pat her hair at school. A hundred tiny ways of letting her know she was *different*, and that is a lonely thing to feel at seven years old, but at least she'd always had her brother.

So she stuck up for Radley. If people gave him shit, she'd defend him – sometimes with her fists.

And now he needed her again. Radley had dedicated himself to the cabal to the exclusion of all else. No girl-friend, few friends outside of his pub quiz team. She was all he had.

'If he finds Dabney Hale, he's dead,' Leonie said very quietly.

'I know.'

'Wherever Hale went, it's nowhere good. And Radley is a fucking *healer*. Not even a very good one! What's he gonna do, lull the most dangerous warlock of all time into a restful slumber?' Leonie felt a flash of anger. Going after Hale *alone* without the cabal or coven was the most reckless thing her brother had ever, ever done in his entire life. Why couldn't he just be boring? *She* was the chaotic one.

Leonie also understood his motivation: much of Rad's work was on rehabilitating the public image of the cabal;

an image very much soiled during Hale's war. Under Rad's management, they were no longer bitter men trying to undermine more powerful witches, but a vital cog in the HMRC machine.

While it was just as much in the coven's interest to find both Hale and Rad as it was hers, they weren't moving nearly as fast as she'd like. If it was one of theirs – if it was Niamh or Moira – they'd have witches all over the world hunting for him right now.

'I have to find him,' Leonie said, effectively shutting down the conversation. 'I can move faster than a whole coven. There are rules about them crossing into other coven territories and—'

Chinara stroked her hair. 'Leonie, my love, we should start talking about what happens if . . .'

She cut her off. 'If he's already dead? No.' She pushed herself off Chinara because she didn't want to be anywhere near this conversation. She pulled an oversized T-shirt over her head. She normally slept nude, but the north was about ten fucking degrees colder than London.

Chinara was no doubt trying to prepare her for the worst, but still, fuck that. 'He is not dead,' Leonie said. 'I would know. He's alive.'

But that was a lie. She couldn't feel Radley one way or another, and how she'd tried. There was nothing, an endless silence ringing in her ears.

Chapter Six

WEAVING

Ciara – Hebden Bridge, UK

And that's what you get, Ciara thought, for underestimating a teenage girl.

Before Theo could so much as flinch, Ciara raised both hands to channel all her mental energy towards her. The slight girl folded at her core and reeled backwards across the room until she slammed into the kitchen sink. She squealed and tumbled to the floor, crockery raining down with her.

A snarl on her lips, Ciara glided across the cottage, looming over her. Her feet made contact with the tiles and she zeroed in on her target.

'Don't!' Theo pleaded, but Ciara's right hand already grasped her forehead.

'*Sleep.*' Theo was powerful, but Ciara had surprise on her side. Theo's eyes widened for a second before lolling into her skull. Ciara didn't let go, sinking her deep, deep out of consciousness.

Satisfied she was out, Ciara flopped onto her bottom, the flagstones freezing cold. 'Fuck,' she said aloud. She cradled her head in her hands. She'd taken her eye off the ball. What now? She couldn't kill her, nor did she have any desire to, that'd somewhat give the game away. Plus, she wasn't a fucking lunatic. 'Shit.'

That only left one option. She rose to her feet. 'Come on, then.' She lifted Theo with her mind and started towards the narrow cottage stairs. The limp body floated obediently after her. Ciara stomped up the steps like an adolescent, and it was all too familiar as she headed for their old room. How two stropping teenage girls had ever coexisted in the smaller room was a true mystery. At the time, it hadn't seemed so bad, their twin beds pushed to either corner.

Ciara swiped Theo's school bag and some laundry off the bed before lowering her. The room smelled of sickly vanilla teenage perfume, and Ciara vowed – if Theo survived what happened next – to take her fragrance-shopping. Life is too short for cheap perfume. She brushed raven hair off Theo's face. She looked serene, like Millais' Ophelia.

This gave Ciara an opportunity to have a look inside. What further gaps could Theo fill? The last few months of her sister's life had been eventful, to say the least. And what of Theo anyway? She had as many chunks missing from her history as Ciara did. Ciara perched on the rim of the bed and held her hands on either side of Theo's temples. 'Let's have a wee look, shall we?'

She closed her eyes and immersed herself, sinking herself past Theo's short-term memory – snippets of the funeral and wake – and into those that had made the sponge layer of her mind trifle. With a lurch Ciara fell forwards into memories that weren't her own. They were vivid, tactual, a reflection of Theo's strength.

She smelled wild garlic first, and then felt the prickle of humidity on her skin. Sulphur too. Demons.

She was in a forest, a forest she knew. Hardcastle Crags.

Then the pain hit. Through smoke and lightning, she saw the frenzy on Helena Vance's face as she tried to tear her – or rather tear *Theo* – apart. The High Priestess was possessed; it takes one to know one, and Ciara knew possession.

Vines and branches were coiled around her throat, arms and waist. Across the woods, the brook somehow blazed with fire, and in the centre of it was her sister. Niamh reached out her hand, squinting through the inferno and started to glow. Ciara recognised this as Vitalis or 'radiance' as a lot of healers called it – the energy they siphon from the elements to heal the living.

And now Ciara felt what Theo had felt that night in the forest; Niamh pouring every drop of herself into the girl. The pain subsided, and she was instead filled with the most comforting inner warmth. Ciara had never felt anything like it. She felt her body stretch, bend and reconfigure; bones and muscles shifting and settling.

Niamh had more than *saved* Theo, she'd remodelled her. Well of course she had. She always did give the most infuriatingly thoughtful gifts.

But this was boring; she'd gleaned this already. Ciara forced herself deeper into Theo's memories. There was a very specific moment when Theo had trusted Niamh; a very nothing night where they'd watched *Pitch Perfect* on the sofa and eaten Quorn fajitas. She went further and saw the first time Theo had arrived at the cottage and, before that, the cage they had housed her in at Grierlings. Ciara shivered. The poor thing had been terrified, and it was a terror she was terrified to revisit.

She went further and felt the sheer, fizzing frustration that led to the destruction of her old school in Scotland. The sky crawled with lightning, bolts licking the roof of the building. Could she go further? Things got darker, like someone was dimming the lights in her mind. Evidently Theo herself did not want to remember much of her life before Hebden Bridge.

Ciara sensed distraction within her own mind and withdrew from Theo's. Her eyes blinked open and adjusted to the muted lamplight. She scanned the room, looking to see if Tiger had entered while she was in the trance.

There was nothing obvious until she became aware of a light rat-a-tat at the window. She drew back the curtain and saw a fat, furry moth beating its wings against the glass. Ciara rolled her eyes in resignation. She was almost surprised it had taken this long. She supposed the sudden burst of magic down in the kitchen had been a drop of blood in the water.

And now came the sharks.

'Go away,' she said aloud.

But how we missed you, dear one.

'I said *go away*.' She returned to Theo's side.

We always had such fun, you and I. I can help you now. This could be easy. Let me help you, sweet Ciara. I can help you remember . . .

And it did.

She now recognised the silky voice: his name was Nybbas. She knew him only too well. A demon of dreams and visions. In the form of a moth of all things. Memories bloomed in her mind, petals unfurling, as the demon worked its spell.

She remembered invoking him in a cheap hotel room in Berlin. It was as if she were there now, the cumin-rich smells from the curry house next door, the scratchy woollen blanket under her body.

The dreams she'd had that night had felt as real as any waking moment; she'd feasted on sumptuous cakes and wines, never feeling sick or full, before one of the best fucks of her life with a man whose face and body kept changing to fulfil her whims.

Then, in years gone by, he'd come to her occupying a feather and a stray cat, she remembered now. Demons can appear as anything they want, within reason, within nature, she knew that. They always find a way. How was it that, almost ten years since she'd last invoked him, and in a different body, he found her so quickly? The stink really does stick.

I can make you better again. Let me in, dear one.

Invoking a demon like Nybbas would be . . . intriguing. While he's not one of the big boys, if a demon has a name, it's by no means power*less*. Nybbas, Belial, even Gaia; these were names created by humans to categorise impossible beings they couldn't ever hope to fully comprehend. But they could *experience* some of them.

Let me fix you. You know what you have to do. Just let me in a while.

Ciara's heart giddied. Even his proximity was drawing images out of the darkness inside of her.

It was tempting. Very tempting.

But as this welcome flashback solidified, she *also* remembered waking up from that delectable dream in Berlin, and discovering four whole days had passed, and that she'd shit the bed.

'I'm not interested,' she said, scarcely convincing herself.

Who is there here to lie to?

She ignored it, turning her back to the window. She

could paper over Theo's memories without needing to invoke a demon. Yes, she'd slept for the best part of a decade, but she was still just as strong as her sister.

The gossamer wings continued to beat against the windowpane.

He's been awaiting your return.

She looked over her shoulder. 'Who has?'

Do you think it an accident?

She stood and stormed to the window. 'What do you mean?'

Let me in and I'll show you.

'I said *no*.' She emitted a psychic blast, swatting it off the window. For so many reasons, she wanted to feel the demon fill her veins. But no. She must be strong. Tomorrow was too important. She sat on the bed and screwed her eyes shut, willing it away. *Fuck off.*

The demon must sense she was serious because, behind her, the wings stopped drumming on the glass.

He'll be with you shortly.

'What?' She dared to look again. 'Who? Dab?'

But Nybbas was gone. For now. Ciara exhaled, half frustrated, half relieved. If she didn't have the meeting at HMRC in the morning, she wasn't sure she'd have such resolve. Today had been gruelling, she'd have welcomed the escape.

That being said, she was quite enjoying Niamh's virgin body. It seemed a shame to let demons put footprints in the snow. She felt strong, perhaps stronger than ever, which raised certain philosophical questions. Witch academics had argued for centuries about whether a witch's power was rooted in her body, or from somewhere more ephemeral. When they'd taken the Eriksdottir test at thirteen, both Ciara and her sister had attained Level 5s, but Julia

Collins once told their grandmother that they'd like to retest Niamh alone. *She showed more promise.*

Ciara refocused on the task at hand. *Weaving.* It was forbidden outside HMRC's Enforcement Division, but a powerful sentient could insert 'memories' into someone else's mind. It wasn't even *that* difficult – she'd done it to Mildred at the safehouse in mere seconds, but Theo was stronger than Mildred. HMRC did it to mundane witnesses all the time. During the war, they wove deepfakes into whole *villages* to cover up their actions: flash floods; freak storms; sink holes; 'gas explosions'.

Ciara conjured the images in her mind first: Theo falling down the stairs in the cottage. She replayed this version of the past over and over in her mind, shoring up the details. She once again placed her hands over Theo's head and started to transfer this convincing lie. With luck, Theo would awake in the morning, convinced she had taken a tumble down the stairs, explaining any bruising from her crash landing in the kitchen.

Weaving in a witch as powerful as Theo took some elbow grease. Theo's psyche didn't *want* memories implanting over real ones. Ciara felt the strain on her own powers, but kept going. With the fiction installed, Ciara moved to the simpler job of wiping the *actual* events in the kitchen – the moment when Theo sensed who she really was.

It was truly a clean-up job; get in and out, and no one should be any the wiser. Ciara read Theo. Seamless. Even Leonie wouldn't see what was real and wasn't. Ciara smiled slightly. Almost ten years flat on her ass and she hadn't lost her touch. She didn't, had never, *needed* demons.

She just happened to like the way they'd made her feel.

Kaur, Sandhya

To me; Roberts, Moira

Hello Niamh

Ahead of the induction day tomorrow, please bring two forms of photo ID and your HMRC registration number if you can find it.

Also, to confirm, the coronation will take place on <u>Tuesday, 31 October at midnight</u>. I've updated the diary. Once the invites go out, we'll start prep. Three weeks! It'll be tight, but the HMRC events team are already well underway on logistics.

We've also had a formal summons from our government liaison in the Shadow Cabinet. They want to set up an introductory meeting in due course.

See you tomorrow.

Sandhya x
Sandhya Kaur (she/her)
Assistant to the High Priestess

Chapter Seven

THE WOMAN WHO WOULD BE PRIESTESS

Ciara – Manchester, UK

The teleport almost knocked Ciara clean off her feet. As her eyes adjusted to the palatial lobby of the HMRC offices, she swayed, but didn't fall. It had been a long time since she'd done that. Goddess, it was monstrous. How, in *centuries*, had no witch improved that method of transportation? Her legs felt like wet spaghetti and she leaned against a mighty marble pillar for support.

Ciara blinked and took in her surroundings. Well, this was all very nice. *Of course* HMRC spent taxpayer's money on fancy offices and not, you know, helping poor witches out of poverty.

'You OK?' Leonie asked, materialising on her left, and then, 'Did you cut your hair?'

'Yeah,' Ciara said bashfully. 'Weird post-funeral feminine urge.'

'It's cute.'

Ciara smiled, despite fighting off a wave of nausea. Over

breakfast that morning – although she now regretted eating a bowl of muesli before teleporting – she'd established that her weave had taken in Theo. Barely injured, she seemed more mortified at clumsily going headfirst down the stairs, and had referred to her as 'Niamh'.

As a further precaution, Ciara had unearthed a dusty jar of *White Sorbus* in a tin under the sink. Why Niamh had any in the house at all was a mystery – it could well have been there since *they'd* been teenagers. The powder – made from desiccated white rowan berries – was once prescribed to temper the gifts of unskilled young witches so they wouldn't inadvertently draw attention to a coven. It was harmless enough. Ciara had added some of the tasteless substance to Theo's porridge that morning *and* sprinkled a little over her sandwich in her packed lunch too. That ought to stop her sneaking around inside her head any time soon.

All was well. For now. She only had to keep it up until they found Hale.

Moira Roberts, Scotland's highest-ranking witch, strode efficiently to the front desk as soon as she was corporeal, her heels tapping across the marble floor. 'Let the oracles know we've arrived, please,' she told the receptionist. Ciara had learned Moira's husband was sick, and Ciara sensed the Cailleach was keen to hand the reins to her as soon as possible to tend to her home situation.

Sandhya Kaur beckoned them through an open security gate. Sandhya had been Helena's PA, and would now be hers. She was a sentient, but a lesser one. It shouldn't be too hard to keep her out. Sandhya handed her a plastic card on a lanyard. 'Here's your security pass.'

'You'd think witches might get something more bling,' Ciara said, accepting the ugly pass. 'A talisman maybe. It's so mundane.'

Moira cackled. 'Oh, Niamh, my girl. HMRC has been squeezing the magic out of witchcraft for decades. It should be their official slogan.'

The pass displayed a stock picture of her sister they must have had on file. Ciara didn't recognise herself at all in pictures of Niamh, never had.

The four of them boarded the lift and Sandhya pressed the button for the fifth floor. Ciara observed the floor plan attached to the wall, taking in as much as she could. If Niamh knew the layout of this sprawling building, then so should she.

Acquisitions & Archive was in the basement alongside the gym. The ground floor seemed to be for logistics: IT, Finance, Human Resources. On the first floor, you'd find the canteen, Boil and Bubble. The second was dedicated to Niamh's old department, Recruitment, Education and Development (RED), while the third housed Events, Community Outreach and Global Coven Liaison. On the fourth you'd find 'Dynamic Workspaces', whatever that meant, meeting rooms and the Teleportation Team. The fifth floor was home to the single largest department; Supernormal Security. That included the oratorium, where they were now heading.

The lift arrived with a ping and they stepped out into the busy, open-plan offices; rows of computer desks, with large monitors suspended from the ceiling overhead. The screens displayed scrolling news from covens around the world: *Sisters of the New Forest celebrate 100 years . . . Santos steps down at Bruxas Brasil in corruption scandal . . . Hale remains at large . . .*

Leonie waved to a group of witches standing around a breakout space. 'All right, girlies?' she called brightly. 'Cunts,' she added more quietly.

Ciara grinned. Only one witch – Robyn Jones – had been sacked over her conduct in the siege at Hebden Bridge. The rest, according to the tribunal held over the summer, had simply been 'following orders'. Sounded about right. She'd checked, and Niamh had never been sanctioned for severing Ciara while 'on manoeuvres'. Far from it, she was about to receive the ultimate accolade: High Priestess.

'Now, now,' Moira told Leonie. 'That's all dealt with.'

'How is the system ever gonna change if you don't change the system?' Leonie fired back.

Moira looked to her, her lips a tight red line. 'And there I was thinking you wanted our assistance?'

Leonie Jackman. Her little partner in crime. Ciara knew enough to know she had missed her. Like any group of girlfriends, little side-units had formed: her and Lee; Elle and Hel. And Niamh. Niamh, Little Miss Switzerland, holding them together like some Blue Peter toilet roll abomination. She had only seen snippets of what happened at the Hotel Carnoustie, but she knew she owed Lee her life. Niamh would have killed her. Perhaps that explained some of the searing rage she'd awoken to: Kill or be killed. And it was exactly *those* sorts of thoughts she needed to hide. If anyone was going to blow her cover, it was Leonie.

They reached imposing double doors. Ciara was intrigued to see inside the oratorium but *assumed* that Niamh already had, so aimed for total nonchalance. Moira rang an entry buzzer and someone opened the doors from the inside. A wave of chill air billowed out into the corridor.

Even as a witch, oracles fascinated Ciara. The strangest of the strange. There was something about the separateness, their monastic lifestyle. They retained remnants of the ancient in a way most witches didn't. She, of course, would *hate* to be an oracle, but they were fascinating.

The oratorium was almost pitch dark, like entering a ghost train, and with all the same jittery anticipation. It was so cold; how did they stand it? She wrapped her arms around herself. Ciara looked up into the domed ceiling, where tiny crystals dangled on delicate chains, refracting what little light there was. She couldn't be sure, but did they . . . hum? She almost, *almost* exclaimed, but remembered who she was.

The room was bigger than she was expecting, with tiered seats leading down to a circular rostrum. A quick headcount, and she estimated there were about forty oracles already seated. None wore wigs on their bald skulls, and all wore austere white cotton jumpsuits. They waited for their guests in silence.

It *was* weird. They were weird.

At the centre of the amphitheatre was a painfully thin woman, the pyjamas hanging off her skeletal frame. Her face was sharp, all angles, her icy eyes slicing through the gloom. Irina Konvalinka. Ciara had seen vague versions of her in Moira's head, enough to recognise her now and to be somewhat fearful.

Ciara had amassed what intelligence she could from materials Niamh had gathered at the cottage in preparation for her new role. Konvalinka – like many witches – was considerably older than she looked; she'd come to the UK during the Second World War as part of an HMRC scheme to protect witches stranded in war-torn Europe. Beyond that, Ciara knew precious little except that this woman was the most powerful oracle in the country. And that made her someone she ought to be careful around. It irked Ciara; were the events in that hospital room foreseen?

'Welcome,' the oracle announced. 'Please, be seated.'

Space had been reserved for them at the lowest tier.

Ciara was glad to see some rough woollen blankets had been left out for the visitors too. She sat and wrapped it around her shoulders like a shawl.

Konvalinka approached her, offering a pale hand. 'Dr Kelly,' she said, her teeth oddly shark-like in the gloom. 'On behalf of all the oracles, we are sorry for your loss.'

Ciara fortified her thoughts. 'Thank you.' She reminded herself that oracles do not see *everything*, they are fallible, their visions constantly in flux as the present diverts the future. Perhaps *a* death was anticipated, or perhaps Helena's actions shattered the course of the future as they saw it.

Only Gaia sees everything from every angle.

The blind woman held her gaze for just a second too long, however, and Ciara didn't care for it one bit. She, of course, *could* read minds and probed deep into Irina's bony head.

Nothing. The woman was a steel trap. Clever little bitch. Fuck. That was worrisome.

'We have much to discuss before your coronation,' Irina said.

'We do.' She sat up straighter. 'But first Radley Jackman. Finding him and Dabney Hale must be our priority over sticking a daft crown on my head.' Ciara sensed Leonie's gratitude; warm, pumpkin-coloured.

'Indeed,' Irina said.

'Have you seen him?' Leonie asked eagerly.

'Did you bring a personal item?' Irina said.

Leonie said she had, and pulled a sad-looking stuffed bear from her tote bag. It had one eye and denim dunga-rees. She handed it to Irina, who held it close to her chest and inhaled deeply. 'Yes. This will help.'

Without a further word, she turned and took her place at the heart of the sanctuary on a slightly elevated nest of cushions. Irina placed the bear before her. 'Sisters,' she commanded. 'See as I see.'

A heavy hush fell over the room. Irina's eyes turned cloudy grey and then pure white. Ciara peeked around and saw every oracle in the room was staring into time, all searching for clues to Radley's past, present and future.

Only Gaia knew when Ciara had last seen Leonie's brother herself. What an annoying, whining irritant he'd always been; always grassing on them for next to nothing. He had a huge thing for Elle as she recalled.

Without warning, she saw him. *Radley*. A memory returned to her insouciantly, as if it were no big deal it had been gone. She *had* seen him, albeit from afar. She'd briefly glimpsed him surveying the devastation after the Somerset Floods.

The floods. Of all the things to come to her; a day she'd rather never see ever again.

Why are you doing this?

On the run, they had just made the derelict Hotel Carnoustie their base in Scotland, and Dabney and the others were celebrating the mass killing of fellow witches with mead and song. Ciara was too weak to dance with the others. She was on a mattress, tired and cold in only a thin satin slip. She had invoked the demon Valac. He'd appeared to her as an infant boy in the rain, begging her for shelter. She had offered it, in a manner of speaking.

Earlier, she had seen it all from afar. At Hale's side, she'd watched from higher ground in the Quantock Hills. Eight of his elementals, arms aloft; summoning torrential rains and hurricane winds from a furious mauve sky, until the River Tone and River Parrett burst their banks. A deluge spilled out over the Somerset Flats, engulfing whole villages. When HMRC and cabal forces arrived, sentients waited in ambush. They never stood a chance.

They are collateral, my dear, he told her, kissing her clammy neck. *HMRC stands between us and true witch supremacy. They are sheep, and we are wolves.*

Had *she* killed people that day? No. Of that she was certain. Ciara had had nothing to do with that. It was needless death; Dab showing off. But by that night, she'd been too far gone to care. She could scarcely lift her head off the damp mattress. She hadn't felt *anything* as the witches were drowned or severed. Nothing. Valac had kept her safe from it all.

'Do you see him?' Leonie asked Irina now, breaking Ciara's train of thought. Ciara almost gasped, grateful that *something* – even that dismal day – had returned from the void. The oracle held up a single finger. 'Silence!' she snapped. 'Wait . . .'

Far behind them, a younger oracle spoke up. 'I see him, sister . . .'

'As do I,' another added.

Leonie fidgeted anxiously in her seat. Ciara reached across her knee and gave her hand a squeeze. It's what Niamh would do. Once upon a time, it's what she'd have done. 'The fuck is taking so long?' Leonie muttered.

Irina now turned to the three visiting sentients in the front row. 'See as I see,' she ordered.

Ciara dared to open her mind a fraction and share in their collective vision. She closed her eyes and felt alien images stray into her subconscious: Radley arriving at an airport . . . but where? She saw him checking into a poxy hotel, again impossible to tell his location. The scene changed to a dingy nightclub . . . a strip club? Behind him she saw a svelte female form dancing on stage. It was . . . familiar to Ciara. Had she been there?

The images were hazy, smoky at the edges. He was alive though. Although that depended on whether or not this was Radley's past, present or future. A final image – a beautiful Japanese woman wearing a jewelled eyepatch which Ciara *definitively* recognised.

The vision receded until Ciara's head was firmly in the oratorium.

'Is that now?' Leonie demanded.

'Time is meaningless to us,' Irina said. 'You know this.'

Leonie sighed and Ciara sensed she was biting her tongue.

'Where is that?' Moira asked.

Ciara waited a moment. *She* knew this woman's identity, but she couldn't say if her virtuous sister would be so familiar. Oh fuck it. 'That woman at the end was Domino.'

Leonie fixed her in a puzzled glare. 'She was Asian!'

Ciara shrugged. 'She's had work.'

'She used to be white!'

'Not that kind of work.'

'Body swapping?' Lee's eyes widened.

Ciara tried to sound as casual as possible. 'That was always the rumour, wasn't it? That she collects pretty girls and swaps between them like designer handbags.'

'How do you know it's her?' Moira asked.

'I sensed it. And the club . . . it all adds up.'

Domino was an old and powerful sorceress. Mad as fuck, and more importantly rich as fuck, but Ciara fully respected her absolute refusal to commit to any specific coven. She was a sole trader, not to mention a soul trader.

Distantly descended from Portuguese royalty, Domino had been establishing her brand of members' clubs for witches and warlocks all around the world for decades. Domino maintained a policy of strict apoliticism that meant they were frequented by the more unsavoury types.

They must have met, even if Ciara wouldn't be able to say where, or when. She just knew.

'There are Voodoo Lounges everywhere,' Leonie said. 'Which one was it?'

Moira turned to Sandhya. 'Get on to Security. Find her *now*.' The assistant nodded and left the oratorium at once. 'Marvellous. With any luck, Radley will lead us directly to Hale.'

'I'm going after him,' Leonie said.

'There's really no need. We'll send a SWAT team.' *Special Witches and Tactics.*

'No!' Leonie argued. 'If Hale knows HMRC is coming, fuck knows what he'll do. He'll kill Rad. Let me go alone, be a little spy. I'll draw less attention to myself. When I find out where he is, I'll let you know, I promise.' Moira was about to shut her down, but Leonie ploughed on. 'Please? Just let me get Rad out of the way, and then Hale is all yours.'

'Remember Somerset,' Ciara interjected. 'That's what Dabney Hale does when someone challenges his manhood.'

This struck home. Moira nodded. 'Aye. OK, then. The oracles here will keep searching and update you as you travel.'

From outside the chamber, Sandhya transmitted into Ciara's head. *We have reason to believe Domino is presently in Bologna, Italy.* Leonie heard too, evidently. She slapped the tops of her thighs with purpose. 'Looks like I'm going to Bologna, then.'

'I'll go too,' Ciara said, perhaps too keenly, but if it meant getting to Dab . . .

Moira, however, looked daggers at her. 'I don't think so, Niamh. We have a meeting with the Shadow Cabinet. It's not optional, I'm afraid.'

Ciara very nearly told her to shove it up her arse, but instead feigned forgetfulness. 'Of course. What am I thinking?'

Moira gave a curt nod. 'Leonie, you'll leave today. I'll give you a twenty-four-hour head start,' Moira said, and Leonie agreed. Moira sent clear instructions to Sandhya: *Sandhya, please alert Coven Italia that Hale may be in the country, and then the CNF to arrange a teleport transfer for Leonie via France.* Leonie was right to look a little concerned; teleportation overseas wasn't nearly as reliable as inland.

'Can I see Chinara before I leave?' Leonie said, sounding as panicked as Leonie ever sounded.

'Of course. Be quick about it. Niamh and I can discuss her coronation alone.'

'Ah yes,' Irina said suddenly before Leonie could even rise to her feet. 'We see it clearly now.'

Ciara's stomach tightened. 'Is that so?'

'Indeed. The future was so uncertain after Helena's death. Some were not certain Niamh Kelly was meant for the coronet.' Irina took a not insignificant pause, a faint smile hovering on her lips. 'Yet before us now is the new High Priestess.'

And that was when Ciara knew she was in trouble. This bitch knew.

Chapter Eight

ARRIVEDERCI

Leonie – London, UK

From behind her desk, Chinara stared blankly at her as she materialised. 'And if there had been someone in my office?'

'I'd have wiped them.' Leonie shrugged, and slid into the guest chair. 'Busy?'

She closed a manila file. 'Yes. I was away from my desk yesterday for the funeral; I'm in court for the rest of the week, so trying to get my ducks in a row.'

Border Free was a non-profit that provided legal assistance to child refugees. Leonie had glimpsed inside Chinara's head at the end of long days, and she held a powerful pride for the work her girlfriend did. It beggared belief that actual *children* who'd been forced to flee warzones around the world even needed lawyers to defend their right to live here, but such was this mean, damp, insular island.

'How did it go up in Manchester?' Chinara said.

Leonie's heart beat a little faster, her fingers drumming on her knees. 'They saw him.'

'They did? Good. Where?'

'He's in Bologna.'

'Italy? What for?'

'I'm guessing Hale got out of the country somehow and went there. He went to see Domino at Voodoo Lounge.'

Chinara pouted slightly. 'That makes sense. She knows all the worst people.'

Leonie leapt in, predicting what Chinara's response would be. 'I'm going there now.'

A pause. Chinara took her reading glasses off and pinched the bridge of her nose. 'I assumed you would. I would bribe you to leave it to HMRC, but I know you well enough to know you cannot.'

Leonie felt the weirdest mixture of love and sadness. 'I have to.'

'I know.' Another pause. 'And I'll come with you.'

'What?' Leonie exploded. 'You can't! You just said you were in court all week.'

Chinara shook her head. 'I'm sure someone can cover for me.'

She knew Chinara wasn't *trying* to guilt-trip her, but the thought of denying orphaned refugees a court advocate was a really fuckin' salient guilt trip. 'No . . . no, I'd feel awful. And anyway . . .' she took a breath because she needed to ask a huge favour. 'I need someone to cover Diaspora stuff while I'm gone.' Kane – her assistant – had a day job, and Leonie couldn't ask them to do everything. They'd picked up so much slack these last few months.

Her eyes widened. 'How long do you think you'll be gone?'

Leonie looked past Chinara at the view beyond her sixth-storey office window. *The* London view, the one on tacky postcards. The Thames glistened like bronze under the meek autumn sun; the outline of the London Eye to her right and Blackfriars Bridge to the left. 'I don't know. I trust Kane and Valentina to keep Black Mass ticking over, but I'd feel better knowing you were in charge.'

Did Chinara know the whole truth? It was very simple – she wouldn't put the woman she loved within a hundred miles of Dabney Hale if she could help it, even if the woman in question was the most powerful elemental in the UK.

Chinara's jaw clenched. 'You're going in search of the world's most dangerous warlock, with no idea when you'll be back. I want to support you, as I always do, but I'm struggling this time, my love.'

Leonie walked around the desk and lowered herself into her girlfriend's lap. She kissed her tenderly on the lips. 'I have no interest whatsoever in Hale. I just want my brother home and then, on this occasion, I'm more than happy to let HMRC take over.'

One final issue. 'What if Hale does find you?'

Leonie shrugged.

'But this is personal, my love.'

Leonie shook her head. 'We don't know that.' They did know that, actually. He really did hate her.

'What about his sister?'

She faked nonchalance. 'What about her?'

'He thinks you killed her, Lee.'

'But I didn't!'

'I know that, but I think he has truly convinced himself.'

It was bullshit. Yes, *technically* Leonie had apprehended Clarissa Hale after the deadly assault on Somerset during the war. Leonie had still been in HMRC and had brought her in after a raid. The fact the girl, only eighteen, had later killed herself in detention at Grierlings did prick on

Leonie's conscience, but she also couldn't see how she'd do anything differently if she got a do-over. Dozens of good witches died in those floods. Dozens more would have died if their campaign had continued.

After Clarissa's arrest, Hale had first sent a warning: a dead capuchin monkey in the post to her old flat in Manchester. She got the none-too-subtle message. Later, he sent a man after Leonie. *That* man she did kill, and *that* was the face that most haunted her.

'All the more reason to go,' Leonie said. 'If he gets hold of Rad, it'll be even worse.'

Chinara had no comeback to that. 'Are you leaving now?'

Leonie nodded. 'I'm gonna grab some clothes from the flat and they're teleporting me.'

'I'm not thrilled to hear that either.'

'I'm going through France; it should be fine.'

Chinara closed her eyes. It pained Leonie to see her in such pain. 'When will all this be over?' she said very quietly. 'When will it just be us?'

'I don't know.' Leonie would not lie to her.

Her partner sighed mournfully. Sometimes the hardest thing in the world was to be supportive. Passion is so much louder than logic or reason, and she could feel Chinara fighting the selfish urge to compel her to stay, to forbid her from going. But that's what eight years of squabbles, fights, make-ups and compromises gets you: understanding. Leonie knew Chinara knew she wouldn't be stopped. Not this time.

'I'll be home soon, I swear.'

'I'm going to love you so hard; you'll feel it in Italy,' Chinara said softly, and Leonie believed her.

Chapter Nine

THE SONG OF OSIRIS

Theo – Hebden Bridge, UK

Theo was alone in the dance studio. Head high, she practised a triple pique turn, her head whipping to a fixed point on the wall so she wouldn't lose balance. Miss Cummings let her rehearse alone; she'd earned that right by being one of the 'good girls'.

Despite its unfortunate title, the 'Pump Studio' had been built with a lottery grant in 2015 so it was one of the nicer parts of St Augustus High School. The floor was sprung for extra bounce and there was a mirror all down one side of the room with the barre. This time last year, Theo wouldn't have been able to set foot in a studio like this. It would have simply been too triggering to look at herself for that long.

Flat on her back, she thrust her hips upwards before placing her hands and pushing up into a backbend. She delved deep inside and used just a little telekinesis to do a kickover to standing. Not the most graceful thing she'd ever seen, but she'd only learned how to do it a couple of weeks ago.

This body. This amazing new body. It made no sense, but it was incredible.

Over the summer, she and Holly had watched *The Little Mermaid*, and Theo knew just how Ariel felt when she looked down and saw her legs for the first time. Only in this case it was a vulva.

Theo walked to the mirror and lifted a leg to the barre to stretch out her hamstrings. It was ironic that she now spent the time she used to dedicate to fretting she was in the wrong body, worrying that it would somehow revert to its original state. She sometimes woke in the night, sweaty and panicked, scared that all this was temporary.

Her outsides now matched how she'd always perceived herself, yet she couldn't relax. At least, not yet. Understanding what had taken place in the woods, the strange exchange between her and Niamh might allay some of her fears, however unfounded they were.

She also felt guilt. The day of her first menstruation could have been momentous, and it was in a small way. At the same time, she mostly felt bad for the countless other mundane trans girls who may never truly get all they wished for. She'd never understood the idiom *never look a gift horse in the mouth*, like who gifts an unsolicited horse, but she got it now. It would be a luxury to simply accept what had happened to her in the woods without this swarm of worries.

Theo, where are you? Holly's voice, a tad irritated, filled her head.

Shit. What time was it?

She hurried over to her bag, dumped in the corner of the studio, and fished out her phone. It was already four. That happened sometimes when she danced; she lost all sense of time.

I'm on my way. Two minutes, she told Holly.

She'd promised Holly she'd go to Annie's cottage with her. Her friend was convinced her dad was up to no good with a mystery woman. From what Theo had seen in his head, she was inclined to agree. It's really hard for mundanes to keep secrets around sentients, and Mr Pearson was guilty about *something*. Theo honestly didn't want to look too hard, scared of what she might see. Sometimes men's heads were scary. Women's too. She had learned, if she was going to be able to live amongst humans, it was best not to look.

Gaia only knew what Holly thought she'd find in Annie's expansive library, but Theo badly hoped their little mission would provide some answers for her too. HMRC hadn't been very helpful at all. They had sent her for a consultation with a witch in Newcastle, who was also a medical doctor, and her unsympathetic vibe had been 'Well you got what you wanted, what's the problem?' More like she didn't know. Theo had read her. The doctor was as baffled as anyone.

Both she and Niamh had been cornered, desperate creatures in the forest that night, under attack from Belial, a demon king. Had the pressure somehow amplified their gifts?

She stared herself down in the mirror. *Nothing* in Theo's short life added up, and this was one more mystery. She didn't know who her parents were, where she came from, why she was so powerful, and now how she'd pulled off this feat of transmutation. A part of her, when it was late at night and she was staring at the grey of the ceiling, remembered Helena Vance's fears: That she was somehow *evil*. That she was the *Sullied Child* that all witches feared.

Ah well, at least she had nice hair. Every cloud and all that.

She gathered her things, slipping her navy blazer on over her dance kit, and exited the studio. Heading towards the car park gates where she said she'd meet Holly at four, she left the Sports Hall and walked the crisp-packet-strewn path on the perimeter of the playing field.

She heard them before she saw them. The unmistakable hyena laughter of teenage boys. She feared them in a different way since her transformation because boys seemed to notice her in a different way. They didn't just want to mock her any more. She felt her shoulders creep up towards her ears but carried on walking.

'It's that new girl,' a male voice said.

'Well fit.'

'Fresh pussy . . .' They started to bray. They didn't know the half of it.

Only then, 'Shut the fuck up you twat.' She recognised that voice. It was Milo Pearson, finishing football practice with the rest of the Year 11 team. Specks of mud dotted his face, but he gave her a tip of his head as they passed on the path. 'You all right?'

Theo nodded and walked on. Milo was the only person, other than Holly, who knew she was Theo 2.0. Niamh had offered to wipe him, to give her a clean start in September, but it didn't seem fair. Actually, Milo didn't seem to care about *anything* aside from football and *Call of Duty* from what she could tell. It was funny, because Year 10 girls *really* liked Milo Pearson, but he seemed to find the whole 'my mate likes you' thing cringe. Which it was.

Anyway, Theo knew – without having to read him – that he hadn't told anyone 'her secret' because there was a trans guy in Year 11 and he got a *lot* more transphobic shit than she did.

There; that stab of guilt again. She was too trans and not trans enough.

'That your girlfriend, Milo?' one of the pack muttered.

'Do you want me to snap your dick off?' Milo said, and Theo couldn't help but laugh. Not that she'd ever really been in a position to know, but in some ways, it looked like being a cis boy was just as much a minefield as being a girl. All the posturing, the willy-waggling. It must be exhausting. She left them to their literal cock-fighting. Both she and Holly had their missions.

When teenage girls are finding their voices, they can be forgiven for misplacing the volume dial. As such, Theo and Holly's full-throated rendition of 'How Soon Is Now' demolished the emerald tranquillity of Hardcastle Crags. The girls trotted down the ramshackle stone stairs to the old watermill. Their high, giggly laughter ceased as they approached.

Annie's cottage soaked up sadness like a sponge. Theo felt it even as they passed through the garden gate. It was like the house had become a focal point for all the grief the coven couldn't quite find the words to convey. There had been a great many happy years here, but all now were tinged with a melancholy set deep in the limestone walls.

It also still smelled strongly of cat piss, even if the cats had moved on to the local rehoming shelter.

'Are you sure we're allowed in here?' Theo followed Holly through the front door into what was once Annie's lounge.

'I don't see why not,' Holly said. 'The sale doesn't go through until next week, so it's ours for now. Mum says the developers want it to be a luxury holiday cottage in time for the spring.'

'That's really depressing.'

'Yeah.' Holly wiped a porthole in the filthy living-room window. 'I don't think Mum wants to sell it, but Grandma wants it sold ASAP. Probably can't wait to spend it all down the bingo.'

'And that's depressing too,' Theo said, turning her attention to the cardboard boxes. 'Where do we start?'

Holly bounded over, now taller than Theo. This week, her bleach-fried hair was bubblegum pink; strictly forbidden at school, but every time she got called in to the Assistant Head's office, Holly used her powers to convince him he was fine with whatever shade it was. 'So these are all Annie's grimoires and almanacs. They're gonna be taken to the archive at HMRC later this week; that's why we have to do it now.'

Theo picked a lighter box off the stack and lowered it to the flagstone floor. She laid out her coat as a mat and sat on it before starting to poke around the contents. This one seemed mostly to be Annie's diaries. 'And you think she had one about what happened to me?'

'She definitely had a book called *The Art of Transmutation*. I remember Mum telling Annie off for letting me look at it. Some of these books are super, super red-band, if you get me.'

Theo frowned. 'You think Annie did Black Magic?'

Holly smiled. '*Never* say that in front of Auntie Leonie. Annie always said that there's no such thing as black or white magic, only the intention in the heart of the witch.'

That made sense. 'I just want to understand what happened in the forest,' Theo admitted.

Holly exhaled and nodded. 'We'll find it. But what *I* need is a forgetting spell . . .'

'Hols . . .'

'Well if you won't wipe him.'

Theo fixed Holly in her frostiest glare. 'Holly . . .'

'What?'

Holly took her hands in hers and half-shook them. 'Theo, please? What's the point in being witches if we don't do anything with our powers?'

The frosty glare persisted. 'Sure. Oh, who else said that? That's right, Dabney Hale.'

That shut her up for all of five seconds. '*You* got to use magic.'

Now that was just pure shade. 'Holly, I didn't *mean* to make this happen. It just did.'

Holly wasn't one for sulking. That was one of the things Theo loved about her. If there was debris on her mind, she just spat it out. Probably wise, given her best friend and aunts were mind readers. 'Sorry. I know. I'm just so fucking vexed, Thee. If he *is* having an affair . . . like what am I supposed to do with that info? Deeply fucking cursed.'

Moral issues aside, Theo wasn't even sure she could. 'I've never wiped anyone! You want me to start with your dad, leave him nice and braindead?'

Over the summer, Holly had become convinced that her dad was either thinking about an affair, or was already having one. She kept seeing a woman – not her mum – in his mind. And guilt, lots and lots of guilt. Guilt is unmistakable, vinegary, mustard yellow.

'He feels so bad all the time. I just think a little spell would help him to forget whoever this . . . slut vulture is.'

'Holly!'

'Sorry. Slut-shaming is bad, I know. I just don't want . . . like Mum and Dad are basically the only parents at school who are still married. I'd like it to stay that way.'

Theo played devil's advocate – metaphorically this time. 'Why? There's a reason everyone's parents split up. They're happier.'

Holly shook her head emphatically. 'Nope. No way. Mum is happy. And so is Dad. I can read their minds pretty well now. But I don't know how to wipe him. Not yet. Maybe one of these will tell me what to do . . .' She pulled another book off the pile and blew dust off the leather book jacket.

'Hey,' Theo said. 'We'll think of something, OK?' Inside every witch there are two crows: one saying you can't use your powers to fix the world to your liking, and another cawing, *why not?*

Holly nodded, focusing on her book. Theo sighed, and started to look for anything on transmogrification. It soon became clear this wasn't going to be a quick task. Night moved in outside the cottage, and Theo brought some candles to life with a flick of her wrist.

The books weren't helpful. Niamh had tried to *heal* Theo, not transform her. At the time, Theo had been struggling to breathe; performing mystical gender reassignment had been the furthest thing from her mind . . . and yet. It was like her body had taken Niamh's radiance and run with it, totally rewriting her, from top to bottom, inside and out.

What am I? Helena, Theo knew, had been scared of her. So maybe she should be scared of herself.

She surveyed the wonky towers of books, and felt dwarfed by the task ahead. There were hundreds of tomes to sort, many covered in thick choking dust. Theo's fingers were black with grime.

'Do you still consider yourself transgender?' Holly asked, out of nowhere. Zero filter.

'Yes,' Theo said without hesitation. 'I was born one way, and now . . . I'm another.' She was worried she sounded a little defensive. 'But there's more to it than that, I guess . . . like Valentina couldn't transform the way I did.'

'You're scared,' Holly said, reading her.

Theo nodded. 'I don't know where my powers begin and end,' she said quietly. *All those prophecies about me*.

'That bullshit was deranged,' Holly said. 'I don't think you're the apocalypse, Theo. We'll find the good shit, we have all night. You're staying at mine tonight, right?'

'Yeah, Niamh doesn't know when she'll be back from Manchester.'

They focused on the task at hand. Annie could have been on an episode of *Hoarders*. One box looked more promising; some of the titles were unmarked, bound with white ribbon and padlocked shut. They had doomy titles like *The Book of Heka*, *Magus*, and *A Taxonomy of Earthbound Daemons*. Theo sighed; any one of these could contain an explanation.

Perhaps what she really needed was a family tree. She couldn't help but feel knowing who her birth parents were would answer more questions than a fusty old book. Her birth name was not Theo. She'd chosen that for herself at about five years old. Up until that point, she'd been 'Adam Wells', a name given to her by her first foster parents. She'd kept the surname as she'd ricocheted through the care system because it was as good a name as any. No one knew who dumped her outside Glasgow City Council in an Adidas holdall, but someone had.

The woman. The woman in her nightmares who had tried to drown her. A familiar nausea gurgled up. No.

Theo couldn't afford to spiral now. She did what she always did, and pushed the vision to the furthest corner of her mind.

As she lifted the hefty *Magus* out of the box, a smaller volume fell from her grasp and skidded across the flagstones. Niamh once taught her that if a tarot card fell from a pack, it was urgently trying to tell you something. She reached for the slim hardback and flipped it over. *The Song of Osiris* was written in elegant, looping art nouveau lettering – she knew because they'd covered the era the week before in Art.

The slight book was bound in a dark blue ribbon which Theo pulled off with ease. She flicked through the sepia pages, the paper silky, expensive feeling. She frowned. She reached the end of the book and leafed backwards. Every single page was empty. It was just a notebook; a very pretty notebook. That, or Osiris's song was an instrumental. She sighed, setting it to one side.

Only then she picked it up again.

It was odd. It was as if the book wanted to be touched. The finish on the cover was almost velvety. She *wanted* it. She wanted to keep it. She ran her fingers over it one more time and decided she would. Holly wasn't looking, and so she slipped it into her school bag. The HMRC archive didn't need empty journals.

'Can you lift me down that box?' Holly asked, pointing up to a shelf. 'It's a heavy one.'

'Sure.' Theo hoped she wasn't blushing. She wasn't sure why she was hiding the notebook, but didn't want Holly to think her a thief. She idly lifted a hand to use her telekinesis. The box hardly shifted. Just how heavy was it? She focused her mind. Lifting a box, any box, really shouldn't be this taxing.

'What's up?' Holly asked.

'Nothing,' Theo said sharply. She narrowed her eyes and held out both hands. She clamped her teeth together and seized the air between her and the box. With a mighty tug, the box toppled off the shelf and crashed to the floor. It split apart and books spilled across the tiles.

Holly laughed kindly. 'Well, *I* could have done that.'

'It was heavy,' Theo muttered, although a horrid knot formed in her stomach. *That* had never happened before.

Chapter Ten

THE HOUSE OF HEKATE

Ciara – Manchester, UK

To the rest of Manchester, the Assize Courts were demolished in 1957 after the formidable gothic structure sustained damage during the war. It appeared to be a private car park with ominous warnings about being clamped, or having your vehicle towed. To witches and warlocks, however, HMRC acquired the remains and converted them into the House of Hekate. As far as records stretched, witches had always lived communally, and, today, Hekate mostly housed the oracles.

While girl power and sisterhood were all well and good, Ciara couldn't think of anything worse as she passed through the perception filter that shielded the grand building from prying mundane eyes. It had all the appeal of a convent school.

On the steps outside the imposing main entrance, Ciara rang the bell and waited for someone to let her inside. There was a bite to the air, the evenings creeping in ever sooner as winter edged close. Ciara had been stuck in a stifling conference room all afternoon, going over the plans to have 'Niamh' installed as High Priestess at Samhain. She'd met every HMRC department head. She remembered literally none of their names.

It's not Imposter Syndrome when you're actually an imposter.

The oak doors opened a fraction and a young oracle stood aside to let her enter. 'High Priestess,' the girl said, bowing her head slightly.

'Not yet, I'm not,' Ciara said, taking in the vast entrance hall. Goddess, it was pretty, but it even *smelled* like school dinners. Down the long, arching corridor, she could see the old courtroom was now a banqueting hall.

Ciara wouldn't want to live in a museum piece, but the reception foyer with its columns and domed windows was certainly impressive, even with the pungent smell: cabbage for dinner, ladies? As the clock struck six, the oracles made their way downstairs from lodgings to the dining room. A procession in white silently filed down the sweeping staircase before her.

This was familiar. She *had* been here before. She recalled her grandmother leading her through these doors. Ciara had been . . . fifteen, maybe? She was wearing a leotard and leggings, and she was sickly nervous. *You're very tall for a dancer, Ciara.* It was on the tip of her tongue. The more she pushed, the less she remembered.

Ciara's phone vibrated in her coat pocket. A text message from Luke asking if she'd be home later to tell him about her first day on the job. She rolled her eyes. Needy puppy. Not sexy. He didn't want to comfort her, he wanted to comfort *himself*, to feel more stable in their pairing. She'd let him dangle.

Mounted on the wall, halfway up the stairs, was the epic portrait of their founder. A gilt-framed oil painting of Anne Boleyn; a 'lost' Holbein, liberated from Hampton Court by her coven before her ex-husband could destroy it like he did the others. The painting depicted her as poised, if a little melancholy, a bonnet covering her chestnut, not auburn, hair. Her posthumous portraits only showed her with red hair because her daughter, Elizabeth, *was* a ginge. Ciara smiled to herself. It figured that she'd retain *that* useless piece of information.

'What brings you here today, sister?' the oracle who'd greeted her asked.

'Where can I find the Head Oracle?'

'She is fasting. She'll be in the palm house,' the oracle told her, pointing the way.

Ciara's footsteps echoed down chessboard tiles away from the dining room. It seemed Hekate had a hollow middle – a garden in the centre of the four wings. She found a discreet exit and crossed to the glasshouse at the heart of the complex.

The botanical garden was familiar also. It was a mottled memory, but seeing it now, she sensed she'd *definitely* been here with Niamh and their grandmother. It was more than the sight of it, it was the humidity, the isolation of this tropical bubble in central Manchester that triggered her. An electric blue butterfly fluttered past Ciara's face.

'Well this is lovely,' she said, shattering the peace.

Irina was meditating, cross-legged in amongst towering palms. Her eyes opened. Ciara assumed she'd known she was on her way. 'I find I see nothing here,' Irina explained. 'I cannot tell you why, but it is a welcome break.' She stood and crossed to a babbling waterfall. She cupped her hands and rinsed her face before returning to the path.

'I won't keep you for long,' Ciara said.

'That's up to you, isn't it?'

Ciara rolled her eyes. 'Let's not fuck about, eh? Does everyone know or is it just yourself?'

Irina smirked. 'Not even I knew for certain until this very moment. Your actions give you away. This is the work of the great warmonger, and – to my grave concern – we were blind to his actions.'

'Belial? He brought me back?'

Irina bowed her head. 'I believe so. We did not arrive at this story at the beginning. There were a great many earlier chapters none of us saw. I fear we have failed greatly in our duties.'

It was absurd. The notion that Belial, the Sword of Satanis himself, would go to the effort for Ciara Kelly, disgraced Galway Girl, was laughable. 'Why would Belial want *me*? Doesn't he have bigger fish to fry?'

'It is not for humans to know demon desires.'

Ciara shook her head. Fuckin' oracles, honestly. 'OK, forget the past, what about now? Are you going to tell Moira who I really am?'

Irina now laughed cruelly. 'And who are you, really? I doubt even you have the answer to that. The wayward. Lost then, and lost more now.'

Ciara held out a hand and, with little exertion, pushed Irina backwards into the bushes. 'I could kill you.'

Irina was unhurt. She picked herself up and brushed her robes down. 'I don't doubt it.'

'You tell me then. Do I?'

Raindrops started to patter on the glass domes overhead. 'When a raindrop lands it can trickle in many directions. There is a course where you kill me, and I have seen it. There are many more where you do not. Water makes up its own mind.'

Ciara stalked her prey. 'If you're the only one who knows, the easiest thing would be to get rid of you.'

'And what of my successor? Will you kill her too? And the next?' Ciara considered this. She hoped she wouldn't be around long enough to find out. 'I could be a powerful ally.'

'Why would you do that?'

'Because *you* could be a powerful ally to *our* cause.'

'And what cause would that be?'

Irina drew breath. 'See as I see.'

Ciara sighed. Must we? She read the oracle.

It all came crashing into her mind as violent, noisy shards: a ruined, derelict city; smoke and dust swirling through the bones of buildings. On the other side of Manchester, a towering skyscraper groaned and then toppled to the left, throwing up a mushroom cloud of dust. Bloodied corpses littered the streets. Sirens shrieked, and people – witches and mundanes alike – screamed in terror.

Beneath Ciara's feet, the tarmac started to split apart, a steaming chasm opened up before her. The world was ending.

An oozing shadow turned the corner of the street, inky tentacles reaching, probing. It had no eyes, this shape, but it had a mouth and it was filled with sharp white teeth and—

'What is that?' Ciara demanded, yanking herself into the present. She blinked, trying to rid her mind of that . . . thing.

'The same visions I showed your sister,' Irina snarled, eyes wide. She gripped Ciara's arms. 'The Sullied Child. Leviathan will rise.'

Ciara pulled herself free of her grasp. 'Oh, for crying out fucking loud! *Theo?* Are you on glue?'

'Helena Vance did terrible things, made terrible choices, but the prophecy remains whether you agreed with her actions or not.'

Certainly, Ciara had been more than a little surprised to find a teenage witch living in her sister's cottage, but over the last fortnight had got a fairly good idea of what she was like: quiet, thoughtful, surprisingly wry for a kid. Leviathan incarnate she was not. 'That girl is not Leviathan.'

'No one is saying she is, but the advent of the Sullied Child heralds the dark dawn of the beast. The clock has started, inevitably counting down to the end of things. The end of witches; of men; of Gaia herself.'

What was *that* supposed to mean? 'So what? You want me to finish what Helena started?' The oracle said nothing but Ciara heard her loud and clear. 'You're fuckin' crazy. I'm not a killer.'

She now flew at her, eyes wild. Ciara felt her spittle on her cheek. 'Liar! I know exactly what you did to your sister.'

Ciara's hand formed a fist and, without thinking, she struck Irina across her face. The older woman staggered sidewards but remained on her feet. Ciara seethed, almost embarrassed at her outburst. What did she know? You can *see* things without *knowing* them and this bitch knew nothing of her and Niamh.

Irina wiped blood from a split lip, leaving a red smear across her chin. 'If you are wise, you shall do as I say. You have the means; you have the opportunity. Kill the child, for all our sakes.'

Chapter Eleven

POWERLESS

Theo – Hebden Bridge, UK

'Listen to this,' Holly said, hogging the book she'd found. She and Holly sat at the Pearson kitchen table. Milo listened in, seated on the countertop and munching an apple. 'It says *the eighteenth-century shamanic healer Indra Kahn, in addition to being able to alter an onlooker's perception of her image, was able to physically reconfigure her body at a cellular level.*'

Theo blinked. 'OK . . . but how?'

Holly flicked over the pages. This tome was newer, glossier – more like an academic textbook. In fact, it looked like a car manual. 'I don't know . . . blah, blah, blah . . . *Kahn is thought to be one of very few recorded cases of a Level 7 Healer.*'

Milo spoke through a mouthful of fruit. 'That's so cool! So you're like a shapeshifter? Like Mystique? Man, that's so sick.'

Theo smiled at his deluded enthusiasm. She *wished* she was Mystique. To be fair to Holly's mundane brother, he'd very much taken his mother and Holly's 'coming out' in his stride, although Elle constantly downplayed their gifts. He didn't even seem especially jealous; it was just one more *girl thing* to him; akin to periods and scented lip balms.

'No,' Theo told him. 'At least I don't think so. It's a permanent change.' If she said that enough times, hopefully she'd start to believe it. She just wanted people to see her as a boring-old-dull-as-dishwater girl, especially now she'd started school. And, aside from the whole powerful-witch/ magical transformation thing, she *was* boring: she liked K-Pop dance tutorials on YouTube; she watched *Friends* on her phone in bed; she pretended to read old grimoires when she really read YA fiction about queer elves. Very mundane for a non-mundane.

Theo asked Holly, *Does he know about your dad and the mystery woman?*

No! Holly glared at her. *And I don't want him to.* Holly twisted in her chair and scowled at her brother. 'What are you doing, Milo? You're such a *lurker*. Why don't you go away and leave us alone?'

Milo smirked. 'I'm *taking an interest*, Hols, don't be anti-social.' Like he was setting up a basketball shot, he threw his apple core at Holly, and it made a moist squish as it impacted with her head.

'Ow!'

'Pound-shop mall-goth.'

'Well why don't you *take an interest* in some porn in your room like you do every other night of the week?'

Milo blushed. 'I don't look at porn,' he babbled. 'Well, I do. But not all the . . . fuck off, Holly!'

Without warning, Elle sauntered into the kitchen from the lounge, wearing a pristine white tracksuit with Ugg boots. 'That's a pound in the swear jar, Milo.'

'Oh for f . . . frig's sake!'

Theo smiled. When she'd had 'siblings' in her foster homes, they'd always been in some way wary of her. Some had been far worse than wary. It had never mattered how 'normal' she behaved, her *supernormal* had got the better of her. Like her innate *difference* ebbed out of her pores whatever she did. The kids she had lived with had either avoided her or been outright hostile. As such, she loved watching Holly and Milo spar. They bickered *constantly* but it was like their own affectionate Esperanto at the same time.

It was also consistently hilarious. Brothers and sisters do not respect boundaries or political correctness. Savage.

As far as she could remember, Theo's *abilities* had started to become evident when she was about six, and her first adoptive parents, the Wells, had turned her in to care. She couldn't actually remember that, but she'd established it later via social workers once she could read their minds. After that, she'd pinballed around various foster homes and then to the care home – the worst of them all. Not once had she slept soundly in an all-boys dormitory.

As such, she found the middle-class, sitcom mundanity of the Pearson home wonderfully exotic.

Elle attended to a macaroni cheese in the oven. 'OK, this is about ready! Milo, off the counter. Theo, love, Holly likes hers with chopped-up hot-dog sausages. Do you fancy that?'

'Holly loves a meaty wiener,' Milo added.

'Milo . . .' Elle warned.

'Shut up!' Holly fired back. 'Jesus, Mum, that's pure embarrassing.'

Elle wiped her hands on a dishcloth, exasperated. 'No, it isn't! It's a sausage! Who doesn't love a sausage?'

Milo cackled and Holly huffed. 'It's OK, I'm veggie,' Theo told Elle.

'Oh of course! Ignore me . . . mind like a sieve!'

'Mum?' Holly asked.

'Yes, love?'

'Can you do transmutations?'

Wearing a polka dot oven glove, Elle placed the piping hot baking tin on a cooling tray and turned to face her daughter. 'I beg your pardon?'

'Not like a glamour. Like, can you use your healing powers to actually change the structure of your bones and stuff?'

Elle crossed the kitchen and plucked the book out of Holly's grasp. 'What are you reading?' She scanned the cover and gave Holly a frosty glare. 'Holly, what have I told you about bringing craftwork home? When you're with Sheila at coven it's fine, but not *here*.'

Theo slipped *The Song of Osiris* into her bag before Elle could confiscate it. Holly rolled her eyes. 'It's just a book! It's not like I'm sacrificing babies.'

Elle bit her tongue, Theo suspected because she was company. She was *mad* though; Theo could feel the red rising in her. 'We have talked about this. Your father and Milo have to live in this house too, Holly, and it's not fair to rub this stuff in their faces all the time!'

Holly looked genuinely taken aback. 'I'm not doing that . . .' she said meekly.

'And haven't you heard of a little something called witchfinders? Hmm?'

Theo and Holly shared a sly look. 'Well, I'll be really careful when I'm in the seventeenth century.' Holly smirked.

Only then, Elle gave her a *very* chilly glare. 'Holly. Enough is enough. No more *witchcraft*,' she silently mouthed the last word, 'at home. I mean it.'

Milo slid off the countertop. 'I don't think the neighbours can hear you, Mum.'

She gave him a clip around the ear. 'And less of your cheek too. Now sit down for dinner.'

The back door opened, and Mr Pearson entered, still wearing his oily overall. Elle held out a hand to stop him. 'No! Get that in the wash please!' Mr Pearson rolled his eyes, but did as he was told. 'Dinner's been ready for ages. Where have you been?'

Theo looked to Holly. Her expression was dark.

'Just don't do anything you'll regret,' Theo told Holly. 'You heard what your mum said about witchcraft. If she knew you used magic on your dad, she'd kill you.'

'I don't want to talk about it,' Holly said, pointedly shuffling the tarot cards.

After dinner, Holly and Theo retired to Holly's room. Holly's taste in music changed weekly, but this week it was Korean boybands and obscure Eurovision entrants. Having changed into their pyjamas, the girls sat, facing each other, on the floor. Holly turned over a tarot card so that Theo couldn't see it.

Theo flexed her neck and concentrated. It really shouldn't be this difficult. Holly wasn't even *trying* to occlude her thoughts. 'Um . . . Five of Pentacles?'

Holly shook her head. 'Eight of Pentacles. Close!' Holly was an incredible artist. She'd made her own tarot deck as a project and the cards were as lovely as any Theo had seen.

'This is so weird. Why can't I see clearly?'

'Maybe it's me. Let's try again.' Holly drew another card from the pack and squinted at it with all her might.

Theo cleared her mind and gently allowed her consciousness to reach into Holly's. 'The Devil.'

'Yes!' Holly said triumphantly, turning the card around.

'Figures,' Theo said wryly. Holly's illustration depicted exactly what you'd expect: a horned, goat-headed man holding a man and woman in chains like puppets.

'See? You're fine!'

'No,' Theo said. 'Something isn't right.'

'Maybe you're getting sick? Mum says she can't use her powers if she's ill.'

Theo shrugged. This hadn't happened before. After the big transformation there had been a week or so where she couldn't use her gifts at all. It was as if the change had totally drained her reserves. But then, bit by bit, she felt stronger and stronger with each passing day. Up until today, she had felt better than ever.

She knew certain people at HMRC were still scared of her. It made her sad, and frustrated that she could be so misunderstood. She wanted to grasp her doubters by the arms and shake them, not that that would go down well. Theo had thought, perhaps naïvely, that now she was outwardly and inwardly female, they would have accepted her the same as any other junior witch. The funeral had been an eye-opener – the whispers and rumours. Witches had looked her up and down with surgical precision, chuntering about how the change was possible, what it said about her powers.

It must be demonic; how could it not be?

Theo was learning that nothing she did would ever be enough. She would, to some, never be 'a real witch' or even 'a real girl'. Now, how to make peace with that?

Holly flung herself onto her bed and changed the music with her phone. 'Theo?'

'Holly.'

'Can I ask a really serious question?'

Oh goddess, what now? 'Yeeeees . . . ?' she replied tentatively.

Holly cleared her throat. 'You don't fancy my brother, do you?'

'What?' Theo leaned in to make sure she'd heard right.

Holly said sulkily, 'Well every other girl at school does.'

Theo thought to tread carefully. For a long time, she'd picked up on the faintest tang of jealousy in Holly if she ever spoke about crushes. Jealousy is sharp, like grapefruit or salt on the tongue. Theo was psychic; she knew that Holly had had crush-adjacent feelings for her in her old form, and no doubt her transformation must have been a headfuck. Now, her friend was constantly asking if she fancied people from school. It seemed like an odd game Holly liked to play with her own emotions. Even so, if Holly did have . . . unresolved feelings, Theo didn't want to cause her upset.

'I can honestly say I've never thought about him like that.' He was *Milo Pearson,* top percentile, and she was a spooky-trans-witch-orphan who'd be lucky to scrape a C in Maths. 'I don't really think of anyone like that.'

'You're so pretty, Theo. Everyone says.' Theo didn't know what to say to that, so said nothing. 'You're just a girl now so you can . . . date and stuff. I'm sure loads of boys – or girls – would want to.'

Just a girl. 'I don't know . . . like, coven stuff is more important to me.'

'But it's not everything!' Holly said. 'You have time now! It's not like people are actively trying to kill you any more, is it?'

Theo smiled. True, that was something.

HEBDEN GIRLIES
Niamh, Helena, Leonie, you

Is Theo stopping here?

Niamh Kelly
Sorry! Yes pls. Still
in Manc. Something came up.

No worries bb. They're all
ready for bed love 'em.

Niamh Kelly
Thanks! See you tom.

Did you get there OK, Lee?

Leonie Jackman
Yep, just left the Italian coven.
Bologna is well nice.

Send pics! There's a fountain
with boobs that squirt water
out of the nips!!!

Leonie Jackman
Do your nips not do that?

Niamh Kelly
Any sign of Hale?

Leonie Jackman
Nope. Stay tuned . . .

Leonie *SURPRISE* 30th
Niamh, Elle, Helena, you

> Sorry to resurrect this ancient group but will you guys keep me posted with any news you get from Leonie?

Elle Pearson
Hi Chinara! Of course. How are you?

> I have been better, my friend. Worried about Lee. That she'll do something rash.

Elle Pearson
I promise we'll tell you as soon as we here.

Niamh Kelly
Xxx

Chapter Twelve

HELLO, KITTY

Ciara – Hebden Bridge, UK

One by one, flames popped to life across the candlewicks, sealing a flaming circle around Ciara, about two metres in diameter. She was naked, kneeling in cool, damp peat. No one would see her, not at this hour, not so deep into Hardcastle Crags. Performing rituals nude was necessity, not a kink. They'd grown up on the urban legend of the witch who strangled herself with a bra while invoking demons.

She would be safe inside her circle of fire. Nothing could enter without an invite.

There was a dull ache deep inside her chest. She didn't *want* to do this, but there was no point in dragging out the inevitable.

Ciara laid the pendant, a simple, sterling silver eye of Horus, flat on the ground before her. A personal possession was necessary to curse her victim. She then took up the steak knife from Niamh's kitchen, and made a cut on her left index finger. She never had been one for ceremonial daggers and the like. Needlessly camp. Ciara smiled as a funny little memory found its way back to her. Her grand-mother's wise words: *Never trust a witch with plasters on her fingers, she's been up to no good, mark my words, girls.*

She let a few drops of blood spatter onto the necklace before drawing the summoning symbol in the dirt; if she was the key, the sigil was the lock. It was a complicated one; she'd had to check in one of Niamh's grimoires before setting out into the woods. She'd honestly forgotten that Theo was staying at Elle's, but perhaps that was for the best. That made it easier to do what she had to do.

Ciara finished etching the sigil into the soil and waited. She was more nervous than she'd anticipated. It had been a while, and it triggered more blurry memories. She hadn't felt this tense about a summoning since her first time, in that dank student house in Durham, the walls and floors scrawled with histrionically large symbols.

There had been someone with her, a man. Not Dabney, someone else.

She couldn't dwell on that now. She'd begun, and she suspected it wouldn't take long to get a response. Her soul was so known to the demons. Even in broad daylight, she could feel them circling her like flies around shit.

Sure enough, through the darkness, she saw the earth outside of the circle ripple and pulse, a swelling just under the surface. Next came the whispers. At first it was un-intelligible, garbled murmurings, but she could soon pick out the odd word in her mind.

It's her . . .

I come for you . . .

I serve you, mistress . . .

I saw her first . . .

These minnows were not the entities she sought.

Overhead, the leaves shuddered on the trees although there was no breeze. A demon can quite easily live in a dead log or stump. An owl hooted somewhere far away. An owl, or a demon that sounded like an owl?

Just outside the circle, a leathery black centipede wove through blades of grass, teasing the edge of her barrier: *Let me inside, Ciara – it's been so long since we have known you.*

Ciara's skin crawled. Or rather, *Niamh's* skin did. This was a shame. Ciara quite liked the unspoiled flesh she was inhabiting, and wasn't looking to share. She repeated her mantra: *you have no choice.*

She was seconds from losing her resolve, and erasing the summons when something caught her attention. A fluid movement between two trees far ahead.

Sensing the apex predator, the minor demons scarpered. A hush fell over the forest.

'Lord Ose, I summon thee,' Ciara said defiantly. A high-ranking demon wouldn't fuck with an unworthy witch, and she'd been out of the game for almost a decade. She squinted into the darkness, past the flickering flames. 'Manifest! I command thee.'

Her nostrils were hit by an overwhelming, meaty odour. Slightly rotten, but mostly . . . boiled . . . the stink of burned flesh. She covered her mouth with her hand, retching. It was acrid. It was, of course, a test. It got worse.

The air around her circle seemed to shimmer and distort. Suddenly the flames on the candles exploded into jets of fire, and she felt her cheeks redden, but she held her ground. Another test. Through the flames, she made out a distinctly feline shape, prowling through the undergrowth. A leopard, lithe and muscular. 'Show yourself, Lord Ose!'

She heard footsteps behind her. She craned her neck and, for a split second through the haze, saw the demon's true form; an emaciated male figure, naked and filthy, with the head and snout of a bald cat. It sunk behind a tree and emerged as a leopard once more, padding proudly through the brambles and leaf litter. The beast looked woefully out of place in Yorkshire.

'I see you,' she said.

I see you.

Its voice had an almost musical quality, syrupy somehow. 'I invoke thee, Lord Ose.'

Its heart is dark.

'I seek to vanquish a witch.'

It seeks my power.

'Lies. You seek my power.'

The demon almost giggled. The leopard maintained its circular patrol some way from her protective circle, vanishing behind trees, slinking in and out of the shadows. *You are known to me.*

'Parts of me are.'

The soiled insides.

That stung. 'Yes.'

The flesh is untouched.

'Yes.'

You lack resolve, witch. It has lost its taste for the kill.

Ciara grit her teeth. 'I do what needs to be done.'

This remorseful heart is infirm.

She would not beg. If she had to, she'd do it without Ose; she had a whole list of backups. Demons, in her experience, just made things . . . easier. Ciara wasn't scared of doing the dirty work, but must not be caught red-handed.

She was already bored of foreplay. 'If you won't help

me, another will; Glasya-Labolas, Andras, Marquis Shax . . . sweetheart, I've had 'em all.'

There it is. She's still there.

Ciara sighed. She said ruefully, 'Fill me up, bad boy.'

Viscous reddish-brown blood bubbled up through the soil and, within seconds, Ciara knelt in a shiny puddle of the substance, her hands sinking into the slush. This was new. Another test? She felt herself being pulled down, the sludge freezing cold around her waist. Her instinct was to claw at the undergrowth to prevent herself from going under. No. She must not show fear. She closed her eyes and waited, sinking further. She felt the stinking effluent creep around her jaw and tipped her head to the sky. She dared to peek at the stars as she was sucked under the surface.

Deep breath.

And darkness.

She was choked for a moment as the ooze flowed into her nostrils and mouth, and then it settled. An icy sensation seeped from inside out and she felt heavy somehow. Then came the pain. A flashing, bright white pain that shot up and down her spine. Her body convulsed, and she fought to keep control of her limbs. Her hands bent all the way back with a nasty clacking noise.

She couldn't scream, prising her lips shut.

She knew it would pass, and it did.

There. This is why you did it. After the pain came the pleasure.

Ciara felt warm all over, the edges all fuzzy. She was a blur, and everything would be fine. Niamh didn't matter. Hale didn't matter. Theo did not matter. Ose was inside her now.

Her eyes snapped open and she was flat on the forest

floor. She could see all the way into the solar system, as far as there was light. And she could *feel*, she could feel *everything*. Every person, and every pet, and every insect for *miles*.

The Ciara in Ciara relaxed, reclining into the deepest parts of her inner self. It was like being on an inflatable in a vast black sea. The water was warm, gentle, endless. She let Lord Ose take control. The sweetest surrender.

He would take care of the rest.

Chapter Thirteen

THE VOODOO LOUNGE

Leonie – Bologna, Italy

What else do you do when you're a solo traveller in Italy? You get a great big bowl of pasta and a glass of red wine the size of your head, that's what. It was chilly outside, but Leonie could chain-smoke on the terrace so had opted for the outdoor seating. There was a heater overhead, and a blanket across her lap. She was itching to get started on her mission but, all in all, things could be a lot worse.

The restaurant was set off a historic piazza, the terrace sheltered underneath the arched walkway on its perimeter. So far, she was impressed with Bologna. It was very pretty and steeped in history, which rendered it both enchanting and enchanted. The narrow, clandestine streets and alley-ways crackled with magic potential.

Since apparating at Coven Italia, she'd checked into a hotel, taking a nana nap to get over the discomforting long-distance teleport, before spending some time sight-seeing. What if she never came again? It'd be a shame not to. She'd chosen a cheap, two-star hostel, though would later invoice HMRC for someplace much fancier, and pocket the difference. She'd learned *that* little trick from Helena, so she wasn't *all* bad.

Sometimes she remembered Helena fondly, and was then forced to remember that she was dead. That just reminded her that the version of Helena that was her friend had died even earlier. That reminded her about Annie. A pinball machine of fuckery, misery pinging from one side of her brain to the other. She took a big gulp of wine.

Domino's club didn't open until eleven, and Leonie was grateful of the calm before the storm. Right now, there wasn't a lot she could do for Radley, except try to relax. The side streets and winding stone stairs of the ancient town centre were a rabbit warren, and Leonie had been content to wander and get lost for a while. There was much to see, and there weren't too many tourists at this time of year to occlude the view. The brickwork had a coppery tinge and the roofs were terra-cotta orange, save the occasional churches or clocktowers with striking turquoise domes. She'd never seen, or felt, anything quite like it. She took pictures to send to Chinara.

London had a lot of history, clearly, but there the old was sandwiched between brand new. Bologna's architecture had been carefully preserved and the walls whispered of generations. The buildings almost vibrated with power, and Leonie found herself tuning in to their heady resonance. There was little wonder witches and warlocks were so drawn to certain cities, she felt almost drunk on it. Or maybe it was the chianti.

The waiter took her pasta dish away and she ordered some tiramisu for dessert. When (almost) in Rome and all that. He returned a few minutes later with a block of the stuff larger than a paving slab, and Leonie suddenly felt a sharp pang of yearning for her girlfriend. She wished they were here together, under different circumstances. Holidays are a great test of romantic compatibility, and both she and Chinara liked a couple of days of cultural sightseeing before taking horizontally to a sunbed with a margarita for the remainder of any trip. A single question to occupy them: *where shall we eat tonight?* Bliss.

Leonie felt uneasy, her appetite for the dessert waning. Was she a shit girlfriend? Probably. *Single-minded* or *hot-headed* was how her (white) teachers had always described her. Rather, she understood it more as having laser focus. When she got a bee in her bonnet, she was unstoppable. Leonie was aware that, in the period of calm just after the war, her spotlight had been focused exclusively on Chinara. The sheer excitement of meeting a woman who was a) a witch and b) a lesbian and c) Black, had been quite the headrush. And, as the stereotype goes, lesbians need little encouragement when it comes to speedy nesting – Leonie ditched Manchester and moved into Chinara's London flat within six months. They got the cat even faster.

But then came Diaspora. Something new to obsess about. And now this. It had been a long time since that spotlight had been fixed on Chinara. And that wasn't right. Leonie had never, ever, doubted her personal sparkle. She had more sparkle in her little finger than most basics had in their whole bodies, but Chinara wasn't getting a lot of it right now. She got the exhausted, spent woman who wanted to crash in front of the TV to watch true crime docs.

She poked at the mountain of tiramisu. When Radley was safely home, she made a silent vow to book a break for them both. Somewhere romantic, just the two of them. No covens, no brothers, no friends. She was acutely aware of the fact they hadn't so much as mentioned the B-A-B-Y idea since the night of the siege in Hebden Bridge. She knew only too well how much *not mentioning it now* was on Chinara's mind. That wasn't cool. Leonie knew that *Chinara* knew that if she were to mention starting a family right now, she'd snap that she *did* have a family in Rad, and he had to come first. She was holding Chinara's wishes hostage.

The clocktower overlooking the square struck eleven, and Leonie remembered the task at hand. In London, she'd sooner die than arrive at the club until at least one, but she wasn't going to party. She downed the last of her wine in one big gulp, and flagged down the waiter.

Even this late, the Fountain of Neptune at the heart of the city was a draw for a few tourists. Elle was right; water really did squirt out of the boobs. A gigantic naked Neptune topped the monument, with several cherubs at his feet, and the lactating mermaids below them. Leonie passed the fountain, putting psychic feelers out the whole time and shielding herself from prying eyes. The entrance to Piazza delle Streghe moved each night, shielded from mundane eyes. After all, no one wants mundanes wandering into witch establishments.

The witches at Coven Italia hadn't spoken great English, but, earlier on, she'd clearly read in their minds how to find Voodoo Lounge Bologna. It was somewhere off this square and finding a glamour enchantment of that scale really shouldn't be that difficult. In fact . . .

Leonie sensed *something* off about a wall to the south of the great fountain. It looked like any of Bologna's peachy stone walls, but it was trying to force her gaze away. Bingo. Leonie reached out and forced her way in, walking straight into the wall.

It wasn't a wall at all, simply a powerful illusion. Leonie walked through the perception filter and found herself in a smaller square; an ornamental garden with its own babbling fountain at the centre. Easy jazz slouched from a chic bar, aglow with candlelight, tables and chairs spilling out onto the piazza. As the music played, a pair of elderly witches sat out front, sipping espresso through thin lips. They acknowledged her with a polite *ciao*.

A herb market, an occult bookstore and a gemstone merchant were on the square too, but all had closed for the night. A witch at the coven had told Leonie to look out for 'the red hand', and sure enough, a buzzing neon finger pointed at the stairs to a basement club on the far side of the piazza. Aside from the hand, there was no signage to the club. You'd have to know to know.

Leonie swore one of the old coffee shop witches tutted at her as she turned down the perilously steep stairs. Harsh. She guessed the clientele were bringing the area down. Leonie found the entrance; a simple door with bars over the window, to be locked. She rang a bell marked *Attenzione*.

There was a honking noise and a click, and Leonie entered a velvet vestibule. The reception area was manned by an outrageously beautiful woman – she *had* to be a model – in a sleek black jumpsuit. Her ebony bob framed her perfect features.

'*Benvenuta, signorina.*'

'Do you speak English?' Leonie asked like any dreadful English person abroad would.

'Welcome to Voodoo Lounge Bologna,' she said with a too-perfect-to-be-real smile. 'Are you an Any Lounge Gold member?'

Leonie tried to read her with little success. 'Do I look like a Gold member?' she replied, not even trying to bewitch the receptionist. She assumed they'd have measures in place to stop that sort of thing anyway.

Leonie had no issue with sex clubs; she'd had great nights at Crossbreed and Klub Verboten as it happened, she took issue with old boys' private members' clubs. This, from what she understood, was more like the latter.

'I'm afraid guests can only be signed in by a Gold member,' the receptionist said smugly.

Leonie was so allergic to snooty cunts it was unreal. 'Very well.' She adopted a fake RP accent like her mum used when she called the GP. 'Do be so kind as to tell Domino that Leonie Jackman from London Diaspora is here to see her. I'm quite certain she'll want to receive me *tout de suite.*'

The receptionist put in a call – the old-fashioned way, by telephone – and relayed her message. Leonie couldn't hear what was being said but the receptionist seemed to give her crumpled jeans, sneakers and baseball jersey a once-over.

'Very well. I can give you a temporary visitor pass.'

'Thank you,' Leonie said. You spin the wheel, and you take your chance. Sometimes it works.

'Your powers won't work once you pass the threshold. House rules.'

Annoying. She'd hoped she'd be able to read Domino and be tucked up in bed by midnight. Hard way it was then. 'Fine with me,' said Leonie and headed for the double doors. The woman pressed a button underneath her desk, and they opened inwards.

An electric bassline, like a wasp trapped under a pint glass, met her first, and was soon followed by the tell-tale interior fogginess of Sister's Malady. It was mixed with the dry ice swirling around her ankles. It was dark, only low ultraviolet lights rimming the floors, and Leonie became increasingly wary as she descended another curving flight of stairs even further into the bowels of Bologna. The music grew louder and louder as she went, and with each step she felt her sentience become duller and duller. She supposed gambling, lying and cheating was that much harder in a room full of psychics.

'Fuck me,' she muttered to herself as she stepped into the main club. Millennia of witches, and the height of decadence was pretty much an upmarket Soho strip club. White lasers skittered through the swirling mist, making elegant silhouettes of the dancers on the podiums dotted through the room. Both male and female forms, all naked, danced for the crowds of witches and warlocks who drank in plush, black velvet booths.

Leonie was going to need a drink. A big one.

It was busier than she thought it would be, considering the lounge had only just opened; the booths were filling up quickly, waiters and waitresses relaying cocktails on silver trays. Not wanting to wait for table service, Leonie took herself directly to the bar. A Black male oracle, and there are *very* few male oracles full-stop, was working the bar. He was blind, eyes palest grey, but moved around his area with finesse. He spoke in English with a German accent. 'What can I get you?'

'Vodka on the rocks please, barkeep.' He poured her

drink and offered to start a tab. Leonie paid cash. She didn't like the idea of leaving her card behind the bar if she wanted to make a swift exit. 'Can I sit anywhere?'

'Anywhere not reserved.'

Leonie could hardly see through the smoke and lasers and the music was, by anyone's standards, too loud. She was getting *old*. How long had it been since she'd been clubbing? She dimly recalled a night in Hackney where Dior was performing but that was at least six months ago. God, Lesbian Bed Death was real.

She did a lap of the floor, ostensibly looking for an empty table, but mostly casing the joint for Domino. Hard to find a woman who changed bodies like most women changed their shoes. The entrepreneur was in London sporadically – she had a lounge off Old Compton Street – and every time Leonie had seen her, she wore an eyepatch. She didn't know if the witch required it, or whether it was to help her clientele recognise her ever-changing face.

There was no eyepatch in sight. Leonie slid into a booth and checked to see if Chinara had messaged. Of course there was no signal down here. No magic, no phone. Great. What were you meant to do? Talk to people? Hideous.

A snake-shaped catwalk wove through the room, allowing the dancers to circulate around the venue. Sort of like a human sushi restaurant, thought Leonie. Pick a plate you fancy off the conveyer belt.

And that was when a spectacle on stage caught her eye. A dancer stepped out of a huge seashell, some sort of modern Venus. Her naked brown skin was covered in minuscule Swarovski gems that glimmered in the lights. She moved sensually, ignoring the pounding music, instead dancing to her own, much more hypnotic rhythm. Her hair – thick, tumbling coils – fell almost to her rear. As she twisted around, Leonie saw first her extraordinary cheekbones, and then a small penis.

Oh. Leonie caught the dancer's eye for a second, and looked away at once, embarrassed. Had she – or they – caught her staring? Leonie felt her cheeks blaze.

'She's exquisite, isn't she?' a voice said as a figure joined Leonie at her table. She *appeared* to be a young, achingly beautiful Japanese woman with a killer fringe and, yes, a diamanté eyepatch. 'Senait is quite a find . . . a true hermaphrodite.'

Leonie recoiled, furious. 'I think you mean intersex, Domino.'

Domino laughed girlishly, batting away her horror. 'Where I found her, they called her "goddess". A remote tribe in the mountains between Ethiopia and Eritrea. They believed her to bring rain to the valley. Her name literally means "One who brings good luck".' Domino spoke with that singular mid-Atlantic accent, placeless. Sort of American, sort of English, somewhat *Moira Rose*.

Leonie raised an eyebrow. Behind Domino, the dancer – Senait – fell to her knees and lifted her arms over her head as she made circles with her pelvis. A group of warlocks leered at her. 'So, you liberated her from a temple to make her work as a glorified stripper? Nice.'

Domino gestured at her harem of dancers with a fey hand. 'This is not work! She's free as a bird! My dolls live very well indeed. We've travelled the world many times over, citizens of the globe. I haven't seen a winter in decades. Soon we shall leave this place for warmer shores.'

Dolls? Fuck that. 'I'm not here for the dancers.'

Domino crossed her legs. She was wearing a skin-tight latex dress with killer heels. 'Oh, relax for fuck's sake, darling, I know why you're here. I wondered how long it would be before someone from HMRC came sniffing around.'

'I'm not HMRC,' Leonie said vehemently. 'I'm just looking for my brother. He came here.'

Domino smiled coyly. This would be so much easier if she could read her. 'A lot of men come here, darling.'

Leonie faked a smile. 'Tall guy, skinny, brown skin? He'd have been asking questions about a man you *definitely* know.'

'Doesn't ring a bell.'

Leonie slapped the table. 'Oh, come off it, Domino! It's fuckin' Dabney Hale. He fuckin' hates women. He hates witches! Why are you defending him?'

Her Cheshire Cat smile widened further. 'Darling, it's business. Everyone's money spends the same. I'm apolitical.'

'I'm not sure killing witches counts as a political stance, babes.'

Domino considered her hungrily. 'I remember seeing you fleetingly at London Lounge and thinking about asking you to join my little family. You were so full of fire. Now here you are, doing HMRC dirty work. Radical Leonie isn't nearly as radical as she thinks she is.'

Leonie opened her mouth to tell her to fuck off, but Domino went on.

'Yes, Hale was here, briefly, and yes, your brother came looking for him. He was too late; Hale was long gone. I don't know where he went, or what his plans are. Nor do I care. Satisfied?'

'Not even slightly.'

'You're a very powerful sentient, darling. I'm sure you'll

find him all by yourself. You're here now, why not enjoy yourself.' Domino looked over her shoulder and beckoned to Senait, who duly sashayed in their direction, moving like silk.

'What are you doing?' Leonie asked.

Domino ignored her. 'Senait, sweet pea, why don't you entertain our special guest, hmm?'

Senait, her expression a little stoned, offered Leonie an elegant hand. She bowed her head and curtsied. 'Certainly. It would be my pleasure.' Her English was good, with an accent Leonie couldn't quite place.

Leonie shrunk into her seat. 'Oh no, I'll be leaving in a sec . . .'

Senait flinched, briefly offended, perhaps. 'Oh look,' Domino said, 'you've upset her now . . .'

Leonie sighed. 'OK, I apologise.'

'Wonderful. I'll have Johan send over Cynar Negronis. House speciality.' Domino rose. 'If you'll excuse me, I have urgent business to attend to. Senait will fulfil your every desire, I'm sure.'

As Domino prowled into the darkness of her club, Senait smiled, and Leonie took her outstretched hand. The dancer elegantly slid onto the banquette. 'Don't worry. I'm not interested in having any desires fulfilled,' she assured the younger woman. Up close, she saw just how young Senait was too. She couldn't be much older than twenty, twenty-one. This was so not her thing. Like, all power to sex workers, but did Leonie personally want to acquire their services? Also, no.

'Do you actually like to be called *she*?' Leonie asked out of politeness. She certainly didn't trust Domino to get it right.

Senait waited until Domino had vanished from sight

and leaned over the table. 'Right, thank fuck for that.'
The supposedly Ethiopian accent was replaced by one
much closer to home. 'You have got to get me the fuck
out of here.'

Leonie blinked. 'What?'

Senait screwed her face up. 'What? You didn't buy all
that Ethiopian goddess bullshit, did you? Babes, I'm from
Bolton. She tells the men that so she can charge more. I
think they think I'm Storm from *X-Men* or summat.'

'I'm so confused right now,' Leonie said.

Senait's tone changed. Instead of girlish and flirty, she
now spoke in a low, urgent tone. 'Do *not* look, but I just
dropped a key on the floor.' Instinctually, Leonie tried to
see where she meant, but Senait grasped her face, then
passed it off as a gentle caress. 'Am I not speaking English?
There are cameras and minders everywhere. If she sees I
stole a key, she'll kill me.'

Leonie believed her at once. 'Got it,' Leonie said. She
also wondered where she'd been storing the key. A petite
waitress arrived at their table with a pair of cocktails.
Leonie waited for her to depart before taking a sip of the
drink; it was bitter, but with a delicious hint of caramel.
'What does the key open?'

Senait shook her head subtly. 'Villa Malora on Lake
Garda. About two hours from here, give or take.'

'That's where Hale is? I don't get it . . .'

'It's not that hard to understand, is it? We're fucking
prisoners and I want out, like right now. Come in the day.
The lazy cunt sleeps all day.'

'Domino?' Leonie felt time was suddenly moving too
fast. 'I'm sorry, I'm really fucking confused, I'm looking
for—'

'I know! Look. You scratch my back, and I'll scratch yours. You get me the fuck out of Domino's way, and I'll tell you where that posh twat Dabberly Hale is.'

'You know where he is? Where?' Leonie demanded, but kept her voice even. She didn't want to attract the attention of the stocky bouncers patrolling the club.

'Nice try.' Senait's posture changed, like she was resolute. 'You get me out first. I need help, and you're meant to be dead hard, or so she says.'

Nothing comes for free. That more than seemed like a fair exchange. One good deed deserves another, but Leonie was troubled. 'Why would you trust me?'

Senait paused. Maybe it was just the big doe eyes, but Leonie's heart broke. Behind the gob, Leonie could see she was scared, really scared. It could even be as simple as the fact they were both equally desperate in this moment, but she reminded her of, well, herself. By this point, Leonie had stopped noticing she was even naked.

Finally, Senait admitted, 'I don't like to brag, but I'm actually an adept. Part oracle, although I've still got my hair, thank fuck. Anyway, I've seen you in my dreams. Visions or whatever. I knew you'd come, and here you are, so I guess I'm pretty fucking hot shit.'

Leonie wasn't sure what to say to that, but this was the only solid lead she'd got from Voodoo Lounge. What choice did she have but to help the girl? 'Villa Malora?'

'Yep,' Senait said. 'Wait for me to leave, and then take the key.'

'Wait! What is the key for?'

'You'll figure it out.' Across the room, a gargantuan bouncer hovered, suspicion creasing his block of a head. Leonie sensed her time was up. 'I hope you liked the

Negroni,' Senait said, her long nails tapping the glass on her way out.

Only now did Leonie see a tiny gold key on the floor.

The key in her pocket, Leonie left Voodoo Lounge and stepped into a chill autumn night. The café bar was now closed, the chairs stacked on the tables, although a weary-looking waiter, at the end of his shift, smoked a cigarette outside. He was a sentient and, using only images in his head, she asked if she could bum a fag off him for the road.

She was through the defences, and on the Piazza del Nottuno, before she realised she was being followed. How? And *who*? Was this Hale's men or Domino's? She was gathering enemies at quite a rate.

They must have left the club after her, or been inside the darkened bar waiting for her. Was that waiter a lookout? She didn't need to turn around to know there were four of them, all male, all warlocks. None was above a Level 4, from what she could sense. There were no mundanes around now. That was either a lucky co-incidence, or the warlocks had moved them on with subliminal suggestion. *Get them out of the way so there'd be no witnesses . . .*

Leonie flicked her cigarette to the cobbles, and struck first. She hexed them, gluing them to the spot, before whipping around to face her stalkers. 'Look,' she said, pinning them down. 'I've had a really long day and travelled from Manchester to London to France to Italy, and I just can't be fucked with your shit, OK? Why are you following me?'

The hulking warlocks, muscle-for-hire, glowered at her, unable to move their feet.

She wasn't ready for the pain. It felt like a demolition ball swinging into her side. It hurt, and Leonie was thrown off her feet, across the square. She awkwardly collided with the wall of the church opposite the fountain, and she felt her shoulder pop in its socket. Fuck. Glittery flecks dancing across her vision, she scanned the piazza. She'd been so pleased with her sassy line; she didn't see the *other* three warlocks coming up on her left.

Ignoring the fire in her shoulder, she got to her feet and, hands outstretched, pushed out psychically, stopping them from getting too close. 'All right, I guess I deserved that.'

One of the men, short, stocky and bald, rushed forward. Almost ripping her shoulder joint out, Leonie manipulated him off the ground and flung him toward the fountain. He landed hard on his butt. Good. 'Stay away.'

The men had her surrounded, her back to the church. The tallest, a thin, vulpine man with a crooked nose, summoned a fizzing ball of static electricity in his palm. If she attempted to levitate *over* the buildings, he'd zap her like a fly. Fuck, fuck, fuck.

They nudged closer. Hand to her head, she clamped her teeth together and tried to hex all seven. She'd done five witches at Hebden Bridge, but that had been a stretch. The warlocks growled, slowed, but they *could* move. She couldn't hold them all at once. 'What the fuck do you want?' Leonie cried; not even certain they spoke English.

The men seemed to be arguing amongst themselves. She quickly read the nearest one, so young he still had acne on his chin. *Hale.* Hale had paid them for this. They weren't supposed to hurt her though. What? Why? That also meant he knew she was following him. Well good. He should be fuckin' scared. 'Stay the fuck back!' she said again.

Fighting against her hex, one edged closer. The skinny elemental threw a bolt of lightning her way and she levitated out of the way. The lightning struck the church and it gave her an idea. She floated down to the paving flags and crouched on one knee. She placed her right hand flat on the floor and, with her left, pushed her assailants away. Two of them toppled like skittles.

Before they could recover, she poured everything she had into moving the *earth*. 'Come on, you cunts . . .' she cried out, siphoning energy out of the air; the water in the fountain; the aged stone walls, and pumping it into the stone floor. Sure enough, the whole square started to vibrate first, then *shake*, almost convulsing. The water in the pond trembled and sloshed over the sides. Tiles started to rain down from the ancient roofs above them.

A crack split the flagstones, a jagged crevice opening across the square. With glee, she saw the look of horror on the elemental's face. Leonie just pushed harder. The windows around the square erupted, showering the warlocks with splinters of glass. One screamed in pain as he got a faceful. The others dived out of the way of the advancing crevices in the ground. They cried to each other in Italian, panicking.

With an ear-splitting, metallic creak, Neptune toppled off the fountain. *Oh fuck, timber.* Leonie grasped the monument, taking hold of the falling statue and aiming his triton directly at the stocky bald one. She shot it at him and he ran. He actually ran. Pussy. Neptune made an almighty clang as he made impact with the piazza.

Another ugly crack erupted the earth and Leonie heard the first sirens. The mundane polizia were on their way.

Water gushed from the broken fountain and clouds of dust filled the concourse. She glared at the furious men on the other side of the crater she'd made.

It was time to go. The warlocks knew they were done, edging away from the carnage, and so was Leonie. Springing up from her calves, she launched herself into the starry night sky.

Chapter Fourteen

RESTLESS

Ciara – Hebden Bridge, UK

Contorting herself, Ciara looked her naked body over in the bathroom mirror. There was a cockroach under her skin. She could feel it tunnelling, burrowing under her flesh. Reaching around, she felt for it. A swollen lump shifted between her shoulder blades and she let out a pitiful whimper. Ciara was itchy all over; she clawed at her arms and thighs, leaving salmon marks. The itch went all the way to the bone. Her arms, legs, hands, feet couldn't stop moving. Her spine felt like a snake in a sack, writhing to and fro. The demon might have relinquished her body, but he had left skidmarks.

She folded to the floor next to the toilet. *There is nothing under your skin, this is all in your head.* She also knew there were those nail scissors in the cabinet. She could gouge it out; gouge out the parasites.

Stop. She had to get a fucking grip. This wasn't the first time she'd invoked a demon. It felt like the first.

Hands trembling, she threw on her dressing gown and guided herself downstairs to the cottage kitchen. Over the sink, she downed pint after pint of water. It was a habit she'd picked up in her student days, convincing herself that anything she allowed into her body could be easily expelled with a glass of tap water.

Wishful thinking. She was supposed to be meeting Elle for yoga in the morning too. Strangely, she found she'd been quite looking forward to it.

Now Ose had left her system, she felt cold all over – that horrible creeping chill the day before the flu kicks in. She wouldn't sleep for hours, wouldn't even be able to lie flat. How had she forgotten this part? She'd been here enough times.

Without warning, she spluttered and coughed up into the sink. It wasn't just water; her stomach was full of what looked like soil and chewed leaves. More clues as to how she'd spent the last few hours. She puked some more, before rinsing it down the drain.

She stared out of the kitchen window towards the lawn, but saw only her – Niamh's – reflection. Her skin was the colour of sour milk, clammy. She ran the tap again and rinsed her face.

When she looked up, she saw woodlice and earwigs crawling over the glass, on the outside. They whispered to her, tittering.

She *could* invoke a lesser demon, some no-name bottom-feeder skulking around the garden. It would fill her just enough to rid her body of the permafrost feeling. No. It was delaying the inevitable. It'd help her sleep now, but tomorrow she'd feel *worse* and someone might suspect.

'Fuck,' she said loudly, stomping into the lounge. She knelt to put more kindling in the fireplace. It wasn't enough, the shivers continued.

She wished she could just tell *someone* everything. The lies were piling up inside of her, fermenting, turning toxic. Her phone sat on the kitchen table, another message from Luke waiting for a response. She swiped it and instead tapped out a quick message to Leonie: *Anything?*

Fucking Hale, just fuck him. Waking her up with nothing but cryptic bullshit. Playing his little games. She almost hurled the phone at the wall, but then she'd be really screwed.

Leonie. She wanted Leonie. She wanted to unload, the way they had as teenagers. Ciara was the first person Leonie had told she was gay; walking home from school after Home Economics. They were both carrying home-made Bakewell tarts in front of them.

But she couldn't. She couldn't tell anyone anything. She was alone. You'd think, by now, she'd be used to it.

On the coffee table was the bronze dish containing the azurite, diaspore and hematite. All great stones for aiding memory. Theo used them to conjure her childhood.

Gemstones were useful for stilling the mind during meditation. The logic went that we hoard everything – every image, every soundbite of our past, if only we had the patience to sort through our inner filing cabinet. The crystals could help with the enormity of that task.

Ciara, arms like rubber, pushed herself onto the sofa, focusing on the chunk of hematite. It was seductively blue-black, like the darkest raven feathers. Ciara cradled the stone in her palm and focused on its core.

Her hands tremored, unable to hold the gem still. Even sitting still was too difficult. 'Get your shit together,' she hissed. Her jaw ached and her throat was raw from screaming. She closed her eyes, waited a minute, and tried again.

Tentatively, her sentience seeped into the gem. It was cool, blue, rational, in there. Quiet and still. She couldn't quite stop her teeth chattering, but let her mind flow through the crystal. Her mind's eye went up and down and around the mineral labyrinth within the rock, and soon it was as if *she* was inside the maze, running her fingers over endless, gleaming tunnels of sapphire blue.

Yes. Yes, this was better.

She idled awhile in these cool hallways, feeling her heart rate return to normal.

Up ahead, Ciara heard voices, laughter. She followed them, half-curious, half-bored. She turned a corner in the crystal and she was no longer in the crystal at all but a derelict, draughty mausoleum in Durham sixteen years ago.

'This, learned friends, is the mark of a very powerful demon.' Dab gestured at the sigil on the floor, holding court as ever.

Ciara recognised the runes from books she definitely shouldn't have read. It was the Mark of Satanis.

Candlelight flickered in Dab's eyes. 'He hath spoken to me.'

'No, he hasn't,' Helena told him, sipping a WKD Blue. They were 2-4-1 at the offie outside the Student Union that week. 'I think Satan might have better things to do than come to a bunch of students in Durham, don't you?'

Dab's eyes blazed, embarrassed in front of the nine members of the Durham Esoteric Society. 'Helena, you promised.'

She shook her head. 'Dab, we could get kicked out of HMRC for even having this conversation.'

'Ooh no! How awful. By unlocking the power of the

Unholy Trinity, we'd be the most powerful coven in the world, Helena. Fuck HMRC and fuck the cabal. It's time for a new era.'

Ciara rolled her eyes. Dabney might as well just get his willy out and instigate a pissing contest. Satan. Sure. 'How did Satan speak to you?' she asked, humouring him.

'In my dreams.'

Convenient. 'But how did he come to you? As Lucifer, Belial or Leviathan?' A fair question, she felt. The most powerful of all demons, the king of demons – Satan – was split, centuries ago, before the advent of the written word. All witches knew the tale. In order to confine Satan to his earthly prison, he was divided into three weaker entities: the lord of temptation, the lord of rage, and the lord of fear. The three fatal weaknesses of man. And woman.

Dabney paraded around the centre of the circle. 'As all three. I saw the true face of the king, Ciara.'

It was too cold for this bullshit. It was interesting how the long-castrated demon only ever appeared to men. Ciara keenly felt the icy stone floor on her rear, even with the extra layer provided by the velvet robes Dab insisted they wore 'out of respect'. Out of respect for who? The dead interred here were long, long past dust.

'There is no room for doubt,' he preached. 'The doubt is the crack where fear gets in. A demon will rip you apart from the inside if you show it fear.'

Across the circle, the newcomer seemed to mirror Ciara's bored expression. It was his first circle with them. A post-grad student, Jude. He was certainly very handsome, even with the hood up. Ciara liked his nose – wide set and a little wonky. She had never had much time for perfect Ken doll types. There was a pleasing asymmetry to his top lip too, a permanent smirk. His eyes were ice blue, his hair sandy blond.

He caught her eye between Dab's legs and gave the faintest suggestion of an eye-roll as Dab droned on and on.

Jude could stay.

So far, Durham was a disaster. She hadn't wanted to be here in the first place and, in her heart, she still yearned to be at the dance school. She was quite seriously considering dropping out at the end of the semester and skulking homewards to Hebden, tail between her legs, or maybe she'd join her sister in Dublin. She missed her.

Ciara didn't even realise that Dabney was addressing her. 'Well?'

'Well what?'

'Are you ready to let an ancient power into your body and soul, Ciara?'

Ciara looked up at Dab, very slowly, and fixed him in a steady glare. 'What the fuck makes you think I haven't already, you arrogant gobshite?' She rose to her feet at the same time as she lifted Dabney Hale off his with a flick of her right hand. She suspended him a few inches off the floor, dangling.

'Ciara, put him down,' Helena hissed, still trying to get into his pants.

Ciara held him up. 'There's something you should know about girls, Dab. The demons like us the best . . .'

Like any dream, the gauzy walls of her mind shifted, and Ciara floated over the scene in the mausoleum, until she realised she was looking up at stars.

Not real stars, the fluorescent stars she'd stuck to the ceiling of their room in Galway. She was on the top bunk, and Niamh was below her. Niamh was trying to muffle the fact she was crying, but Ciara could hear the sharp, wobbly intakes of breath.

'Niamh, are you awake?' she asked kindly, knowing full well she was.

'I don't want to go,' Niamh said, and Ciara didn't have to read her to know what she meant.

'It'll be fine,' Ciara said, hoping her sister didn't read her. 'It's just Nana's house.'

Niamh said nothing for a moment. 'What's going to happen to us?'

Ciara hung upside-down off the top bunk and saw Niamh's face half-buried in her pillow. 'It's what Mam and Dad wanted.'

'Do you think they can see us?'

'I don't know,' Ciara said. It was a comforting thought, the notion that the people we loved stay with us in some form after they died, but she suspected that was all it was.

'Where do you think we go when we die?'

'I don't know that, either.'

Niamh looked up at her. Even in the gloom, her eyes were pink and sore-looking. 'I think they're here. Like there's something inside us, isn't there? Something that makes us us. Maybe they'll move on when we go to Nana's.'

'Move on where?'

Niamh shrugged.

Ciara looked down at her softer, gentler half. 'At least we're still together. And we're going to be the best witches in Hebden Bridge.'

Niamh smiled slightly. 'Let's always live together. Even when we're grown—'

Ciara's neck spasmed, rudely jolting her out of the trance. She blinked, her eyes adjusting to the soft firelight. She didn't like where that was going. She pushed herself off the sofa and crossed to the kitchen. The tiles were freezing cold on her bare feet.

She saw young Niamh's face again and pushed it out. Fitting that *she'd* come back for the guilt trip. Ciara guessed if she wanted her memories restored, she'd have to take the rough with the smooth.

And talking about smooth: Jude Kavanaugh. Fuck. How on earth had she forgotten *him*? Every girl remembers her first time and her best time, and Jude was – on different occasions – both. With sadness, Ciara found these memories – like so many others – were now in tatty fragments. What happened to him? She couldn't even remember how it ended.

Still, thinking of Jude caused a different sort of restlessness. It had, after all, been a decade.

How odd. Libido. She'd been awake for over a fortnight, but now she felt *desire* awakening. It was almost surprising; she'd forgotten the urge.

Jude. Some of the old *feeling* returned to her now. Heartache is like smelling an old perfume again for the first time in years. A sort of exquisite melancholy. She couldn't *fully* recall their time together, but she remembered the *surprise*, the delight of it. The giddy joy of finding someone who likes you as much as you like them. Not to mention the sex. It's always the quiet ones. She saw, or rather felt, glimpses of their nights; the way he threw her legs up, bent her over the sofa.

He dominated her and she allowed it; a game they played together. That sense of being *taken*, devoured. Ciara didn't relinquish control very often, least of all to men, but with him . . .

A different sort of itch. Much harder to scratch.

She could – naturally – see to herself but tonight she craved the unpredictability of a partner. Her thoughts turned to Luke. Why starve when there's a fridge full of food?

Ciara had no difficulty in finding Luke's address on Niamh's phone. Still over-charged with Ose's power, she levitated high over Hebden Bridge with little effort. She felt weightless, almost non-corporeal. She hovered a moment over the tiny town, considering the little firefly lights of the cars and lorries travelling down the A646. She breathed in the insignificance of the sea monkeys below for a moment before plunging towards Pecket Well.

Since she was last conscious, they'd adapted the old wool mill into swanky flats by the looks of things. She landed gracefully outside the entrance and tried the main doors. Locked. Was this the maddest thing ever? He'd most likely be sound asleep, and there were the additional moral issues surrounding consent. Here's one for the philosophy majors.

She both was and wasn't Niamh. Luke thought she was Niamh, and the body *was*. Niamh was very much dead, so couldn't consent one way or another. Was this, in fact, necrophilia?

There wasn't a Judy Blume novel about this dilemma that she could recall. Is it wrong to fuck your dead sister's boyfriend if you've taken possession of your dead sister's body? *Are You There, Satan? It's Me, Ciara.*

Fuck it, she was horny, and it was her body now. When you buy a used car, you fucking drive it. She pressed the bell for Apartment 6 twice.

Her foot twitched, waiting for a response. Finally, she heard him clearing his throat via the entryphone. 'Who is it?'

'It's me,' she said. Honesty is the best policy, after all.

'Come on up!' The door honked and she hurried up the stairs to the third floor where he was waiting for her at the door in sweatpants and a vest. He did a double take on seeing her. 'You cut your hair!'

She'd forgotten that bit. 'Yeah. Fancied a change.' He stood aside to let her into the flat. It was a standard boy flat: Stormtrooper helmet, check; *Pulp Fiction* poster in a frame, also check. 'You got anything to drink?' she asked.

'Niamh Kelly, are you drunk?' he asked with a smile.

Fuck. Did she still look possessed? Drunk was far easier to explain. 'Maybe a little. I had some wine. I'm grieving, like, you know?'

'Whatever gets you through it. I've got some wine, I dunno if it's any good.' He went to the kitchenette and rummaged in the cupboards for wine glasses.

Ciara scoped out his broad shoulders in the vest, the curve of his spine and firm rear. He clearly knew his way around a gym. He wasn't overly plucked and preened though, and she liked it. His back was a little hairy, which felt only right for a man his age.

The wine could wait. She stalked after him and slipped her hands under his elastic waistband. He was naked underneath and she reached for his cock. It had a decent heft to it. 'Oh, 'ello!' he said.

'Don't talk,' she said simply. Little to nothing of what men said during sex was worth hearing. 'Fuck me.'

She pulled him towards the bedroom door. Like so many witches, Ciara would be quite content if all males were blinked from existence, but until then, it was what it was.

She tugged Niamh's sweater over her head and slid out of her jeans. There would be no coquettish striptease; she wanted him all over her. He went to kiss her, but she swerved it, going to his neck instead. To kiss his lips *did* feel like a betrayal, even after everything. She tugged the vest over his head and smothered his chest, his nipples, with kisses, bites.

He pushed her onto the bed, still warm from where he'd slept. He stooped to his knees at the side of the bed and ate her out. Ciara moaned, genuinely, remembering how exquisite these brief earthly joys could be in the right hands. His tongue flicked against her clit and she forgot everything anew. She spread wider and grasped his hair, driving his face hard into her, suffocating him.

He gasped and pulled away, wiping his face on his forearm. He kicked off the tracksuit pants and sank on top of her. 'Fuck me,' she said again. She seized his buttocks and pulled him inside her. Oh fuck, that was good.

Now he moaned, building speed. He went to kiss her again and this time she offered her neck. His lips nuzzled her all the way up to her earlobe. It tingled. 'Faster,' she told him. She'd always been a believer in if you're gonna do it, *do it*. She wanted to get fucked *hard*.

The bed squeaked and she could feel an orgasm building within, ready to erupt. She pushed him off her, accidentally using her powers a touch. She flipped him over and climbed on top of him, easing his dick in. She was soaking wet.

She wasn't far away, and neither was he, she sensed. She rode him, touching herself at the same time. With her other hand, she traced his muscular chest all the way to his throat. She wrapped her fingers around his thick neck and squeezed. His eyes bulged a little, but he didn't look displeased at her move.

Bet Niamh didn't fuck like this.

She squeezed harder and harder and she rode him faster. Her skin burned and prickled all over. Oh fuck, she was gonna come so fucking hard. It was going to break the sky in two. His face turned red. She laughed. Maybe there was still some of Ose lingering in her veins because it was funny. She laughed and laughed. She was going to fuck him to death.

Chapter Fifteen

PILLOW TALK

Ciara – Hebden Bridge, UK

She awoke to the smell of frying food. Her mouth was sealed shut like she'd swallowed superglue. She peeled her dry lips apart and dared to open her eyes. Luke's curtains were thin, sheer drapes that did little to block out the morning light. That said, she didn't feel as awful as she thought she might. Now, it really did feel like a hangover. Her hair hurt.

Weird though; it didn't feel how she remembered it feeling. Was that because it was so long ago, or because Niamh's body was . . . it didn't bear thinking about. She groaned and rolled to the cool side of the mattress. She squinted at her phone. Almost eight.

In the kitchen, Luke was singing along to the eighties radio station. No one needs Human League before coffee. He appeared in the doorway, carrying a mug. 'Hey, I didn't know if you needed to be up for work or not?'

'Hence the singing? That was my alarm?'

'Sorry. I brought you a coffee though.'

She gladly accepted it. He steered for a kiss again. 'Morning breath. You'll die.'

He perched on the rim of the bed, already dressed in cargo pants and a dark green GREEN & GOOD T-shirt. 'Last night was awesome,' he grinned. 'You should get tipsy more often.'

Ciara took a deep slurp from the mug. Good sex and good coffee, she could see why Niamh had recruited him to the cause. She reminisced on their session. She'd pretty much passed out after they'd both come at the same delicious moment. Any dark thoughts of snapping his head off like a dandelion had evaporated the second she orgasmed.

She smiled slyly. 'Oh, are you secretly one of *those*?'

'One of what?'

'Those men who want to be dominated and humiliated? Like women to tell them they have tiny dicks, and spit at them?'

He laughed, his baritone almost shaking the windows. 'I wouldn't go that far! Just . . . didn't see it coming.'

'Thank Gods for that,' she said, taking another sip. 'I always think it's a sure sign of Mammy Issues.'

In his head, there was an explosive flash of pain so white-hot that Ciara almost spilled the coffee all over the duvet. Startled, she looked harder, but saw nothing, like his past had gone into retreat. Fuck, maybe there *was* a Mommy Dearest somewhere in his past. Whatever it was, it was buried very deep. Nor did she especially care to know more. She wanted a fuck, not therapy.

'You OK?' she asked.

'I'm fine. I've made scrambled tofu. I hope it's OK.'

Ciara tried to look inside his head again, but it may as

well be tofu. Most mundane men didn't have an awful lot going on upstairs, and there's no point erecting a diving board above a puddle. Ciara sighed. 'That'll be great, thanks.'

He returned to the kitchen. Maybe shagging him was a nuclear mistake. She cursed her recklessness. Ah well, soon she'd be long gone, and he'd be cry-wanking himself to sleep. In the interim, he was a good fuck. Rare. She didn't want to cut off her nose to spite her vagina.

He carried a plate of tofu, avocado and sourdough toast into the bedroom. 'Here you go! Hey, are you about tonight? They're showing *Poltergeist* at the cinema. The original, obviously.'

She took the plate from him. 'I . . . um . . . what night is it? Wednesday?'

Now he looked shocked. 'Oh fuck, I can't tonight. I'm meeting the lads. Shit.'

'Another time,' Ciara told him, tapping her head. 'I'm sure I can persuade them to show it again.'

Her phone caught her eye, ringing silently on the bedside table. Luke handed it to her. It was Moira incoming. 'I'd better get this,' she said. 'Hello?'

'Oh morning, Niamh, I hope I didn't wake you.'

'I was up.'

'Just a quick call to let you know. I don't quite know how to tell you this, but there's been an accident . . .'

'What?' Ciara feigned shock.

'I've heard from the House of Hekate and, um, last night Irina Konvalinka died. All very sudden. It looks like she fell down that huge staircase – I've said for years it was a Health and Safety risk. Poor thing broke her neck. They found her this morning.'

Ciara sat up straighter. Ose. A demon able to take control

of a human entirely. He must have launched her down the stairs. Neat and tidy, too. Ciara hadn't dared to tell the demon *how* to do it, only that he must. 'Gosh, that's awful,' Ciara said robotically. 'I'm so sorry to hear that.'

I wonder if she saw it coming.

Chapter Sixteen

DOWNWARD DOG

Elle – Hebden Bridge, UK

Melissa's treacly voice washed over Elle's body. *And let your arms and legs just melt into the floor. Shavasana. Empty your mind of the to-do list. Slow your breathing into gentle tides.*

Elle found the switching off the hardest part of her weekly yoga class. The bending and stretching were fine – she'd now even mastered Crow Pose – it was the to-do list she couldn't shake. Her colleague, Caz, was off on mat leave so they were one community nurse down, and Elle had taken on one of her routes. Milo needed a new winter coat before the weather properly turned; the sleeves of his old one finished halfway up his arms like Lurch. She had to ensure Annie's cottage was fully empty by next week at the latest. All that, and Holly's insistence on fully exploiting her powers like some sort of rabid coven activist. Maybe it would be best if she and Theo didn't spend *quite* so much time together. It might be easier if she found a little mundane friend.

Shit. She'd failed to relax yet again. One more thing to feel like a failure at. How was *that* meant to relax her?

'When you're ready,' Melissa purred, 'gently open your eyes. There's no rush. Meditate for longer if you need to. Raise your hands to your third eye . . . and namaste.'

Well thank goddess that was over. Who has time for just laying still? Elle sprang up like a jack-in-the-box and rolled her yoga mat into a sausage. She wished Melissa a good week. The yoga teacher was further proof that not *all* witches have to be immersed knee-deep in HMRC drama. Melissa was only a Level 2 healer, granted, but – as far as Elle knew – her girlfriend didn't even know she was a witch. Most of Hebden Bridge didn't know. You don't have to wave a flag or wear a cape. What's wrong with just being a woman who is also a witch?

As the rest of the class – mostly yummy mummies, it must be said – filed out of Calderdale Yoga Centre, Elle tiptoed barefoot to Niamh's mat. She was looking a little worse for wear, sweating profusely. 'You all right, babe?'

'Bit of a hangover, my friend, I won't lie. I came from Luke's.'

Elle grinned. 'Oh aye?'

'Stop! It's nothing.' Niamh stretched her arms overhead before gathering her things off the studio floor.

Elle quite enjoyed seeing Niamh all lovestruck and coy. 'Have you got any time for lunch?'

Niamh shrugged. 'I suppose so. I'm a lady of leisure theoretically until they stick that crown on my head.'

They collected their shoes from the racks, and Elle zipped a Lululemon gilet over her matching yoga kit. They headed, yoga mats tucked under their arms, towards

Market Square. It was a perfect autumnal day outside, both sides of the valley starting to turn. 'So Luke, eh?'

'What about him?'

'It's getting serious . . .'

'It absolutely isn't,' Niamh said with finality.

Niamh Kelly was impossible. If she was going to toss Luke Watts in the bin, she might as well get fitted for a wimple and become a nun right now. 'What's wrong with him? He's tall; he's handsome; he's got his own business. Hell, you even told him you're a you-know-what and he didn't freak out.'

Niamh tied her hair into a stumpy ponytail as they walked. Elle liked it shorter. 'It is what it is,' Niamh said, oddly dismissive. 'I'm about to get real busy, aren't I?'

'Is it about Conrad?' Elle asked as gently as she could. 'Because, you know I loved him, but it's been almost ten years, doll.'

Niamh stopped a second, a frown crinkling her forehead in a way that Elle's didn't, thanks to the wonders of Botox. It seemed like she'd forgotten something. 'No. No it isn't Conrad.' She looked blank. 'Elle, can I ask a question? How did Conrad die?'

Now Elle was confused. 'What do you mean?' There was no easy or nice way of wording it. 'He . . . died in the war. Ciara killed him.'

'I know that. I mean . . . how did she . . . do it?'

What a question, honestly. 'I . . . I never asked. It's not the sort of thing you talk about.'

Niamh looked puzzled, which puzzled Elle. If anyone knew what happened to Conrad, it was Niamh, she'd found him after all. But Elle had seen PTSD in both witches and mundanes alike. It took many forms, and had many symptoms, and it wasn't like in the films. Yes, she'd treated soldiers on returning from Afghanistan, and witches after the war; but she'd also treated a teenage boy who'd developed PTSD after a bad trip on mushrooms, and a woman who'd fled domestic abuse twenty years earlier yet still flinched every time she heard a door slam.

Elle reached her healing hands towards Niamh. 'Can I . . . ?'

Niamh recoiled. 'No, no I'm fine. I just . . . I'm fine.'

'Sure?' Niamh assured her she was. Elle looped her arm through Niamh's, and they carried on towards one of the many, many cafés in town. 'It's such a cliche, isn't it? *He'd want you to be happy.* But Conrad really would – he worshipped you. And I *know* you, Niamh. Luke makes you happy, I can tell. I'm not psychic, love, but I've known you for twenty-five years!'

Niamh stared at her trainers. 'He's not so bad.'

Elle had an idea. After her grandmother had died, one of the other nurses at the Health Centre had loaned her the most wonderful book: *The Power of Now.* Jill would never know if she lent it to Niamh. 'Did I tell you about the book I read after Annie passed on? It's so good. I'll lend you it, if you . . .' On the other side of the bridge, she saw Jez emerge from the wine shop on Crown Street. 'Is that our Jez?'

'Looks like,' Niamh said.

'Oi, Jez!' she shouted at the top of her lungs and hurried to catch up with him. 'You drinking on the job now?'

Jez, for a moment, looked surprised but then grinned. 'I were thinking about it, aye!'

They met halfway, outside the Shoulder of Mutton, and she gave him a peck on the cheek. 'What are you doin'?'

'I'm taking the early lunch today because Gary has to leave at three.'

She looked at the tote bag of booze in his hand. 'What's the wine for?'

He nodded at the window. 'They had an offer on, so I thought I'd grab a couple of bottles.'

That sounded about right. She tactically planned their Ocado shops for fifty-one weeks a year, but as soon as Christmas or barbeque season came around, Jez suddenly transformed into Jamie friggin' Oliver. He'd bulk-buy very specific ingredients for recipes they'd never use again, and this was why her cupboards were full of expired jars of harissa or fish sauce.

'I'm gonna grab some lunch with Niamh if you wanna join us?' Elle turned to her friend. 'If that's all right?'

'Of course,' Niamh said. She still seemed spacey, however. Must be low blood sugar.

'I better not,' Jez said. 'I'll grab a sarnie and eat at the garage.'

'No worries. What time are you home tonight?'

'Usual. I'll take Milo to footie if you want.' They kissed again, and he darted away in the direction of his van.

'Right!' Elle announced. 'What we having? Oooh, do you know what, I really fancy one of those big halloumi salads at The Old Gate . . . what?'

Niamh squinted after Jez's van as he drove away.

'Niamh?'

Niamh blinked and looked at her. 'Right, OK.' She paused. 'You know what, fuck it. Here's a question: if you knew Luke was cheating on me, would you tell me?'

It felt like the cobbled street was somehow coming up underneath her feet, the rug being pulled. 'What? Yes, I would, I suppose.'

Niamh's lips were tight, her face sour. 'In that case, you should know Jez is shagging a woman from a hotel.'

Chapter Seventeen

THE DOLLHOUSE

Leonie – Lake Garda, Italy

Shielding herself from mundane eyes, Leonie soared over the vast mirror of Lake Garda. The expanse was a doomy slate-grey today, angry clouds tumbling down off the mountains, leaving a cottony mist over the water. The air up here was a tonic; squeaky clean, and Leonie sucked in healing lungfuls as she skimmed the surface with the tips of her boots. Her shoulder ached from the fight. A couple of co-codamol helped, but she needed a healer ASAP.

She'd got out of Bologna as fast as she could. Having destroyed a sixteenth-century statue, causing a minor international incident, Leonie thought it best *not* to ask Coven Italia for further favours. They were hard at work, convincing the media the 1566 statue of Neptune had been struck by lightning.

After a light breakfast in Bologna, Leonie took the first fast train to Verona – impressed as ever with how much nicer European trains are than poxy English ones – and FaceTimed Chinara. 'What do you know about this girl?' Chinara, at the gym, had asked.

'Not a lot. She's intersex. She was essentially trafficked from what I could tell.'

'Do you trust her?'

Leonie mulled on this. 'Yes. I really do.' Sentience went deeper than reading minds. Sometimes it really was about the vibes, and her instincts rarely failed her. Theo: good vibes. Helena: bad vibes. See?

'Then I trust you,' Chinara said. 'But be careful. Domino is *not* one to fuck with.'

Amen to that. This close, she could scan the houses and villas lining the lake. Some of them were touristy hotels, others were vacant holiday homes that spoke of grotesque wealth. She sensed Domino's distinctive, shifting aura in a palatial villa on the water's edge.

'Villa' sold it short – it was a renaissance mansion with pillars out front and a rampart running around the top of the house. The masonry was the same pastel pink shade as many of the buildings in Bologna, but this one also had a custard yellow trim, lending a sugary, gingerbread cottage facade. And as much as Leonie sympathised with the witch in any fairy tale, she also knew to be cautious.

Leonie slowed her flight. She brought herself down to earth softly, landing on a private jetty off the gardens where a gleaming speedboat was docked. Domino enjoyed her toys – dolls, boats. Leonie crouched behind a mottled balustrade wall and removed her rucksack, stowing it behind some bushes. She scanned the palazzo. The thoughtwaves were somnolent, telling Leonie most of the house slept. Good.

Leonie ducked further as a figure emerged from the side of the house. A mundane male, but one with a gun. She did a more thorough sweep and she sensed two men – both awake and, she guessed, both armed guards. She focused her mind on the first. He was hungry. Musing mostly on when he could get to his packed lunch, which today was his Nona's leftovers.

'*Sleep*,' Leonie whispered.

The guard staggered, steadying himself against the wall. He blinked doltishly before sliding down onto his bottom, and his head lolled onto his chest. Leonie sensed the other guard was in a car parked on the driveway on the other side of the mansion. He was even easier to send to sleep, given he was already seated.

Almost too easy. Leonie felt at least seven lifeforms inside the house, and all of them were witches or warlocks. If they awoke, she'd be in trouble. If the guards were strolling around the lawns, that suggested that there weren't motion alarms outside. She would chance it.

Feeling hugely conspicuous, she prowled across the plush green grass as if she were in the SAS. If the SAS wore hot-pink leopard-print ripped jeans and Blondie T-shirts. The mental image was so ludicrous, she almost laughed at herself. She darted onto a sun terrace and more cautiously approached the double French windows. Leonie peered through the glass to look inside. The room beyond the doors looked to be a study or library of sorts.

A red light high on the wall blinked. There was nothing she could magically do about the alarm. Tech was disappointingly witchcraft incompatible, but she *could* do something about the people who'd hear it. She could temporarily make them deaf.

What was less certain was how long she could render them so. That meant this had to be a really quick job. In and out. Leonie focused everything she could on locating Senait based on her aura last night, but the lifeforces within the house were damp, foggy, muddled somehow. Human soup.

Leonie braced herself. As soon as she did this, a count-down started. Three, two, one . . .

She punched hard with her mind, shattering one half of the French windows. The second after she stepped into the parlour, the intruder alarm started. *Nothing to hear here.* Leonie seeded the *idea* of silence throughout the house, transmitting the single, lullaby notion to anyone within range. *Everything is quiet.*

Leonie flew directly for the stairs. If people were sleeping, that felt like the safest bet.

She froze in her tracks as she heard the tell-tale sound of nails clicking on the marble floors. The biggest rottweiler she'd ever, ever, seen trotted insouciantly around the corner from the bottom of the sweeping staircase. As their eyes met, it was almost as if both Leonie and the dog did a double take.

Remembering its job, the dog dropped a rawhide chew from its mouth and growled at her.

'Oh fuck,' Leonie muttered. Animals were *way* harder to control in some ways. Their energy was so chaotic. You couldn't reason with them. She crouched – very gingerly – to the dog's level, all the while mindful she couldn't let the alarm go from her mind. 'Here, girl. Who's a good girl?'

The dog growled some more, but didn't leap for her. *This* was why she was a fucking cat person. Unless there was a fucking tiger hiding somewhere. She held a confident hand out. She'd seen dog people do that. The dog padded closer. Close enough for Leonie to get inside its head in any case. 'Sleep, doggy . . .'

The rottweiler sat, first on her bottom, and then all the

way down to the floor, resting her head on her mighty paws. 'Gooooood girl! Sleep!'

Leonie exhaled for what felt like a very long time once the dog had closed her eyes. She refocused her mental energy on suppressing the whining intruder alarm. Would it trigger a further mundane security unit? She hoped she wouldn't find out. She stepped over the sleeping dog and hurried up the stairs.

Fuck, she was out of shape. When all this was over, she really needed to start going on runs with Chi. She reached the landing out of breath and with a sweaty top lip.

An upstairs mezzanine overlooked the grand entrance hall and featured a warren of corridors and connecting doors. Leonie was spoiled for choice. She closed her eyes and let her mind figure it out. Senait possessed the most unusual aura. An air witch, certainly, but with an earthy undertone. Like dew and winter dawns. Where *was* she?

There.

Leonie swung herself off the banister towards a closed double door. She tested the ornate handle and found it unlocked. She slipped inside a dusky bedroom. In the low light, Leonie saw a grandiose four-poster bed with drapes drawn down all sides. Inside the cocoon, a form was tucked up and sleeping. Leonie, now closer, ensured she stayed that way, pulling the woman further under. It was unmistakably Domino. If she'd had more time, she would have been curious to see her original body and discover if she was white. Leonie was willing to bet any money in the world she was. The way she switched ethnicities so flippantly reeked of white privilege; all the beauty, none of the oppression. But, with the alarm sounding, she couldn't dally.

Aside from the ostentatious bed, and a chaise longue with Domino's discarded clothes strewn across it, the main bedroom was empty. Leonie looked to her left and saw a door to an adjoining suite, or perhaps an en suite. She tiptoed through the murk to the next room, which was even more shadowy.

Leonie sensed six auras in here, but couldn't see in the gloom. Her hand groped for a light switch along the wall. She flipped the lights and gasped, almost dropping all the psychic plates she was spinning.

They were like coffins. Glass coffins.

Subtle floor-level lighting cast a silver glow around the windowless chamber. At first glance, it was a walk-in wardrobe. One wall housed rails of clothing, another shelves for an enviable Gucci, Hermès and Chanel handbag collection. There was a display board of eyepatches; and a whole wall for shoe racks. But Leonie was far more concerned with the large glass cases in the centre of the room. They were laid out horizontally in a neat row, one box after the next.

In the first slept the striking receptionist with the Louise Brooks bob. She *looked* asleep, but Leonie felt the resistance coming from the glass cabinet. The framed edges were gilded wood; Leonie guessed they were laced with mistletoe. It would explain why she couldn't accurately trace Senait from outside; the wood was dampening the 'dolls' powers as well as hers.

They were prisoners. Each of Domino's 'dolls' was sealed in the way Helena had once kept her collectable Spice Girl figurines pristine in their packaging. *They're worth more if you keep the boxes.*

Senait was in the fourth cabinet after the receptionist and two other stunning young women; one a cherubic blond, one a pale redhead who reminded her a little of Niamh. In the final two were the Japanese face Domino had worn yesterday, and a final, South Asian, girl with waist-length raven hair. She wanted to puke but swallowed. Her throat tight, Leonie cast her mind back to Domino's idle offer of a place in her troupe at the Voodoo Lounge. This could have been *her* sealed in a glass case.

Intuitively, Leonie knew this was the lock that would fit the key Senait had left behind. She took it from her pocket and ran her fingers around the mistletoe frame until she felt a tiny jewellery box lock. *This* was why Senait needed her; it couldn't be opened from the inside.

Leonie inserted the key and twisted until she felt a satisfying click. Carefully, she raised the glass lid. It was hinged and held itself open.

'Senait?' she whispered. When there was no response, Leonie placed two fingers to her temple and sent a clear message deep into her subconscious: *WAKE UP*.

Senait's eyes fluttered open, confused at first, and then wide awake. 'Wow. You actually came. Faith in humanity restored.'

'Quickly,' Leonie told her. 'Get dressed. We haven't got much time.'

All the dolls were dressed in functional black vest and short combos. Leonie helped Senait clamber out of the glass coffin. She was unsteady on her feet for a second, but quickly crossed to the clothes rails and pulled out some unremarkable cotton pants. 'Get as much as you need,' Leonie told her. 'You're not coming back.'

Senait nodded and grabbed more items, shoving them into a Louis Vuitton holdall. Leonie hovered on the threshold to the main suite, eyes fixed on the sleeping shape in bed. Finally, Senait pulled on some socks and Adidas trainers. 'I'm ready.'

'Come on!' Leonie pushed her out into the bedroom,

tiptoeing past the four-poster. Only then, as she cast a look over her shoulder, did she hesitate. 'Wait,' she breathed. 'What about them?' She nodded at the five other captives.

Senait's eyes widened. 'I don't fuckin' know. Some of them like it here, she's minted.'

Fuck. 'Does she control their minds?'

'No, she can't do that.'

That didn't mean the other women *wanted* to stay. Women stay in worse situations without being hexed. Do not ask why an abused woman didn't leave, ask how her abuser kept her there. She wouldn't leave the others stuck in those cases, defenceless; she couldn't.

Leonie raised her left hand and slammed out. All five coffins shattered and she steered the glass outwards, away from the dolls. She saw their eyes snap open. Her spell was broken. 'Run!' she told Senait, grabbing her hand.

They fled the bedroom, their footsteps echoing down the marble landing. Behind them, she heard a raspy scream. She looked over her shoulder: Domino was awake, a silhouette sat upright beyond the veils. 'Who dares?'

Leonie and Senait almost tumbled down the stairs in their haste. 'The mirror!' Senait cried. Leonie had noted the enormous hallway mirror on her way in, but now she saw the outline of a woman materialise in the glass. 'It's a conduit!'

Sure enough, Domino – in her own body this time – stepped through the mirror into the hall, intercepting them. Her frame was that of a very elderly, emaciated woman, her satin-clad spine hunched over. And yes, as Leonie had suspected, she was white – if very dangerously tanned. Her leathery face had seen many surgeons. Her skin was stretched over her skull, cheeks and lips swollen with fillers, making her head look much too big for her body. Her eyes squinted out past puffy, lumpen cheeks. Leonie couldn't say if the platinum blond hair was a wig or not. Either way, Domino was furious. She jabbed a talon-like fingernail towards them. 'You fucking ungrateful little bitch,' she sneered at Senait. She could scarcely part her taut mouth to speak.

'Let us go, Domino,' Leonie said defiantly. 'She wants to leave.'

'I bought the bitch, she's mine.'

'It doesn't work like that,' said Leonie. 'Step aside. You can't beat me in a fight, and you know it.'

'The arrogance of youth,' Domino said. She levitated off the floor and, from the kitchen, a swarm of chef's knives and cleavers flocked like birds around her, poised to attack. 'Now get upstairs, Senait. You signed a contract.'

'Go fuck yerself.' Bolts of lightning shot from Senait's palms, right at Domino. The old woman bore the full brunt of the blast and she was smashed into the mirror. Leonie felt the impact in her calves. The glass shattered with an almost musical gong, cymbals clashing. The elderly witch flopped to the floor like a crumpled silk sack. Senait looked to Leonie. 'Storm from *X-Men*. Right, can we get some food, I'm starving?'

Leonie stared at Senait, agog. 'Let's get out of here.' The rottweiler was starting to stir beside her.

The pair ran past Domino and into the study. Leonie could feel her essence well enough to know the woman was alive. It was up to the other dolls to decide their fate while their mistress was unconscious. Over the burglar-alarm, Leonie heard another type of siren – and it was getting closer. The alarm *must* have triggered security.

'Can you fly?' Leonie asked Senait as they pelted towards where she'd hidden her stuff.

'I'm a bit shit at it, to be honest.'

'Get hold of me,' she commanded. Senait wrapped her arms around Leonie's neck, and she lifted them both off the lawn. Shrouding them both, Leonie took flight once more over Lake Garda. 'Where are we heading?' she shouted over the wind.

'Turkey!' Senait called in her ear. 'Istanbul.'

'Turkey? Why?'

'That's where whatshisface is going. It's where they found it.'

Leonie was in no mood for guessing games. 'Where they found what?'

Senait answered as if it were the most obvious thing in the world. 'The Seal of Solomon.'

Chapter Eighteen

OF BOYS AND MEN

Theo – Hebden Bridge, UK

A gas van sailed past them, and as it did so, the driver – a twentyish guy with a face you'd forget in seconds – craned to get a better look at them. His head did the full *Exorcist* twist. There was a hunger in the way he looked at them. He looked too long.

Theo had noticed this a lot since her transformation. It made little difference whether or not they were in their school uniforms. She also didn't waste any time on *which* of them the driver was interested in. It mattered not, they were just two McNuggets in his Happy Meal.

She did, however, wonder if he'd got a kick out of noticing her noticing him. Surely he can't have thought that a fifteen-year-old girl would see him ogling her, chase after his van, jump in it, and wank him off. He can't seriously think she *wanted* to be stared at? No. It can only be that he'd somehow got off on making her squirm.

She knew, from her time in foster care, the way boys spoke about girls when they thought there weren't any present. Do they grow out of it, do they grow *into* it, and is it all of them? It was not unreasonable, she felt, to want boys to find her appealing but for them not to seek to subjugate her.

As it neared the end of the road, Theo gave the gas van a cheeky shove with her mind. The driver slammed on the brakes and she suppressed a smile. Served him right. Eyes on the road, mister. She was also pleased that her powers seemed better today. Maybe it was a hormonal thing.

Holly, luckily, didn't seem to notice either the driver's *lustful stares* or the emergency brake. 'Did Niamh say where they were going?' Holly asked as they turned into the Pearsons' driveway. For a family of witches, there wasn't a lot of life in their front garden. It was entirely paved in Indian sandstone and the privet hedges were neatly pruned.

'Nope. She just said she had to go somewhere with your mum.' Theo sighed. 'She's different since Ciara died.' With a nauseous, creeping dread, it was starting to feel like Niamh was putting distance between them. She'd been pass-the-parcelled around so many postcodes, you'd think she'd be used to it, but she thought she'd finally found a home. To lose it now didn't bear thinking about.

'It must be, like, a LOT,' Holly said. 'Milo is a pain in my arse, but I'm not going to literally kill him.'

'Niamh didn't kill her,' Theo said defensively, but Holly shot her a premium *bitch, please* expression as they entered the hallway. 'OK, she didn't *mean* to.' Theo didn't know if that was true, but she knew for certain that Niamh felt very, very badly about what happened during the war. Every day, her head was full of a swirling, watery grey: regret.

'Shoes off!' Holly said, so well trained. Everything in Elle's home was Mrs Hinched to within an inch of its life.

Everything – the walls, the carpets, the furniture – was the same muted grey shade – not *unlike* regret now she thought about it. Each room had a slogan stencilled onto the walls. The hallway catchphrase was, predictably, *There's No Place Like Home*, and that was about as witchy as anything outside of Holly's room.

They headed directly to the kitchen (*If You Want Breakfast In Bed, Sleep In The Kitchen!*) to scope out the food situation. 'Mum's probably left us individual Tupperware portions,' Holly said, leaning into the enormous fridge.

Theo heard someone thunder down the stairs overhead and Milo burst into the kitchen, shirtless and wearing only grey sweatpants. Theo averted her gaze at once, not willing to become her nemesis – the pervy van driver. He was really buff though. She allowed herself like a *millisecond* of a glance.

'Ew!' Holly barked. 'Could you please get dressed? My friend is right there!'

'It's *only Theo*,' he said, and Theo felt really good about herself. 'I was waiting for you to get in. Mum says we can have pizza and put it on her card.'

'On *Wednesday*?' Holly looked as shocked as Theo had ever seen her. 'Wow, something must be up.' She looked to Theo now. *Do you think Mum knows?*

'Can you feel them?' Theo asked aloud. 'Where are they?'

'I can't find them, can you?'

Theo cleared her mind and let her consciousness unspool. It's a strange sensation, like having flotsam brush against your legs in the sea. She *could* sense a Niamh-like presence, but it wasn't strong. 'I think they're close, but I don't know where.'

Milo leaned against the kitchen island, a look of mild disgust on his face. 'That shit is so fucking freaky.'

'Swear jar,' Holly sniped.

'Fuck off.'

Twenty-five minutes later, the pizzas arrived and they gathered around the coffee table in the lounge because while the cat's away, the mice will eat in the lounge without plates or cutlery. Holly put *A Nightmare on Elm Street* on the 77-inch wall-mounted TV.

While waiting for the food to come, Milo had put on a T-shirt so Theo could at least look in his direction without getting an itchy neck. What was that about?

'Did you finish the transmutation book?' Holly asked, wiping her fingers on kitchen roll.

'Yeah,' Theo said. The title had set out how the practice of transmutation – changing the physical self – was achieved mostly by powerful healers, more or less using the physics of teleportation: pulling molecules apart and putting them together again in a different order to resemble something else from the natural world. But this took an enormous toll on the witch, and was nearly always temporary – although there was a notable case of a Scottish witch in the 1800s who is said to have rebelled against an arranged marriage by turning herself into a cat, and living out the rest of her days in that form. 'I don't know if it explains what happened in the woods.'

Holly pulled a tatty little paperback book out of her school bag. 'I read this in fifth period Physics.' It was called *The Witch, Elevated* by Samantha Bourne. 'She says a witch's strength can go up by as much as three levels when she's under extreme stress.'

'That's so sexist,' Milo said through a mouthful of pizza. 'How do you know she's talking about a woman?'

Holly looked at him with horror. 'Are you thick? All witches are women.'

'Well . . .' Theo interjected. Living proof that things aren't always so binary. 'We call male witches "warlocks".'

Milo, for the first time, lowered the masculine bravado shield just a fraction. 'Mum says it's too late for me. She'd know by now.'

Even Holly must have picked up on the hint of sadness, of being deemed unspecial. 'Well, if it makes you feel better, Mum wishes I wasn't a witch either, and Dad is scared of me.'

Milo didn't deny that.

'We need glasses for the Coke,' Holly announced, springing to her feet and breaking the melancholy.

'Can't we just drink out of the bottle?' Milo said.

'Ew no, that's passive kissing.' Holly returned to the kitchen, leaving Theo alone with her brother. He looked her way and half-smiled. She felt a weird prickly heat spread across her chest, like she was blushing inside.

'You want another slice?'

'No,' she said. 'Thanks.'

This was awkward. How long did it take to get some glasses? Before her transformation, she'd been scared of Milo. Cis boys had always treated her worse than any girl; to them she'd been an aberration; the feminine male. Now, she wasn't sure how she felt. Not *scared*, but then again, she could probably make him walk off the edge of the cliff if she so willed it, so there was little she feared full-stop.

'Would you know if I was a warlock?' Milo asked.

She shook her head. 'I don't know.'

'You're more powerful than Holly, right?'

'Yes,' Theo said simply. It wasn't a brag, it just was.

'Can you look inside my head?'

Theo smiled, daring to look him straight in the eye. 'I could, but I won't, don't worry. Think your worst.' She was quite proud of the little quip. This was possibly the most she'd ever spoken to a boy. Ever.

He crawled around the coffee table and leaned towards her. 'No, go on. I want to know.'

Theo got the sense Holly might not like how chummy they were right now. She could hear her clattering around in the kitchen.

She didn't need to touch Milo to read him, but he was right there, and it was easier this way. She placed her fingers delicately on his temple. She was surprised by how warm he was, how soft his skin. She closed her eyes.

When you read mundanes, it's like flicking through *Heat Magazine* without paying for it in WHSmith because you half want to know why Posh is mad at Becks. It's all snippets and images, two dimensions, not three. Milo was no different. She saw football, so much football. He like *really* loved football and all its associated numbers. He also liked working out – another pastime all about the numbers – reps and calories and weights and gains.

She saw his body as he saw it in the mirror. He was almost *angry* at it. He wanted everything *better* than it was now.

She saw girls. He liked girls as much as he liked football. He was trying *very* hard not to think about pornography, but it was all there: girl on girl mostly, some from the point of view of a faceless man. But aside from the perfectly natural hunger that was sex, it seemed he liked the *company* of girls too, finding many of his male friends tiresome. Their *banter* sickened him as much as it would her. So why persist, she wondered. He joined in, even if he didn't mean it.

Snow Vance-Morrill was in his head too. Predictable, Milo. And Amber Taylor from Year 11.

And Theo Wells. It's very disconcerting to see yourself the way others see you. Why was she in his head? A day in the summer. She'd worn short-shorts and a child's Jigglypuff T-shirt, much too small for her, because she thought it was quirky. She and Holly had hung out in their garden, their legs kicked up behind them as they lay on their front, floating daisies out of the grass. She hadn't even been aware that Milo had seen them.

'What are you doing?' Holly said loudly, carrying three tumblers to the table.

Theo let go of his face and moved herself away from Milo. 'I'm sorry. You're not a warlock,' she said.

Holly pulled a face. 'You already knew that.'

Theo wasn't sure if Milo was disappointed or not. She saw no evidence that Milo was a warlock, but there was no mistaking what she'd felt when she found those memories of herself. He thought of her. He thought of her in a *way*.

He looked now. She briefly looked too before turning her attention to the enormous television. The only question was, if she knew how he felt, did *he* know how he felt?

Kaur, Sandhya

To me; Roberts, Moira

Hi Niamh

Just to let you know, we're finalising dates for the Shadow Cabinet meeting in Whitehall. It is likely the day after tomorrow, keep your diary clear, please.

Also, Events is drawing up a list of singers who could perform at the coronation. Florence sang at Helena's – do you have a preference?

Best,
Sandhya
Assistant to the High Priestess [she/her]

Kelly, Niamh

To Kaur, Sandhya; Roberts, Moira

Siouxsie. Or Kate. Literally no one else.
N xxx

Chapter Nineteen

HARMSWORTH HOUSE HOTEL

Ciara – Hebden Bridge, UK

The last time Ciara stayed at a hotel, she'd had her brain ripped out by her sister, so this was an enormously triggering experience. Her legs ached, squashed up in the passenger seat of Elle's tiny Fiat 500. A steady drumbeat of rain hammered on the roof as they waited at the furthest edge of the car park away from the entrance. Night was falling fast, and Ciara watched as yellow lights blinked on behind the leaded windows.

Harmsworth House, built in 1627, had once belonged to a powerful lesbian witch, Lady Elizabeth Harmsworth, but even her status as landed gentry hadn't spared her a drowning in the seventeenth century along with so many others after the Pendle clusterfuck. Now it was just another stately home repurposed as a wedding venue in the summer months. Ciara and Niamh had worked the odd waitressing shift here one summer, and it wasn't even a very nice hotel – all dust ruffles, tartan and oppressive wood panelling. The whole place reeked of mothballs from what she recalled.

Elle's hands gripped the wheel, knuckles white.

'I shouldn't have said anything,' Ciara said when the silence became too much to bear. 'Let me wipe the memory from your head, Ellie.'

Elle finally turned to face her. She seemed to be considering her offer. Ignorance is bliss, and all that. As she spoke, she sounded slightly drunk, or like she'd just woken up from a hundred-year hibernation. 'No. I . . . um . . . I think I knew. I pretended I didn't know. Jez . . . he sometimes will just drop everything and dash out "with work". Who needs a mechanic in the middle of the night? OK, yes, I can see that people might, but this was different. I knew.'

Ciara's heart felt heavy in a way it hadn't for a long, long time. Of course Elle knew. There was steel under all the marabou, always had been. 'Ellie, I'm so sorry.'

'Not your fault. Does Leonie know?' Elle's face fell. 'She does. She must. Why didn't she say?'

Ciara shrugged. 'It's not an easy thing to say.' She could only assume Niamh was well aware of this too, and opted not to tell Elle. Cowards. The pair of pussies, sparing themselves from an awkward conversation. She could see how she'd hurt Elle, but she hazarded the pain she'd inflicted today wasn't nearly as bad as what Jez had done and would continue to do if left unchecked. Sooner or later, Elle would have found out. Ciara had saved her some time, and a woman's time is priceless.

Loving men is truly a weakness. Elle was better off rid. The men she had loved lingered in her mind like aftershave on bedsheets: Jude, Dab, *Conrad*.

One night over the summer break from college, Ciara had been so drunk, she'd fallen asleep in a bus stop in

Todmorden. It was raining. She was wet but did not feel the cold, high on vodka and a demon called Carabia, who'd appeared to her as a nest of spiders. She was still deaf from the experience. She didn't really know where she was, or the man who came to help her at first. She couldn't hear him saying her name. She opened her eyes and into focus came Conrad, her sister's new boyfriend. She was visiting from Dublin and had brought him over to meet Nana. She was old now, and she'd had a fall the previous winter.

Why are you here? she'd asked, reaching for his face.

Her ears were ringing, but she dimly heard his voice. Ciara? Are you OK?

Yes. I am fine. You can go.

I can give you a ride home? Should I call Niamh?

Oh no. Niamh would be so cross. My sister is very well-behaved, you know.

Gods, that was weird. These little dribs and drabs returning to her of their own accord. It was like, the more she forced it, the less likely it was to happen, but nor did she like these nostalgic surprises.

Elle's voice snapped her out of her reverie. 'Is he in there?'

The van parked outside the hotel certainly suggested that, but Ciara scanned the hotel regardless. 'He is.'

'Are they . . . ?'

'Thankfully no. He's hanging out at the bar.' Ciara wondered if that was actually worse. It wasn't just a hit-and-run, they were *talking*. They had in-jokes, and this secret made a delicious clubhouse-for-two.

'But they have?'

'Yes.' Ciara didn't even have to look very hard; Jez's

head was a snow globe. 'He's very guilty, but he can't stop.'

'Because he loves her?' Elle started to cry. A fat teardrop ran down her cheek and plopped onto her chest.

Ciara didn't answer, but yes, he did. It was stronger than garlic. He was obsessed with this Jessica woman, infatuated. What he felt to his family was *commitment* – although that is a sort of love, Ciara supposed – dedication. It was powerful. He had told Jessica he'd leave Elle, but it was a lie, he had no genuine desire to do so. 'He won't leave you,' Ciara said, focusing on the positive. 'He won't. He wants both.' Of course he did. He was a man.

She read Jessica too. She loved Jez, and she loved the *pursuit* of Jez. The way she contorted herself into the most appealing version of herself; all the things she didn't say lest they scare him away. The fictional role of Sexy Jessica was almost a part-time job. No whining, no ultimatums, no pubic hair.

It made Ciara acutely morose. Where do we learn these behaviours?

'So what am I supposed to do?' Elle said, her voice cracking. 'Just ignore it? Turn a blind eye to my husband shagging some skinny slapper in a hotel? Forbid him from seeing her? How do I drop that one into conversation?'

'I can make you forget this,' Ciara said more forcefully. 'Or I can make *him* loathe her if you want. Or I could kill his sex drive, or—'

'No!' Elle shot back. 'That is not what our powers are for, Niamh! We cannot just fix things, fix *people*, the way we want them. Look at what happened to Helena! We do not have carte blanche to do whatever we want!'

But that's exactly what they did do. Witches did not,

should not, follow the rules. Mundane rules are for the mundane.

'And aren't you forgetting a key detail? Jez is mundane. It's against the law.'

Oh, that old chestnut. *The Treaty*. It was funny how HMRC wheeled that legislation out only when it suited them. 'Elle,' Ciara said. 'Didn't you use magic on Luke?' She saw the incidents quite clearly in Elle's mind. '*Twice?*'

'That was totally different, and you know it! He'd have died twice!'

Ciara sympathised with those first HMRC witches who, no doubt, got real sick of listening to 'Greensleeves', but they took literal magic and created a code of conduct precisely no fucker asked for. The only difference was now, witches could only use magic to support whatever cause HMRC decided. Respectable witchcraft.

During the war, hundreds of mundanes had their minds altered to forget what they'd seen. Witches lived long past their natural lifespans with the help of healers. He was a prat, but Dab had always had that part right; it's a strange sort of puritanism that saw witches swear off witchcraft.

If you can, then do.

'Do you think I'm stupid?' Elle muttered.

'No,' Ciara said. 'Not one bit. He betrayed your trust.'

Ciara could tear this hotel apart and bury them under it. Imagine hurting Elle fucking Device. It'd be like kicking a puppy. Even *she* wouldn't go that far.

'I don't know what to do,' Elle said, staring at the rain as it coursed down the windscreen. 'I just don't know what to do.'

And she didn't, her mind was a swirling, shifting mass, like liquid mercury. Ciara's head started to hurt, like the metallic sludge was pushing at the edges of her skull.

Worse, a ghastly bloodlike taste clogged the wall of her throat. This was rage. Pure rage, velvety claret, and molten hot in her veins. She'd never seen this in Elle before, not ever. Something primal stirred within her.

Even Ciara was scared.

She gasped for air, and quickly withdrew. 'Elle, are you OK?'

'No,' the woman said, still gripping the wheel, looking ahead at nothing.

In that moment, she felt oddly grateful for the hunk of Yorkshire granite that was Luke Watts. At least you knew where you stood with a rock of ages like him.

Chapter Twenty

THE WORKING MEN'S CLUB

Luke – Huddersfield, UK

Luke hated this shithole. What the fuck even was a 'working men's club'? He'd never questioned it as a kid, but now he thought about it, it made little sense. Most men of working age work, but the majority don't frequent dank single-sex cellars.

To add to his discomfort, he was wet. Even running from the car had left him drenched, cold drips running off his brow.

Just the clink of snooker balls politely greeting each other turned his stomach. How was it, over a decade after the smoking ban, this dingy basement pub hadn't got the message? The carpet was tacky underfoot as he made his way to the bar. He'd driven in, but he wouldn't get through this without a pint in him. He briefly toyed with the idea of asking for a glass of wine or a gin and tonic, just to see what sort of toxic shock it'd elicit from the other patrons.

Linda, the only woman in the venue, was here to serve. She poured him a pint of stout with muscular arms and took his money. There was a faded dolphin tattoo on the top of her hand. 'Yer late,' she said, peering at him through clumpy, electric blue mascara. 'They've started without yer.'

Luke inhaled, and braced himself. He approached the rows of chairs all facing the screen. He hoped the darkness might hide him, but no such luck.

'Oh, His Highness has bothered to show up then?' A tall man with a beak nose and a receding hairline stood at the front of the little viewing, illuminated by the skittish white light of the projector. 'What time do yer call this?'

Luke stared him down. 'Sorry, Dad,' he said, and went to take a seat on the last row.

'Get yer arse up here. It's you we're waiting fer, ya twat.'

He swam through a fog of cigarette smoke, pork scratchings and BO to reach the front. The Club was all men, mostly over fifty, but increasingly their sons and some of *their* sons too. Luke had wondered at one time if their movement had one generation left in it, but it was startling to see the renewed zeal some of the kids had. Young John Ackroyd was only nineteen and already had the 1727 tattoo behind his ear.

The final *official* execution of a witch in the British Isles, and when the work of the Working Men had officially begun.

Luke took his reserved space on the front row. 'What is it you wanna know?' He took a mighty gulp from the pint glass.

Peter Ridge did not need to point the clicker at the laptop like a gun, but he did. A PowerPoint presentation started on the screen. HEBDEN BRIDGE: THE NEW PENDLE? 'You tell us, matey. We're all ears.'

His father beckoned for him to take the floor. Luke parked his drink on an already sodden Tetley's beermat and turned to face the audience while Peter took a seat. Luke jammed awkward hands into his pockets. Major high school flashbacks: freezing, statue-still at Harvest Festival, poem in hand.

He cleared his throat. 'I feel like I'm repeating myself at this stage. You're wasting your time. I've been undercover in Hebden Bridge for almost three years and I'm yet to see any *real* evidence of witchcraft in the town. You know what it's like, it's full o' hippies. They like candles and vegan food and crystals. They aren't witches like we know witches.'

And it was a good job none of this ugly bunch *were* witches or they'd know he was lying through his teeth. There was a stiffening of the audience though. It didn't matter how often he repeated his 'findings'. They didn't believe him.

'Lads, think about it. If you were a witch, would you live anywhere near Pendle? It's . . . naff! It's all tourist museums, and tea towels, and fridge magnets. And they know *we're* still out here, searching for 'em. I'm telling you. Yer barking up the wrong tree.'

There were very few Working Men left. Fewer witches too. The war had been an eye-opener. On one hand it had uncovered that there were many more live witches than they thought, and it had demonstrated just how dangerous they were. On the other, their civil war did all the heavy lifting for them. Luke had been young, but he remembered his dad and his mates lapping it up as the witches killed each other, saving them the bother. Those left saw themselves as clearing up the remnants of a dying breed, still hosting quarterly meet-ups like this one.

Big game hunters. In Huddersfield. The Working Men had, naturally, started up north, where witchcraft flourished away from the prying eyes of the big cities down south. Each year, the various witchfinder chapters around the UK, and some from Europe, met up at Chester Racecourse for the Away Day. Fuck they were a tedious bunch. Luke still remembered the precise day where he realised he just didn't give a shit about their obsession.

And it was long before he clapped eyes on Niamh Kelly.

Peter stood once more. 'Luke, my son, I don't know if you need a trip to Specsavers or what, but how do you explain this?'

He pointed his clicker at the laptop and moved the slideshow forward. The photo was grainy but seemed to show a cyclone approaching the valley. His father clicked through the next slide and there did look, if you really squinted, to be human forms inside the tornado.

'How do I explain what? That could be anything. It's a shite photo, Dad.'

'Then what about that?' The next photo showed the aftermath of the siege; the gap where the bridge used to be before Leonie destroyed it.

'The weather? The fact it were hundreds o' years old?' Around his father, his accent became ten times broader. If he toned down his accent, they'd accuse him of being soft.

'And then there's this.' A photo of Helena Vance filled the screen. 'We'd been watching this one for years and then, just like that, she vanishes without a trace. Where is she?'

Luke didn't have a convincing lie for that one. No lie could be as insane as the truth. *Well, Dad, they burned her alive.*

Peter came to his side and addressed the audience. 'Before we sent Luke in, we identified twelve potential hags in Hebden Bridge.' He brought up the next slide and there she was on the third row: Dr Niamh Kelly, potential 'herbalist'. The irony was nine of them really were hippies with candles from what Luke had ascertained. Of the women on the board, only Niamh, Lillian Vance and Sheila Henry were witches as far as he knew.

'I have found zero evidence . . .'

Luke was cut dead by the next picture. It was another shit picture, but it definitely showed Niamh, Theo and Holly meditating in the woods. The yellow rays beating down on Niamh's face suggested it had been taken at some point over the summer. 'Who took this?' he asked.

'We did.' Mick Ackroyd nodded at his son. 'Our John has a drone.'

He had to play this next part very carefully indeed. 'Well . . . what did you see? All I can see here is three women sat in a circle.'

'Look at 'em!' John spat angrily. He had a vicious little mouth, like a chihuahua. 'As if that's not fuckin' hags!'

'Did you see any of the Five Signs?' Every Working Man knew them: Change in eye colour; the ability to cloud judgement or cause forgetfulness; human flight or levitation; conjuration; telekinesis. 'Well?'

'We didn't get owt on camera,' Mick conceded.

Thank fuck for that. He knew Niamh was more careful than that. 'Look. I've been watching that woman for years . . .'

'Aye, I bet you 'ave,' Roger Barraclough leered, and Luke fought the urge to punch his last three teeth out of his skull.

He ignored the comment. 'She's . . . a little different.

Eccentric. Quirky, yes. But she's not a witch, she's a vet. What? Are we just stalking women now? Is that our MO?'

Peter took charge. 'Here's what we're gonna do: I want us working shifts every weekend. We'll draw up a rota. All we need is three pieces of concrete evidence on any o' these hags and we got 'em.' There was a gruff titter of approval from the audience. 'The last drownin' were nearly ten year ago. I say that's far too long. What do you think?'

Now the audience really went for it, cheering and clapping. His father only needed to do the bare minimum to whip them into a frenzy. Their eyes were hungry, famished. The pack dogs were starved and wanted fresh meat. They wanted a kill.

For Luke, ironically, it had been an article in the *Guardian Weekend* supplement magazine: 'How I Escaped a Cult'. It was the first time he'd read words like *deprogramming* or *exit counselling*. He had grown up around Working Men and had never known any different. He didn't realise there were men in the world who didn't make a hobby out of hunting witches, *women*.

Most men didn't even know witches were *real*. To most it was nothing more than a Halloween costume.

He'd gone from 'going through the motions' to meeting Niamh. It was embarrassing, shameful, how it had taken getting to know 'one of the good ones' to counter years of hatred. He'd been a fool. But it was not his fault. It wasn't. He had been a *child*. It had taken him even longer to accept that.

As the crowd dispersed; heading for the snooker tables or the bar, his father grabbed Luke's arm. 'Oi, wait up a minute.'

'What? I've got to get back to Hebden Bridge and it's getting late.'

'Why? You seein' *her*?' His grey eyes glinted like stainless steel, even in the low light.

'What's that supposed to mean?' Play dumb. Luke had a good face for playing dumb, open, kind, almost golden retriever like.

'Do you think I'm fucking daft or somethin'?'

'No . . .'

'I'm not blind neither.' He came closer, lowered his voice. His breath smelled of beer. 'I can't keep covering for you, Luke. Do you think I don't know what it's like? What they can do to a bloke's head?'

Luke stared at his feet, the way he had when he was little. What is it about parents that sends us through a time tunnel? 'It's not like that . . .'

'How the fuck do you know what it's like? If yer spendin' time with a hag, yer mind's not yer own, is it? She can make you believe whatever she fuckin' likes. You better promise me now, son, that you'll not get close enough to let her control you the way your mother did to me . . .'

'I would *never*,' Luke Ridge barked in the older man's face. 'I *won't*.'

HEBDEN BRIDGE GIRLIES
Niamh, Helena, Leonie, you

Leonie Jackman
And I am in Romania. It is pretty.
I do not care bc have not slept in 2 days.
Great cabbage rolls tho.

How are you getting on?
We miss you here!

Leonie Jackman
Off to Turkey to find a magic ring bbz.

Niamh Kelly
What?

Leonie Jackman
For real. Seal of Solomon.

Who?

Leonie Jackman
Exactly.

Niamh Kelly
Meanwhile, I'm off to meet the PM.

Leonie Jackman
Cunt.

No way! Good luck! Get a selfie. Before you ask, Lee, no, I didn't vote for him.

Niamh Kelly
How are you getting on, Ellie?

Yeah, I'm fine. All good xxx

Chapter Twenty-One

THE SEAL OF SOLOMON

Leonie – Bucharest, Romania

'This is us,' Leonie said, nodding towards the *next* train, the fourth since they left Milan. At least this was the final leg of the journey. Senait looked as tired as Leonie felt, neither had truly slept last night on the overnight train from Vienna to Bucharest, but they had both agreed this way was safer than risking either Milan or Istanbul airport. Between Hale and Domino there were so many targets on them. Nor did she want to involve Coven Italia, or the smaller covens of Turkey.

As Turkish politics grew more conservative, they'd seen clamp-downs on women gathering for magic. The national coven of Turkey was disbanded in 2017, and Leonie didn't trust that the remaining indie groups were free of warlock interference. It was safer to keep a low profile and, with any luck, Hale wouldn't see them coming.

As they boarded the sleeper train, Leonie flashed a sanitary towel at the conductor; making him see two train tickets to a station just outside Istanbul. He directed them to an unoccupied first-class compartment. They'd travelled a long way, and Leonie's interrailing days were long behind her. Besides, they needed the privacy. The first-class berth was far from luxurious as it was: two benches that folded out into bunks in a cramped sardine tin.

While Senait used the toilet further down the carriage, Leonie took the opportunity to FaceTime Chinara. She answered right away from their living room in Camberwell. 'My love, are you OK?'

Leonie nodded. 'We're leaving Bucharest in a bit and we'll be in Istanbul by dawn.'

'You look so tired,' she said kindly.

'You have no idea. I'm deceased.' A day of aimlessly roaming the city, waiting for the direct train, hadn't helped. It was hard to care about sightseeing on two hours of fractured sleep. 'How was court?'

'Not great. We lost a deportation case.'

'Cunts.'

'I know. I've come home to lick my wounds and get greasy chow mein.'

Leonie smiled. 'From the bougie one or the really gross one?'

'Oh, darling, I wanted the *really* greasy, four-pound noodles.'

'Nice! How's the cat?'

Chinara flipped the phone around and she saw Midnight Miss Suki was curled up on the cushion at the end of the sofa, a cosy black pom-pom. It was a massive tit-punch of homesickness. She wanted to go home. She suddenly wanted to be anywhere but on yet another train, baby-sitting a runaway. 'We both miss you,' Chinara said. Leonie found she couldn't speak or she'd cry forever. 'But you're getting closer, Lee, don't give up now.'

Leonie nodded, again not daring to speak.

'Find him, and kick his ass all the way back to Grierlings. Hale, not Radley.'

'I got that,' Leonie said, smiling. The door to their compartment opened with a screech and Senait returned. 'That's Senait.'

No one else would have noticed, but Leonie registered a certain curiosity in Chinara. It was safe to assume she wasn't thrilled that Leonie was sharing a cramped bunk with an exotic dancer, but Leonie also knew that Chinara would *never* admit to something as petty as jealousy. She wouldn't even express *concern* over another woman, aware of how controlling that can seem. And if Leonie went to lengths to reassure her girlfriend, that'd just make her seem more guilty. Best to leave well alone. Nothing to see here.

Still, Leonie – after the adrenaline from the lake house had subsided – felt she'd Done The Right Thing in liberating Senait from Domino's grasp. 'I'd better go,' she told Chinara. 'HMRC sent a bunch of stuff about this seal for us to read.'

Chinara smiled. 'Homework. Welcome to my world.'

'I love you,' Leonie said very pointedly, just in case Senait was getting any ideas. Leonie and Chinara had a *relaxed* approach to monogamy, but this was neither the time nor the place. As extraordinary as the circumstances were, Senait was a survivor of trafficking as far as Leonie was concerned, and she needed to be the grown-up.

'Can you still feel my love all the way over there?'

'I can.' Leonie smiled and they said their goodbyes for the night.

Senait sat on her cramped bunk and folded her legs. 'Aw yeah, look at all this shit I found in the buffet thing. You want sandwiches? I got 'em! We have corned beef – minging, but I thought maybe you'd be into that.'

'Ew, no.'

'I also have salt beef or roast beef.'

'So . . . beef?'

'That's all they had sandwich wise, *but* I have every flavour of crisp on earth, plus this fit-looking chocolate cake thing.' Senait popped open a plastic tub and got stuck in, shovelling the cake in her mouth. 'Don't worry I got you one too.' She smiled, her teeth brown.

Leonie yawned. 'Great, thanks.'

'Were that your wife?'

Leonie nodded. 'She's not my wife. At least, not yet. She will be.' And, of that, Leonie had never been more certain. She didn't want a wedding in a church or any of that shit, but she wanted to celebrate what they had in a way that everyone could see it.

'What's she like?' Senait asked, progressing from cake to some onion rings. A cursed combination, but Leonie said nothing.

She felt shy for some reason. 'She's, um, she's amazing. I don't know how else to say it. I'm so fucking lucky to have her.'

'She's lucky to have you too, don't put yourself down! You're still a ten.'

'Well I don't know about that,' Leonie said, feeling about eighty years old. She was honestly astounded sometimes that Chinara put up with her. She decided to change the subject before she got weepy. 'You know we've been on trains for the best part of a day, and I barely know anything about you.'

Senait brushed crisp dust down her thighs. 'What do you wanna know? I'm an open book, me.'

'OK,' Leonie sighed. 'Where do you come from? Really?'

'I said, Bolton.' With that, she opened a Dr Pepper and took a big swig. Where did she put all this junk, she was a twiglet. Her own metabolism had turned on her the day she hit thirty.

Leonie prodded further. 'You were born there?'

'Yep.'

'And you knew you were a witch?'

'Yep, since I were little.'

'Are you registered with the coven?'

'Dunno, to be honest.'

Gods this was painful. 'Senait! You gotta give me something! Is that even your real name?'

She sat forward. 'Yes. Sorry, I just hate talking about my past – and don't be looking in my head, neither.' The chance would be a fine thing; she was remarkably cagey up there. Leonie sensed flashes of raw emotion – big, bright fireworks of giddiness, or annoyance, but nothing nuanced, no fine print. She sighed. 'Look, it's just embarrassing mostly. My mum was a psycho; my dad was a wet blanket. I got expelled from school because my teachers were CUNTS. Left home when I were fifteen and never looked back.'

That was all hauntingly familiar to Leonie, with certain gender roles reversed.

'When I met Domino, I was podium-dancing in Ibiza. I thought I had it made. A chance to dance all over the world, meet rich people, eat fancy food. I wanted one of those Chanel bags with the little Cs on. I didn't realise she wanted to wear my fucking body like a onesie, the mad bitch, but by then it were too late. I'd already signed the contract.'

Leonie read her for lies. She didn't sense anything amiss. 'OK. Well, where next?'

She shrugged. 'I've got some mates in Turkey. I'll help you find this bloke and then hook up with them, I guess.'

Leonie didn't want Senait getting anywhere near Hale if she could help it. Perhaps it was how much she reminded her of Herself Circa 2012, but she felt weirdly protective of her. 'You don't have to come with me.'

'As if! I owe you one, don't I? Anyway, now I'm free I'm fucked if I know what I wanna do next. Might as well make myself useful.'

That sounded familiar too. Sometimes the prospect of being able to do anything is so overwhelming you end up doing nothing.

Leonie offered a sympathetic smile. 'Yep, that's freedom. Choices can be pretty scary. It's like when you leave school, all of a sudden no one's telling you what to do any more, and everyone acts surprised when you just stand there looking confused.'

'Right?' Senait looked a little panicked; as if the enormity of things was hitting.

'If nothing else, you're a fucking powerful witch . . . you can be whatever you want.'

Freakishly limber, Senait hoisted her foot up in front of her chest to inspect a toenail. 'I dunno. Since I was, literally, a baby, everyone told me how different and special I am. My parents, doctors and nurses, Domino. I do *not* feel different and special. I'm dead boring. I guess I get a job and some money. I might have a go at being a normal person.'

'You'll *never* be a normal person,' Leonie said. 'And thank Gaia for that, eh?' Senait managed a smile. 'And you know you always have a home at Diaspora – my coven for witches of colour. Always. And we have a whole community who can help with housing, or work . . . I mean it. Come to London.'

It was all in her eyes. Leonie sensed a deep sadness in her, almost yearning. Almost everyone, however chaotic, has *home* within them. Even Theo possessed a certain belonging since Niamh had introduced her to Hebden Bridge, to witchcraft. Senait had nothing. Truly homeless. Contrary to her claim, she was a closed book.

'Nah. I've been to London. Not for me. Saw a pigeon eating some KFC off the bone. Cannibalism, man.' She stared out of the train window. 'You know I said I had visions? I'm gonna live by the sea.'

'Yeah?'

'Yeah. In my mind, when I'm in bed, I can hear the sea, like, juddering over pebbles. When I hear that in real life, I'll know I'm home. Easy.'

Leonie grinned. 'Brighton, babe. Check it out.'

Beyond the window, Bucharest station started to move, or so it seemed. They were on their way.

Now Senait changed the subject. 'Did your friends write to you?' She pointed at the computer.

Leonie wasn't sure she'd call HMRC her friends, but she said they had. Sandhya had emailed her everything the archives had on Solomon and his legendary seal.

There was also the news that the coven was even further in disarray because Irina Konvalinka had fallen down the stairs and died. Brutal. Leonie had only ever spoken to her a handful of times, and the woman was a fucking human icicle, but it was still bad news for the coven. If her best friend wasn't about to become High Priestess, she might have revelled in HMRC coming apart at the seams. Instead, it felt ominous somehow.

'What do they say?'

Leonie clicked on the file that Sandhya had attached. Oh, just the forty-three pages to scroll through. Luckily, Sandhya had written a shorter precis in her email. Leonie shook her head. 'Sandhya says it's all hearsay.' Senait looked confused. 'As far as the coven knows, the notion of a magic ring that controls demons is a total myth.' She scanned the email. 'Like, people can't even agree on whether or not King Solomon was real.'

From the information, it looked as if Christians, Muslims, Jews and witches all had a slightly different interpretation of him. Some thought he was the Arabian king of what we now call Israel; some thought he was a prophet; others thought he was a symbolic invention – an amalgam of various powerful men in history. There was certainly precious little archaeological evidence to suggest he truly lived.

'Warlocks think he was a warlock,' Leonie said. 'But they would, wouldn't they? They want *anyone* on their team. They say Bowie was a warlock.'

Senait nodded. 'I know that story.'

'Bowie?'

'Solomon!'

More surprises. 'You do?'

'Yeah, my dad was a drip, but he was also a warlock. Solomon was the king with the ring.'

In the PDF, there was a supposed illustration of an ornate signet ring, tiny jewels dotted around a pentagram. 'Warlocks say a lot of things,' Leonie said. 'Usually, when you do a little digging, you find out there was a bunch of witches doing all the heavy lifting behind the scenes. The *Seal of Solomon* was probably a witch, not a ring.'

That said, she could understand why Dabney Hale, of all people, would believe the Legend of the McGuffin. What do you get the warlock who has everything? Posh white men love nothing more than 'exploring' countries and 'liberating' indigenous artefacts. The British Museum doesn't have a lot of British shit in it, look at it that way. It all fit with everything she knew about Hale.

However, that logically led to the next question: what did he intend to do with it? He was already the most dangerous warlock in the world. The last time he declared a war on witches, hundreds died. No witch who'd been in Somerset that day would forget the bodies floating like trash down the flooded streets. She still remembered Julia Collins slitting her own throat at solstice.

And he'd done all that without a magic ring.

Him becoming more deadly didn't even bear thinking about.

Chapter Twenty-Two

THE CORRIDORS OF POWER

Ciara – London, UK

It was customary, so as not to scare them, Moira explained, to travel to meet the Prime Minister the mundane way: by train. And so, Ciara was forced to tolerate Moira's company all the way from Manchester Piccadilly to London Euston. At least this gave her an opportunity to shake off the lingering chills following the encounter with Lord Ose.

She didn't feel good about it, but Konvalinka had to die. What fucking choice had she had? There was no way Ciara was going to let someone hold that much power over her. She hadn't done what she'd done to Niamh just for some bald nosy twat to fuck everything up.

Ciara wasn't sensing any desperate sadness from any other witch at Irina's demise. Served her right, the frosty cow; maybe she should have been a bit nicer. The oracle had implored her to kill Theo. *Nice try, you fucking fanatic. Do your own dirty work.*

It troubled her. Was *that* the grand cosmic reason she'd

been revived? As an assassin? It didn't quite check out; when Helena visited her at the safehouse, she couldn't have known that her own attempt to kill Theo would fail. Ciara wondered if Hale had access to oracles and had foreseen Helena's downfall. What was she? Plan B?

Well fuck that. She liked Theo.

The train, a Virgin Pendolino, was too hot, stank of meat and tilted precariously as it sped south. Ciara wasn't sure if it was the demon hangover or genuine seasickness making her nauseous. Moira also used the two-hour journey to bring her up to speed with this side of HMRC. Ciara was on her third Americano of the day.

'The Shadow Cabinet consists of twelve people,' Moira explained. 'Six witches or warlocks, and six mundanes. That's the way it's been for over a century.'

Code-named the 'Shadow Cabinet', the cohort contained the handful of lucky mundanes who were briefed on the existence of witches and warlocks. It was part of the treaty of 1869 – the coven would cooperate with government but on a strictly need-to-know basis. The more mundanes who knew of their work, the more likely it was someone would panic and go Full Pendle.

Moira went on, 'The coven is one of a number of secrets revealed to a fledgling Prime Minister the day after he or she wins an election: the truth about Diana, Lord Lucan, UFOs, BPV – oh, the so-called "vampire virus", the Loch Ness experiment and us: Her Majesty's Royal Coven.'

'I'd like to be a fly on that wall.' Ciara smirked. 'Can you imagine? *All those things your mummy told you weren't real, well, guess what?*'

Sandhya travelled with them, fielding emails about Irina's burial mostly, but also keeping tabs on Leonie and updating both Ciara and Moira when there was news.

Apparently Dabney was searching for fairy tales. Sounded about right. Somewhere in the annals of her mind, his grandstanding about the Seal of Solomon was familiar. It should be her searching for him. She didn't trust what he could do to Leonie.

Once more, Ciara swallowed a mouthful of vomit before taking a sip of coffee. 'Go on then, fill me in. The new Prime Minister. Should I be intimidated?'

Moira guffawed. 'Absolutely not. Well, perhaps we should *all* be very afraid. Once again they've handed the keys to an absolute simpleton.'

'What? The *Good Guy*?' That was all Ciara knew of him. After years of accusations of being the 'Nasty Party', Guy Milner, with his perma-tan and sparkling veneers was supposed to mark a new centrist dawn for the Tories.

'His real name is Fabian,' Moira told her. 'He changed it twenty years ago because they felt it was too posh to win over northern voters. Seemingly it worked. Eton educated . . .'

'Big surprise.'

'Banker for a minute in the noughties, then a stint at the *Financial Times* and then politics. Nothing ever changes does it?'

'What's his stance on witches? When was he told?' As Ciara understood it from the reams and reams of notes Niamh had inherited, the existence of HMRC was limited to only those six lucky mundanes. Internally, they were referred to as *Project Eve* in order to conceal their true nature. Most MPs and civil servants thought it was 'something to do with women' and nothing more.

'He was elected last December and met Helena twice,' Moira said, applying some dreadful peachy lipstick in her compact mirror. 'I've met him once. I think it would be fair to say he's still adjusting.'

Sandhya cleared her throat. 'Keep an eye on Harkaway.'

'Who?'

Moira nodded. 'Eric Harkaway, his chief political adviser. Milner can't wipe his arse unless Harkaway briefs him.'

'Got you. Is he one of the six who knows?'

'Yes,' Sandhya said, and – from her tone – it sounded like this might not be the best thing in the world.

'Anything else I should know?' Her question was partly drowned out by a train announcement heralding their imminent arrival into London.

'I don't think so,' Moira said, gathering up her papers.

Sandhya, however, leaned in close so only she'd hear. 'Helena wasn't a fan of Selina Fay.'

'Who?'

Her question was answered a short black cab ride later. It would have been quicker to walk, given the traffic in central London. The hackney carriage eventually pulled up outside the Ministry of Defence, a stern cube of a building on Horse Guards Avenue. The entrance was guarded by two formidable abstract sculptures: both women, naked.

'They're called Earth and Water,' Moira told her. 'In recognition of our work. Fire and Air were supposed to be installed on the other side of the building, but they ran out of money. Typical.'

The fabled Selina Fay greeted them in the empty lobby, her heels clacking noisily down the gleaming floors. The foyer was almost a mirror image of the grand interior of HMRC in Manchester, only here the marble columns were a solemn black. The precise symmetry of the hall, the floor tiles, the uniform – somehow authoritarian – leather armchairs that flanked both sides of the vestibule, unnerved Ciara. That, and the security men with the guns.

Ciara knew she was getting older if senior HMRC witches were as young as Selina Fay; she couldn't be much older than twenty-six or twenty-seven. She sensed power emanating from her all the same, she was an adept. Petite, even in heels, and trying too hard with letterbox red lipstick, and girlboss skirt suit. 'High Priestess!' she said with all the fake cheer of a Greeter at the GAP. 'At last!'

'Not yet,' Ciara reminded her. 'Call me Niamh.'

'Welcome to Whitehall. If you want to follow me, we're just in a private meeting room.'

'Is he necessary?' Ciara cast side-eye at the armed guard who shadowed them.

A faint smile crossed her lips. 'Can you blame them?'

The trio followed Selina up the escalator and along endless, identical grey corridors. It was oddly quiet, crypt-like. Selina treated them to a tour-guide running commentary of their surroundings: 'Since the Ministry of Defence moved in to these offices in '64, we've always conducted these meetings in Historic Room 24. It was moved here from its former address at Pembroke House and reconstructed piece by piece because it's impervious to our . . . skills.'

Fay (because 'Selina' felt too informal for this business-like woman) held a door open and Ciara stepped inside the conference room. It was like stepping into another building entirely – more like a fussy old hotel by the sea with its chandeliers and chintzy wallpaper. As soon as she crossed the threshold, Ciara felt her sentience drop off a cliff. The walls, she guessed, were laced with a herb, resin or oil to deaden her gifts; likely mistletoe. She understood why the mundanes would want to be on a level footing, but that didn't mean she liked it. On the bright side, she could drop her own defences for a while, knowing the other witches were at an equal disadvantage.

The Prime Minister and his team were already seated at a large conference table in the centre of the room, awaiting their arrival. They stood to greet them. Ciara recognised the Prime Minister off the TV right away. He looked more like a TV doctor than a politician. Was his hair plastic? He reminded her of a Justin Timberlake doll she'd had as a kid.

He stood to greet them, opening his arms wide. Ciara wondered how many body language experts had trained him. 'Dr Kelly, how wonderful to meet you at last.' Ah yes, Ciara could quite easily see how he'd won his landslide. Mums and nanas must love him. 'Tea?'

Ciara asked for another black coffee and took her seat at the table. This was so surreal. She'd once been threatened with expulsion in Year 9 (for making a necklace out of tampons which she thought was quite funny, truth be told), and here she was, sat opposite the Prime Minister. If only she could share the irony with someone. Leonie would *die*.

Milner was accompanied by a young aide, whom she sensed was gay without needing her powers. A gay Tory. So baffling, Ciara could hardly wrap her head around it. On his other side were a shrewd-looking redhead in an ill-fitting suit, his collar too loose for his pencil neck, and, finally, a tired-looking woman.

'Ladies,' Milner said. 'These are my colleagues, Eric Harkaway – my chief adviser – and Elaine Piggott, who is the human counterpart to Miss Fay.' And *that* was who she reminded her of – Miss Piggy. That name was an unfortunate coincidence. 'Sorry, is *ladies* the right word to use? What should I call you?'

Moira said nothing, deferring to her. Ciara smiled. 'We're *human*, Prime Minister, relax. We're just more powerful than you are.'

'Oh, I don't know about that,' Harkaway said, somewhat brittle. Right away Ciara understood Helena's reservations. So, he was actually in charge. Got it. It made a sort of sense. As Ciara understood it, Milner was the fourth Prime Minister since Niamh had put her in a coma. *Someone* was needed for consistency.

'Very well.' She smiled even more sweetly to annoy him. 'Different then.'

'Certainly.'

Selina Fay stepped in. It was, after all, her job to be the bridge between the organisations. 'As ever, Prime Minister, Her Majesty's Royal Coven will be working behind the scenes to ensure *our* world doesn't collide with yours. We'll protect you, so you can protect us.'

Milner seemed to stifle a yawn. 'Of course! That's the way it's been for what? A hundred years?'

'Over a hundred and fifty now,' Moira added. 'Longer informally.'

'Oh, I was meaning to ask. Shouldn't it be *His* Majesty's Royal Coven following the sudden death of our beloved monarch?' Milner made a great show of heartfelt regret for about a second, and then awaited their response.

Ciara dived in. 'Our coven was formed in honour of the wrongly executed Queen Anne Boleyn. In solidarity, we have remained Her Majesty's Royal Coven ever since, regardless of whomever is on the throne.'

'I think we'll have to see about that,' Harkaway muttered quietly, making a note of it on his pad.

Ciara wanted to reach over the desk and slam his pea-head against it. A reigning monarch hadn't met – knowingly – with a witch in *decades*. Was it any wonder Hale wanted to abolish the whole fucking thing?

Milner went on. 'I'm very much looking forward to your coronation, Dr Kelly. Always time for a bit of pomp and pageantry, I say!' Gosh, his teeth were very white. It conjured to Ciara the Cheshire Cat. 'Do I get an invite?'

'Perhaps we could turn our attention first to the events of the summer?' Harkaway once again interjected, sliding an agenda along the table to Milner. 'For decades, Whitehall has turned a blind eye to coven matters, partly, I think, out of fear and ignorance. I, however, would prefer to know precisely why half of Hebden Bridge was destroyed in some sort of skirmish. We can't merely ignore such incidents. The cost of repair alone ran into the millions.'

The witches at the table stiffened. 'That's just what it was,' said Moira, choosing her words carefully. 'A skirmish.'

'Which led to you summarily executing the previous High Priestess?'

'Exactly,' Ciara added. 'It doesn't get much more definitively dealt with than that.'

'Good!' Milner said. 'That's great to know.' He paused. 'Although, are we allowed to execute people these days? I thought . . .'

Fay said, 'Coven Law was retained under the 1869 treaty in certain circumstances.'

'*But*,' Harkaway chimed in, 'it's critical that you know, going into this role, Dr Kelly, that a *skirmish* on the scale we saw ten years ago – a *war* amongst your people, will not be tolerated again. Your actions must not impinge on the general public.'

'I couldn't agree more.' Contrary to previous thinking, Neanderthals and Homo Sapiens had coexisted on earth for ten thousand years or more by cheerfully avoiding each other. Ciara felt the same was necessary for witches and mundanes.

'I think what Eric is trying to say,' said Milner, 'is that it was only during your little . . . civil war, that we realised quite how . . . *talented* you ladies are.'

Ciara didn't like feeling unprepared. Having been asleep for so long she'd perhaps forgotten the very first rule their nana had taught them as little girls: never trust mundanes. While mundane children are read cautionary tales about big bad wolves and, well, wicked witches, young witches are taught about Pendle, about Salem, about King James.

She regarded Harkaway coolly. What was his problem? It could be as trivial as the public purse. HMRC was very, very expensive. But was it more than that? Any mundane with knowledge of witches would be wise to be mindful of their power, but sometimes that mindfulness becomes *fear*, and fear is dangerously close to *hate*. She needed to get close to Harkaway outside of this room so she could find out.

At times like this she all too easily understood Hale's position. Why on earth did they waste time negotiating with these inferiors? If so minded, she could snap their spines with a flick of her wrist.

'Are you scared of me?' Ciara asked with her most disarming, girlish smile. She couldn't stop herself. She even tilted her head coquettishly.

'Should we be?' Harkaway fired back.

Moira intervened. 'Prime Minister. Her Majesty's Royal Coven exists to serve Crown and country. It's what *we* do. No witch joins the coven to undermine the work *you* do.'

Harkaway rested his chin on his thin fingers. 'And what about the witches who *aren't* in HMRC?'

This man was a problem. Ciara wondered if *she* should be scared.

After another forty-five minutes of excruciating tiptoeing around witchphobia, the Prime Minister was whisked away to cut the ribbon on a food bank that people only needed because of his government's policies.

Ciara was starving, ravenous, after her night with Lord Ose. At the very least, HMRC could cover a nice lunch at The Northall before they headed north.

Over lunch, they finalised plans for Ciara's coronation – it would take place at Samhain in a fortnight's time. The joke was getting less funny. Ciara didn't know if she could actually go through with it if the time came. She had assumed she'd be long gone by then. What the hell was taking Leonie so long? She made a mental note to check in with her later.

When both Sandhya and Moira had to take calls, Selina Fay seemed pleased. 'I'm glad we have a moment to ourselves.'

Ciara was busy mopping up leftover jus with more bread. 'Uh huh?'

Selina dabbed her lips with a linen napkin. Somehow, the lipstick had remained more or less flawless. 'Outside of my role at HMRC, I run a little group on the side?'

'Another coven?' Even Ciara knew that was expressly against the rules. That was how Leonie had been forced out when she wanted to pursue Diaspora.

'Oh no, no, nothing like that! It's more of a movement than a coven. It's global, mostly online, although we do have monthly meet-ups or brunches sometimes. I was hoping we could maybe take you out some time after the coronation to talk about things.'

It was no wonder Helena went demented if this was what her life was like. Was she being *lobbied* right now? 'And what *things* is that?'

'Are you familiar with the Trad Witch movement?'

Ciara groaned internally, and didn't care if Selina read her. This sounded like an internet thing. Perhaps the most disconcerting thing to occur during her nine-year sleep was the rise of social media. Pre-coma, what was merely irritating was now a cancer on the flesh of society, from what Ciara could tell. 'I am not.'

'Well!' Selina beamed. 'We're a group of witches who welcome progress, but wonder if some traditional values with merit were swept away with the tide if you like.'

'Traditional values? Like burning women alive in the Pipes? Because we still do that apparently.'

Selina pretended to laugh. 'No, we're more concerned with the legacy and integrity of witches. Did you know that next year is projected to be the first in recorded history that *no* girls will take the oath at solstice? None! Niamh, we're fading away. I don't know why HMRC isn't speaking on this.'

'What is it you think we should be saying?' A horrid feeling in her gut was telling her where this was headed.

'Simply that unions between witches and warlocks should be celebrated! Rewarded even.'

'*Unions?* You mean *fucking*, right?' Ciara let out a bitter laugh. 'Sure thing! I'll work up a breeding programme on the train.'

Selina flinched. 'I was hoping the most powerful witch in the country would appreciate the sanctity and purity of the craft.'

As soon as some cunt says *purity* it's all over. 'I do. I love being a witch. I don't condone eugenics.'

The lacquer was starting to chip. Selina carefully folded her napkin and put it to one side. 'You're putting words in my mouth, I think.'

Ciara felt her own aura blaze scarlet. 'Is that where we've landed?' she snarled before taking a sip of sparkling water to cool herself. 'Hundreds of years, and dozens of covens, and you want me to start mandating the choices witches make with their bodies? You're a disgrace to the coven and you're a disgrace to women.'

Selina recoiled like she'd been slapped. 'Well, I—'

'No. If you mention this again in my vicinity, I'll remove you from your post. Is that clear?'

Selina wilted. 'Yes.'

'Yes, *what*?'

'Yes, High Priestess.'

That was when Ciara understood what a different sort of power felt like. The power of *status*. She rather liked it.

The train home was a subdued affair. Either the entourage was tired, or they had genuinely run out of things to say to one another. Sandhya and Moira caught up on their emails, Ciara mostly stared out of the window.

What a bleak day. Everyone she'd met had been a uniquely different flavour of awful. And they called *her* a bad guy. At least she didn't pretend to be anything other than who she was. Body-swap notwithstanding.

Magic and politics were oil and water. Today had only cemented a theory she'd held since she was a teenager: the sheer notion of HMRC was fundamentally flawed. The witches who'd signed the 1869 treaty were insane to think mundanes and witches could work together. In the end, it seemed, mundanes benefited and witches were exploited. Look at MK-Ultra. Look at Novichok. And no matter what anyone said, the witches only acquiesced under the veiled threat of persecution like in the olden days.

Her phone vibrated and she took out Niamh's phone. Mobiles had *evolved* during her time in a coma and she'd had to be very careful not to give herself away by appearing clueless. She wasn't quite sure why everyone was so amenable to phones collecting both your fingerprints and face, but there you go. People are stupid.

The text was from Luke. *What time are you home? You wanna get together or are you chilling with Theo?*

Although she would not, she was surprised at how much she *wanted* to see him. She allowed her ego an adolescent giddy moment (*he likes me!*) before pouring water on the urge. What was the point? She stared at the message for a minute. She really wanted to see him. But no.

Chapter Twenty-Three

SHIPS IN THE NIGHT

Theo – Hebden Bridge, UK

Theo was about to take herself to bed when she heard the kitchen door open then close downstairs. Even up in her room, she sensed Niamh was in no mood for talking. A barbed, mauve aura almost physically pushed her away. She guessed she'd never really seen Niamh stressed; maybe this was a taste of things to come. Nonetheless, Theo tied her terrycloth gown at the waist, and headed downstairs. She missed Niamh and wanted to see her.

She found her necking vodka from the bottle next to the fridge. Niamh swallowed, blinked and stared her down. 'Long day.'

'Are you OK?' Theo asked, hovering at the foot of the stairs. Tiger remained in his basket. It was a little weird; he normally made such a fuss of his mum when she returned.

Niamh gave a half-arsed shrug. 'I'm going to wash down a co-codamol with this, and take a bath until the inner buzz kicks in and I fall into a medicated sleep.'

Theo wasn't sure if she was serious or not. She couldn't

read her. It was like Niamh was holding her mind tightly shut, and Theo didn't feel anywhere near strong enough to prise through the dam. 'There's some cottage pie in the fridge. Vegan. I, uh, made it for us. I didn't know if you'd have eaten. I did text . . .'

Niamh took another shot of vodka. 'And I said I'd be late.'

Theo cursed her neediness.

In her time, Theo had lived with eight foster families. This was the pattern. They'd welcome her at first and then, realising her inherent strangeness, they'd become wary, then cool, then retreat altogether. The more they pulled away, the more she'd chase at their heels, looking for crumbs of affection. She could feel herself becoming annoying, bordering on loathsome and simpering, but it was desperation.

She just couldn't believe it was happening here, with Niamh. *Not again.* 'I . . . did I do something wrong?'

Niamh put down the bottle and steered her through to the cottage lounge. 'I'm sorry. No, you've done nothing wrong, and I'll microwave the shit out of that cottage pie in a sec.' She sat Theo down on the sofa. 'It really has been a colossal motherfucker of a day. High Priestess: zero fun, it transpires. No wonder Helena lost her damn mind.'

Theo lapped up the attention. Now she had her, she wanted as much Niamh Time as possible. 'What happened?'

'I can't say. Shadow Cabinet only.'

Ah. 'OK.'

Niamh recoiled a little. 'Are you trying to read me?'

She hadn't – she couldn't. 'No. I told you. I don't know what's happening, but my powers . . . I can't . . .'

Niamh pulled her in for a hug. 'Hey, now, don't fret.

Very common for powers to fluctuate with hormones and whatnot.' Niamh withdrew and smoothed her hair down. 'Tell you what, why don't I make us both some cocoa?' She smiled broadly.

Chapter Twenty-Four

GAMBLERS

Elle – Hebden Bridge, UK

It felt a lot like mourning. A notion of her husband had died. A version of Jez was dead.

When she woke, she could, for a few blissful seconds, believe Annie was still alive, and that Jez was who she had thought him to be. But reality soon hit and she found herself lying next to a clone who has sex with twenty-somethings; a man who lies to his wife; a man who couldn't possibly care about his family. She wasn't sure what to do with him, this stranger.

It was scary, having an imposter in her bed.

'Mum?' Holly asked, a spoonful of Cheerios hovering in front of her face. The kitchen Alexa played the Radio 1 Breakfast Show. Elle hadn't heard a word, and barely heard Holly now. 'What's wrong?'

'Nothing,' she said instinctively. Elle quickly changed the subject. 'You need to get a move on. You'll be late for school.'

Holly looked at her for a moment, and Elle knew exactly what she was doing. Elle filled her head with the potent image of Agatha Halliwell and her colostomy bag – her first house call of the day. Holly stopped poking about inside her mind very swiftly.

Nonetheless, Elle felt her hand being forced. It was only a matter of time until Holly saw the truth in one of them. Pretending there wasn't a problem wasn't an option.

Elle walked to her car and took a deep breath before pulling out of the drive. Once she was past the gate, she left Home Elle behind and tried to focus on being Nurse Elle.

That morning, Elle had eight patients to see across the Calder Valley. She liked her job because she got to make people happy. Even though some of her patients were really very poorly, they were always glad to see her. To her regulars, she was more than a district nurse, she was a friend. Some of the older ones didn't get many knocks at the door and – even with the NHS higher-ups trying to schedule every minute of the day – Elle found time to join them for tea and a chocolate digestive. Leaving was sometimes hard; the patients didn't want her to go. You'd be amazed how many of them thought of a strange ache or pain to tell her about when she was one foot out of the door.

Her calls took her mind off the inevitable. It wasn't the sort of job you could daydream through and, before she knew it, it was lunchtime. She parked up outside the Co-op and crossed the bridge to Jez's garage on the other side of the river.

She loved the smell of Pearson's Motors. Engine oil and grease and petrol and tyres. It was so masculine, exotic somehow but, more than that, it was the smell of Jez. It felt like her heart was dying, it really did. A rose drying out in her chest, the petals turning brown.

There were two cars in the garage, although neither was presently attended. Gary and Tomas must be on lunch. Radio 5 Live was on, always, and Elle headed for the office. She heard his voice; he was on the phone. When he saw her, he looked semi-surprised and held up a finger. 'Yep, love, that'll be ready any time after five. Thanks, love, bye!' He hung up and sidestepped his messy desk to greet her. 'Are we havin' lunch today or summat?'

Elle shook her head. 'No.'

'What's up?'

The words no one *ever* wants to hear. 'I think we need to talk, don't you?'

Even mundane men can read women occasionally. Every drop of colour drained from his sickly face. 'Fuck, Elle . . .'

'Please don't try to explain. You must have known this would happen.' He knew at least two of her friends, and one of his own children, can read minds.

'It's not what you think.'

'You're having sex with the receptionist at Harmsworth House.'

Somehow he grew even more pallid. 'Just hear me out—'

'What is there to say?' *Sorry* fixes a lot, if you mean it from the heart, but not everything. Elle's throat felt like it was getting tighter by the second. The words came out oddly low, strangled. 'I suppose the only thing I want to know is why you'd carry on, even knowing what we can do? You *must have known*,' she repeated.

'I, um, I don't know.'

The poky office shrank in around them, the silence taking up ever more space. '*I don't know?*' Elle winced. 'I think you do.' Tears stung her eyes.

'I don't know what to say to you . . .'

Her heart was beating up around her ears. 'We've been together for almost *twenty years*, Jez. Half my life. I was a girl.'

'I'm sorry . . .'

OK, maybe *sorry* didn't help after all. '*Sorry*. Sorry you did it, or sorry you got caught?' Elle felt a shift at her core. She was getting angry, deep scarlets pulsing through her body. There was a taste like batteries on her tongue. 'The word you needed, Jez, was *no*.'

Jez looked like a shamefaced little boy, and she *hated* him. Was this how he got out of trouble as a kid? He made himself look *cute*? She did not find it even slightly loveable.

'Shall I tell you about *no*? About all the things I didn't do because of you and the kids? You know when they say "the tip of the iceberg"? That's all you see, Jeremy. The *hours* I spend on that house, on meals, on shopping, on cleaning, on laundry. Those holidays – do you think they plan themselves? Are you even *aware* of how much I do? How much I gave up? I was a Device witch before I met you. I hid myself for twenty years, and for what? For you to shag someone else anyway.'

'No, I know! Elle, you're the best wife and mum in the world, I just . . .' He paused and took a cautious step away from her. 'Elle, what's happening?'

The room too, was turning red, the walls almost pulsating with raw heat ebbing from her. Her voice didn't sound like her voice. 'You *just* what? You felt you deserved another woman as a treat? For all *you* do? What is it you do, Jez? Because of me, you've been able to cruise on autopilot for most of your adult life. You do the bits you like, the parts that suit you.'

Her husband's back spasmed and he fell to his knees. His face twisted in pain. 'Elle, what are you doing? It hurts!'

Whatever radiance was flowing from her skin lifted Elle off the floor. It was almost as if her energy had become gelatine and it suspended her mid-air. This had never happened before, and she couldn't control it. In the small space, waves of dry heat ricocheted off the walls, sealing her inside a cocoon of her own rage. 'I do those things because I love you. I didn't mind because I thought you loved me too.'

Veins bulged from his forehead, his skin turning pink. 'Babe, I do love you, stop! Please!'

How could he? How could he love her and also *her*? Sex is one thing, but love is exclusive. 'Don't lie! If you loved me, you would have known how much this would hurt me. You would have *cared*. You would never have . . .'

Jez could no longer speak. His mouth hung open and his eyes bulged. In a way, Elle was glad this was finally hurting him. He should feel what she was feeling.

'I was a girl.' Tears rolled down Elle's face and into her mouth. They were hot, salty. 'I gave myself to you. I gave you all of me.'

Her skeleton seemed to quake within her. Radiance gushed from her, distorting the whole room. White heat shimmered. She couldn't see properly, but everything started to change.

Everything in nature is made from *matter*. Fundamentally everything is the same, which is why witches don't consider themselves better than anyone, or anything, else. Elle saw the truth of that now as the lines began to blur. Matter shifted. She was coming apart.

Jez, his jaw locked, screamed. A ghastly noise he'd never made before.

What did you do for me? What have you sacrificed? Nothing. You couldn't do the one thing you promised. All you had to give was loyalty.

Distantly, she heard car windscreens shatter. The shutters to the garage crashed down. As Elle altered the matter in the room, gravity in turn shifted; the shit on Jez's desk – paperwork, a stapler, his laptop, countless takeout coffee cups – started to drift around the office as if they were underwater. His office chair melted into a noxious puddle of black liquid.

Why did I have to do so much, and you so little? Is this how you thank me?

And that was what really hurt. She'd been taken for a fool. She had been a fool. She was a fool. She heard them all now: her mother; Annie; Niamh; Leonie; even Helena. They had warned her, in so many ways: *don't lose yourself in him.*

Yet she had. Entirely. She was his additional limb. She had made herself his.

Elle screamed and screamed and screamed until she blacked out.

She came to face down on the oily lino of the office floor. She felt solid again, like her body was one whole thing, and not a thousand fragments. Her throat was sore, her lips cracked. She was surrounded by debris and smashed glass. The office stank of melted plastic and coffee.

What happened?

For a minute, she had thought she was dead. She'd blacked out. Never had she felt anything like that. Yes, she'd turned her powers on other witches twice in her life, but whatever *that* was had never happened before. Aching all over, she pushed herself up into a seated position.

'Jez?' she said, hoarse.

And then she saw what she had done.

Chapter Twenty-Five

NORMAL GIRLS

Theo – Hebden Bridge, UK

What was the point of homework? It wasn't like Niamh got home from the vets and tended to further sick animals. Why was it they had to do *extra* work of an evening? Was this supposed to prepare them for adulthood? It was all busywork, too. There was no way the teachers were going to entrust them to learn anything they might rely on in a test.

Regardless, Theo completed her maths homework at Holly's dining room table, both of them doing the bare minimum to scrape by. 'What do you think you'll do after school?' Holly asked.

Theo blinked. She was still adjusting to life as a girl and a witch. Wasn't that enough for now? 'I don't know.'

'I'm going to join HMRC,' Holly said confidently.

It had crossed her mind too but, 'Isn't HMRC a bit ACAB?'

From the adjoining lounge, Milo laughed. 'Oh as if you even know what that means,' Holly shouted through. 'But yeah, I see what you mean. It'll be different once Auntie Niamh is in charge.'

Theo shrugged. 'I doubt it. She was in a foul mood when she got home from London yesterday.'

'Yeah?'

She thought to last night, to Niamh's coolness. 'She's not herself at the moment. I don't know why, it's weird.'

'Can't you have a sneaky read?'

'She's more powerful than me,' Theo said, although that was only half the story. Right now, she could hardly read Milo, and he was a mundane. She'd tried at school, too, but when she tried to read people, she was only picking up the slightest essence of what people were feeling. It really was just the headlines: *I am hungry*, *I am bored*, *I am pissed off*.

Something was wrong, but she didn't want to say it aloud in case that somehow made it permanent. Previously, she'd been able to see a reflection of precisely what other people were thinking – have whole conversations telepathically.

Although the hot chocolates with Niamh were lovely, Theo had barely slept the night before, anxious. One question ruminated in her head: is this the price of being a girl? It was *The Little Mermaid* all over again. Moreover, is it a price worth paying? Before she'd known she was a witch, *all* Theo had wanted was to be a girl. Now it seemed like a hugely unfair trade-off: you can be the girl you always wanted to be, but you'll lose most of your power.

The irony wasn't lost on her. Not one bit.

Holly, apparently able to read her just fine, reached for Theo's hand. 'It'll be OK,' she said.

Will it?

They were interrupted by the back door slamming shut. 'Hi, Mum!' Holly shouted.

Elle appeared in the doorway, looking flustered. 'Oh hello, Theo love,' she said. 'I might have to ask you to go home in a minute, if that's all right? Will Niamh be home?'

'I think so . . . ?'

'What's up?' Holly said, suddenly serious. Theo wished she could read whatever it was Holly could see in her mother. 'Mum?'

Holly caught her eye. *She knows. She must.*

'I'll go . . .' Theo said.

No. Stay. I want you to stay. Holly wasn't having any of it, and now Milo hovered in the archway to the lounge. 'Mum?'

'Where's Dad?' Holly said, now white as snow. 'Just tell us.'

Theo suddenly wished someone would teleport her out of the house. You could crack the air with a fist.

Elle perched on the big cream leather sofa in the lounge. 'Your dad has gone. He's left.'

'What?' Milo exploded. 'Are you serious?'

'Yes, I am. I'm so sorry.'

'What do you mean, he's gone? Gone where?' Holly followed her into the living room.

Elle closed her eyes and then massaged her eyelids with her fingers. 'He . . . he's met another woman.'

Holly said nothing, but gave Theo a knowing glance.

'No way!' Milo said. 'He'd never just leave.'

'Well he did, and he has!' Elle snapped before composing herself. 'I'm sorry.'

Milo now turned on his sister. 'Did you know about this? Did you read his mind or whatever?'

Theo wasn't saying *anything*. She awaited Holly's reply. 'No. No, I'd have said.'

Elle shook her head. 'It doesn't matter. I need you both to know this is not your fault, OK?'

'He didn't even say goodbye? When will we see him?' Holly's eyes shone with tears. Theo didn't know what to do. Should she just slip out of the door and leave them to it?

'I, um, I don't know. I think they've gone away together.'

'Where?' Milo said.

'I don't know precisely . . .'

'Well that's bullshit.'

'Watch your mouth!'

Milo went to argue, but Holly got in first. 'I don't understand. Why would he do this?'

'Because he's a fucking coward,' Milo announced as he stormed past Theo towards the kitchen. A moment later, they heard the back door slam once more. The whole house seemed to rattle, and a framed family portrait slipped over on the mantelpiece above the fire. It was almost too on-the-nose somehow.

'Mum?' Holly said, her voice trembling. 'Why can't I see in your mind?'

'Because I don't want you to!' Elle said. 'This is all . . . very unpleasant, Hols. I only just found out about this; I swear. I need some time to process things, and what have I told you about snooping in other people's heads without consent. Stop it, Holly, just stop!'

Holly looked gravely wounded. 'OK. I'm sorry.'

Theo said nothing, wishing she could will herself deaf for a minute.

Elle stood, hands on hips. 'Holly, I'm sorry. It's fine. It's all going to be fine. Wait here. I'll get Milo.'

Elle trudged wearily in his direction. The second she was gone, Holly turned to Theo. 'She's hiding something. Did you read her?'

Theo shook her head.

'Theo, please? You're way more powerful than I am.'

Theo could only shake her head. 'I'm not. Not any more.'

She wasn't expecting Milo Pearson to be waiting for her outside the cottage when she got home. Autumn had crept up on them, and it was night by six o'clock. Milo mustn't have taken a coat when he stormed out and he looked frozen stiff, squatted on the front steps. 'What are you doing?' she said. 'You'll get hypothermia.'

She led him around to the kitchen door – the one they used – and ushered him inside. 'I dunno,' he said. 'I didn't know where else to go. I can't go to my mates.'

'Why not?' Theo flicked a lamp on. Niamh wasn't home yet, it seemed. She didn't even know where she was.

'As if I'd talk to them about it. Like *my dad left my mum for another woman*. That's girl stuff.'

Theo was at once horrified by the toxic masculinity and yet delighted to be included in the category of 'girl'. It was still a novelty.

Tiger climbed out of his basket and did a perfect *downward-facing dog* on the kitchen floor. 'I should take him for a walk. Do you want to come with me?'

He agreed, and Theo lent him a hoodie Luke had left at the cottage. Luke was a giant while Milo was lean, muscular. There wasn't a team at school he wasn't on. In the winter he was in the football first squad, and in the summer he took part in district athletics. It was hard to say if Theo hated sport because she'd always been excluded from it, or if it simply wasn't her thing.

They walked in companionable silence at first, following the road up out of Heptonstall – past Ted Hughes's old house and towards Hardcastle Crags. It was a crisp, cold night, clear, the indigo sky full of stars. It felt like winter for the first time that year, and Theo remembered how much she preferred the dark, the secrecy, of the season. They walked single-file up against the haphazard stone wall, wary of cars that sped up the country lane. They went slowly, letting Tiger sniff as many blades of grass as he liked.

Theo sensed he *wanted* to talk, but couldn't find the words. 'Did *you* know?' he asked eventually. 'What my dad was up to?'

'Yes. No. We suspected,' Theo admitted. 'Don't get mad at Holly.'

He said nothing for a second, kicking a stone across the road. 'I won't. Not her fault my dad's a fuckboi.' He paused. 'Do you think he'll come back?'

'I don't know. For that you'd need an oracle!' He didn't seem to get the joke. 'To be honest, even when I could, I mostly stayed out of people's heads. People, um, didn't think very nice things about me before I changed.'

'Yeah?'

'People thought I was a freak.' It was telling – not to mention depressing – how differently she was treated now that she looked a little more Disney. Of course it was nice to have compliments, but Theo wasn't sure she'd ever forget how she was treated when she'd been a mute, gender non-conforming trans witch with behavioural difficulties. It proved, beyond doubt, that people are both mean and shallow.

An owl hooted somewhere close by and they stopped to listen, sitting on a section of broken wall. She let Tiger's lead go long so he could roam in the empty field awhile.

It was cold, but not so cold she wanted to go home just yet. In fact, she felt nocturnal.

'Was I a dick to you?' Milo asked.

'No more than anyone else.' In truth, Milo had barely acknowledged her in much the same way he only spoke to Holly to torment her.

'I'm sorry if I was.'

'What? Now that I look like this?' Theo had been genuinely gobsmacked at how boys had descended on her as if she was a fresh kill when she started at St Augustus.

'More the witch thing than the trans thing, if I'm honest. I'm not looking to get turned into a frog.'

Theo laughed, properly laughed, for the first time in ages. 'I'm not sure I can do that. Maybe a healer could,' she mused.

'That's what blows my mind. You guys have this whole world. It's so cool.'

'You think?'

'Are you serious? You're basically *The Avengers* or something. Even my *mum* is badass.'

She laughed again. 'What would you do? If you had my powers for a day?'

He mulled on this a moment. 'I would . . . want to know what you were thinking?'

'Me?'

'I would want to know if you like me.' He gazed out across the black meadow, unable to look her in the eye. 'Because I like you.'

Even in the gloom of evening, she could see him blushing deeply. 'What?' That was the other thing with being a formerly mute gender non-conforming witch with behavioural difficulties – she didn't think anyone was ever going to like her like that.

Theo found herself mute once more. She wished there was a script for this, or that they taught it instead of fractions at school. *This* would be way more useful.

Milo shrugged, his ears touching his shoulders. 'I'd find out if you wanted to, like, go out with me sometime?'

Theo exhaled and her breath formed a big cloud between them. 'Well you didn't need witchcraft to ask me that,' she said. As intoxicating as this conversation was, and it really did feel the same as when she got tipsy after her oathtaking, she had to follow girlcode on this one. 'Milo, I honestly think Holly would kill me.'

He nodded, hiding his disappointment by climbing off the wall and continuing up the lane. Theo reeled Tiger in and followed. He said as she caught up to him, 'But do you though? Like me like that?'

Theo did not want to lie, so said nothing at all.

Chapter Twenty-Six

INTIMACY ISSUES

Ciara – Hebden Bridge, UK

When she and Luke got to the cottage with more Indian food than they knew what to do with, Ciara was surprised to find it empty. A few moments later, Theo returned home with the dog, and, after a little needling, informed her she'd been on a walk with Milo Pearson. Made sense. Theo was quite captivating in a certain Beetlejuice-era Winona way. It was only a matter of time before boys started sniffing around. 'Will he be joining us?'

'No, he had to go home. He wanted to make sure Elle was OK.'

'Why? What happened?'

Theo looked to Luke, but Ciara assured her it was safe to talk. Theo relayed what she knew about Elle's marriage woes. 'Did you know that Jez was . . . ?'

'Who do you think told Elle?' She made a mental note to see her friend ASAP. There was clearly more to it than Theo knew. Had she actually thrown him out? Or had he really eloped with Anal Jessica? Gods, this was very 2001; inserting herself in Elle Device's boy dramas.

Nothing ever changes. Guiltily, given the circumstances, she found she quite liked this nostalgia.

Puzzling on this, Ciara role-played Niamh. Being Mum, she set out the various curries, dals, naan breads and rice on the kitchen table for the others to help themselves. She went for aloo gobi and sag paneer (not vegan, but fuck it) and a couple of chapatis. They ate in the lounge, some superhero movie on in the background. Forks and plates clinked, and they drank Diet Sprite, and Ciara felt good.

She had the scantest fragments of her parents, of Galway, left. Was this what it was like? Family? She frowned. This was familiar.

A Chinese, not Indian, takeaway. Spring rolls, chow mein. This cottage. Niamh and . . .

Conrad . . . she kept forgetting his fucking name.

'Niamh?' Luke said, and she blinked dumbly at him. 'Huh?'

'Do you want to try some of the sweet potato and pea?' He offered her his plastic dish.

'No, thank you.' Is this what normal people do? She tried to recall *any* significant part of her history, but much of it was what she'd plucked from other people: Leonie or Elle's version of the Ciara origin story, and that was hardly reliable.

'What's up?' Theo asked, no doubt trying to read her. Ciara was still sprinkling *White Sorbus* over all her food, but maybe she'd have to up the dose a little.

'Nothing,' she lied. 'Just trying to get my head around the High Priestess stuff.'

'Did you really meet the Prime Minister?' Luke asked.

'Yep. Total cunt.'

Luke almost choked on his naan.

'Did you see what he said about trans kids?' Theo said.

'He wants to make laws preventing under 18s from getting our healthcare.'

'That's how he got in,' Luke said. 'All sorts of gimmicks to win votes: banning protests; caps on refugees; "Christian values" in school assemblies. What does that even mean? Nothing that actually does anything useful. People are so fucking mean.'

Ciara thought back to their meeting in Whitehall. 'It's not so much Milner I'm worried about. He's a glove puppet, and there's a hand up his arse. He won't have come up with those things himself. It's the rest of the Shadow Cabinet. I don't trust them, I'll have to . . .' She stopped herself. She wouldn't *have* to do anything, because she wouldn't be around to find out. Who *would* become High Priestess? Goddess, would that rancid Fay woman go for it? Of course she fucking would, the thirsty little leech.

'What?' Luke asked, licking sauce off his thumb.

'I'll have to keep a close eye on them.'

What if Hale didn't turn up? She was getting comfortable, perhaps *too* comfortable. If she stayed much longer, she could see herself convincing herself it was safe. If Leonie, or Moira, or even Theo learned who she was, it'd be the Pipes. Instantly. And that was without them figuring out what had happened to the oracle.

She couldn't be Niamh forever. Could she? She looked at Theo, and the dog, and the man, and the group chat notifications on her phone. She had friends here. Here, she was loved.

There were worse things she could be than Niamh.

Luke looked down at her, into her eyes, while he was inside her, her calf resting over his shoulder. She screwed her eyes shut. 'Hey, look at me . . .' he said, pelvis rocking on top of her.

She tried to give him the Niamh Experience, to mirror his gaze, all demure and honey-like, but it was too much. It was like he was trying to read her, and he wasn't even a witch. She pushed him off her and climbed on top. She rode him, instead focusing on his impressive chest. He groaned, but she'd lost her momentum now. If sex is Snakes & Ladders, she'd just slid down to the start.

As if he sensed this, Luke threw her off and twisted her over, entering her from behind. He went fast, pummelling her. Now *this* she could vibe with. She felt herself reaching boiling point and, with her face pressed into the pillow, she came hard.

Spent, he collapsed beside her, catching his breath. She could see sweat glisten on his forehead. 'What was that?' he said.

'What was what?'

'Is it me, or can't you look men in the eye during sex?'

'Am I being evaluated?'

'No! I'm just worrying you've got what the kids call *The Ick*.'

'This conversation is giving me *The Ick*.' That wasn't a very Niamh thing to say. Ciara scolded herself. 'Sex is sex. We shouldn't have to be the people we are in real life.'

'I agree. Am I getting you off though?'

She'd give him that, many men wouldn't even think to ask. 'You are. And if you weren't, I'd get myself off, don't you fear.'

'Too right.' He propped himself up onto his elbows. 'I remember when we were at school, us lads were so scared that girls were faking it.'

Ciara looked in his eyes this time. 'How awful. We were scared we'd get raped.'

'Fuck. Heavy.'

She patted his face. 'Don't worry, Big Boy. I'd have you throw yourself out of the window before I let that happen.'

His expression changed. 'You could really do that?'

'Of course. It's called a hex.' This was good. She couldn't keep him, so she might as well terrify the poor thing. 'Luke, what is it you think witches are? It's not *Sabrina*. We are the weapons of an ancient goddess.'

'I . . . I thought you didn't use your powers on, what is it you call us?'

'Mundanes? We don't as a rule.' Niamh never would. Ciara had done. It was funny. Control over the bladder is so precarious. 'We do in self-defence.'

'From who?'

'From *whom*. Demons mostly, I guess. Rogue witches like my evil twin. Until a few decades ago there were still active witchfinder cells in the UK, you know?'

'Really? No way.'

'Yeah. Sad misogynist bastards. The excuses men will find to kill women. Usually it's a family thing, like fathers passing it down to sons.' She saw a flicker of a man – his late father – in Luke's head. He didn't talk about his family much, but she understood there had been bad blood, and that his father was dead. There was a stepmother in Spain too, she believed. He didn't think about his birth mother at all. 'According to the HMRC there aren't any active cells any more. I think they have a watch list.'

'Wow. Scary stuff.'

'Not especially.' Mundane men were the least of her worries.

'You know what I don't get.'

'What?'

'The oracle thing.'

'The oracle thing?'

Luke propped himself up. 'Do you know what's going to happen? Like, in the end?'

Ciara chuckled. 'No spoilers.'

'Seriously though?'

'Only Gaia sees it all. Every decision we ever make, and every decision we *don't*. Limitless outcomes, freewill blah blah blah.'

'So the future can change?'

'The future is what we make of it.' She ran her fingers through his thick hair.

Luke, no doubt overcome by a cocktail of post-orgasm hormones, passed out swiftly, leaving Ciara rolling from her front to back like a rotisserie chicken, her skin itching. When it was clear she wasn't going to fall asleep naturally, she headed to Niamh's stash of contraband under the kitchen sink to see if there was some Lullaby No.5, or even a tiny sniff of Sandman.

There was no Sandman (or Valium, for that matter), and although she did find dried valerian root and lavender, she definitely didn't have the patience to distil her own batch of Lullaby. It wouldn't be as effective, but she added a little of the valerian to some chamomile tea and headed to the lounge. In the bowl next to the television were Theo's meditation crystals.

Where was the harm?

Ciara set the bronze dish on the coffee table and sat before it, cross-legged. This time she selected the azurite. She let her eyes go lazy, thinking only of the impossible blue-greens. It was like water, like ice. No feathers, it was feathers, like a peacock or a . . .

A blue tit. Its wings were bent and broken. Its eyes were open, staring at nothing. They were shiny, black.

What happened to it? Niamh asked. Do you think it fell out of the tree?

They had only a small garden in Galway, walled in at all sides, but they did have an apple tree that was great for climbing.

The cat must have had it, Ciara told her sister. And if it hadn't, it soon would, she thought. Niamh turned on her heel and ran towards their home. Ciara stayed. Out of curiosity, she felt for it. Does a dead thing feel different to a living one?

The local coven in Galway had spent a long time observing her and Niamh, both together and apart. 'Games' secretly designed to test their fledgling gifts. The adults were careful of what they said, but Ciara could read them enough to know that the elders thought she and her twin were somehow special. Adepts, so they were. Ciara liked it, being sort of famous in their town. And they were only eight. One day, every witch in the world would know Niamh and Ciara Kelly.

Ciara understood they were special because they were two sorts of witch at the same time, and that was very rare indeed. They could read minds, move objects just by looking at them and they could heal things. In one of the games, Ciara had made a rotten apple fresh again.

How was this poor bird any different? Their craft tutor, Franny O'Regan, spoke of 'radiance'. Borrowing life from A and moving it to B. It wasn't complicated. Everything around her was buzzing with life, how hard could it be to put some in the blue tit?

The bird rested between two flourishing rose bushes. A to B. Ciara knelt in the grass and sank her fingers into the dry soil. She closed her eyes and waited until she got a sense of the life down there. It was teeming with it, though she felt how the radiance of the roots, the worms, the soil itself, seemed to veer around the bird's body. The dead thing almost repelled life. Never one to be deterred, Ciara steered the radiance toward it, ignoring the yellow flashes in her mind; stop signs.

She opened her eyes and saw the blue tit start to twitch as she forced radiance through it. She was doing it! Only then she stopped to question if, or how, the bird would stay alive. Living things create their own radiance, so how—

Someone seized her wrist, twisting her arm backwards. Ciara yelped. The bird died again.

Just what do you think you're doing? Her mother's voice was low, serious, as she dragged her across the lawn towards the house.

Nothing, Ciara said, knowing it must be plainly obvious.

Her mother swung for her, slapping her across her bare legs. It stung. Niamh watched sheepishly, framed by the patio doors. What is the matter with you, Ciara Kelly? Miranda clamped her hands on Ciara's arms, squeezed them tight. She hissed in her face: Why can't you just be good like your sister?

On the sofa, a tear ran down Ciara's face. Sad, from a sad dream.

I sometimes think there's a cog loose inside me, Jude said after the first time they had sex. It was in her room in halls and they were a helix in her single bed. She was hot, so hot, but didn't want to let go of his damp body.

What do you mean? She looked up at him from the pillow of his chest.

I want to be a good person, Jude said, his breath on her forehead. But I just can't stand other people.

Ciara laughed.

I mean it. I wish them harm. Not you. You're different. I feel special.

You are special, Ciara. Seriously. Dabney is all ego; Helena is insecure. They are the least deserving of power but they have it because of luck, because of the families they were born into. You should lead us.

What? You think I should be in charge of the coven?

I think you should be in charge of everything.

Ciara recoiled, swiping the azurite off the coffee table.

She wasn't alone. Catlike, she sprang onto the sofa, pulling her feet in close to her body. 'Who's there?'

The room was dark, only leaden moonlight creeping in under the curtains.

This presence was familiar somehow. A demon she'd invoked before. 'Show yourself,' she commanded.

In the corner, behind a cheese plant, there was a figure. Ciara squinted into the darkness. It didn't move. It had the body of a man, but she could also make out leathery wings, like those of a bat. 'I said, reveal yourself.'

The demon said nothing, only waited.

Ciara dared to climb off the sofa, and crossed to the light switch. She hit the light, fearing it wouldn't work. The overhead light came on, and the figure was gone.

Chapter Twenty-Seven

THE TEMPLE OF THE QUEEN

Leonie – Istanbul, Turkey

The Grand Bazaar was a labyrinth and Leonie couldn't remember what Mehmet looked like, it had been years since he'd been in London. After a good night's sleep in their hostel, she was relying on sentience more than sight to guide her through the thronging marketplace. In other circumstances, she'd have loved this; Anatolian music, the bouquet of incense and spices and leather, but right now she was merely hot and bothered.

She turned to Senait. 'Seriously, I can do this alone if you want to find your friends?' Apparently, Senait had some musician friends she'd met on her travels through the city.

She shook her curls. 'No. We stay together for a bit,' she said breezily, inspecting some silk scarves that hung outside a stall.

Typical oracle shit. 'I beg your pardon?'

'Didn't I say? We travel to like a mountain thing together. There's snow on top. It's cute.'

How Niamh mentored young witches was a true mystery. Exhausting. 'Well, thanks for that info . . .'

'You're welcome!' She grinned. 'So is he here?'

'My guy at the cabal said so . . .' Leonie had used a secure messaging app to keep in contact with Nick Bibby from the Warlock's Cabal in case, by some miracle, Rad got in touch with him.

Mehmet Yalchin was a warlock with dual nationality, splitting his time between London and Istanbul. Nick had suggested that if Radley had come to Turkey, he'd have almost certainly looked up his old cabal colleague. He also said his family owned a bunch of stalls here in the souk.

Leonie pushed her mind as far as she could. There were other witches and warlocks in the bazaar. None as powerful as her or Senait, which was a blessing. She was still tired after the journey; she was in no fit state to face Hale at present. She was also mindful that, after the attack in Italy, Hale definitely knew she was tailing him. They had to tread carefully.

Mehmet Yalchin, make yourself known.

At once, she felt a spike. Someone had heard her. 'This way,' she took Senait's hand. They hurried past a busy café, and took a left past the jewellery district. The signature she felt grew stronger. In her mind's eye she saw dozens of glass lanterns hanging from a ceiling. She saw what he saw.

She counted twelve rows of shops before they arrived in what seemed to be the furniture stalls. The bazaar was essentially a very pretty, old-timey mall, albeit one with narrower, arched corridors. A catacomb of capitalism.

And there he was. A stocky man with a heavy brow waited in the entrance to a lantern shop carved into the outer wall of the arcade. The warlock gave her a subtle nod and beckoned them inside. It was exactly as she had seen in her head; the shop sold multicoloured hanging lanterns as well as some other ceramics; tagine dishes and the like.

He pulled her into a hug, slapping her back jovially. 'Leonie Jackman! Well I never!' Mehmet retained his Tottenham born-and-bred accent.

'It's been forever,' she said. 'Mehmet, this is Senait.'

He shook her hand with vigour. 'You're a sight for sore eyes, ain't ya?' Senait, like all very pretty people, shrugged it off.

'Do you know why I'm here?' Leonie said.

'I can take a wild guess, yeah.'

'Well? Is Hale in Istanbul? Is my brother?'

Mehmet took a look around in the forecourt before pulling down the shutters so they wouldn't be disturbed. 'I could get in deep shit for talking to you.'

'Why?'

Mehmet shifted uncomfortably, wiping his neck with a handkerchief. 'People are picking sides again, doll. He's got a lot of supporters over this way, you know. And not just in Turkey.' That was what worried her. Nowhere in the world was safe for witches, not ever, and you'd be a fool to think progress equals protection, but Hale's credo had gained traction outside of the UK. Turkey, even now, was that fabled gateway between East and West. On the other side of this country were Georgia and Russia – complicated nations as both historically enforced witches into state servitude – but also Syria, Iraq and Iran – where while there was a long, proud tradition of magic, there was also friction between witches and state.

And Hale knew he'd find willing supporters.

'Warlocks?'

'Mostly. Some mundanes too.'

'Why?' Leonie said, exasperated, although she already knew the answer: Because they were men. 'Actually, never mind, it doesn't matter. Is he here or not?'

'Yes,' Mehmet muttered. 'Hale, at any rate, no idea about Radley.'

Shit. 'He hasn't been in touch?'

'No. 'Fraid not.'

Nor had Leonie felt his presence since they arrived. 'Where's Hale?'

'I don't fraternise with them sorts, Leonie, you know me.'

Leonie rolled her eyes. 'Oh come off it, Mehmet, who the fuck do you think you're talking to?'

He had the sense to look abashed. 'OK, if I *was* gonna, there's some bars in Tarlabasi.'

'I have friends there,' Senait said.

'You wanna watch yourself in that part of town.' Mehmet grimaced. 'It's all thieves and prostitutes and trannies.'

Senait raised a brow coolly. 'Then we'll fit right in.'

Leonie laughed aloud.

Something else flashed through Mehmet's mind; a landscape rather more rural than inner city Istanbul. She saw mountains, sand. 'What aren't you telling us, Mehmet?'

Mehmet sighed, knowing he was outmatched. 'Rumour has it he went to some archaeological dig in the mountains outside Ankara. I don't know why.'

Leonie looked to Senait. Snowy mountains. 'We do,' she said. 'Is it far?'

It was not. They took a high-speed train from Istanbul to the capital, Ankara. It was mercifully air conditioned. 'You think you'll stay in Istanbul?'

The younger woman shrugged. 'Maybe. For a bit.'

She was such a stray. 'Look. Why don't you come to England with me? We have a huge coven, and they can help you settle.'

'Maybe,' she said again, and Léonie let it drop. After they'd checked out this dig, she'd take Senait to these pals in Tarlabasi and figure things out from there.

On arriving at Ankara, the pair made their way out of the train station and got a cab to drive them to the north of the city, to the rural town of Memlik in the foot of the mountains. Their driver went much too fast, swerving manically to avoid scooters and bikes, leaving a trail of dust in his wake. For perhaps the first time, Senait looked scared.

The mountain range soon loomed before them. It was craggier and rockier than it was a sandy, Arabian desert. Just as Senait had foreseen, the foothills were shrubland while the highest peaks were capped with snow and shrouded in fine cloud. She told the driver to stop. They would fly the rest of the way. Leonie was confident she could shield them out here where it was quiet.

Clutching Senait tightly, Leonie stayed close to the hillside so she wouldn't overshoot the archaeological site. She needn't have worried; she saw the location in the distance almost as soon as they left the village. The whole area was protected by high metal fences, and there was a fleet of jeeps and trucks parked up. Leonie also spotted a security guard patrolling with an enormous German Shepherd.

Landing safely inside the dig site, Leonie focused on keeping them shielded. It was easy enough, guiding the guard's attention elsewhere. The dig crew, maybe thirty of them, were diligently invested in their tasks. They

seemed young to Leonie, and she thought they were probably students, or recent graduates. It was a hot day for
October, and Leonie noticed that – out here at least – even
the women wore shorts and vests.

An angry Turkish voice shouted across the dusty plateau.
Shit. They were rumbled. How? Leonie turned to see a
woman striding towards them, a wide-brimmed sunhat
concealing her face. Leonie read her. She was a sentient,
although a low-level one. Enough to sense their presence,
but maybe not even enough to know she was a witch.

'I'm sorry,' Leonie said. 'I don't speak Turkish.'
Unfortunately, being a sentient is no replacement for
Google Translate. Leonie could read emotions in people
easily enough, but – even internally – we shape our inner
worlds, define ourselves, with language. And Leonie only
knew English and the remnants of GCSE French.

'Who are you? What are you doing here?' The woman
spoke perfect English. She stood before them, gloved hands
on her hips. Her shirt and cargo pants were filthy but, up
close, the woman was quite stunning. She was a little
older than Leonie, perhaps forty or forty-five with a long,
black ponytail streaming to her waist.

Time for the old Jedi mind trick. 'We're from UCL. I
was told you were expecting us.' Leonie slid her truth
deep into the woman's mind, waiting for it to take root.

'Oh of course!' she said suddenly. 'My sincere apologies!
Too much sun! I'm Professor Zehra Darga from Oxford.
This is my dig, pleasure to meet you.'

Leonie smiled slyly at Senait. 'Thank you so much for
offering to show us around.'

'Not at all. Follow me!'

Professor Darga led them to the excavation site. It was
quite the chasm they'd dug into the land, ladders dropping

to tiered levels, deeper and deeper into the earth. Darga chatted away as they made their descent, animated about her field of expertise. 'You can see why we'd want to keep it quiet,' she said. 'This could very well be the most significant archaeological find in generations. It could reshape our understanding of history, religion, mysticism, *everything*. Come on in.'

It wasn't really taking shape. All Leonie could see were a few ruined walls poking out of the dirt. Imagine being this excited about bricks and rocks. She faked a broad smile. 'Amazing!'

Professor Darga led them to the eroded remains of a fancy doorway half-embedded in the hillside. The stone plinths were engraved with what could be snakes.

'There were a number of earthquakes that could have sunk the temple,' Darga went on. 'AD17, or perhaps the Constantinople event of 557. We'll never know, but the artefacts we've recovered from the tomb lead us to believe we're eight or nine hundred years before Christ.'

Leonie looked around the musty chamber they were now in. 'It's a tomb?'

'Almost certainly.'

'Is there a mummy?'

'Hopefully!' Darga said gleefully. 'We anticipate finding a burial chamber.'

'Who do you think it was?' Senait asked shyly.

Darga's eyes sparkled, even in the gloom of her torchlight. 'That's the big question, isn't it? Is it *her*?'

Leonie frowned. 'Is it who?'

'Isn't it obvious?' Zehra Darga beamed. 'The Queen of Sheba!'

Chapter Twenty-Eight

DADDY ISSUES

Luke – Hebden Bridge, UK

Niamh had seemed a bit off it that morning, so Luke popped into Fleur De Lys on Crown Street to get her some flowers. Yes, it was basic but who *doesn't* love flowers? He wished someone would get him flowers, to be honest. They weren't especially fragrant but, as he left the shop, he stuck his nose in the bunch anyway. He hoped she'd like the ones he'd picked: an autumnal mix of orange roses and brassica.

'Them for her?' Just his voice made Luke flinch, half expecting a clip around the ear. His father waited outside, both hands restraining the latest in a long line of bull-mastiff hounds in a butch leather harness.

He'd known his father was in town because he had a tracker hidden in his car. He used them to monitor the Green & Good fleet, and he'd realised a couple of years ago he could use the technology to learn if there were other witchfinders prowling around Hebden Bridge. Luke was honestly surprised at how easy it had been; you can get them from Halfords, and the GPS device linked to an app on his phone. Piece of piss.

'What if they are for Niamh?' Luke said, ignoring the dog and walking around them. His van was in the car park just around the corner. He'd not paid for parking and the bastard traffic wardens were like hawks in the town centre. He wasn't stopping for anyone, least of all his dad.

Peter followed. 'Don't push yer luck, son.'

Fuck him. He wouldn't try anything here. Luke purposely crossed the street to join a convoy of infant school kids on their way to the library. 'Why are you here? You'll blow my cover. You're supposed to be dead, for fuck's sake. What if someone sees?'

He held the dog away from the noisy procession of children. A couple looked rightly wary of the beast. 'Well, if there int any hags in Hebden, it dunt matter, does it?'

'Go home, Dad. Your spies will let you know if I'm turned into a toad.'

Peter grabbed his arm and the dog growled. 'Oi. You listen 'ere. If I think for one second, you're shackin' up with a hag, I'll . . .'

'You'll what?'

His flint eyes blazed. 'I'll fuckin' drown the cunt is what.'

Luke believed it. After all, he'd drowned his own wife, hadn't he? If the mother of his son wasn't safe, who was? 'You can't. She isn't like Mum. She's the town vet. She has friends . . .'

His mouth curled into a cruel smile. 'No family though, has she? No parents, no grandparents, sister's dead. Niamh Kelly ant really got anyone to miss her, has she? No one except you.'

With hindsight, it was painfully obvious to see how his dad had cut his mum off from her family in the earliest days of their relationship: moving her halfway across the country; making her feel it was them against the world – no one else understood their love. That's the way they operate. Luke tried desperately to keep his composure, but felt it slipping. 'Dad. Niamh is not a witch, I promise.'

'The Ackroyds think different.'

'The Ackroyds don't know their arse from their elbow.'

Peter reached up and tapped his cheek. 'If you don't want yer bird goin' int tank, you better find us some *real* hags, ant yer? And fast. Got it?'

Was that an ultimatum? 'What is that supposed to mean?'

'It means the only reason you've not had yer head kicked in by the lads is because yer my son. They're gettin' impatient. Find us a witch, or I give 'em Niamh Kelly. Do you hear what I'm saying?'

Luke looked to his feet, feeling about twelve years old and three feet tall. 'Loud and clear.'

Chapter Twenty-Nine

SEPARATION

Elle – Hebden Bridge, UK

Thankfully, Gary wasn't the sharpest tool in the garage. He was a sweet man, but a drinker, little broken capillaries mapped his bulb nose. Jez had given him more chances than most people have had hot dinners. Now, he shook his head, running a hand through his mop of grey hair. 'I just don't get it, Elle love.'

'You and I both, Gary,' Elle said, very honestly. She didn't get it either.

'I just don't understand how he could do this to you and the kids.'

Elle shrugged. She was right there with him on that one. 'I don't know what to tell you. I think I'm going to have to close up until I hear from him.'

Gary surveyed the silent garage. Elle felt wretched. He'd worked here since *before* Jez acquired it, and Elle was leaving him professionally homeless. What else could she do? 'There's only so much I can do if I can't get in the office,' he admitted.

'And no one else has a key?'

'No. We never locked it, to tell you the truth.'

Good. That was something, at least. No one would see what she'd done. The last three cars they'd worked on had been repaired and collected. Elle had no explanation for why all the glass had shattered during her outburst, but luckily neither Gary nor young Tomas had pushed it. Maybe they thought she'd smashed them in anger. It seemed – for now at least – everyone accepted her version of events: Jez had run away to an undisclosed location with some nameless woman. Depressing that it was so believable, really.

'I'm so sorry, Gaz. I'll make sure you're paid until you find another gig, or we'll open again when . . . when I figure some things out.' She couldn't pay the mortgage with her part-time work alone. She might need to hire someone to run this place. Or sell it. But that was for later. She had far bigger problems than mortgage arrears.

'Aw, you don't need to do that, Elle, love.'

If he said or did one more nice thing, she'd cry. 'No. It's the least I can do. I'm going to lock the place up for now. I'll give you a glowing reference, obviously, if you want to look for a new position.'

Gary nodded. 'Aw, thanks, love. Right you are. You let me know if you need a hand with anything.'

There was that one more nice thing. Elle burst into tears. She hid her face with her hands. Mercifully, her tears made the garage sufficiently awkward for Gary to pat her arm and make a quick getaway.

The large shutters into the carports were already down, but she locked the 'little door' too once he'd gone, before retrieving the key to the office from her handbag. Once more, her heart plunged somewhere below her stomach. It kept happening and it left her struggling to breathe every time.

What was she going to do? Sooner or later, *someone* was going to question Jez's whereabouts. His mother was dead (not a bad thing, the old cow had always hated Elle and thought they married too young. On reflection, she may have had a point) but his father still lived just outside Huddersfield. Elle watched a *lot* of both true crime and police procedurals on TV. She knew they would quickly learn his mobile was still in the area and that he hadn't used his credit cards. Hell, his van was still parked outside the garage. If someone, anyone, went to the police, she was going to be in serious trouble.

Unless . . .

Well Niamh or Leonie could work a little enchantment, couldn't they? Never, in twenty years, had she asked them for anything. They could gently allay any concerns a police officer might come to her with. They could even make Alan Pearson forget he ever had a son . . .

No. Elle scolded herself. That was monstrous thinking. Moreover, that plan of action would involve her having to tell her best friends what she'd done.

The worst thing by far was the *fear*. What if it happened again? What if Holly or Milo pushed her too far someday, and she snapped? She swallowed a fresh wave of nausea and prepared to enter the office.

The lock was old, perhaps damaged when she'd . . . lost control. She tugged on the handle while she turned the key and eventually it twisted open. She closed the door behind her and switched on the strip light. It flickered to life with a ting-ting-ting and then a buzz. She saw it and flinched. No change, although she hadn't expected there would be.

Not like a living statue can move.

Could you even call *it* a statue?

He did *not* look like a museum piece; a sensual Michelangelo carved out of clay or marble. This *thing* was formed of stone, but that was where the similarity ended. If anything, it was more like a stalagmite jutting out of the office floor. Stalagmites go up, stalac*tites* come down, like tights. She'd never forgotten.

And in the craggy rock, there was a face. His pained face was mottled, pocked and rough, like corroded sandstone. There was no real definition to his limbs – the arms connected to his torso. If she hadn't known, she'd have barely recognised the boulder as human, but – if you knew how to look – there was her Jez. Eyes screwed shut, mouth open in a silent cry.

Elle could not explain what had happened yesterday. She had no idea *how* she had done it. To fundamentally change his matter from flesh to stone was well beyond her. Well beyond any witch she'd ever heard of. She was only a Level 4, for crying out loud! She dimly recalled her grandmother talking about transmutation and, of course, she'd discussed it with Niamh following Theo's transformation. That was different though; Theo's body reconfigured itself but she was still made from *human* cells. Rocks are mineral or plant-based, for Gaia's sake!

To be able to do this, to change his body on a molecular level, *terrified* her. And she had no clue how to reverse what she had done. None at all.

Elle touched his cold, stony face. He was alive. She felt his radiance deep inside the structure. It was Jez, still.

'I am so sorry,' she said, and she was.

She had finally become the thing he feared. The thing *she* feared she'd been all along. The Wicked Witch of West Yorkshire.

HEBDEN BRIDGE GIRLIES
Leonie, Helena, Elle, you

Yesterday
Hey, how you getting on?

Today
Lee? Ellie?
Are you both dead?
I didn't mean that obvs.
Pls don't be dead.

Chapter Thirty

THE DANGER ROOM

Ciara – Manchester, UK

Ciara stepped into the lift at HMRC and pressed the button for the fifth floor. The doors slid shut and she heard the voice. Like that of a little girl, shivering.

Can you help me?

Ciara was alone in the lift. She looked around the narrow elevator and saw an air vent in the ceiling. There was an entity in there; coldly malevolent, like the dark at the bottom of a well. 'Go away,' she told whatever it was.

But I'm so cold. The voice was so sweet, so sad. *And you killed to help the other girl.*

Oh yes, they see it all. 'I said go away.'

Please let me in. You once did. I can help you. I can help you to remember.

Ciara was tired. She didn't want to be here. The urge to cry took her by surprise. She couldn't remember the last time she wept, even as a kid. How did all these demons know her by name? She knew, from Elle and Lee, that things weren't . . . great for her in the years leading up to the war. How bad did it get?

Don't you want to know who called upon your home last night? I know.

They *always* tell you what you want to hear. That's what demons do. 'Who was it?'

Let me in, Miss Ciara.

'Tell me—' The doors opened on the fifth floor, and her ten o'clock appointment – Emma Benwell – was waiting on the other side. Ciara shut up, caught in the act.

Recovering her wits, she managed small talk until they were safely ensconced in what was to be her office. Benwell, the Acting Lead Oracle since Konvalinka's *accident*, sat primly on the other side of Helena's old desk throughout the meeting. Ciara hardly heard a word she said; she had one of *those* inflectionless, monotone voices that were very hard to listen to. Ciara concluded the interview. 'How old are you, if you don't mind me asking?'

'I'm thirty-two,' she said earnestly. 'But I joined HMRC at eighteen. And I don't think you're technically, or legally, allowed to ask me that question.'

Prissy bitch. Ciara read her and – as messy as oracle's minds were – she was confident that while Emma had met Niamh in passing, she didn't *know* her well enough to suspect anything was amiss. 'And your appointment is foretold?'

'Yes. It was seen many years ago, although . . .'

'Although?'

'In the reverie, I appeared somewhat *older* when I took on the role.'

Ciara didn't flinch. 'Would you rather I promoted someone else until you have a few more wrinkles?'

'No! I'm honoured to serve my coven.'

Ciara smiled. 'Good!' If Emma was their most powerful

individual oracle, she was only an O4. God, it's always so tempting to ask them for spoilers, but she'd seen too many witches and warlocks go batshit crazy trying to steer their destiny towards or away from what had been forecast. Look at fucking Dab. *I am the future of witch-kind, one day all witches and warlocks will follow me as their rightful leader.*

She looked at her phone surreptitiously. Still nothing from the group chat. Maybe she really ought to worry. About both of them.

The entity she'd witnessed in the cottage last night had unsettled her, and it took a lot to do that. She'd been scared.

Was it even real, or just another flashback? She hoped the latter. Invocation: Just Say No. It fucks you up. As a teenager, dabbling had felt decadent and rebellious, two fingers up to Niamh and the coven. Admitting that now was faintly embarrassing.

She didn't want to return to that, and didn't like whatever that presence was last night. She'd hardly slept, afraid to close her eyes. At some point, she must have nodded off, and everything feels bleached and clean by the light of morning.

Satisfied Emma wasn't an immediate threat, Ciara dismissed her. 'Just be careful,' she told her. Emma lingered in the doorway. 'After what happened to Annie and Irina. They do say these things come in threes.'

Emma went rather pale and left her office.

Slip of the tongue. It was not *her* office. *It could* be, a mischievous inner voice told her. She told it to fuck off. Right now, it was an empty shell; all of Helena's effects cleared out. Ciara wondered where all her stuff had gone. The Vances, Helena's parents and daughter, were still down south as far as she knew. How old would her daughter be now? Ciara couldn't even remember if she'd met her.

The desk drawers and bookshelves were all empty. Purely hypothetically, what would Ciara do with the office, given the chance? Round desk for one thing, so everyone felt equally important. Curtains, red noir velvet, for texture and warmth. Scented candles; oud and amber. And art, new, exciting art, commissions for up-and-coming witches, not these inspirational teamwork photos Helena had up.

Of course, that was all academic, because soon Leonie would have news and then it'd be time to go. Although . . .

Fidgety, Ciara crossed to the window. It went without saying that Helena had the best view of Manchester, the sun glaring off the side of the glass monolith that was the Beetham Tower and across the rest of the metropolis. Ciara had forgotten how *cool* Manchester was. She'd taken it for granted growing up close by. Sure, Afflecks Palace market wasn't quite the mecca it had been when she was fifteen (where else could a girl get her neon fishnet tights, combat pants and incense sticks?) but the new Northern Quarter had undergone quite the evolution while she slept.

In the 00s, when they'd first been allowed to start getting the train into the city, it had been the part of town you'd get mugged in; now it was all cocktail bars, coffee shops and art spaces. With Niamh's bank balance, gentrification was quite fun. Bless whoever got rid of the need for PINs. Ciara was having a blast just tapping Niamh's cards everywhere she went.

There was a knock at the door. Sandhya looked panicked. 'What's wrong?'

'I . . . the Prime Minister is here.'

Her heart stalled. 'What?'

✶

And naturally he'd brought the whole entourage with him. No sign of Selina Bay; Ciara *hoped* the witch would have at least had the decency to give them some warning had she known. Harkaway hovered at Milner's side, along with a pair of anaemic aides in cheap-looking suits.

'Ah there she is!' Milner said jovially as Ciara entered the lobby, Sandhya at her side.

'I must apologise, Prime Minister. I wasn't aware we were due a government inspection, given we get forty-eight hours' notice for such an event.' Ciara parroted precisely what Sandhya had told her in the elevator. Had she known, she probably wouldn't have worn jeans and a Nirvana T-shirt. She was only in the office at *all* for her meeting with Emma.

'Gosh! Goodness no! This isn't an inspection! I'm in Manchester for the keynote at the Northern Powerhouse Conference tonight, and it occurred to me I'd never seen inside your HMRC building. It's lovely, isn't it?' Milner grinned and this all felt very rehearsed. Harkaway, Ciara noted, didn't look away from his phone once. 'Perfectly informal! Just being nosy!'

Ciara smiled tersely. If she denied them entry, they'd think they had something to hide – which by and large they didn't – but nor did it feel right to allow mundanes into their sanctum. 'Very well,' she said, and saw even the receptionist's eyes widen.

The aides can't come in, Sandhya told her. *They haven't signed the Occult Secrets Act.*

'Your assistants will remain here and have their memories wiped. Our location is Shadow Cabinet only, after all. You had no right bringing them here. It contradicts the terms of the treaty.'

'You can wipe our memories?' Milner's shit-eating smirk faltered.

Ciara smiled. 'We can do a great deal more than that, Prime Minister.'

'Then what if you wipe *our* minds?'

'Prime Minister, we'll simply have to trust one another.'

This time, Harkaway did look up at her, contempt in his eyes. He didn't bother to conceal it. Oh, this was all his doing, of that Ciara was certain. What she was less sure of was how worried she should be. While lots of mundanes down the years have hated witches, the vast majority of them were entirely powerless to do anything about it. This one, though, had the ear of the most powerful mundane in the country. *That* was a concern.

This little tour mattered more than Ciara would have liked.

By the time they reached the lift, Ciara had telepathically told every witch and warlock in the building to look lively. They were in the midst of a government inspection; whatever Milner deemed it.

They started on the top floor at the oratorium – no doubt the 'wowiest' stop on the tour. 'Crikey, isn't it strange?' Milner commented in hushed tones as he surveyed the darkened theatre, and that did about sum it up. Outside of the oracle's space, Ciara imagined the biggest shock was how *dull* it all was. HMRC was an office like any other. They had coffee machines and soup-splattered microwaves in kitchenette areas, hot-desking and tiered breakout spaces. Only one woman in the whole building fully understood how to operate the photocopier. It was – in every sense of the word – mundane.

They continued down the building, Ciara sensing Milner's boredom deepen with every floor. Harkaway was more interested; his curiosity never waning. He seemed determined to find a smoking gun.

Archive & Acquisitions was full of cool things, but wasn't especially cool to look at: all their antiquities were boxed up and mothballed for the most part. An elderly warlock, Edward Okeke, was in charge of the department. He tended the basement space like it was his garden, and Ciara was delighted at the very real prospect that he might bore their guests to actual death. She deferred to him, allowing him to get out some of their more precious artefacts: Peter Stumpp's belt; some rusty nails from the crucifixion; the knot of Isis; a singing sword. Tourists love that old crap.

Ciara thanked Edward for his excruciatingly thorough show-and-tell and concluded the tour.

'What about the gym?' Harkaway asked.

'What about it?' Ciara replied.

'Is it a gym like any other?'

'More like a Pokémon gym,' Ciara said glibly.

'I beg your pardon.'

'It's a space where witches can hone their skills safely,' Sandhya explained.

'Oh marvellous!' Milner clapped. 'May I see?'

Ciara scowled slightly. 'We aren't dancing bears, Prime Minister, we don't perform for peanuts.'

'I don't think it's an unreasonable request,' Harkaway started towards the gym at the other end of the basement. 'If there was to be a critical supernormal event, the Prime Minister needs to be reassured that HMRC are equipped to handle it. We place such trust in you.'

'I confess I am rather curious to see you ladies in action,' Milner added.

Ciara sighed. She'd rather do it here than have them tracking witches in the field. In that moment, she caught herself almost *caring* about this fucking coven. Goddess, why was she even *here*? If Ciara at twenty-four could see her now, she would assume she'd dropped acid. 'Very well,' she said through gritted teeth, 'I'll see who's available.'

She turned to her assistant. *Find some young, pretty witches who aren't too threatening to these chodes.*

Sandhya spluttered, and very quickly arranged to have a healer and an elemental come down to the gym to meet them. Ciara had never seen the training room before, and was somewhat nosy herself. It turned out to be a large, windowless room; exposed brick on all sides, and kitted out like those very masculine bodybuilder gyms. Here, though, the weights and kettlebells were moved by tele-kinesis. At one end of the hall was a series of man-shaped targets pinned to the wall. She saw Harkaway eye them with suspicion.

The healer, Giovanna, could barely conceal her disdain as she perfunctorily revived a wilting spider plant before returning to her desk in RED. Deborah Asher, an experi-enced elemental from Coven Liaison, obliged in a display of firepower. She conjured a swirling ball of fire in the palm of her hand before hurling it at a straw dummy at the furthest end of the room.

The mannequin went up like poor Guy Fawkes, himself an elemental incidentally. See? That's what happens when warlocks attempt to function without the help of witches. As Ciara understood her history, had they waited for the witches, James I and his witch trials could well have been prevented. Fools.

'Gosh, how wonderful,' Milner beamed, watching the dummy smoke after Deb extinguished it. 'We could use you ladies in the armed forces.'

Ciara blinked a moment before laughing nervously. 'Oh, sorry! I didn't realise you were kidding.'

Now Milner looked even more gormless. 'I wasn't.'

Harkaway cleared his throat. 'Prime Minister, NATO forbids supernormal involvement in the military, although that's not to say *some* nations don't flout that rule.'

'Ah I see.'

'And more to the point,' Ciara added, 'no self-respecting witch would allow herself to become a weapon of the state.' She smiled sweetly again, more sugar on the Frosties.

Deborah waited for further instruction. 'Thanks, Deb,' Ciara said, letting her off the hook. 'You can head upstairs.'

'Is that it?' Milner asked.

'*Is that it*? She just made fire with her bare hands.'

'A flamethrower can do that. I was expecting something a bit more, well, *Avengers*.'

Ciara looked to Sandhya. *Oh, for crying out loud. Shall we?* The pair of them pushed themselves off the floor, hovering halfway between that and the ceiling. 'Better?'

'Gosh! You can fly!'

'It's not flight as much as it is telekinesis,' Sandhya told them.

In for a penny. Ciara reached out and lifted them both into the air too. Milner looked down at the floor with childlike wonder, while Harkaway's mouth sucked in like a dog's arse. It looked like he was trying really, *really* hard to keep his cool. 'See?' She brought them all down to earth with panache.

'And that's what sentients do?'

'They can control minds, too,' Harkaway bleated, 'isn't that right?'

'How so?' Milner asked.

'Care to demonstrate?' Harkaway's flint eyes never left her.

'Very well,' she said through a clenched jaw. And just

like that, Ciara was over it. These men were maggots and they ought to know their place. They wanted a parlour trick? Fine. What would it be? She looked around the vast room for inspiration.

She reached inside their heads and got creative. There were air vents and air conditioning ducts running all across the ceiling. Focus. *What if . . . ?*

Water. It started as a trickle, leaking in through the vents, and running down the walls. Soon, a torrent was spurting through the grate with a noisy whoosh. The mundanes saw as she saw, turning to look at where the noise was coming from.

Milner looked to her, the car showroom veneer faltering for the first time. The Botox allowed a few creases on his forehead. 'Is this real?' Ice-cold water surged around their feet, lapping over their polished shoes. 'It's freezing!'

Ciara cocked her head. 'Is it? Is it in your head or am I an elemental? Feels real, doesn't it?'

The torrent continued, the room rapidly filling. Within seconds they were submerged to their knees. Even Ciara felt the chill spread up her jeans. Man, she was good. Harkaway seemed to stare her out. 'It's only an illusion.' He grimaced.

Milner, on the other hand, turned and waded towards the door. Ciara sealed it shut.

She was vaguely aware of Sandhya trying to speak to her telepathically. She ignored her and carried on.

Mundane minds are so easy to convince. The water continued to gush from the vents, swilling up around their waists. 'That's enough,' Milner said. 'Make it stop.'

Instead, she made it deeper. She adjusted the glamour and the water was now at their chins.

'Can you swim, Prime Minister?' They were now

floating, or at least that's what Ciara had them believe. 'Psychosomatic reactions are as real as anything. If your mind believes your body is in trouble, it'll force your body to react accordingly. Hold your breath . . .'

They reached the ceiling, and there was nowhere left for them to swim. Milner's cheeks puffed out and he tilted his head to stay above the surface. Harkaway screwed his eyes shut as if he was trying to wake himself from a bad dream. Ciara pictured herself suspended underwater. 'So you see, this is what a witch could do to a, let's say a renegade warlock. I could convince him to stop breathing until he died.'

The sheer horror on Milner's face made it all worthwhile. She ended the illusion and they were exactly where they were the whole time, stood on the gym floor, bone dry. Milner gasped for air.

'How was that for you? Wanna go again?'

Only then Ciara realised what she'd done. Harkaway smiled slightly and she saw she'd made his point for him. She'd just convinced the Prime Minister that witches are a deathly threat. She was the fool, and Niamh would never have been.

Chapter Thirty-One

THE QUEEN OF SHEBA

Leonie – Ankara, Turkey

Zehra held an LED lamp aloft as she led them down endless narrow tunnels. Leonie ran her fingertips along the stone wall, and they were wet to the touch. They must be deep underground now, and Leonie sensed more than a little claustrophobia stirring in Senait. This far down, the air smelled old, furtive somehow. It was a powerful space; Leonie heard millennia in the rocks.

Zehra waited outside a final antechamber. 'Are you ready?'

Leonie guessed, wherever they were going, they'd arrived. 'Am I ever.'

Zehra stooped to duck through the entryway. Leonie cast a quick look at Senait and followed. On the other side of the opening, Leonie found she could stand up straight and the air was cooler still. They were in some sort of crypt, the ceiling held up by crumbling pillars.

As her eyes adjusted to the gloom, Leonie saw Zehra proudly standing next to a formidable statue.

'She's beautiful, isn't she?' Zehra exclaimed, angling her lamp up towards the effigy's face.

No, Leonie thought, but she didn't want to piss on Zehra's chips, as *she* was clearly besotted. The statue depicted a woman, her stone face neutral in that way Leonie had always found slightly eerie. She rode an elephant, although, in her arms, she held what was clearly a serpent. Very Britney. The snake coiled around her naked form. 'What makes you think it's her?' Leonie said, instead of answering. 'The Queen of Sheba?'

'The dates about add up. This is all conjecture, of course, but look at this.' Zehra held the lamp over writing carved into the wall of the tomb.

'What language is that?' Senait asked.

'We think they're early Anatolian hieroglyphs. They're reminiscent of inscriptions found on the Marash Lion, which we estimate came about seven hundred years later. You have to understand that writing as a concept was in its infancy, and where there is writing it was usually to denote a name. Here – we think this symbol means "queen".'

Leonie considered the statue's knowing expression. 'How do you know she's *that* queen?'

'Truthfully, we don't,' Zehra admitted, a little deflated. 'But there's scant agreement on who she was, or where she was from, in the first place. Some people think Sheba is what we now call Yemen, while others believe she was the queen of Egypt or Ethiopia.'

Senait nodded. 'In my dad's stories, the queen was called Makeda.'

Zehra's face lit up, even in the dark. 'Please, go on.'

Senait shrugged, a little coy. 'I don't know much. Just a story he used to tell me at bedtime.'

'What did he say?' said Zehra.

'That once there was this beautiful queen who learned of a wise and powerful king in the East.'

'Solomon?' Leonie asked.

Senait nodded. 'Makeda wanted to see this kingdom for herself, so went to him and took him a gift: a stone pillar thing with the secrets of the universe carved on every side.'

Secrets of the universe, or the secrets of Gaia? 'She was a witch?'

Zehra bristled slightly at the term. 'Historical figures are often imbued with otherworldly powers in legend; I wouldn't take it too literally.'

'They say she could see the future,' Senait said.

A Black witch queen *two thousand* years ahead of Anne Boleyn. Leonie couldn't wait to get back to HMRC and tell them about this. 'What happened when she found the king?'

Senait carried on her tale. 'Solomon fell in love with the queen, obviously - because she was flawless, a ten, stunning - while she stayed at his palace. One night, she . . . drank forbidden water and got knocked up.'

'*Forbidden water*,' Leonie said doubtfully. 'Oh that old chestnut.'

'Immaculate conception is a motif across many cultures,' Zehra added. 'Go on.'

'So King Solomon foresaw that the child would be king of Ethiopia, so Makeda returned, and he gave her a ring as a token of faith.'

That got Leonie's attention. 'A ring? The Seal?'

Zehra recoiled at the word *seal*, her brow creased. She seemed suddenly perturbed. 'There was a man here . . .'

Leonie looked to Senait, who knew exactly what she was thinking. 'Professor Darga, did a man come here looking for a ring?'

Zehra's mind was a swirly, muddy mess. Leonie knew

at once that Hale *had* been here and wiped her. 'I'm not sure.'

Leonie couldn't recover the memories. 'Professor Darga, did you find a ring in the tomb? Could it be Makeda was buried here with it?'

Zehra smiled once more, although Leonie heard sirens in her mind. She was suddenly wary of them. Why? 'Well, that's our holy grail. The legendary Seal of Solomon. But no,' she said quickly. 'We haven't found any jewellery to speak of. We haven't found a body either, so it could be that this was all a monument to the queen more than a burial chamber.'

Leonie wondered how an Ethiopian queen would end up in Turkey, but didn't suppose Zehra would have any answers. It was rich though, all this history. A witch queen and a warlock king. They might not have used those words to define themselves, but the exchange that took place – the pillar for the Seal – was telling, as was the fact that witches, for generations, bred with warlocks to ensure gifted offspring. It all added up.

She wasn't supposed to be enjoying this. It wasn't a history field trip. Guiltily, Leonie reminded herself why she was standing in this cavern. All these miles and she still didn't have a scrap of an idea where Radley was. She couldn't, and wouldn't, entertain him being dead. She didn't know Hale well, but there was enough of the Bond villain about him to make Rad, or her, suffer. A quick death wasn't his style. That was his whole thing during the war – he never killed *anyone* himself, he got other people to do his dirty work.

Zehra now eyed them with suspicion. 'Who did you say you were again?'

Leonie quickly re-established the lie in Zehra's mind. 'You've been very helpful, thank you.'

'Not at all. Plenty more to sift through. Imagine if we did find the Seal. That'd put us on the map, wouldn't it? Allow me to show you the way out.'

The sun was dangerously bright as they exited the labyrinth of tunnels under the hillside, and Leonie shielded her eyes. Zehra wished them all the best with their fictional PhDs, and asked an undergraduate assistant to show them off site.

Once they were alone, Senait asked, 'Do you think Hale got the Seal?'

Leonie shook her head. 'No. I think if he had what he wanted, we'd know about it.'

'So, what do we do now? I'm starving.'

Leonie wiped sweat from her brow. 'Nothing. Dinner will have to wait. That woman is hiding something and I wanna know what. We're going to watch her because I bet Dabney Hale is watching too.'

Chapter Thirty-Two

TEENAGE DREAMS

Theo – Hebden Bridge, UK

If Theo could not be made to care for football when she was a boy, she certainly wasn't going to show enthusiasm for it now she was a girl. Nonetheless, she found herself sitting in the sheltered seating on the side of the football pitch watching a mud-splattered Milo in the drizzle.

She did not have a clue what was going on in the game. It would be very Cool Girl for her to understand the offside rule – because the boys kept screaming OFFSIDE – but Theo would rather use that mental capacity for potions, rituals and the history of the coven.

She'd only agreed to come because – even with her powers at their depleted level – she could sense Milo's worsening heartache over his father's vanishing act. When she'd seen him at lunch, eating alone outside the sandwich bar in the canteen, he'd been about to skip class and blow off the rest of the afternoon. 'But what about your football match?' she'd asked.

'I don't care,' he'd muttered, and she knew it must be *bad*. Milo *loved* football, all its *gossip* too; tittle-tattle about where players were rumoured to be going filled his head a lot of the time. He loved it like she loved her craft.

'You should play. It'll cheer you up,' Theo had told him, and he said he'd play if she came to watch. What else could she do? That was how she came to find herself gradually freezing to death on the bleachers.

At half-time (goddess, how was there more?) he came and sat with her in the stands. 'You enjoying it?' he asked. 'Did you see that cross I made to Stevens?'

'Um, yeah.'

He gave her a doubtful glance. 'OK, I can't read minds, but I heard that. You bored?'

'Sorry!' She didn't want to whine, but it was also Baltic out there.

'You can go if you want.'

'No! I want to see if you win.'

'We will,' he said without a trace of doubt. 'Oh, by the way, Gooner's having a party at his Friday night, if you wanna come?'

Theo frowned. 'Did Gooner actually invite me?'

'Not exactly, but he said I could bring anyone I want to, and I want to bring you.'

She sighed. 'I thought you had a thing with Olivia Metcalfe?' As if she was gonna break girlcode, even if the girl in question was as vile as Olivia Metcalfe.

Milo rolled his eyes. 'No, Olivia tells people we have a thing. Big difference.'

'Milo, I don't know . . .' Her answer, honestly, was a definite NO, but she didn't want to hurt his feelings. She'd only seen house parties on TV, and no good came of them.

'It's just a party.'

'You go to a lot of parties. To me, any party is very alien.' She added, more quietly: 'I hear what people say about me.'

As she was a new girl entering Year 10, rumours had started as soon as the new term started. Naturally. One of the rumours amongst the girls of St Augustus was that *Theo used to be a boy*, but it was no more or less persistent than *Theo is a whore*, *Theo is a gypsy* or *Theo's a witch*. Two of them were true, but she did question why people were so unnecessarily cruel. What was it about school that made everyone so fucking nasty? Survival of the shittest.

Before her powers had started to wane, she could very clearly read the *threat* she posed to other girls. It didn't matter what she did, wore, or how much she tried to sail under the radar. A high school is not a nice place for a teenage girl to be. The sheer panic of it all, the constant thirst for reassurance: *am I getting this wrong?* Other girls observed and ranked Theo's beauty, her thinness, but also zeroed in on minute comparisons: wrists, thigh gaps, hair, eyelash length. She'd once overheard Olivia Metcalfe making fun of Elsa Moore's 'farmer knuckles'. What the fuck?

And for why? What resource were they competing for? Beauty is limitless, but friends and boyfriends were apparently finite within the boundary of their school. Theo felt their collective exhaustion – or at least she *had* until this week. The boys, the straight ones in any case, did not have quite so many frustrations on top of their academic woes, although they certainly rated *male* approval over any attention they got from girls. Interesting, she thought.

'So?' Milo shrugged.

'If we go to a party together, people will start saying stuff about us.'

'Do I look like I give a shit what people think about me?' Milo said. He smelled good, salty somehow.

'That's because you're already very popular.'

'Probably *why* I'm very popular. Everyone else at this school is a winnit. Why would I care what they think?'

'A what?'

'A winnit. A bit of shit that gets stuck to your arse.'

Theo laughed. The word was funny. Using what little power she still had, she closed their conversation off from anyone else within earshot. 'Does it not bother you that I used to be . . . different?'

'You still are different,' he said, swigging nonchalantly from his water bottle. 'I don't understand literally any of this witch stuff, but no one else *ever* has to know how you were before, right? You can just wipe it out of their heads forever?'

He meant well, but that sounded a lot like he thought her past was best kept hidden. But she *had* kept it hidden, and continued to do so, so she was just as bad, wasn't she? What a cautionary tale she was; truly, happiness is not skin deep. Theo shrugged. 'I don't know right now. My power . . .'

'It'll come back. Ask Niamh about it. She'll help you.' Theo wasn't so sure of that. They'd have to be in the same room, for one thing.

Milo's hand brushed against hers. Maybe on purpose. This was as scary as everything that had happened to her over the summer. She hadn't even started to think about her life *beyond* becoming a girl. That had been her only goal. It turned out there was a whole lifetime of stories waiting for her after that happy ending.

What now?

Theo wanted not to attend Gooner's party, but she also wanted to be around Milo. She was about to fob him off when she saw Holly watching them from the other side of the football pitch. Her face was stormy.

'Shit,' Theo muttered.

'What?' Milo said.

'Holly.'

'What about her?' Milo followed her gaze, but Holly was already marching towards the school buildings. 'I don't give a flying fuck what she thinks either.'

Theo stood. 'I do.'

Milo would have to fend for himself. Theo squelched across the spongy, sodden field, every step trying to suck the Doc Martens off her feet. She headed towards the main driveway of the school in hopes of finding Holly at the bus stop.

St Augustus was a depressing place. The original school building was a Victorian redbrick (their school had once been a workhouse), and despite its history, it was at least an impressive building. When the school had expanded in the sixties and seventies, they'd built ugly pebbledash cubes around the older structure. The classrooms had low, false ceilings made from foam squares, and the windows steamed up every lesson like a sauna.

Sure enough, Holly was trudging past the science block towards the bus turnaround, dragging her feet. 'Holly! Wait!'

Holly kept walking. Theo tried to stop her telekinetically but found she could not. Holly turned to her, a scowl on her face. 'Did you just use your fucking powers on me?'

'I tried,' Theo admitted. 'Just to get you to stop.'

Holly winced and Theo felt an invisible force shoving

her. She stumbled, her shoulder blades scraping on the pebbledash of the Home Economics block. 'Ow!'

'Maybe I'm stronger than you now,' Holly said, her expression hard.

Theo said nothing. She wasn't going to get into this in front of the school, even after hours. Also, it was her best friend.

'I'm sorry,' Holly caved first. 'That was babyish.'

'We shouldn't use our powers on each other,' Theo conceded. 'I'm sorry.'

They stood awkwardly for a moment, all elbows. 'Don't date my brother,' Holly said simply.

'Holly . . .'

'No. When have I ever asked you for anything? I didn't tell anyone you were a girl . . .'

Theo tilted her head. 'You told your mother.'

'She threatened to read my mind!' Holly threw her hands up. 'I helped you get away from Helena; I helped you research what happened in the woods; and now I'm asking you to do one thing. There are six hundred boys at this school, date any of them except Milo! Please!' Her eyes were wet.

'Why?' Theo asked, and judging from Holly's face, that wasn't the right answer. Theo, as much as she'd like to, just didn't fancy girls so there wasn't a lot she could do about that. But if she had to date *anyone*, wasn't it better that it was someone Holly knew?

'Because I hate him,' Holly said, her voice echoing around the empty quad. 'I *love* him because he's my brother, but he has also been mean to me my whole life. I need you to see he's horrible too, even if he's nice to you. Theo, please. With everything that's going on with Mum and Dad, I just can't deal with this too.'

She was shaking. This was something Holly needed.
Theo nodded. They had both taken an oath at solstice.
An enemy of my sister is mine. She had no choice but to
leave Milo well alone.

Roberts, Moira

To me

Evening Niamh

Just checking you got my email earlier?

Various rumours circulating re the Prime Minister's unannounced visit to HMRC. Obv clearly unacceptable but similarly, we need to be especially cautious. Am sure once you're settled in, we'll hear much less from the Shadow Cabinet fingers crossed.

Just FYI I've attached the most recent official guidance on using magic against mundanes. Maybe worth a refresh? Should you need further clarification, do let me know.

M x

Sent from an iPhone

Chapter Thirty-Three

DOWNTIME

Ciara – Hebden Bridge, UK

What do adults do of an evening? As a teenager and then at university, she'd spent every waking hour with her friends, or with Jude. Old episodes of *Friends* or *Spaced* in his bed, eating cheap and nasty sweet and sour chicken balls from the place next door to his student house.

Do you want the last chicken ball? she'd asked him, and he smiled up at her. After a moment, he said, I love you. And she said, I know – because – Han Solo. He laughed, and said, I fucking knew you were going to say that.

She had loved him. She remembered now. She, Ciara Kelly, had once been in love. *Where did he go?* She almost daren't find out. To lose what they'd had must have hurt like fucking hellfire. Maybe she was better off not knowing.

Now, it seemed, everyone had *family* to spend their evenings with. Is that why people get married? So someone is forced to amuse you until you die?

Ciara sat alone in the kitchen, bathed in the light of her laptop. Sandhya had sent over the outlines for her grand coronation ceremony but she couldn't bring herself to open the attachment. That'd mean it was real. Circumstances were starting to feel out of her control, a runaway train. She didn't like it.

Next to her computer was the most stunning bouquet of flowers from Luke. The man had taste. The card read: *I hope you know how happy you make me.* The cynic in her, telling her he liked how hard she made him cum, couldn't entirely drown out more wholesome feeling. She felt sort of . . . proud and glowing. She made him happy. Her; she did.

She couldn't entertain this. She was getting soft.

She needed a distraction. Ciara couldn't even indulge in novocaine TV because Theo was meditating in the lounge, gazing at her crystals.

The girl was trying to establish why her powers were fading. Ciara *almost* felt bad for poisoning her, but needs must. It was a bit fucking late for regret.

Ciara considered her. Her eyes were closed, face serene. What would happen when, not if, Ciara left. Would she go to Elle? Hard to tell, given that Elle wouldn't even reply to the group chat at the moment. The more likely outcome was that HMRC would be forced to step in as she was under sixteen. Another witch orphan floating around the system, the way she and Niamh had been uprooted from Ireland and plonked here with their grandmother all those years ago.

Nursing a glass of Merlot, she raked through the cat litter tray that was her memory for scraps of grief. She knew she *should* be sad about her parents. They had been killed in a car accident. A drunk driver drifted across the lanes and hit them head-on at seventy miles an hour. Killed on impact. That told Ciara how they died, but not how she felt about it; that was one more memory destroyed by Niamh. She imagined she'd been sad. If she hadn't cried, she hoped she'd been smart enough to fake it.

Her father was pure hilarity. He did Foghorn Leghorn and Kermit the Frog.

That she remembered. She half-smiled, and finished her wine.

Her mother. Red hair. Thin. They'd inherited her looks. Ciara saw her mother reading Niamh a story in bed. *Gobbolino, the Witch's Cat.*

Ciara was jealous of them. She remembered that too, the horrid little heartburn. *Fuck this.* She stood swiftly, ditching her glass in the sink.

Ciara didn't see the harm in listening in to Theo's reverie. Well, she did – it was a grotesque violation, but it was infinitely preferable to spending time with her own moth-eaten quilt of a past. She tiptoed to the lounge and found Theo cross-legged in front of a dwindling fire in the hearth. Ciara sniffed out the younger girl's unique thoughtwaves, and let herself be pulled with the riptide into her mind.

That fucking flat again. Whenever Theo regressed, the same dingy apartment made an appearance sooner or later. Even Ciara flinched from it. There was a woman, and Ciara knew as soon as she saw her the ravages of possession: the puce, pocked skin, the thinning hair, her sinewy limbs. You see, when you're losing days on end to the thing that's inside your body, you don't think to eat, sleep or wash. Some demons push their human hosts to breaking point and beyond. Why would they care? Fast fashion; another cheap mortal skin to wear like a Primark dress, and then cast aside.

A baby screamed and screamed and screamed. It was

awful, cutting right through Ciara. The vision was lucent, half-formed. Like a ghost, Ciara drifted through a wall into a mildewed bathroom. The bath and basin were a drab, olive green. Through swirling steam, a soaking wet baby writhed on its back on top of a towel. From the next room, Ciara dimly heard voices. The woman, she assumed the baby's mother, was talking to someone else, although she couldn't make out what they were saying over the howling infant.

Ciara tried to move her feet, but found she had no feet. She was incorporeal, and barely able to steer her consciousness. Once more, Ciara found herself slightly afeared of Theo. If her memory had somehow stored these early images, she was a powerful witch indeed.

Ciara forced herself to move within the memory. Could she? Yes. Somehow she knew the layout of the alien apartment and left the bathroom. She followed the voices to a lounge. It was in a similar sad state to the rest of the flat: wallpaper peeling, black with mould. There was a dented floral sofa with greasy yellow patches where heads had once rested, and a black glass TV stand as a coffee table. At first, Ciara thought the room was empty, only then a cold breeze drew her attention to the open balcony doors. She was just in time to see the weary-looking woman climb onto the balcony railing and drop over the edge. A pebble down a well.

She shouted, but no sound came out.

Instinctively, Ciara raced to grab her but—

But . . .

But instead, Ciara found herself swinging her legs on the London Underground. The heels of her lilac Kickers drummed on the base of the seat. The other commuters looked annoyed. Her mother told her to stop.

Her mother. This wasn't Theo's mind any more. It was hers.

This is a Piccadilly Line service to Cockfosters. They were surrounded by business people in suits with cases, and punks, and monks. They didn't have many of those types of folks in Galway. This was *so* exciting for Ciara because to go somewhere without Niamh was rare—

What? No. Ciara felt drunk and a little hungover at the same time.

That didn't happen.

She was sure of it.

She'd never been to London with her mother. She didn't go to London until she was at St Augustus. They'd gone on a school trip to the Natural History Museum.

She recoiled from her reverie, the armchair feeling somehow too solid under her very real bottom. Fighting a sudden urge to vomit, she forced herself over to the kitchen sink. She hunched over the enamel; the plughole comfortingly close.

Over her shoulder, Theo was still in her trance state, features passive. Ciara rubbed her temple and drew a deep breath. Not for the first time, she wished Niamh had killed her, just got it over with. To exist as a colander was painful, like everyone else in the world knew a secret she wasn't in on, and she was the secret. What *was* that? Her hands were shaking. They had teleported her from Manchester to Hebden Bridge; maybe she still felt out of sorts.

She stooped and yanked open the cupboard under the sink. She took the little vial of Excelsior she'd found in Niamh's stash and rubbed some into her gums. If that didn't perk her up, nothing would. Better. She felt the instant head rush between her eyes, followed by the gentler fuzz-buzz in her muscles.

She took Niamh's phone from next to the flowers, and went into the garden so as not to disturb Theo.

Luke answered on the second ring. 'Hey you.' She loved how happy he was she'd called. It was like being a teenager again, those early days with Jude when everything felt *Dawson's Creek*. 'Y'all right?' he asked.

'Yeah. I got to hang out with the Prime Minister today.'

'What? No way!'

'Yep.'

'Did you take the opportunity to slap him in the face with a wet cod?'

Ciara laughed. 'Well . . .' In a roundabout way . . .

'What yer doin' now?'

'Not a lot. I wondered if you wanted to come over?' What else was she going to do?

'Ah, that'd be mint, but I've, um, got plans tonight.'

She was surprised at how quickly the sour of jealousy cut through her. She knew to hide that. Boys don't like girls that get jealous. 'Oh yeah, some little chickadee on the side?'

'Nah. A friend of mine needs help with some shelves.'

If she'd been nearer, she'd have known if that was a lie. It was startling how quickly her mind was doing these things to her. She'd only fucked him twice, for crying out loud; what hormonal nonsense was this? Luke Watts did not matter. He was a stress toy at best, something to squeeze. She did not care if he was shagging some other girl, for she would very soon be fucking some other guy, most likely in Cuba, maybe Brazil.

Inside the cottage, she saw Theo stir, her shadow moving around the walls. Ciara headed into the kitchen. 'OK, then. If you get done early, you know where I am.' Goddess, that sounded needy.

'Aye, I'll text later.' At that her heart perked up a little and she hated herself. You can become addicted to anything that makes you feel good.

Busying herself, she made hot chocolate for herself and Theo – taking care to remember which mug she added the *White Sorbus* to – and they watched television for a while. Incredibly, the very same episodes of *Friends* she'd once watched with Jude were still in rotation. Theo sat between Ciara's knees, on the floor, while Ciara French-braided her hair. She remembered the way she and Niamh used to do this. It made her sad, although she found keeping her hands busy quieted some of the chatter in her head.

'What shall we watch?' Theo said, flicking through the seemingly endless options on Niamh's TV. Ciara was careful not to say anything too granny-ish, but before her coma, there'd been no such thing as 'streaming platforms'. The sheer choice was overwhelming. She needed a list to keep track of what Niamh had seen and what she ought to catch up on. 'There's a documentary about the Pendle trials on Amazon,' Theo suggested.

'Is that not triggering?' Ciara smirked. 'And anyway, Annie always told us they had it coming. Two witch families basically sold each other out to the mundanes and they all got hanged for their efforts. You can't ever trust a mundane.'

'Even Luke?'

Fuck, she had her there. 'No. I think Luke's one of the good ones.' They could rely on him at least.

Chapter Thirty-Four

RETURN TO THE WORKING MEN'S CLUB

Luke – Huddersfield, UK

It was the most dreadful feeling, a fist around his throat. Ironically it was his father's words he kept revisiting. A conversation from a long, long, time ago, when Mum had been alive. His dad was once a steelworker and, when the works closed, he was in direct competition for jobs in Sheffield with his former colleagues. Luke so clearly remembered how quickly his father shelved any notion of fraternity. 'It's dog-eat-dog son. When you have a family you'll understand.'

And now he had a family – of sorts. Anyone who saw him and Niamh and Theo out walking Tiger together would assume they were a family unit. They had to come first. And that meant it was time for dog to eat dog.

Fuck. There was no justifying this. What he was about to do was unforgivable. He knew that, and would not seek forgiveness if she ever found out what he'd done. He could feel the light dimming in himself. No way back.

The Working Men's Club basement was thick with

Benson & Hedges, as always. Peter had gathered everyone for this special meeting, and was running through the notices: mostly a list of women the WMC suspected of witchcraft. It was just a list of women they didn't like: unmarried women; lesbians; transgender women; women with mental health issues.

Luke heard little of it over his guilt. However much he tried to square it, this was human sacrifice. In this case it wasn't to appease some god or goddess, but these pathetic, bitter, little men. Maybe what he ought to do was kill his father. He didn't doubt that he could: he'd drug the dog – he'd nicked some *Sandman* from under Niamh's kitchen sink weeks ago, knowing he might need a way to get past the creature sooner or later – and kill Peter Ridge in his sleep. But then what? He'd heard enough true crime podcasts to know everyone always gets caught these days, and he'd be sent down – or the other witchfinders would have his scalp – and then his little family would be even more vulnerable. He could keep these hounds off Niamh and her friends if nothing else.

So here he was. The worst thing he'd ever done. He didn't see any other way. It wasn't like he could tell Niamh the truth after all this time; the lie had snowballed far out of his control.

'I'm sure you're wondering why I called this emergency session. Well, our Luke has *finally* come up with the goods,' Peter said pointedly. 'Up you come, son.'

Luke felt sick. All he could hope was that she was a very, very powerful witch. He hoped she killed them all, the fuckers. He turned and about thirty expectant faces looked to him, that same appalling hunger in their eyes. He hovered next to the projection screen.

His father's gaze was the worst of all. He was enjoying this, making him squirm. But then, he'd always been a cruel man. Most of us only get one set of parents, and, as a kid, Luke hadn't visited many other homes. How was he to know his normal wasn't normal.

Luke had never forgotten the time, an average Wednesday, when he'd been served venison kidney and spuds. The offal swam in grease on his plate and tasted of piss. He'd been five or six at the time, and couldn't bring himself to swallow the chewy flesh. With every mouthful, his stomach tried to toss it up. He knew now it wasn't OK to force a child to sit alone at a dining room table, in the dark, until every mouthful of food was gone from the plate. *It'll make you big and strong.* Luke had cried and cried, but remain at the table he must. It was a little after eleven when he managed to swallow, and keep down, the last mouthful of kidney.

Peter glared at him now the same way he had that night. 'Don't keep us waiting, son, spit it out.'

Luke cleared his throat before beginning. 'I wasn't sure for a long time, but I think I finally have evidence of real witchcraft in Hebden Bridge.'

'No shit, Sherlock!' Mick Ackroyd heckled from the back row, and there was a naughty schoolboy snigger from the audience.

'Evidence was difficult in this case. As you can see, she has perfectly legitimate reasons to be performing group rituals.'

Behind him, the kindly face of the Reverend Sheila Henry appeared on the screen. There was yet more murmuring in the audience. 'How does that work?' One man asked, pointing at where the white collar would go.

'I have no idea,' Luke said, and he didn't. When Sheila

prayed to God was it in fact Gaia she spoke to? Did it matter? Were they really *that* different? Niamh had explained their belief system to him, and it appealed. Everything came from and returned to the earth. There was no angry father figure in the sky for the witches. For obvious reasons, Luke could get on board with that.

'What evidence have you got?' someone else shouted.

'Next slide,' Luke instructed, and they came to the video. He'd had it for months. One of his delivery drivers had asked him to take a look at some unusual dashcam footage. He pressed play. It was grainy as fuck, but showed one of the Green & Good vans making its way down Market Street past the Baptist Church when, blink-and-you'd-miss-it, a female form flew diagonally downwards past the car, and onto the steps at the church's entrance. Luke replayed the video in slow-motion and it was clearer, if not clear. Sheila coming in to land. She'd been very care-less. Luke understood they could 'shield' themselves from human eyes, but not from CCTV.

He'd told his bewildered driver that it must be an error, a glitch with the camera and filed it away. Luke had been in Hebden Bridge for three years now, hiding these little tell-tale fragments. He had a whole folder for Niamh alone: she was careful, but did insist on using her garden for witchcraft.

The audience exploded, demanding the clip be replayed so they could see the witch in action again. Flight was on the long list of signs they were trained to look for, but to see it on video was porn every witchfinder could hate-wank at for years to come. They had it. *Proof.*

Today, he'd sifted through what evidence he had and made his terrible choice that afternoon. Who was the eldest? Who'd had a good life? Who was strong enough to take them on and win? It was playing god, and it made him squirm. He didn't know much about Sheila. She was a vicar; she was a lesbian. She had a wife, Joanne.

What have I done?

It was too late now. Couldn't get the genie back in the lamp.

There were more pictures of her to scroll through. Pictures with her LGBTQ youth group; pictures of her marching at Pride. A part of Luke had cynically known her being gay would rile up the WMC further, distract even more from Niamh.

Peter took over. 'Right, calm down! I know! It's great stuff. Sheila Henry is active in *women's groups* in the community. It's possible she could lead us to other hags in the area.' He now turned to his son. 'Luke? You gonna bring her in?'

He was being tested and he knew it, but that was a step too far. 'Why bother? Just because she's a witch doesn't mean she's doing any harm. Leave her be.'

The room exploded until his father held up an arm. 'Thou shalt not suffer a witch to live. Brainwashing them kids? No harm? You want yer head checkin', you do. You'll bring her in.'

'No. Sheila doesn't know me, why would she come with me?'

Peter rolled his eyes. 'Oh give over. As if I'd trust you anyways. I reckon Stevie's got it covered.'

A red-haired, sunburned man in the front row grinned. 'PC Steve Brent at your service.' Another man patted him on the back.

Suddenly Luke felt very sick. He could lie and tell himself someone would have caught Sheila out eventually, but he knew they were far more likely to catch Niamh at it.

'Ey, Jack,' Peter said. 'You've never seen a dunkin' have yer?'

'No, mate,' the teenager replied.

'Yer in for a treat.'

Luke felt like the whole sweaty basement was capsizing. He sat down, but the floor continued to lurch. Anticipation of what would follow rippled through the audience and everyone started talking over each other. It was like a kindergarten class had just been told they were going on a school trip. *When? Where? How would it happen? There hadn't been a dunking in years.*

Luke dared to look over his shoulder only to be greeted by an enormous photograph of a smiling Sheila in her dog collar. He didn't even see Peter hovering at his side. 'Luke, son, I want you to meet someone.' A short, stout man with thinning hair was at his father's side. 'This is Ralph Barber.'

'Hi.' Luke didn't recognise this man. They all looked alike; chinless and frustrated.

Peter looked to the newcomer. 'Well?'

Ralph squinted at Luke a moment. 'It's hard to say. You've trained him well.'

'The fuck is this?' Luke asked, straightening himself.

'Ralphie Boy is a warlock.' Peter clapped him on the shoulder. 'He can read minds and I'm very curious to know just how long you've been sitting on this video.'

'Are you fucking kidding me?' Luke immediately pulled up the walls in his head, the way he'd practised his whole life. He guessed if he'd kept *Niamh* out all these years, a male witch shouldn't be an issue.

'If I find out that you've been keeping things from me . . .' Peter hissed, leaning in so close Luke could smell the stout on his breath. 'I'll say this for hags; at least they have the right idea when someone betrays a coven . . .'

'Are you threatening me?'

'I am, yeah.' His dad tapped his cheek with his palm and skulked away.

Ralph lingered, shrugging his round shoulders. 'I don't get it,' Luke said. 'If you're one of them, why the fuck are you here?'

Ralph didn't flinch. 'I just really fucking hate those bitches.'

Kaur, Sandhya

To me; Matas, Veronika

Hello Niamh

Just wanted to introduce you to Veronika from the events team. Do you have any ideas what you'd like to wear? Westwood have offered – they designed a gown for Helena, and make the HMRC capes. Do let Veronika know if you have any strong feelings, and let her know your dress/shoe size.

Best
Sandhya
Assistant to the High Priestess [she/her]

Kelly, Niamh

To Kaur, Sandhya; Matas, Veronika

Hiya

I'm easy. Some Stevie Nicks looking wafty witchy stuff? I'm a 10 dress, 7 shoe.

Ta xxx

HEBDEN BRIDGE GIRLIES

Niamh, Helena, Leonie, you

Leonie Jackman
Sorry I've been AWOL. Still in
Turkey. Think I'm on the right track.

Niamh Kelly
But you're OK?

Leonie Jackman
Yep. Getting closer to Hale.

Niamh Kelly
Really?

Leonie Jackman
Yeah.

For Gaia's sake BE CAREFUL.

Niamh Kelly
Elle! You're alive! I was about to
send a search party!

I'm sorry. I'm finding things hard.

Leonie Jackman
What's going on? Did I miss something?

Chapter Thirty-Five

BREADCRUMBS

Leonie – Ankara, Turkey

Jez had left Elle. Fuck. She wondered if her threat to him at the last solstice had hit home. Well good. Elle would hurt for now but at least that absolute turd of a human was flushed out of her life. She hadn't put that sentiment in the group chat.

At sundown, Zehra Darga and her crew left the dig site. The students piled into a University of Ankara minibus, while Darga had her own filthy jeep. She left alone, leaving clouds of sand and dust in her wake.

'Can we get some food now?' whined Senait. 'I really fancy a kebab or summat.'

'Oh my goddess, soon!' Leonie had never known anything like it. She thought *she* was bad.

Leonie and Senait watched discreetly from a shallow cave in the rocky hillside. As the sun melted behind the mountains, the sky turned almost neon pink, with flashes of Malibu orange. If only they could have stayed to watch the light show conclude. Instead, the witches took flight, following the archaeologist towards the city.

Zehra's car drove into the capital, itself quite stunning by night. In the centre of the citadel, the minarets and dome of the Kocatepe mosque were illuminated, while the proud fortress castle looked down on the city from high on the hillside. Yet, far below, the car continued out of town, away from the hubbub of the street cafés and markets.

Leonie was growing tired. Keeping herself and Senait above the car and shielded was exhausting work, and her shoulder was still fucked from Italy. She'd need to land soon.

The jeep slowed as it entered what seemed to be the slums on the outskirts of Ankara. It looked like a shanty town, at stark odds with the handsome city to the south. Ramshackle houses, some little more than shacks, leaned perilously against the dusty hillside below the fort. Was this where the professor lived? If she was visiting from Oxford University, that didn't fit. They'd have her staying somewhere three-star at least, right?

I need to go down, Leonie told Senait. She brought them to an unsteady landing on an empty strip of narrow road.

'I can help,' Senait said, and a thick sandstorm whirled in. Soon the street was half-hidden by dust. Aside from a couple of skinny cats weaving between the bins, there wasn't anyone around to see them.

This way. Leonie turned the corner just in time to see Zehra step out of the jeep. Swinging her rucksack onto her shoulder, she jogged over the road, and ducked down a narrow alleyway between the shacks. *Follow her.*

Keeping them shielded, Leonie and Senait followed her down a rat-run of alleys, worn stone stairwells and snickets. The professor seemed wary, checking over her shoulder as if to ensure she wasn't being followed. Eventually, in the middle of the rickety labyrinth, she came to a stop outside a crumbling home. It looked derelict, but then so did a lot of these streets. Zehra took a final, cautious, look around and slipped down some basement stairs.

'The fuck's she doing?' Senait asked.

I told you she was up to something, Leonie told her directly.

'Are we safe?'

I don't know. Be ready.

Leonie missed Chinara so hard. She took for granted how safe she felt around her. If she were here, she wouldn't be feeling so . . . well, fucking terrified. *Come on*, she said, hoping she sounded brave.

She led the way. At the bottom of the stairs, she found a metal grille covering a rotten door. It was locked from within. Leonie planted her feet, raised her hands, and telekinetically ripped them off their hinges. *Ready?* Behind her, Senait conjured a ball of fire in her palm to light the way, and Leonie entered.

It was a cellar, dank and dark. Gods, it looked like a fucking Prodigy video down here. The plaster was peeling from the rust-stained walls and it reeked of mildew. This was exactly the bit in the horror movie where she'd scream at the dumb bint to get the fuck out.

It was empty. A rotten door was propped against the frame at the far side of the room, but that only led upstairs to the rest of the ruined house. 'Where'd she go?' Senait asked, her face glowing amber in the light of her flame.

There was nowhere for her to hide. She listened for footsteps overhead, but all was silent. 'What the fuck?' Leonie said aloud.

'Did she teleport?'

Leonie took a deep sniff but smelled only damp. Teleportation usually left a slight sulphur odour. She did, however, sense magic, a little like sentience . . . but different. She'd felt it before, it was familiar. It was on the tip of her tongue . . .

And then, in the centre of the cellar, she saw the puddle. It looked innocent enough – basements flood all the time, but the weather was bone dry. *That* was what it reminded her of – Annie Device's well. 'It's a water conduit . . .' she said to no one in particular.

'What?'

'The puddle. It's . . . not a puddle. It's a tunnel.'

'To where?'

Leonie shrugged. 'Only one way to find out.'

She took a step towards the water. 'Wait!' Senait said. 'Are you high? That could go anywhere.'

In Senait's mind, Leonie saw a flash of Hale at Domino's club; his wolfish smile. But that didn't connect. 'Zehra's a witch. I sensed some power in her. I trust her. I think.' Senait didn't look convinced. 'Stay here. If I'm not back in a couple of minutes, come after me, ready to fight. OK?'

Senait nodded, her big eyes like pools in the scant light.

It had been over a decade since she'd been through a water conduit, and she hadn't especially liked it then. Leonie held her breath and stepped into the puddle.

She plummeted. As soon as her head went under, she was submerged in total blackness, although it wasn't as cold as she'd feared. She felt the fluid whoosh around her, just for a moment, and then there was light.

She gasped for air and opened her eyes. She was on the other side of the conduit, wherever that was, kneeling in a shallow fountain. Quickly taking in her surroundings, she saw a beautiful moonlit courtyard, the fountain at its centre.

And then she saw she was surrounded. Women, and women with power at that. Stern faces glared down at her. Instinctively, Leonie held up her hands in surrender. She couldn't fight numbers like this, nor did she want to. She slowly climbed to her feet, the water in the pool coming up to her calves. 'I'm sorry! I'm sorry! I don't want trouble.'

No one said anything, until: 'We knew you would come. It was foreseen.' The crowd parted, and an elderly woman, the most powerful witch Leonie had ever felt, stepped forward. Leonie was almost bowled off her feet, the air around this woman seemed to shimmer like heat haze. An apricot scarf was draped loose over her head, silver hair cascading well past her waist. A sleek lioness trotted obediently at her heels, and Leonie took a step backwards because it was a fucking lion.

'Where am I?' Leonie said, although she somehow knew the answer before the reply came.

'My child,' said the woman, her ocean-blue eyes twinkling. 'Welcome to Aeaea.'

Chapter Thirty-Six

THE ISLAND OF THE WITCHES

Leonie – Aeaea, somewhere in the Mediterranean Sea

Leonie waited for the punchline. 'Are you for real?'

The priestess surveyed her coolly. Yes, she was definitely for real. The old woman was barefoot, her dress a simple white linen, but her wrists and neck laden with colourful charms and bangles and chains and beads.

'Aeaea,' Leonie *butchered* the pronunciation, 'is a *myth*. Everyone knows that.'

Zehra Darga sidled up alongside the priestess, towelling off her hair. 'As the expert, I beg to differ.' She spoke into her leader's ear. 'She followed me here.'

'I, um, mean you no harm,' Leonie said, because that's what you say in situations like this if films are to be believed. 'I'm sorry,' Leonie admitted, not least because there were some powerful witches on the courtyard. 'But there's a powerful warlock out there and he came to your dig site. He wants—'

'My child, we know what he wants,' the priestess said gravely. She held out a slender hand to help Leonie out of the pond. 'Come get dry. My name is Calista, I am the Custodian of Aeaea. We have much to discuss.'

'No kidding.' Again, the witch was not kidding.

The air was hot, not humid, and a salt kiss of a breeze swept in from the sea. The sun was almost set. Crickets chirruped in the shrubs that spilled onto the higgledy paths, and cicadas hissed. In very different circumstances, Leonie would have assumed she was on holiday. It was hard not to crave a shot of ouzo and some tapas.

Senait walked alongside her. She'd fetched her through the water conduit when she'd established the coast was clear, and both had been taken to a small hillside villa and given towels and dry clothes – linen dresses not unlike their hosts.

Now, with Calista, Zehra and the terrifying pet cat leading the way, they were given a guided tour of a place Leonie had thought a fairy tale: the fabled island of witches.

'Is this it?' Leonie whispered to Senait. 'Is this the place you saw in your dreams?'

Senait looked spellbound. 'I don't know. How . . . just *how*?'

The *power* in that water conduit was unlike anything Leonie had ever experienced. If this truly was Aeaea, it had carried them hundreds of miles.

From the fountain, they were steered off the courtyard and up well-worn stone steps to the temple, if that was the right word. It was dilapidated but dignified, once palatial: vine-strangled columns held the roof aloft, while the floors were dusty marble. The temple was crumbling, ancient, with deep cracks chasing across the walls and flagstones. Torches, candles, and lamps lit the concourse; Leonie saw no evidence of electricity.

Once inside, there were further noble columns, and an intricately tiled floor, but Leonie's eyes were drawn first to the paintings that filled every inch of the walls: women, witches. The friezes depicted what could only be witches; the way they harnessed the weather; communed with plants and animals; healed the sick. Leonie saw a picture of two women holding a baby and smiled. The representation the ancient Greeks needed.

'This is so sick,' Senait breathed in awe.

At the centre of the main hall, there was a long table where most of the island's inhabitants were now drinking wine, eating, chatting. A diverse group of women, all ages, all races. Leonie didn't sense malice in these witches, more wariness. Perhaps they were right to be wary. They had invaded a sanctuary, uninvited.

Leonie sped up to catch Calista. She was old, but the woman could move. 'I'm sorry, I'm gonna need a second, this is a fucking trip. Sorry about my language.' She clamped a hand over her mouth. This didn't feel like a place she could be herself. The closest thing she was ever going to get to church. 'Where are we, *really*?'

Zehra opened an intricately painted door that led to a dark passageway. In the torchlight, Leonie made out winding stone stairs, heading downwards into the bowels of the mountain. Zehra lingered at the top of the steps. She and Calista seemed to speak psychically, but kept Leonie out. She guessed, knowing women and witches, they were deciding if they could trust her. 'Come with us,' Zehra said finally, and started down the stairs.

'Aeaea is real,' Calista said as she descended the spiralling stairs, lightly using the damp walls to support herself. 'It always has been.'

'Where is it?' Senait added.

'That shall remain secret. The island doesn't want to be found.'

Now Leonie looked to Senait, eyes alight in the torch flame. 'What about Circe . . . ? Does that mean she's real?'

Calista smiled, deep lines creasing her face. 'Women have been custodians of the island for untold generations. One guardian passes the secrets to the next when she dies, but one thing never changes. For however long there are witches, and however long there are *women*, we will need this place. For protection.'

'From men,' Senait said.

Calista tutted. 'Men are not a monolith, child, remember this.'

'Hashtag not all men,' added Leonie quietly.

'The great lie of Belial,' Calista said. 'That men deserve the world, and women deserve men. It is up to the fathers to decide whether they share the lie, and the sons to decide if they believe it.'

'But yes,' Zehra said. 'Women have a natural predator, and it is man.'

'So Aeaea is like a women's refuge?' Leonie said. 'For witches?'

'When a witch needs Aeaea, she is here for them, and so am I,' Calista said. 'Always, until my last breath. I came here as a lost soul many decades ago . . . and remained, taking the mantle of guardian when our beloved sister Gia passed. When I die, it will be someone else's turn, and someone else's after that.'

'The island finds you,' Zehra told them, the stairs winding down and down. 'When I first came to England in '94, I met a charming young man who turned out to be far from charming. Do you know I almost gave it all up; my dreams, my ambitions, to suit him?' Leonie listened, rapt. 'One night, when things were at their worst, I drove to the coast, to Beachy Head, and I thought about ending things, I did. Only then I heard a voice, the voice of the *island*, in my head I somehow knew the way out, and the way here. The island found me, and tonight, she found you two.'

'I have seen this place,' Senait said. 'In my dreams.'

Leonie took her hand and gave it a squeeze. Just maybe Senait was a homing pigeon who'd found her way home at last.

Growing dizzier with every turn, Leonie lost count of how many stairs they went down. They must be deep inside the hills by now. She was reminded of the cavernous musk of the ruins in Ankara. Eventually they came to a stop outside a circular stone door, like the entrance to a vault. Zehra passed her flaming torch over the Hellenic script carved in its surface.

'I show you this because I feel I must,' Calista said, her voice echoing. 'The oracles said you would come, and that it was part of how things must be, but I offer you a choice, Leonie. You can turn away, and leave this fight to us.'

Leonie didn't hesitate. 'No. Dabney Hale is a threat to all of us.' She chose her next words carefully, mindful of how long she'd hesitated before taking action against Helena. 'This isn't your fight or mine, it's *ours*.'

Calista bowed her head slightly. 'Very well, then enter.'

The witch slid her right hand into a shallow bronze dish. The oily fluid it held glowed from within, jade, then magenta, and violet. The stone door rolled aside with a gravelly rumble. Leonie gasped when she saw what was held inside.

It made sense when you thought about it. A crown, at the end of the day, is a very large ring. Still, Leonie had thought it would be grander. As it was, it was a simple band of dull, ancient gold, inscribed with intricate symbols all the way around. 'That's the Seal of Solomon?'

'We believe so,' Calista told her, and Leonie entered the vault to get a closer look.

It wasn't a vault; it was a shrine. The crown sat atop a statue not dissimilar to the one in Zehra's crypt. Another naked woman, but this one was newer, carved out of marble, instead of legs, her lower half was that of a snake. She rose up off her coiled tail, like a cobra.

It was interesting comparing their Queen of Sheba, to Eve, to Lilith, and how these motifs repeat throughout history. The woman, and her serpent.

Leonie had always been taught of, and had dreamed many times, the mysterious snake woman – Gaia in her earthly form – who had risen from a desert lake and bestowed magic on the first witches. This statue was the feminine divine she'd always imagined. Maybe it was tiredness, but Leonie was oddly moved. She swore that, just for a second, she felt something holy, Gaia, in her heart. A tear ran down her face and she brushed it aside with the back of her hand.

Almost amber in the low torchlight, the statue loomed over them, wearing the Seal on her head. Her expression was impassive. 'We unearthed it about four months ago,' said Zehra, gazing adoringly up at the artefact. There was a note of resignation to her voice. 'It's timeless, pristine. It's the archaeological find of the century – of any century – but the coven has to come before my ego. It will be safe here.'

'What does it do?' Senait asked.

'I have never worn it,' Calista admitted. 'None of us dare. Scripture tells of immense power; total dominion over demonkind. In turn, this grants the wearer limitless power. The sort of power no witch – or warlock – should ever possess.'

'Why?' Leonie asked. 'The right witch could—'

'Could what?' Calista seemed to peer directly into Leonie's soul. 'End suffering? Prevent war? Admirable aims, yes. But how will you do that? You are saying this witch would impose her design over the entire world. Remove free will entirely? Why not kill all menfolk, do us all a mercy? No. Who is to say what is the *right witch*? One person's right is another's wrong. Absolute certainty is the language of fools, and the demagogues who exploit those fools. We are women. We are fallible, all, and welcome of it.'

Shamed, and corrected, Leonie nodded.

'The Hale man is powerful,' Zehra admitted. 'He came to the dig. I think I was able to keep him out of my head. At least, I hope so.' Well, she'd fooled Leonie, so she must be more powerful than she seemed.

'We move the water conduit around the city to protect ourselves,' Calista added. 'Though we remain on alert.'

'You're right to be,' Leonie said. 'Dabney Hale is one of those despots you mentioned. He wants the Seal, and he's *definitely* the wrong sort.'

'Can you stop him?' Zehra asked. 'Is your coven with you?'

Leonie assumed she referred to HMRC, and that was complicated. She didn't want to admit she wasn't officially here at their behest. 'I'm gonna try. I'm gonna find him, and stop him. I'm thinking at this stage I might have to kill him.'

'And would you do that?' said Calista sombrely.

Leonie felt slightly drunk at the prospect, not in the

good way. The hangover of remorse. She'd killed people during the war: two rebel warlocks. Jason Ellis and Carlo D'Agostino. She had severed them, snuffed out their consciousness before they could kill her. She hadn't wanted to, but nor – in the fire of the moment – had she hesitated. It had been them or her, and she rated herself. Didn't mean she'd got used to it. 'We tried containing him. Clearly that wasn't enough.'

Calista took her hands in her own warm palms. 'If you help us to protect this seal, then you are a sister of ours.'

'I promise. He's not getting this crown.'

Calista smiled for the first time. 'Thank you, child.'

'You said you have oracles here?' Leonie asked. 'Can you see my brother?'

Her smile faltered, and she started out of the altar room. 'You must be hungry. You've travelled far. Come, let us eat.'

With the Seal of Solomon safely in its vault, Calista led them upstairs to the temple. It was a mindfuck. Women – dressed in modern clothes – chilling like the ancient Greeks. A freckled redhead played Joni Mitchell on an acoustic guitar while her audience sang along, or drank wine. A couple of kids ran around the fountain courtyard, playing with some (regular cat) kittens.

Leonie liked it here. Who wouldn't? It was female nirvana, Shangri-la, Eden. For the first time in days, weeks, she felt her spine and shoulders unclick. She exhaled, realising just how much she'd been holding in.

Would she want to live here? A world without men? No. She liked a lot of men. Cis men, trans men. Calista was right, good men are, well, good. Good men like Rad. Radley was many things; a fusspot, a stickler, yes, but he was fundamentally a *good* man. Even here, in paradise, Leonie couldn't relax. Not right now.

'This way.' Calista led them down a lamplit clifftop path, away from the temple. They came eventually to a paved terrace, an olive grove with sweeping views of the ocean. The moon rippled on the black sea and there was nothing on the horizon, aside from a lonely lighthouse at the tip of a peninsula. As its pale light swept over the waters, Leonie wondered if it was *more* than a lighthouse, somehow working to keep Aeaea cut off from the rest of the world. Further up the hill, gay music and laughter drifted down from the sanctuary.

A table was set for them with wine and meze. Everything looked, and smelled, divine, and Leonie found she was ravenous. Calista beckoned them to sit, and she tucked into some hummus, tearing at a flatbread with vigour. Senait, not at all herself, timidly picked at some olives and fried calamari. 'Are you OK?' Leonie asked her.

Senait nodded. 'Peachy keen, jelly bean. I'm just knackered, man.'

'Do you think this is the place you saw?' She turned to the others. 'Senait thinks she saw Aeaea in her dreams.'

'Maybe she sang to you the same way she sang to me?' Zehra said, dipping into what looked like taramasalata. 'What are you running from?'

There was a brief, tense silence and Calista seemed to consider Senait closely. 'I think I was meant to come here,' she said, half hiding behind a little tumbler of white wine.

'I think so too,' Calista said knowingly as she scratched the lioness – Nyssa, she was called – behind the ears. 'Gaia. Gaia sees the saga in its fullness. She doesn't make mistakes.'

Leonie observed the older woman observe Senait. Calista was an adept, maybe even a Level 7. Chinara was a 6 – the only 6, besides herself, she'd met in real life. Sitting next to Calista here, Leonie almost felt the urge to move away, like her radiance needed a seat of its own at the table.

Now they'd stopped a minute, Leonie felt a mass of tiredness almost crushing her to the chair. She honestly wasn't sure how she'd found the energy to make it this far. But it was like if she admitted tiredness, her entire being would unravel and she'd weep for two weeks straight. She would keep thundering on, powered by hatred for Hale and love for Radley.

'What do you know about my brother? Please?' Her voice tremored a little on the last beg-word, and she took a deep breath in through her nose.

Calista took a sip of wine before beginning. 'He is alive.'

'He too came to the dig,' Zehra added.

Leonie tasted more sweet hope than she had since she left London. 'Really?'

'Yes. He also sought Hale.'

'Did he find him?'

'I know not,' said Calista. 'Though now he is somewhere cold. I see him. Somewhere white with snow . . .'

So, she must have the power of sight. 'Do you know where?' Calista shook her head. 'Is he at least safe?'

'I'm afraid I have no further answers. Sadly, the magic that keeps others out of Aeaea keeps me in. My sight only reaches so far. I am healer first, seer second.'

Leonie felt the hope drain as soon as it had returned. *Where are you, Rad?* She cast the thought over the shifting satin of the sea. She returned to her meze, half-heartedly dipping the flatbread into some baba ghanoush.

'You were familiar to us, you know, even before Calista saw you,' Zehra told her, reaching past her for some halloumi. 'You're *famous*,' she added with a cute smirk.

That went some way to wake Leonie up. 'What? No! Really?'

Zehra eyed her. 'Everyone has heard of HMRC. The largest coven in the world. And you broke away to start your own. Impressive.'

'Impressive or crazy,' she replied.

Calista leaned closer. 'You are a phenomenal witch. You will change the future, Leonie.'

Leonie raised a brow. 'Is that official?'

'I have no doubt,' the witch said.

Calista reached for her hand, and Leonie took it. She felt her shoulder glow warm within, the older woman healing her wounds. 'I dunno. I just figure if I lay the foundations now, things might be better for the next generation. I owe it to the Black witches that came before me, too. It's my turn, and I just hope someday soon, it doesn't feel like a fight any more. You know what I mean?'

'Quite. We share that vision, you and I.'

That assumed there would be a next generation. With each creaking turn of the Earth, that seemed ever less certain. War, disease, climate change; and that was just the mundane stuff without adding demonic prophecy to the mix. And Leonie thought about Chinara again. Their conversations about starting a family, and how that'd fallen by the wayside as soon as Radley went after Hale.

'How is that?' Calista asked, letting go of her hand.

Leonie rotated her shoulder backwards and forwards. 'All good! Thank you.'

'I'm afraid, with that, I must ask you to excuse me. I am an old woman and I grow tired,' Calista said. 'I sense I am not the only one. Senait, child, will you walk me to the villa?'

A little puzzled, Senait dabbed her mouth with a napkin. 'Of course.'

'I wish to talk with you. About your future, and the island.'

Leonie caught Senait's hand as she stood. 'Are you OK? Do you want me to come too?'

'No,' she said quickly. 'It's fine. I'm good.' Calista waited for Senait to link arms with her. Senait looked back at her. 'Hey, Leonie? Thanks. You know, for everything.'

Leonie nodded. Calista then said, 'I will see you with the dawn. I trust Zehra will keep you entertained.'

'I shall do my very best.' Zehra stroked her hand a moment too long. Leonie read her intent loud and clear.

The flirtation wasn't a big deal. The very first time Leonie and Chinara had slept together, it had been established during the charged all-nighter that monogamy didn't work for either of them. What a fucking night: it had been them, a picnic blanket, and a sultry July night in the sand dunes of Aberffraw, on Anglesey, in the middle of the war. Between orgasms, they'd talked and talked until the sun came up out of the Irish Sea.

By demolishing those strict rules, any notion that they *owned* or *policed* one another's appetites, they'd mostly found contentment as a happy twosome. Leonie liked the occasional night at a kink club, whereas Chinara found them cringe. They sometimes had threesomes – or more-somes – though their rules of non-monogamy (no one in their home; no overnighters; no mutual friends; no one either of them veto) sometimes felt as much of a hassle as monogamy.

Leonie knew Chinara had a lover in Lagos, although she hadn't seen her in years, and Leonie mostly just enjoyed having the option to make out with a hot girl in a club if she met one. Goddess, she certainly didn't have the capacity – mentally or practically – for *dating* multiple women. Absolutely not; that was a lot of hormones to manage. And think of the WhatsApp admin. Think of the *cost*; dating is *expensive*.

But sex is not sensible, or rational. Sex is a magical thing; libido a force unlike anything else. Right now, Leonie felt the familiar cerise energy building in Zehra. She sensed it *strongly*. It was up to her now to respond to it or not.

Zehra shuffled closer. 'Am I being too much?'

Leonie smiled. Zehra *was* a sentient. 'Not at all.'

'You have an open relationship?'

'I do.'

Zehra nudged in a little closer until they were almost nose-to-nose. When Leonie didn't pull away, Zehra kissed her. Her lips were warm, soft and full. Leonie kissed her back and it *was* lovely, but . . .

'My gosh, your head is so full,' Zehra said, smiling.

'I'm sorry,' Leonie said. 'It's not you—'

Now Zehra laughed, a gorgeous throaty laugh. Suddenly, more than a fuck, Leonie craved a cigarette. Of course, Zehra heard this desire, and reached into her handbag. 'Here.' Leonie took a Marlboro, and Zehra lit it for her. She took the deepest drag of her life. 'Yep, that hits the spot.'

Zehra laughed, and lit her own. 'Tell me about this magnificent woman I see in your mind.'

'My girlfriend, in London.'

'And?'

'Her name is Chinara,' Leonie said, and unexpected tears ran from her eyes. You know when it all creeps up on you? A sob broke her throat. She looked up, and saw constellations glitter above them. It was so beautiful, but, without Chi, it was just white dots in the sky.

Zehra shushed her. 'She sees the same stars, the same moon. She cannot be so far away under the same sky now, can she?' Zehra took her hand, sisterly this time. 'You love this woman.'

Leonie sniffed, and wiped the tears from her cheeks. 'More than anything,' she said. 'She is my strength. Everything I do is for her. She is my first, and last, thought. Every day. I don't deserve her. I don't.'

'I do not believe that,' said Zehra softly. 'You are full of love, and you love *hard*. I'm not sure I've ever been loved so hard. I hope one day I feel it.' Zehra kissed her one last time, a chaste goodbye. 'Sister, you are loved.'

Leonie rested her head on Zehra's shoulder, and the witch stroked her hair until she fell asleep in her arms.

Chapter Thirty-Seven

KURT AND COURTNEY, NIAMH AND CONRAD

Ciara – Hebden Bridge, UK

Ciara was in the bath. Her phone was perched on the wooden shelf thing, on speakerphone to Elle. 'I wanted to check on you after what you said in the chat. Are you OK, darl?'

She swore she heard Elle shrug at the other end of the line. 'Not really.'

It wasn't like Elle to be so closed. This would have been easier if she could read her in person. Perhaps she should go over. 'Why didn't you say something? I could have . . . well, not cooked but I could have carried the takeaway. I could have brought you a Müller Rice.'

Elle managed a tiny chuckle.

'It's custard flavour too.'

'Thank you,' Elle said. 'Sorry I've been AWOL. You've been so busy.'

That sounded like a fib. 'Ellie?'

There was a significant pause. 'Niamh, I feel like I'm dying.'

And Ciara got it. To Elle, it really must feel like the end of the world, a wound she wouldn't heal from. Because she'd been a kid when she got together with Jez, she hadn't spent her twenties getting dumped every six months and developing that tough, calloused hide. She didn't have experience in stitching up a broken heart. Selfishly, Ciara wondered if this was what it felt like when she and Jude split – assuming they had. 'What can I do? Do you wanna . . . like hang out?' That felt like a thing Niamh would do.

'Nothing. I'm exhausted, I'm upset, I just want to be by myself. I'd be terrible company.'

This wasn't the Elle she used to know. Always the last two awake at the sleepover. She fed off gossip like a hummingbird. 'OK. But will you call me tomorrow? I'm worried about you, girl.'

Elle assured her she would, and hung up.

The water was getting tepid, but Ciara wasn't ready for bed. She topped up the bath and added a little lavender oil.

Steam swirled around the bathroom. She liked the water almost too hot to stand. From downstairs, she'd brought a small chunk of diaspore gemstone. It sat expectantly on the bath shelf next to her phone. Ciara inhaled through her nostrils.

She wasn't sure what to think. Her meditations were disturbing her more than she'd like to admit, but it was interesting, almost academically, that memories supposedly 'destroyed' were coming back to her. As she understood it, to be severed meant you were permanently disconnected from your own consciousness, never to retain it. Now it seemed as though the leaves had fallen from the tree, but they were still there, inside her, waiting to be collected.

It raised questions about self, about memory, about her

soul. And all those things are bigger than us, Gaia-size concerns. And that made them scary.

Still, Ciara never had scared easy. They were her memories – at least she hoped they were – and she wanted them, even if they were smashed fragments. She remembered Helena once wittering on about kintsugi – the Japanese art of glorifying cracks and mends in gold lacquer. Taking broken items, and actually celebrating the damage. The lies people are willing to tell themselves when their pottery is fucked.

She focused on the diaspore. The stone was clear, palest green. She stared to its core. The washed-out hue reminded her of apples, springtime. Linen on the line. Lime cordial and freshly mown grass and . . .

The curtains of the house in Claypath. Her second-year house. It was always cold, always. There was a mottled, black damp patch above the window in the shape of a cat's head.

She and Jude were naked in bed, legs knotted, listening to Nirvana. Heart-Shaped Box.

'You know,' Jude said as she lay with her head on his chest, 'everyone says that Kurt wrote a bunch of Hole songs, but it's highly likely that Courtney wrote with Kurt on Nirvana shit too.'

'Of course they say that,' Ciara added, still euphoric in her post-orgasmic state. 'She's a woman. How could she possibly have a single lyric in her kitten-filled mind?'

'I bet she's a witch.'

'You think?'

'I bet he was too,' he said. 'They have that energy. The way they were obsessed with each other. The way they were inevitable.'

Six months ago, Ciara would have balked at that, but she'd gulped down the Kool-Aid of late. Jude was her world, and she knew that was fucked, and she didn't care one bit. In fact, she positively wallowed in the infatuation of it all. She used his toothbrush; she ate his spunk; she wouldn't sleep without him and, best of all, he felt the same. She ran her fingers along the muscular groove that ran over his hip and into his groin. 'Do you think we're inevitable?'

'Yes,' he said without hesitation. 'I always wondered why and now I know. I know why I'm a warlock when neither of my parents are. I know why I changed my mind about Durham at the last minute. I know why I wake up in the morning. It was you. Gaia knew.'

'She's good like that,' Ciara mused.

'I feel powerful with you. I never felt it before.'

'Me too,' she said quietly. Finally, finally someone that was hers and hers alone. He'd never met Niamh, she was away in Dublin, and didn't seem to care to. It was just the two of them. Here, like it had got off the train at Durham station, was her future. Everything suddenly made sense.

He freed himself and reached for a cigarette. 'Are we gonna go to Dab's thing?'

Ciara sighed. 'That would mean leaving this duvet.'

'You make a compelling argument.' He lit the cigarette. Ciara didn't smoke but she loved that he did. He tasted of them. 'You think he can do it though?'

She rolled onto her back. 'Invoke Astaroth? No! Dabney couldn't invoke a parking ticket.'

'He did,' Jude said softly, like he shouldn't be telling her that.

'What?'

'I saw him.'

'He invoked Astaroth?'

'No! Some lower demon. Nameless.' Jude paused to take another drag. She liked the way his lips stuck to the tip of the cigarette with a tiny pop. 'Still pretty cool though.'

Ciara propped herself up onto her elbow. 'What happened?'

'He spoke in some language none of us recognised. Some sort of demoniac tongue.'

'He could have faked it!' Ciara duly made a weird gurgling sound. 'That was demoniac for "pass me that water".'

Jude laughed, and passed her the glass from the bedside table. 'I believed it. There was this weird smell – eggy – and his eyes turned black. It wasn't like he was speaking; it was like something was speaking from within him. It was fucked up. But cool.'

'How, though?'

Jude climbed out of bed and fetched his rucksack. 'Book learning . . .'

'Latest Dan Brown?' He handed her a slender notebook. It was icy cold to touch, clothbound. She flicked it open to the title page. 'The Song of Osiris. What is it? It's empty.'

He shook his head. 'Not if you know how to awaken it.'

Ciara stroked the creamy pages and felt a shiver run up and down her spine. What did it have to say? She wanted to know. 'So what? You use this to summon the demons?'

He shook his head again. 'That's the maddest thing,' he said. 'I always thought witches had to go looking for *demons . . .' He crossed her bedroom to the narrow window. 'When, in fact, demons come for us . . .'*

With a pale hand, he drew aside the curtain. Ciara gasped and pulled the duvet over her breasts. The thin window was crawling with dozens of fat, furry moths, their white wings beating urgently against the glass, little legs looking for a way in . . .

Ciara sat up in the bathtub, realising too late that she'd slipped under the surface. She gasped for air, pushed matted hair off her face. 'Kiki?' her sister called from outside the bathroom. 'Are you all right in there?'

That voice. *Her* voice. No one else in this whole world called her that. Ciara was winded.

This wasn't real. It couldn't be.

But it felt real, realer than a memory. The soapy water around her was now lukewarm. She could *smell* the pomegranate and patchouli bath oil. 'What's happening?' she muttered.

'I've made tea when you're ready,' Niamh called.

Ciara looked for the chunk of diaspore, but she wasn't in the present. She was still somewhere in her past, with no clue how to find her way out. It was horribly like being in the sickbed at the safehouse, that sense of being hermetically sealed inside her broken body.

She climbed out of the bath and wrapped a towel around her. She looked in the mirror and very nearly gasped a second time. She looked *horrific*. Her skin was sallow and covered in red pimples. Her eyes were sunken and there was a scabby sore on her lower lip. She was thin too, thinner than she ever remembered being.

She tried to place herself into her own history. She was at the cottage, but an adult. That meant it was somewhen between leaving for Durham and, well, now. Had she returned at some point? She had no memory of that.

On autopilot, she crossed the landing into their old bedroom, where there were still the narrow twin beds for twins. The walls were still covered with posters of the Manics, Garbage, Linkin Park, and the last Spiceworld one that Niamh had insisted they keep up for old times' sake. Ciara had coloured all their eyes in with a black marker pen and crossed traitor Geri's face out.

She dried off, changed into a terrycloth robe, and headed downstairs to the warmth of the lounge. A fire crackled in the wood burner. Niamh carried a tea tray through from the kitchen to where a gorgeous man was already seated on the sofa, wearing jeans and a muscle-hugging teal sweater. How had she forgotten how fit he was?

Conrad.

He smiled kindly, and dimples appeared in his cheeks. He moved over to make room for her. 'Feeling better?'

'Yes,' she said, the scene progressing quite out of her control. She was passive in all this. She wanted to wake up but found she couldn't snap herself out of it. Every ounce of her wanted to retreat.

Niamh was so infuriatingly beautiful, even in sweats, her mane of hair glossier than an Irish Setter in a Pedigree Chum advert. She handed her a steaming mug. 'Drink this.'

'What is it?'

'*Vivica* tea. It stinks, but, you know, it helps.'

Ciara dimly recalled being forced to drink it by their mother when they were sick. A cure-all worse than any cough medicine. Nettle and turmeric amongst other things.

'She once tried to make me drink it,' Conrad grinned. 'Vile stuff.'

'It really works!' Niamh protested.

'Sure.' He gave Ciara a wink.

She could not have felt more like a third wheel. 'Thank you for letting me crash,' Ciara said, blowing on the cup to cool the concoction.

Niamh looked puzzled. 'Don't be an eejit, it's your home too. Nana left it to us both.'

Ciara felt that wasn't entirely out of choice.

'You can stay as long as you want,' Conrad added.

She took a sip of the *Vivica* and fought not to gag. It tasted of the smell of garden compost. Niamh leaned in closer and tucked her hair behind Ciara's ear. 'What happened with the guy? Jude, was it? You seemed so happy? Do you wanna talk about it?'

Ciara couldn't bring herself to say it, not that there was much to tell. 'He's gone.' One day he was there, and the next he wasn't. No calls, no texts, no nothing. She'd actually been sleeping with Dab for the past few months. Rebounding. The sex was wild, but she often muted him by making herself temporarily deaf. A sure sign, she felt, that she needed help. There's a certain allure to scraping below the bottom of the barrel, caking dirt under your nails. How low can you go?

'I've, um, been seeing Dab.' Ciara heard herself say.

'Dabney Hale?' Niamh winced. 'Isn't he trying to start a cult of warlocks?'

Ciara didn't have the strength to explain, so she simply shrugged. Conrad didn't have to be a sentient to read Niamh. 'I'll leave you ladies to it,' he said, heading upstairs to give them privacy.

Niamh took her spare hand. 'Ciara, what's going on? Please tell me. You look awful. Is it drugs?'

Ciara laughed bitterly. 'I wish! At least they have clinics for that.'

'Whatever it is, HMRC can help.'

She laughed again. Could her sister possibly be so naïve? For witches they were so fucking puritanical. The things she'd seen, the things she'd done, while possessed – and those were just the things she was cognisant of. The coven wouldn't look kindly on her actions. The remorse manifest physically, twisting her spine. It had to stop.

Niamh's phone rang. She turned it over and looked at the screen. 'Fuck, I need to get this, I'm on call.'

Her twin took the call and Ciara worked on keeping the tea down. It took a surprising amount of effort, like each sip was batted right out of her stomach.

'Shit,' Niamh said. 'My partner is out of town and there's an emergency – a Dachshund got into a stash of chocolates.'

'It's fine. Go. The sausage dog needs you more than I do.'

'Will you be OK?'

Ciara assured her she would be. Niamh gathered everything she needed and headed for the surgery.

She'd got this far. That in itself was a miracle. Until that morning, when she'd fled, she'd been living in one of Dabney's family homes in Oxfordshire. The mansion had become his base, sort of a commune for disenfranchised witches and warlocks. The demons, the orgies, the blood. So much blood. The whole house was soaked with blood; the bodies buried in the expansive grounds, under the rose beds.

Her spine twisted again.

She should have burned it down. She should have killed him.

Suddenly feeling acutely sick, Ciara raced upstairs and hunched over the loo. Burning up, she pressed her cheek to the rim of the toilet bowl, letting it cool her skin. She was overcome with sleepiness and wondered if she could sleep right here.

'You OK?' Conrad asked softly. He filled the bathroom doorframe.

'Not really,' Ciara said, forcing herself to sit up. 'Does she hate me?'

Conrad didn't need to ask who. 'You're the mind reader, not me,' he said with a grin.

She managed a meek smile. For a mundane to joke about witchcraft with such ease was rare indeed. Where on earth had Niamh found him? He sounded American, but she understood they'd met in Dublin.

'But no. She doesn't. Not at all. She missed you.'

'She went away too,' Ciara said defensively. 'Although I guess she came back . . .'

'True. I guess we only came here because of your grandma, but it's weird how quickly it felt like home.'

Yeah, that was Hebden Bridge for you. Come for the day, stay forever. 'Let me help.' He came closer, and hooked his arms under hers. Either he was strong, or she was emaciated, but with one swift movement, he lifted her up and rested her on the side of the tub. 'Better?'

Ciara, with what little power she had, read him. Maybe she didn't need to, it was written all over his face: He felt *sorry* for her. How dare *he*, a mere mundane, pity her, a fucking adept. 'I'm fine. Just go.'

He smiled a little. 'You're exactly like she described you.'

This guy was pushing his luck. 'Oh yeah? What did she tell you about me?'

Conrad shrugged. 'Tough, independent, hilarious. She was always very proud of the fact she had a twin. She always says you're the cool one, the rock star.'

She huffed ruefully. 'You know what? It's only cool if you actually get the fuck out and become a rock star. I'm back here with nothing. I've done fuck all. Nothing.'

She saw she'd embarrassed him. 'Can I get you a drink?'

Why not replace one vice with another. 'You got vodka?'

'I don't drink,' he said quickly, 'but Niamh might have some in the kitchen.'

'You don't drink at *all*?' she said in disbelief.

'Alcoholic dad,' he said as if that was all the explanation necessary.

'Oh so you know,' Ciara said. 'You *know*.'

Once more, Ciara slipped under the water in the bath. She gripped the sides and pulled herself up with a gasp. Only this time, she was pulled under again. She felt it, something ice-cold, wrap around her legs. It felt prehensile, its tentacle flesh almost barbed.

Still gripping the rim, she screamed. 'Theo!' she managed to yelp before she was tugged back under the surface.

Was this real?

Somehow the body of water was vast, like she was being dragged into a dark, endless abyss. Ciara tried to see what had her, but there was only shadow. The light of the bathroom candles grew more and more distant as she was pulled further and further in the black ocean.

Ciara, it is almost time. The voice was like cream in coffee. She recognised it, but couldn't say how or from where or when. Sensually deep, wholly demon. *We have such dark designs for you.*

No. There would be no more. Ose was the last.

She fought, clawing at the water with her arms and fingers. She felt her lungs constrict. Couldn't hold her breath a second longer. She burst.

Until hands grasped her wrists and pulled her out of
the water and over the edge of the bathtub.

'Niamh!' Theo's face was pale, fraught. 'What's wrong?
What happened?'

Ciara gasped for air, coughing and spluttering. 'Oh my
goddess.' She tried to regain her wits before Theo could
read her. 'I . . . I, um, fell asleep and slipped under.'

Theo reeked of scepticism as she wrapped a towel
around her body, rubbing her dry. 'Are you sure? The way
you screamed . . .' Ciara looked at the perfectly innocent
bath. Nothing out of the ordinary. The water sloshed end
to end, settling. The chunk of diaspore now seemed rather
less harmless.

'I guess I had a nightmare,' Ciara said. Theo didn't look
convinced.

What the fuck had happened here? That was twice now:
the apparition in the lounge and now this. Worse, she
could not say if either happening was real or imagined.
She shivered and Theo rubbed her arms harder.

We have such dark designs for you.

No more. Ciara was done feeling lost. She had to know
why she was here.

Chapter Thirty-Eight

GRAVE MATTERS

Ciara – Hebden Bridge, UK

The Vance Mausoleum was located in the churchyard which neighboured Helena's old home. The old manor house was dark, dormant, although Ciara sensed someone, a caretaker perhaps, was looking after the place while the Vances completed their shame-exile in Cornwall.

It was a little after 2 a.m. Theo was sound asleep, unaware she'd even left the cottage. Ciara had taken more Excelsior to power through. Enough was enough.

She landed in the graveyard, untroubled by the thickness of the night. Witches are of the night. She oriented herself, and started towards the mausoleum. Helena had, more than once, shown off the ostentatious burial plot; all the proud Vance witches and their warlock husbands. The structure didn't seem so impressive now they were grown-ups; a squat structure, weathered and grey, even by moonlight. The gate was guarded by a pair of snarling stone griffins, their expression glum from erosion.

Ciara held out a hand and shattered the chain sealing

the entrance. She pulled the door open and entered the tomb. No fear, no sir.

Lies. She was more nervous than she could ever remember being. This was a terrible idea, but the only one she had.

Lighting a candle, Ciara sat cross-legged on the cold floor. She felt nausea burn her stomach. The inside of the mausoleum was even more dismal than the exterior. Water had seeped in somehow, green slime running down the rear wall. In the feeble light of the candle, Ciara scanned the plaques neatly placed on both sides. One, to her left, was notably newer than the rest.

HELENA JANE VANCE
1983 – 2022
29TH HIGH PRIESTESS OF HER MAJESTY'S
ROYAL COVEN

Ciara hadn't done this for a very long time, at least that she knew of. The irony was, they'd last done this at Vance Hall, at a sleepover when Helena's parents were out one night. Leonie and Elle had covered all the mirrors in the house with bedsheets or towels before they'd gathered in Helena's luxurious bedroom inside a salt circle. What teenage witch hasn't attempted this little stunt?

That was because only an arrogant, inexperienced witch would play with these spells. Death magic. Necromancy. The world of the dead was not of Gaia, or Gaia's daughters, and thus witches have no control over spirits. Ciara could be about to make a dire situation ten times worse.

She'd brought everything she needed from the cottage. She poured table salt around herself and lit another candle. She placed a mirror, a hand mirror from Niamh's room, on the floor in front of her, next to a photograph of Helena she'd peeled from a photo album. It depicted Helena, Niamh and Lee in happier times. Outside the Louvre pyramid; a girl's trip to Paris at some point. Ciara hadn't been invited, clearly.

She was ready.

Emptying her mind, she felt for life in the graveyard. Even this late, the valley was teeming. Lots of options. A family of bats roosted in the eaves of the now derelict rectory. Ciara summoned them. Soon enough, she heard their leathery wings beating. They darted about the mausoleum circling her.

Come.

A bat, a juvenile male, flew willingly into her hands. It was a tiny, impossible thing really. It was sweet, squeaking in her palms, and Ciara was grateful for its sacrifice.

Back then, at the sleepover, it had been a gerbil. Life summons death. On the last breath, a little door opens.

Ciara killed the bat swiftly and it knew nothing but peace. Opening its throat with her nail she let blood drip onto the glass of the mirror. She cast the body aside, and drew the sigil with her finger. Like riding a bike. She remembered that book Jude had given her all those years ago. It had taught her things no witch ought to know.

'Helena,' she said. 'Make yourself known.'

Ciara was proof that there is matter *inside* a body, even if that matter is non-corporeal. A soul, a ghost, a spirit. Her body was buried in Bluebell Woods, but the *real* Ciara was what now resided in Niamh's old frame.

Where does that essence go when the body dies? No one, and certainly not Ciara, knew, but this wasn't just a slumber party trick. She'd seen it work.

The things that live inside us don't always go far.

'Helena, you know why I'm here. If you're here, come out.'

Ciara tilted the mirror, looking over each shoulder. Taking care to stay inside the salt circle, Ciara stood and turned around, her eyes never leaving the reflection. She saw through the open door into the graveyard; a new moon and the black trees on the horizon.

She completed a full rotation, seeing nothing in the hand mirror. The candles blew out and Ciara smelled smoke. Choking, black smoke filled her nostrils.

She covered her mouth and nose. 'Helena? Are you here?'

Ciara felt she was not alone. She held her breath. She told herself she was in control. All she had to do was break the mirror, her porthole into the spirit realm. That's the thing with opening a door. It can be crossed from both sides. You can see into the beyond, and the beyond can see back.

She heard a muffled, snuffling noise. 'Hello . . . ?'

Crying. Someone was crying.

'Helena?' Ciara tilted the mirror around the crypt.

She almost passed her by. Ciara gasped. If she tilted the mirror downwards, there was a form pressed into the darkest corner of the mausoleum, between the wall and a stone sarcophagus. Ciara crouched, her back to the figure. In the mirror, she saw her own face reflected and, behind her, what was once Helena Vance.

Ciara's throat was sore. 'Helena?'

Not her.

'Then who are you?'

No one.

Her face was pressed against her knees, her face and hands terribly burned, and black with soot. The Pipes.

Only her eyes and teeth caught the moonlight. It was enough. Of course, demons can look like *anything* and they do so love to play games. Another reason why this was clutching at straws – it could all be fake news. Ciara would tread carefully. 'You look like her.'

No name.

'You are Helena Vance, High Priestess.'

She is gone.

She looked so small. Had she always been so tiny? The piteous thing cowered, hiding her scorched face. The effigy was right, in a manner of speaking. This was *not* Helena Vance, at least not the Helena Vance she'd known; proud, determined, ambitious. Ciara said, 'You brought me out of a coma. Why?'

The hazel eyes now looked at her. There were only fine wisps of hair left on her burned scalp. Ciara backed away from the edge of the salt. Just in case.

The demon made her do it.

'Belial?'

Somewhere out in the night, Ciara heard a deep, guttural laugh. She gripped the mirror tight. 'Why would he do that?' Belial was *Satanis*, the most powerful of all the demons, and she was . . . nothing. 'Tell me!'

You are puppets. They need mortal hands. It's not just Gaia who sees it all. They have been waiting for centuries. Now is the time. The great undoing has already begun.

'What does that mean?'

Like dominoes they fall. Helena, Annie, Niamh . . .

This thing knew them. It knew what she had done. 'Shut the fuck up.'

You will bring ruin. It's too late to stop it. Your path is chosen.

She shook her head. Ciara remembered what Irina had

shown her. The streets tearing apart, skyscrapers tumbling. The end of things as they are now. That wasn't her doing. It couldn't be – to be honest, that sort of destruction looked like hard work, and she was fundamentally lazy. 'You're lying.'

Suddenly spry, the figure launched itself at her with a hiss, and Ciara tumbled onto her side, slipping outside of the salt circle. She felt ice-cold fingernails touch her cheek before she scrambled inside the lines.

The charred face filled the mirror, eyes black. A foul, rotten-egg stench filled the crypt.

The voice was male, and deep, so deep she felt it below her ribs. Belial.

I will devour you, cunt.

Ciara screamed and with one heavy swing smashed the mirror against the floor as hard as she could. 'No!' For a second, a feral roar, and then, silence.

She regained her breath and the rank odour dissipated. There was no one here to be tough for, and so she drew her knees to her chest, the same way the frail husk that was once Helena Vance had done.

Ciara was scared. She wanted the coven. She wanted the coven to keep her safe. She couldn't do this alone.

She needed a friend.

Chapter Thirty-Nine

COLD LIGHT OF DAY

Leonie – Aeaea, somewhere in the Mediterranean Sea

Leonie snoozed contentedly, halfway between sleep and the day. She dreamed the most vivid dream of her life.

She slept naked in a dense tropical forest. The air was close, humid, dewy. She felt warm and safe, almost swaddled by nature: insects, birds, somewhere high overhead a monkey chattered in the palms as it swung from tree to tree. Abundant greens twinkled all around, emerald and jade. She'd never been here before in real life, but it felt real, like she could run her fingers through the mulch beneath her. Columns of honey amber light cut through the canopy to the forest floor. There was a decadent, almost cocoa-like, aroma to the air.

A rustle in the undergrowth. Leonie knew she ought to be scared, but she knew nothing but oneness with this jungle. She was safe here.

The snake was the largest she'd ever seen, yet she remained unafraid. She welcomed it. An anaconda or a python, perhaps, weaving through the undergrowth. Inquisitive, it rose from the ground, searching her out. A forked tongue darted in and out, tasting the air around her. Its muscular body was as thick as her thigh, and it moved fast, strong.

Leonie considered it. It was beautiful; its scales the most vivid neon green in a rainforest made of green, its eyes curious and yellow.

It was here for her.

She opened her legs, let the creature writhe over her. The snake covered her, coiling around her frame, and they became one entity.

The woman, and her serpent.

Leonie woke in a cool bed with a start, oddly aroused. As crazy as it was, it was a shame the dream had ended. She felt a sudden disappointment. It had felt very real. Her body crackled with a strange energy, almost pins and needles.

She stretched out across the mattress. Slats of golden sunlight cut through the wooden shutters and somewhere close by she heard the hiss of a sprinkler in the bushes outside. No wonder she'd dreamed of snakes.

After a good sleep, Leonie felt renewed. She only half remembered Zehra walking her to one of the little cabins dotted around the outskirts of the main temple. The room was spartan – a mattress on a stone plinth, and no air-con on Aeaea – but it was clean and had everything Leonie needed. Today, she could take on the world. One of those rare mornings where you sincerely believe that everything is going to be A-OK. She'd kill Hale, find Rad, get him home and then spend every single day with Chinara and as many mini-Chinaras as she wanted.

But first, breakfast. After her exertions last night, Leonie was famished. Nothing is better than a hotel buffet breakfast.

Leonie.

It was Calista's voice, in her mind. Short, curt, serious.

Then, from closer by, she heard a scream. Not a childish, playful scream. A scream.

Despite the late morning heat, Leonie's blood ran cold. She swung her legs off the bed, bare feet touching tiles. She still wore the white and red dress from last night. She was now alert, wide awake.

Leonie, help me. We've been found.

Not wasting another second, Leonie ran out of the cabin and onto the winding pathway that led to the sanctuary. Again, she heard a scream, and a crash, like a platter or tray rolling across the flagstones. The Greek sun was blinding.

Leonie raced uphill, and had only taken a few strides when she saw a heap of robe and hair splayed across the path. 'Oh shit, no.' She threw herself down to crouch at her side, skinning her knee.

She rolled Zehra over.

Her eyes were empty, her lips parted. No blood. Leonie tried to read her but there was nothing. She could only pray the severing had been swift, painless. 'Fuck!' Leonie cursed. She breathed unevenly, fighting the urge to puke. No. Not this. She stroked Zehra's beautiful face. What the fuck? What the fuck was going on?

Another scream, this one followed by a male voice, barking orders in what sounded like Russian.

Leonie sprang to her feet and, staying low, cautiously approached the pergola-covered courtyard where she'd first arrived on the island.

She ducked behind a thick column as a hefty man, all muscles and beard, dragged a witch out of the sanctuary by her hair. She screamed at him, telling him she didn't understand what he was saying. Leonie was about to hurl the brute across the concourse, but she was beaten to it.

There was a feral snarl and Nyssa, the lioness, dove at him, clawing, biting, at his face. He went down, letting go of the girl, and she ran for the olive grove.

In here. Calista again. Leonie used the distraction to slip past the thug and into the sanctuary. Nyssa had him by the wrist, almost pulling him down the stairs like a chew toy.

Inside was a mess. The table and benches were upturned; glasses and plates smashed to smithereens. There were two more dead witches strewn across the floor. One old, one the redhead with the guitar from last night – the Joni fan. She scanned the hall for Senait, panic levels rising. She was nowhere to be seen, which was a relief. Leonie wanted to howl, to rip the roof off.

Calista, where are you? She knew she would hear her.

With a scrape, one of the painted walls slid aside to reveal a hidden antechamber, a sort of panic room, Leonie guessed. Inside Calista crouched with some of the children. Leonie darted inside to join them, the panel closing behind her.

Only then did she see Calista was gripping a blood-soaked silk around her arm. 'They took my hand,' she breathed.

'The Seal.' Leonie looked towards the cellar.

'There was nothing I could do,' she said mournfully.

Leonie took a look at the wound. Dots of blood spattered to the floor. 'Can you heal this?'

She shook her head. 'I do not know, child. I am weak.'

She looked to the young witches huddled in the dark. 'Are any of you healers?'

A little Chinese girl, maybe eleven or twelve years old came forward. 'I am.'

'Help her.' Leonie went to leave.

'Leonie, wait! Stay with us,' Calista said. 'He'll kill us all. This chamber is shielded by a powerful charm, they won't find us here. We will need you in the battle yet to come.'

'I have to find Senait. And it's time someone told Dabney Hale *no*. Stay here. If anything happens to me, find Chinara Okafor. Find Niamh Kelly. Got that?' Calista understood but urged her to remain. 'Open it.' Leonie was resolved.

Leaving the priestess-hole, she hurried across the ruined banquet hall. Fresh screams came from the fountain yard. This reminded Leonie of the war, those seconds in which you had to see, evaluate and act within split seconds.

She strode into the sunshine.

Four men. Four big men.

Two terrified witches running for the villa.

'STOP!' Leonie screamed. Using the whole fist of her mind, she sent a wave rippling across the terrace. All six bodies were knocked down like bowling pins, too stunned to counteract her move. Arms out, she held the men – warlocks all – down, pressing their faces into the soil or shrubs. She let the women stand, pacing past them. 'Get inside! NOW!' she cried through gritted teeth.

She yanked one of the warlocks out of the bushes and threw him across the yard, pinning him up against one of the stone columns. His feet dangled mid-air. Leonie prowled closer, choking him. He was clean-cut, chisel-jawed, his eyes a cool blue-green. 'Where the fuck is Hale?' He gurgled a sentence in Russian and she understood the *fuck you bitch* sentiment only too well. Leonie squinted, and burst one of his eyeballs like a grape. It trickled down his cheek. He squealed like an animal. 'Try again, motherfucker.'

A chill breeze sliced across the garden and Leonie whirled around, ready to fight. She let the hulk slide down the column. He crawled away, clutching his face.

A billowing, black smog spiralled around the fountain, gradually taking on a human shape. The shadow became Dabney Hale, and he wore the Seal of Solomon upon his head. He waved at her, using Calista's severed hand.

Leonie raised both arms and threw him backwards with her mind. Everything she had, full throttle. Just fucking kill him. Why chat first? He recoiled a couple of paces, when he should have been punched through the wall and the one beyond that. Leonie altered her stance and hurled even more at him. He scarcely budged, only pausing to toss the bloodied hand into the fountain. Change of plan, she tried to enter his head, start the process of severing him. She couldn't even sense his mood. Leonie faltered, unsteady on her feet. How . . . ?

'I suppose,' Hale said wistfully, 'King Solomon required protection from the women in his life too.' He was as polished as she'd ever seen him, smartly dressed in a navy suit, crisp shirt, open collar. Taller than she remembered. His hair was still long, and she guessed a trip to the barber wasn't his first priority after breaking out of prison.

Leonie diverted all her power into protection. She needed to keep him out of her head. 'Leave them alone.'

'No,' he said, like it was the most obvious thing in the world.

'You didn't have to kill them, Dab.'

'Never trust a witch.' He cast a glance over his shoulder. 'They'll have your eye out.'

'There are *children* here.'

His stance changed. 'Oh relax, Leonie, this isn't *Game of Thrones*. I didn't kill anyone. It's not my fault if some of the boys got carried away.' He tapped the Seal. 'I got what I wanted.'

'Why are you doing all this?'

'I'll catch you up en route.'

Leonie winced. 'What?'

His face grew more serious. 'It wasn't just the Seal I wanted, love. Why else do you think I paid Senait to bring you here?'

Leonie felt the floor under her feet collapse like a trap door. Her knees almost buckled. 'What? No way.'

'Where is the wee scamp?' he said, looking past her into the villa. 'I guess she didn't want the other half of her money after all. There's no pleasing some people.'

It took her brain a second to process his words. 'I don't believe you.'

Hale grinned. 'You fell for a pretty face, darling. The stripper? I paid her an awful lot of money in Bologna.'

'No,' she said again.

'I knew full well these witches had the Seal, and I knew they'd trust you. You're quite famous these days, you know? I just had to get Domino's little friend to convince you to follow the trail. You led us right here, love. I paid her half upfront and the rest was to be on completion.'

'No . . .'

'Poor, trusting Leonie. You never were the brightest star in the sky, were you?' No. No, she'd read Senait a hundred times and . . . just no. 'You gave us time to trace the water conduit.'

'I don't believe it.'

'What? You think she's coming to save you? You've been played, Leonie. That's the problem with your childish, pseudo-feminist nonsense. *All men are bad, all women are good*. How's that working out for you?'

Leonie glared up at him, readying another killer blow. He'd let down his defences sooner or later, they always did. His heavies gathered at his side. They were big, mean-looking bastards; three, four and then *six* of them materialised. Powerful too, for men. Leonie was surrounded. She couldn't fight this many warlocks. They'd crush her like a bug.

'Round up the remainders,' Hale told them.

'No!' Leonie barked. 'Please, Dab.'

'Have them call the cavalry? I don't think so, not when I'm so close.'

The men moved towards the sanctuary. 'Wait!' Leonie pleaded. She would beg if it meant saving the others. 'If that crown makes you as powerful as it's supposed to, just fucking wipe them. They won't tell anyone if they don't remember anything.'

He seemed to ponder this.

'Dab, you got what you came for.' Her voice wobbled. 'Where's my brother? Please?'

A smirk crossed his lips. 'You'll see him soon enough.'

At least that meant he was alive. Maybe there was hope for him, if not her. For her, this was it. 'Why not just kill me?' she said, shaking her head. 'Just get it over with.'

Hale smiled, his white teeth dazzling. 'Oh gosh, no! Leonie! We go way back. As if I'd kill you while you slept. I've got something *much* more exciting planned for you.'

Chapter Forty

HEART OF STONE

Elle – Hebden Bridge, UK

A little after dawn, Elle returned to her husband and placed her hands on his stone face. He was alive. Living things and dead things are as different as different can be, and Elle would know.

She hadn't slept at all. Not a single minute. She didn't sense any pain, but was her husband dying inside this shell? Starving, or dying of dehydration? But rocks have no need to breathe, eat, sleep.

Elle did what she would do with any seriously ill patient. She channelled her radiance – her strength – into him. She held her hands over where she thought his heart was and let it flow. The air around her skin glimmered and she tingled all over.

Soon, though, she grew tired, nauseous. She'd given too much of herself away. Almost spent, she leaned on the hideous formation, pressing her cheek to the cold granite. Still, she hoped if she gave him enough, it would reverse the transformation. She kept going. Her radiance, naturally, was human; perhaps it would return him to his natural state.

The air smelled sweet, almost like toffee. She was hot, sweat running onto her lips. She did not rest. *Come back, Jez, for crying out fucking loud.*

She stumbled backwards, and slid down the wall. She might have even blacked out for a second or two. When Elle opened her eyes, there was no change at all. Jez remained a gargoyle.

She had no idea how much time she lay on the filthy linoleum. Could have been hours, could have been minutes. Eventually she pulled herself upright and took out her phone. It was funny, more than ever she wished Helena was still alive. She'd have been so bloody rational. She'd have fixed it, moved heaven and earth to find an answer.

Leonie wouldn't have judged, either. She'd have done *worse*.

Her only option was Niamh, though. Goddess knew what she'd think, she was so unfailingly kind and compassionate. But then, she *had* told her about Jez and his bit-on-the-side. Elle wished she hadn't.

It was time. She had to tell *someone*. If Jez was able to feel in there, if he was aware of all this, well, it was hardly worth thinking about. Time was of the essence. She couldn't do this alone. That acknowledgement was not one mothers were supposed to admit.

She sighed and dialled Niamh's number. She answered on the third ring. 'Hey, doll, how's it going?'

'Niamh, I need to see you.'

A pause. She must really sound unhinged. 'Ellie? You OK?'

'Not really. I should have told you last night. Meet at the café?'

'Sure. Which one?'

Elle paused. Which bloody one did she think? 'The usual.'

'The Tea Cosy?'

'Yes.' Like they ever went anywhere else. That was a bit random, as Holly or Milo would say, but she was too frazzled to give a shit right now. 'How soon can you be there?'

'Um . . . give me half an hour. I'll get in the shower.'

Elle hung up and picked herself off the floor. It was now almost nine in the morning. She must have passed out after all, lost some time.

She went to the – frankly disgusting – toilets and splashed some water on her face. The walls were papered with various pictures of topless women – Page 3 Girls – with the heads of female politicians glued onto their bodies: Angela Merkel, Theresa May, Kamala Harris. Why? Elle didn't understand men at all.

She looked at herself in the mirror. She looked *awful*. It was startling how gaunt she looked. That was stress for you – the ultimate misery diet. She'd called in sick from work. She wouldn't risk harming someone in the community while she was this exhausted. Even Milo had asked if she was OK this morning, a rarity.

Holly was devastated her father had left. Ironically, she was in such a mess she didn't seem able to focus her powers on reading Elle's mind. Lucky, but her luck would run out, and soon her daughter would sense what was really going on.

She finished up in the bathroom, drying her face on scratchy paper towels. She collected her handbag and decided to wait for Niamh in the café. Caffeine would either help, or tip her over the precipice into madness.

Elle was so wrapped up in her thoughts, she *almost* didn't see the woman scurrying away from the garage as she emerged into the blinding light of day. Even from behind, Elle recognised her. Well, the balls on this one, honestly. 'Can I help you?' Elle called after the retreating figure.

Jessica Summers, receptionist at Harmsworth House hotel, turned to face her, her dyed jet-black ponytail skimming her rear. She was all lip-filler and Oxo cube contour. Elle's head swirled with insults: blow-up doll; Pound-shop Kardashian; Reject Barbie. Underneath all the makeup, she was so young. Twenty-two? Twenty-five, tops. That could have enraged Elle, but rather she felt disgusted at Jez; what was he doing? It was just *sad*. Did shagging someone so young boost his ego? Surely he merely looked ancient next to her, a pervy uncle.

'I, um, I was . . . the garage is shut?' she said pitifully.

Elle bit the inside of her cheek. She would not let what happened to Jez inside that workshop happen again. 'It'll be closed for the foreseeable.' She fought to keep the shrill off her voice.

Jessica nodded and went to leave, before plucking up yet more youthful courage. 'People . . . people are saying Jez has gone?'

'Is that right?' This bitch *knew*. She had known the whole time that Jeremy Pearson had a wife and two teenage kids, and yet she had still . . . what sort of a woman does that to another woman? A child, perhaps. A girl whose heart hasn't yet known pain. Or just a selfish little shit.

She recalled everything Annie had taught her about sisterhood and solidarity, how it transcends all petty squabbles, but would even her grandmother have expected her to welcome this tacky magpie into the coven?

'Yeah . . . people are saying he's left town?'

'What's it to you?' Elle forced herself to blink sore eyes.

She must look intense, judging from the look mirrored in Jessica's own expression.

The younger woman shook her head. 'It doesn't matter.' She almost left, but then added. 'Are you OK?'

Am I OK? Really? There was a very real urge to rip this woman's hair extensions off her scalp, but Elle was more shocked by what she found beneath that urge. Jessica's eyes were filling with tears. Elle felt bad for *her*. What the hell? The ultimate woman's curse: Sympathy.

Elle took a long, steadying breath before continuing. 'My husband has disappeared with another woman; how do you think I feel right now?'

Jessica's lip trembled. 'I would want to kill her.'

Elle just nodded. More or less right. 'I'm fully aware it takes two to tango, but I do keep asking myself how she could do it. She must have known it would hurt.'

A tear now ran down Jessica's face. 'Maybe she was in love with him.'

A laugh popped out of Elle's mouth. She couldn't help it. Maybe the answer really was that simple and she'd been overthinking it. Love doesn't play by the rules. Never has done. Love is like diarrhoea: it can't be helped, it can't be contained, and it's often messy. As a nurse, Elle knew that better than anyone.

They say love is blind, but it *makes you blind*. There were so many things Elle had pretended she couldn't see. Now the girl shivered in front of her, and Elle pitied her, she did. Oh, who was she kidding? Elle used to be this girl. Twenty years ago, she'd have stepped on any girl to get what she wanted, and she had wanted Jez more than anything else in the world. And she'd have done it all while proudly wanging on about girl power.

Now neither of them had Jez, and whose fault was that? He had played them both for fools. He had wanted it all, and now no one had anything.

The sky was dark and heavy and, sure enough, a veil of freezing drizzle blew sideways across the car park. It about summed up how she felt.

'I've been such an idiot,' Elle said. 'I should have listened to my friends when they told me not to build my world around a man. They were right. Now the middle's fallen out of it.'

Jessica Summers nodded. Maybe she was learning that golden rule for the first time. 'You've got the kids.'

'Yes, I do,' Elle said, oddly victorious that she had a piece of Jez this girl, with her diving board false lashes, did not. 'They are my world.' Jessica said nothing. 'I pity this *woman* he's run off with. He'll only keep trading her in for younger models while they'll have him. That's the problem with Jez. He thinks he's still twenty-one. It's all a mid-life crisis – you know he's forty this year. This *woman*, she wants to find a bloke her own age; someone who can give himself to her and her alone.'

She nodded again. 'I'm sorry,' she said.

'So am I, love. So am I.'

Elle held it together until Jessica was far out of sight. She walked past the Co-op and onto Market Street before bursting into tears. She tried to keep it in her throat, but found she could not. It all came out in a big ugly woof. She cried so hard; she couldn't breathe. She saw people looking her way, and that made her feel even worse.

At first she assumed it was some kind stranger, offering her a tissue, but then she was pulled into an embrace. 'Hey, what's wrong?' It was Niamh. 'I came straight down.'

Elle couldn't even begin to explain. She buried her face into the taller woman's bosom and wept.

Niamh rubbed her back and held her tight in the street, right outside the Italian restaurant. 'Whatever it is, let it all out. Better out than in.'

Elle felt the innate healer in Niamh stir, some of her radiance passing into her own body. It was soothing, until Elle realised what was amiss.

This wasn't Niamh.

Niamh's radiance was sedate, blues and willow greens, like a shallow Mediterranean tide. This was very different, swirling, marble violets and almost phosphorus jade. She pushed her away.

Radiance, to a witch, is as distinctive as a fingerprint. But . . . how? It wasn't possible. Annie had told Elle her whole life that *anything* is possible for a witch. Oh shit.

She really was an idiot. *Ellie.* Only one person had ever, *ever* persisted in calling her that, however many times she protested.

Ciara.

Chapter Forty-One

BARGAINING

Ciara – Hebden Bridge, UK

Elle pushed her away, looking up at her with clouded confusion. Her stare hardened. In her mind, one word, loud and clear.

Ciara.

Elle backed away, down the street.

Fuck. FUCK. At once, she shielded them. This could get unladylike.

'If you do anything, I'll scream,' Elle said.

'It won't make a difference.' Ciara held out both arms and summoned Elle into her grasp. She tried to resist, dragging her feet along the damp pavement, but Ciara was stronger. The little blond flew into her arms and Ciara lifted them off the ground at once.

Ciara gripped her tight, ignoring her screams. Right now, she just had to get them somewhere she couldn't make a scene. They flew higher and higher over Hebden Bridge village.

'Put me down!' Elle cried.

'You sure?' Ciara said. She released her. Eyes wide, Elle

plummeted a few feet with a blood-curdling scream, until Ciara caught her with her mind again, compelling her into a tight embrace.

'Ciara, please!'

'*Hai si ja*, hold tight!'

Ciara careered through low, lingering cloud cover until they came to rolling green pastures below. She didn't have any desire to drop Elle Device to her death. She descended towards an empty field. The rain was heavier now, a biting wind whipping it in her face like needles.

The second her trainers touched wet grass; Elle turned and seized her wrist, and Ciara felt the most horrific wave of nausea swell from inside her guts. A high-pitched whistle rang in her ears and she was overcome with a dizzy sensation worse than any seasickness. She toppled to her knees. How the fuck was she doing this? Ciara's head throbbed; her vision dotted with vivid orange flecks. 'Ellie, stop!' Ciara begged.

Elle didn't stop. 'You're not Niamh. Where's Niamh?'

'Stop!' It was all she could say, and even that hurt. Was fucking *Elle* going to actually kill her? Mortifying. Hardly able to breathe, Ciara held out a hand and blindly pushed at anything and everything as hard as she could.

The agony ceased as Elle was hurled across the field. She landed on her arse a few metres away.

'Elle, I don't want to hurt you!' she called, wiping the rain from her face. 'I need your help.'

Elle got on her feet, smearing mud across her sweatpants with her hands. 'Yeah, nice try!' she said sarcastically. 'Stay where you are! I've never severed anyone, but I reckon I could give it a go.'

Ciara rose too and held her hands up in surrender. They stood ten metres or so apart, mirroring each other's defensive stance: a stand-off. She wasn't even sure what the rugged hillside was; farmland, she guessed. 'I don't want to hurt you,' she repeated. It was that sort of clinging drizzle, and her hair swung about her face in soggy ropes.

'Are you still evil?'

Ciara rolled her eyes. 'Really?'

'What did you do to Niamh? I could *always* tell the difference, and that's her body, but . . . it's *you* inside. I know it's you.'

Ciara took a deep breath. Fuck. This wasn't how she'd envisioned her great coming-out moment but the encounter in the Vance Mausoleum had rattled her and she needed someone to talk to. Maybe Elle had done her a favour, forced her hand. No more pretending.

Elle's eyes narrowed. 'Where's Niamh?'

What else could she do but tell the truth? 'It was Helena.'

Elle looked like she was waiting for a punchline. 'Helena?'

'She was possessed.'

'We know.'

'I know you know. She came to the safehouse and gave me a vector stone. I don't know why, I swear. I was in a fucking coma, there wasn't a lot I could do about anything, was there?'

'Why would she do that?'

'Fucked if I know. What do you think I've been doing for the past few weeks? I even tried asking Helena herself.'

Now Elle looked *really* baffled. She massaged her temples. 'Look: Where. Is. Niamh?'

'She's dead,' Ciara said truthfully. 'She didn't survive the transfer,' she added, less truthfully. 'I guess my old body was too damaged.'

Ciara saw Elle had stopped listening after *She's dead*,

and that was fine with her. Elle wasn't psychic, she didn't have to worry about her catching her out that way. 'I'm sorry,' Ciara said, for all it was worth.

'Oh my goddess . . . Niamh, no,' Elle said, staring down at the grass. All the light, all the 'bubbly' she associated with Elle was gone. Her face was ashen. 'We buried her. All this time. Why . . . why didn't you tell us?'

Ciara scowled. 'Why do you think?'

Elle said nothing, it didn't really need saying. Ciara Kelly, at the very least, belonged in Grierlings, and if a sentient uncovered what she'd done to Niamh or Irina, she'd get the Pipes.

'So you're just going to pretend to be her for the rest of your life?'

'Why not? It's worked for a few weeks now. I fooled *Leonie*, for fuck's sake.'

Like it was the most obvious thing in the world, Elle said, 'You're not Niamh.'

That stung more than Ciara would have liked. 'I can be.'

'No, you can't.' Elle snapped. 'Niamh was kind, and caring, and—'

'Oh spare me. I am familiar with the miracles of Saint Niamh, thanks. I especially enjoyed the parable where she ripped my soul out and left me in a vegetative state for the best part of a decade. Kind. Caring.'

There was nothing Elle could say to that. They faced off, neither budging. A gust of wind cut across the valley and Elle hugged her arms.

'What now?' Ciara asked.

'What?'

'You gonna grass on me?'

'*Grass on you?* This isn't like when you used to steal Urban Decay from Boots, Ciara.'

'I didn't want this,' Ciara said with a shrug and, in a way, that was true.

'Really? I don't see them dragging you kicking and screaming into being High Priestess.'

'Which, if you think about it, is pretty funny,' Ciara tried for a laugh. Elle blinked at her. 'Well, I can't be fucking worse than the last one. She killed your grandma.'

'You have a point there.' It might be her imagination, but there was a tiny suggestion in her lips that said Elle at least saw the irony.

Ciara took a step closer. Elle didn't retreat. She was getting somewhere. When they were kids, sometimes Ciara had enjoyed spending time alone with Elle. They weren't an obvious match, but it worked. Elle Device was so terminally uncool, that you didn't have to pretend to like Blur *or* Oasis around her, and they'd unironically watch *The Little Mermaid* or *Aladdin* free from judgement.

Ciara let her senses creep inside Elle's mind. 'I can't bring Niamh back. If you want, turn me in to HMRC, but what good will that do? They'll just stick me in Grierlings. Or the Pipes.'

Elle dwelled on this fact, but there was turmoil underneath too. Her head was a *mess*. Everything was the most disgusting mixture of grey, green and bile yellow.

'So?' Ciara ventured.

'Ciara, I don't know! Gods! What am I meant to say? Welcome home? It's been almost ten years, and . . . and before that you were . . .'

Ciara took another step closer. *Jez.* Her thoughts were of her husband. Jez and *guilt.* 'Elle?' she said, probing further. In all the chaos she'd almost forgotten that Elle had summoned her with urgency. 'What's happened?'

Her eyes widened. She really did look like a Disney princess. 'What do you mean?'

Ciara saw more clearly. Flashes of the garage, of Jez, of . . . some sort of . . . rock. 'Elle, you can't lie to me. What did you do?'

Just when she thought she'd seen it all. It took a lot to shock Ciara, and yet. 'How . . . well, how?' She ran her fingers across the stone face. It was real, and unsettling, to say the least. The expression was . . . haunting. The poky garage office even smelled dank, cave-like.

Elle was all cried out, a tissue wrapped tightly around her fingers. 'I don't know.'

'You did this?' Elle nodded and sniffed. 'Elle, this is incredible. I've never seen transmogrification like it. I've read about it in grimoires, but . . . this is next level.'

Elle lingered by the door, like she was scared of her own creation. 'Is he in pain?'

Ciara scanned the statue – Jez – for signs of life. 'No,' she replied. 'I don't think so. He's alive.' Elle seemed relieved to hear that. 'But alive like a tree is alive, I don't know if he *feels* anything.'

Ciara felt her phone vibrating in her handbag. It was Theo calling. Whatever it was would have to wait. She dismissed her to voicemail.

Elle urged her. 'Can you help? Can you fix him?'

'Elle, I wouldn't know where to begin. Aren't you only a Level 4? How the fuck did you do this?'

'I don't know!' Elle now screamed, flying into Ciara's space. Thick snot dribbled down to her lip. 'I don't know and I don't care, just turn him back!'

'I can't!'

Elle scraped her greasy hair off her face, desperate for

answers. 'What about Theo? She changed her body. Maybe she could . . . ?'

'No,' Ciara said tactfully. 'Her powers have faded since that night, but you can't tell anyone about this. You shouldn't have told me. Elle, you turned a mundane to stone. Can you imagine if HMRC finds out? You broke the Witchcraft Act.'

Elle shook her head. 'So what do I do?'

The cold, hard cynic in Ciara rejoiced. She had collateral so juicy on Elle that there was no way she'd reveal *her* secret. She had her exactly where she wanted her.

But the seventeen-year-old Ciara inside Ciara just saw her old friend in desperate need. It was instinct. She actually wanted to *help*, an urge that shocked her as much as anyone.

'What do *we* do.' Ciara gave Elle's shoulders a supportive squeeze. 'We'll work it out together. Help me figure out why I'm back and I'll help you heal Jez.'

For once, she meant it.

Chapter Forty-Two

BLOOD

Theo – Hebden Bridge, UK

'I'll be fine I promise!' Theo said brightly, even though she was pretty much seething. Fake it, fake it, fake it. The older she got, the more faking she did. Toddlers just lay on the floor and wail. She still *wanted* to do that, but couldn't.

Her algebra homework was fucking impossible and, once more, Niamh was about to abandon her. Theo was certain she wasn't imagining it any more and, to use Holly's catchphrase, she was triggered. She suspected it was only going to get worse with the coronation around the corner.

Theo tried to read Niamh as she flitted around the cottage. Maybe if she was distracted she'd get a glimpse. There was nothing. Just a certain *urge*, itchy feet, as if Niamh wanted to get far, far away. From her?

Who knows, maybe things *would* improve once the ceremony was out of the way? Theo couldn't shake the feeling she was a disappointment; not so much the Sullied Child as the Flop Era. Her power had once been so concerning that Helena had tried to kill her. Now, Theo could hardly float her biro over her homework.

'And you'll be OK making yourself some dinner?' Niamh asked as she put a lip-balm and her phone in a handbag. She was meeting Elle for cocktails at Nelsons; apparently Elle needed cheering up. She was sure there was more to it. She couldn't read Niamh thoroughly, but knew when someone was keeping a secret. It was all in the body language, the vague answers to her questions.

Maybe she was protecting Elle. Holly and Milo were in pain since their dad took off, but, to Theo, he was no great loss. He was kind of a douche. 'Sure, I'll find something in the fridge,' Theo said, failing to keep a hint of sadness out of her voice.

'I know,' Niamh said, reading her mind, no doubt. 'I'm a fucking dreadful Supply Mother.' Niamh slipped into the dining chair opposite. 'What's wrong? Tell me.'

For the first time in a while, Theo felt she had Niamh, still, right in front of her, not flitting around like a wasp. 'It's nothing . . .'

'You can't lie to a psychic.' Niamh smiled. 'You're worried about your home.'

Of course she was petrified of losing Niamh. She'd lost everyone else in her life, ever. Niamh was the best thing that had ever happened to her, she was clinging to the woman for dear life. But Theo was keenly aware that Niamh was just being kind. There was nothing legal holding them together. The day she got bored of her, or scared of her, who knew what'd happen.

'It's not just the cottage,' Theo said, although she did adore this house. 'It's you. Sorry, that's so cringe.'

'We . . . I lost my parents too, remember. I get it.'

'You had your sister.' At that, Niamh tensed up. Maybe she shouldn't have said that.

'That I did,' Niamh said sadly, and then she sighed, like

she was resolute. 'Listen: Only Gaia knows what the future holds, but this is your home and I've . . . I've got your back. I remember what it was like; coming here and not knowing anyone. You . . . remind me of how I was, once upon a time. OK? I'm not going to let anything shit happen to you.'

Theo couldn't read her, but she seemed sincere. 'Thank you. Niamh, you changed my life. You *saved* my life. I hope you know how much I—'

There was a knock at the rear door and Milo sauntered into the kitchen. Theo frowned. Was she missing something? 'Mum's outside in a cab,' he announced.

'I won't be late,' Niamh told Theo. 'Things will be less manic after the coronation, I promise, and we can chill then.' She gave her a kiss on the crown of her head even if it felt oddly stiff. 'I meant what I said.' Theo felt her spirit bloom. She'd needed to hear that. Niamh smiled, and left the way Milo had arrived. As they crossed, Niamh looked Milo up and down, like she was assessing his suitability for her. She blushed.

'What are you doing here?' Theo asked.

'I got a lift with Mum.'

'That's *how* you got here, not why.'

He shrugged. 'I was bored.' He crossed to the fridge. 'Has Niamh got any good stuff to drink? Coke or whatever?'

She ignored that. 'Where's Holly?'

'Fuck knows. She's the last person I'd wanna hang out with.'

Theo pushed her homework to one side, and Milo joined her at the table with some pressed apple juice Luke included in their delivery box. Before he could swig it from the bottle, she stood and fetched him a glass. 'Milo, I told you. This . . . isn't a thing.'

'What isn't?'

'Don't be cute. It's not cute.' He just looked at her and it was cute, actually. 'Look. I literally took an oath promising to put the coven before any man. You are "man". Holly is my sister.'

He slumped in his chair; legs splayed wide. 'Well, that blows.'

Theo didn't admit it was also far less scary to keep him at arm's length. Honestly, she had not anticipated any sort of – you know what – in her future. Until four months ago, she'd been a freaky pariah. This would . . . take some getting used to. What if she kissed weird? What if she did it wrong? What if she had dog breath? Never mind Leviathan, *this* was scary. Better to kick it into the long grass, a situation for twenty-year-old Theo. That seemed like a good age to do the whole boyfriend thing.

'I'm here now,' Milo said. 'You wanna get some food?'

'There's stuff in the fridge, help yourself.'

Milo rummaged around behind her while she quickly completed her homework. He unearthed some veggie lasagne leftovers and started making a salad and garlic bread. 'Are your powers up-and-running yet?' he asked, chopping away. 'I fully need you to read my mum. She's definitely tripping off her tits on something.'

'No,' she said, admitting defeat on the indices worksheet for now. 'If anything, they're getting worse. It's embarrassing.'

'Better than having no powers at all.' He returned to the table with his chopping board. 'Do you know why?'

'Nope.' Theo ran a finger down the spines of the mountain of books on the table. 'These were all hopeless. I have no idea.'

He asked if they were all witching books and she told

him they were. 'These all sound sick. *Nocturnes*, how do you even say that . . . *Dwolcræft? The Song of Osiris . . .*'

'That one is especially shit,' Theo said. 'It doesn't even have words in it.'

He took it off the pile and flicked it open. 'It's blank.' He grabbed her biro and grinned. 'Let's fix that . . .' He swiftly drew a spunking penis and balls on a blank page, only the pen didn't work, failing to make even an indentation on the paper. 'Your pen is fucked.'

'No, it isn't, I just used it on my homework.'

She plucked the biro out of his hand and scribbled on the edge of her Maths worksheet. 'See?'

Milo had another go at writing on *The Song of Osiris*. Once again, the pen wouldn't comply. 'That's weird.'

Theo agreed. This time, she took a pencil out of her pencil case and tried to scribble on the notebook. Nothing. 'OK, that *is* weird.' She ran her fingers over the pages. The paper didn't feel any different to any other sort.

'Maybe it's enchanted. Maybe it's haunted.'

Theo blinked. 'Sure. Why not?'

She used witch logic; the book was blocking her? Could only sentients read it? She was a sentient, though. Surely there wasn't a magic word, that'd be naff. *Abracadabra*. Objects *can* be enchanted – like the well in Annie's garden. A mystery to solve. Cool. Maybe she'd given up on *The Song of Osiris* too quickly.

Milo's chair scraped on the stone tiles as he returned to the cooking. 'Have you got, like dressings and stuff for the salad? I'm trying to eat dead healthy. I want the full six pack.' He patted a very toned stomach.

Theo was more focused on her discovery. 'Um, try the top cupboard.' She added a couple of drops of ink to the page from her art supplies. The liquid ran off the paper as if it were waxed or laminated. 'Shit.' She mopped up the excess with a tissue.

Milo clattered around, a bottle falling out of the cupboard and rolling across the counter. 'Sorry,' and then. 'What's *White Sorbus*?'

Theo was hardly listening. 'What?'

She turned and saw him holding one of Niamh's little brown jars. 'What's *White Sorbus*?' he repeated.

'No idea. Niamh has loads of bottles like that.'

'This one was with herbs and stuff.'

She smiled. 'They're all *herbs and stuff*. We're *witches*.' He unscrewed the jar and gave it a sniff before offering her the chance to do the same. 'I'm good, thanks.'

He left it on the counter and returned to his salad, slicing a cucumber on the chopping board. 'OK, I don't actually really like salad, because it's fucking rabbit food,' he said, 'but I'll do like cucumber and tom – ow fuck!' he cried.

'What?' She twisted around to face him.

'Fuck, shit, I cut myself. It's bad.'

Theo went to help. 'Let me see.'

'Have you got some . . . ?' He reached for the kitchen roll, and she got a good look at it. Blood, purply-red and gloopy, trickled into his palm. Shit, it did look bad.

Theo said urgently, 'I can heal you.' Well, she hoped she could. It certainly wouldn't hurt to try.

'It's really bad,' he said again. As he held out the wound to her, blood dripped onto the table; droplets spotting on her homework and books. 'Fuck, sorry.'

'It's fine. Give me your hand.' She took his wounded hand and sandwiched it between hers. His skin was soft, warm. She felt some of his blood pool in her palm.

'Sorry,' he said again.

'It's OK,' she whispered, focusing. 'Does it hurt?'

'A little.' He nodded. 'Your hands are nice and toasty.'

She smiled up at him. Healing was all about pushing your radiance into another host. As soon as their skin touched, she felt their energies stir. She could do this. Her hands, and then his hands, started to glow, a warm, golden shimmer. She concentrated, steering her latent energy into his finger. This shouldn't be taking this much effort. Why was she struggling so much?

Sure enough, after a moment, the gash in his index finger began to repair itself. 'No way . . .' Milo said, and then. 'Whoa look!'

'What?'

'Your book!'

Theo tore her attention away from his hands and looked at the table. Droplets of blood had splattered across *The Song of Osiris*. This time though, the fluid was absorbed into the pages, gradually revealing the most beautiful handwriting Theo had ever seen. Line by line, red script appeared as if some invisible hand was writing before her eyes. 'Oh wow . . .'

And *The Song of Osiris* was silent no more.

Chapter Forty-Three

CORPSE REVIVER

Elle – Hebden Bridge, UK

'What are people drinking these days?' Ciara asked, flicking through the sepia menu pages attached to the little clipboard.

'What?' Elle asked.

Nelson's Wine Bar was a cute basement bar in the centre of town. It was run by a nice lesbian couple, and served yummy little vegan tapas-like small plates. Very trendy, very Hebden. She'd often come here with Jez on Date Night.

Ciara looked to her expectantly. 'Like what's the *in* cocktail? I'm a little out of the loop, remember.'

'I don't know,' Elle said, struggling with all this. Ciara was babbling away, giddy, as if this were highly normal circumstances. 'What are you doing?'

Ciara stopped. 'What do you mean?'

Elle gestured around the bar. 'This? With everything that's going on?'

'Isn't this what women do? We get dressed up and go for cocktails.'

'Sure, until you realise that *Sex and the City* isn't a documentary.' It wasn't like Elle to be cynical, but here they were. Twenty-four hours had passed since she'd learned the truth and, now the dust was settling, Elle wasn't at all sure about playing Happy Families with a murderer. She'd accepted Ciara's invitation and deigned to put on some makeup, but only because she didn't trust that she wouldn't turn her over to HMRC if she refused. 'I assumed, when you said cocktails, you meant . . . *potions?*'

'I meant cocktails.' Coy, Ciara half-hid behind the menu. 'I dunno. I guess, now the cat's out the bag, I was excited, OK? Is that a crime? I wanted to catch up properly. It hasn't been easy sneaking around.'

Elle couldn't believe it. Ciara Kelly, vulnerable and meek.

'Ha!' Ciara said suddenly, bravado mode restored. 'Corpse Reviver No.2! Perfect! You know what you want?' Ciara flagged down their waiter for the night, a bearded hipster with neck tattoos and a nose ring. Ciara ordered her drink, and Elle opted for a Porn Star Martini, as ever.

Ciara's head twisted to watch the waiter return to the bar; his rear notably pert in his circulation-stopping trousers. 'Oh he's cute!' she said.

Elle rolled her eyes. 'He's gay!'

Ciara tapped her head. 'Doesn't have to be tonight.'

'Ciara!'

'I'm kidding, obviously! Gods!'

Elle suddenly panicked. 'Shit, I called you . . .'

'Doesn't matter,' she replied. 'I shielded us when we came in. We can speak freely, counsel.'

Their cocktails came swiftly, and Elle downed the shot of prosecco that came alongside hers. She needed it. Annie, Helena, Jez and now Niamh. Come to think of it, she couldn't remember the last time life had felt average. *Mundane.*

'So,' Ciara said. 'Fill me in.'

'On what? Ciara, I'm finding this all a bit . . . surreal.'

Ciara raised a brow. 'You wanna try living in someone else's body.'

'Stop! Please! It's *Niamh's* body! You took Niamh's body.' Elle sighed. 'What I can't wrap my head around is why you'd bring it here. You could have gone a thousand miles away and hidden, but you walked into HMRC instead.'

She took a studious sip of her drink. 'I had to know.'

Elle caved, too nosy to resist. 'Know what?'

'Ooh that's strong.' Ciara took another sip. 'Everything – why I'm back; why now; who I am. I forgot half my life.'

'I guess I can help with that,' Elle offered, relaxing a smidge. 'What do you remember?'

Ciara nodded gratefully. 'I remember growing up here. I remember taking the oath, but after that, things get ropey.'

'To be honest, after you left Hebden Bridge to go to uni we lost touch.' Elle fiddled with her coaster napkin. 'I always got the impression that, well, you sort of *tolerated* me.'

Ciara, wearing Niamh's face, looked a little hurt. 'What? That's not true.'

'You and Leonie. You were a lot cooler than I ever was. And I wasn't as into craft stuff.' Yes, Helena had used her much of the time, but at least that made her feel needed.

Ciara reached for her hand, but Elle withdrew. 'Elle. You were the best friend a person could have. I love the bones of Lee, but if I needed someone in an emergency, you were the one I could count on. A girl needs a girl she can rely on.'

'Reliable.' There were worse things, she guessed. 'Anyway. I know from Helena that you got to know Dabney Hale at Durham.'

'What about Jude?'

'Your boyfriend?'

'Yes. Did you meet him?'

Elle shook her head. 'No. None of us did, not even your sister.' Ciara hmmed thoughtfully. 'But you were besotted. You fell off the edge of the earth.'

'Red flag.'

'I know that now. I didn't then.' She'd done the same with Jez; built her home out of straw. A cautionary tale: keep your boyfriends close, but your girlfriends closer.

'Did I come back here at some point?'

Elle nodded. 'You did. You stayed at the cottage with Niamh and . . . you were in a bad way. It was pretty scary, to tell you the truth.'

Ciara just took another sip of her cocktail.

Steeling herself, Elle asked the question she really wanted to ask. 'Why did you kill Conrad?'

'I don't know,' she said sharply. She'd hit a sore spot. 'I don't know, so don't ask. I don't even fucking remember it, why do you think I asked you that time?'

She couldn't help but feel this alliance was a huge mistake. Yes, they had a whole lotta history, but she was a *killer*. A *murderer*. Was she supposed to conveniently forget that detail? That was part of the problem with Ciara: she was charming, outrageous, hilarious. She made *you* feel more rebellious just by being in her aurora. Two minutes in her company, and you'd forgive the fact she scratched your Dido CD or left your Tamagotchi on the train. But this wasn't so easily forgotten or forgiven.

She had killed Conrad, an innocent mundane, not to mention one of the loveliest men she'd ever met, in cold blood.

'Maybe I should just go.' Elle pushed her chair to leave.

'No!' Ciara snapped. Other patrons didn't look their way, her spell working. 'Ellie, I need you. And you need me, remember? I'm not the only one using magic on mundanes . . .'

Elle sighed and sat down again. At least her fuck-up was accidental. 'Fine. Let's say I play along; what are we going to do?'

Ciara smiled, satisfied she'd won her over. 'OK, hear me out. This might sound bananas, but hang on in there.' And then she revealed her masterplan. 'I think Dab could fix Jez. He is the most powerful warlock there ever was and, let's face it, he owes me one.'

Sure, why not throw oil on the fire? 'Hale? Are you insane?'

'Probably!' she said, smiling. 'But, the way I see it, Hale is the solution to both our problems. He brought me back for a reason.'

'It's nothing to do with me. I just want my husband.'

'Whether we like it or not, Dab is powerful. If anyone can figure out what happened to Jez, it's him. Help me find him.'

'Ciara, no.' Elle had met Hale once or twice when they were teenagers. He was a prick then, and a bigger prick now. She dealt with a lot of his handiwork during the war. God, the clean-up after the Somerset Floods didn't bear thinking about.

'Can you think of an alternative? Maybe move Jez into your garden as a water feature?'

Elle said nothing.

'Why do you think I'm playing along with the priestess shit? The coven will shove him in Grierlings the second Lee finds him. Then, we can *make* him help us.'

Elle took a sip of her drink. It was delicious, the passion-fruit syrupy on her teeth. 'No offence, but I think you're being a little naïve where Hale is concerned. He's your ex after all.'

She grew more serious. 'I don't know exactly what happened during the war, with him and me. But . . . he hurt me too.' Ciara's expression hardened. 'He doesn't control me. He never did. Elle, you have to trust me on this.'

There was the problem: Elle didn't trust her. As much as she wanted to, only a fool would. Elle shielded her thoughts the way her grandmother had taught her to. That was Elle's gift; let them think her a fool. Ciara couldn't charm her way out of this one. Elle would play along for now but after Jez was restored, and they'd put Hale in Grierlings, she'd make sure Ciara was in the next cell over.

She downed the rest of her martini. 'Another?' she said.

Chapter Forty-Four

THE CUCKING POD

Luke – Halifax, UK

In a disabled toilet in a derelict Toys 'R' Us, Luke vomited. When there was nothing left in his stomach, he puked horrid yellow bile. It burned his throat and nostrils.

He flushed and rinsed his mouth out under the cold tap.

How was he ever going to live with this?

Luke couldn't fully remember the day his mother disappeared. He remembered his father thrusting him into the back of his van with a Nike holdall full of clothes, and telling him he was going to live with him now. There hadn't been time to even think about it, much less protest, or cry, or beg. His mum, he was told, was going away for a long time.

A really long time. He'd stopped asking when she was going to come home after the first year or so. He'd have been about six years old. It was only later, when he was eleven or twelve, that his father had finally told him his mother's fate.

Angela Ridge had confessed to witchcraft, and she had been drowned.

That was as much detail as Luke had ever wanted to know because by that point he had wholeheartedly believed witches were the evil, monstrous, whores of Satan. He'd only been told the truth once his father knew he'd think she had it coming, so he'd never asked the *why*, *how*, *when* questions.

Had she endured *this*?

He left the toilet, located at the end of a long, dark, staff-only corridor, and found his way back to the shop floor. The old megastore – disused for a couple of years now – was on a retail park outside town. Pets at Home and Dunelm were still going strong, but nothing had, as yet, moved into the defunct toyshop. Keith Powers, a witchfinder of the Working Men's Club, was a key holder for the whole trading park, and he was well liked enough that the other security guards and their dogs had agreed to take a few hours off.

Luke accidentally stepped on Batman's head. A cardboard cut-out, a remnant of the toy shop. Shopfitters had cleared out most of the warehouse; it was a shell. Only a few empty shelving units remained, although some kids must have got in at some point and scrawled shite graffiti squiggles over them. Electrical cables hung down from the ceiling like vines, and the few light fittings that were still installed strobed. Below, about sixty men milled around, beers in hand, waiting for the show to start.

Some men from the Working Men's Club, and a great many more he didn't recognise, stood around the contraption. Witchfinders from cells all over Europe had flown in for this event. The Working Men's Club was only one chapter of a very splintered movement. Once, many centuries ago, there had been a council of witchfinders, but – and no doubt Niamh would say this was all too predictable – squabbles and power struggles had broken out and now there were many, disparate groups: the Working Men's Club covered the north of England; The Hammers were based in the south; Slains Boys in Scotland, and so many more.

And then, of course, the flag-waving, Bible-bashing Noblemen from America. Big Jock Romaine had flown all the way from Texas. He was especially popular within their movement, with quite the presence on the Dark Web. His sidekick was filming the events tonight and they'd no doubt be uploaded later for his followers to wank over.

Romaine mugged frantically for the camera like some sugared-up TikTok brat. 'This is your bro, Big Jock, right here in Halifax, In-Ger-Land for the first British dunking in almost twenty years. Can you believe that?'

Luke swallowed more bile. One of those last women drowned had been his mother. Big Jock went on. 'I'm here with our brother from the York-Shire Chapter of the Working Men's Club, Peter Ridge. What can you tell us about the hag, my man?'

His father, wearing a three-piece tweed suit and tie especially, stepped forward. He was stiff before a camera, but visibly proud, holding himself taller. 'Well it was actually my son, Luke, who gathered the evidence we needed.' Peter beckoned Luke to join him but he gravely shook his head. 'Her name is Sheila Henry. Especially repugnant woman, passing herself off as a local vicar if you can believe it?'

'No fuckin' way! Fuckin' blasphemous cunt. Working with kids and shit like a fuckin' groomer, man.'

'It is a disgrace.'

There was some motion from close to the dunking tank. Jock returned to the camera. 'Let's get this show on the road.'

The audience was composed almost exclusively of white men, from spotty teenagers to men well into their retirement. It had taken Luke an embarrassingly long time to notice that most witchfinders are white, and even longer to question why. You didn't have to go very far online to encounter the assumption that all Black or Asian people are automatically involved with witchcraft or occultism. That had ever been the case: Luke had dug out old ledgers of suspected witches from bygone eras and – surprise, surprise – guess what a lot of the targets had in common.

Another individual stood out from the crowd for a different reason. Luke vaguely recognised him, but he wasn't sure it was from the Men's Club. This man wore an expensive suit, albeit an ill-fitting one, and shoes so polished they shone. His pencil neck was much too skinny for the shirt he wore. His hair was strawberry blond, but his face was unremarkable. His expression was sheepish, like he badly wanted to be invisible. He seemed to be watching the clock, checking his phone rather than engaging with his fellow witchfinders. There honestly wasn't time to worry about his identity now.

With an electric hum, the machine whirred to life. It was beginning.

Luke couldn't bring himself to look at Sheila, already strapped into the device. The witchfinders had some rich donors, including some notable names from the aristocracy, happy to anonymously give to the cause. Over the decades, the Dunking Pod had been updated, modernised, but it still looked like it was straight out of Frankenstein's laboratory.

This incarnation was an expertly modified fairground attraction. One of those dunk tanks, where you hurl a beanbag at the target and some poor person plunges into the pool below. Only now, above the Perspex tank, they'd welded a medical-grade chair, complete with leather-bound arm and leg restraints. Sheila's hands were encased in lead-lined gloves and there was a scolds' bridle strapped around her face. A metal bit was lodged in her mouth, pressing down on her tongue.

Witchfinders believed this would stop a witch from using her powers. Luke knew otherwise, but couldn't say anything without giving Niamh – or himself – away.

He dared to glance upwards. Although no doubt still woozy from being drugged in the back of PC Brent's car, Sheila looked directly at Luke, her blue eyes watering.

She spoke to him: *Luke, please.* He heard her voice so clearly in his head. What was it Niamh called the ones who could do that? Sentients. *You have to stop this. I won't survive the tank, I'm not an elemental.*

He wasn't sure how to communicate. He felt tears sting his eyes. He filled his head with how sorry he was, how he was desperately trying to protect the woman he loved, and her adopted little sister. He also told her how he knew that didn't make this right, that she was totally innocent.

These men kill women. I am begging you. Think of my wife.

He backed away. He couldn't watch this. He bumped into someone. His father. 'Oi, where you goin'?'

He blinked at him. 'Nowhere.'

You can stop this, Luke.

How? How could he possibly stop this thing he'd started? There were about sixty men congregating around the tank. He couldn't fight them all. It was too late. The wheels had started in motion the second he handed over that dashcam footage. He wanted to kill himself. He could think of no other way to get rid of this feeling.

'Sheila Henry, of the Metropolitan Borough of Calderdale,' Peter started. 'You stand accused of witchcraft, how to you plead? Nod for guilty. Shake for not guilty.'

Sheila didn't move for a second, of course unable to speak. Her forehead gleamed with sweat. A thick silence squeezed all the air out of the room.

After a moment, Sheila slowly, deliberately – proudly even – nodded. The male audience gasped in horror. The whole point of the tank was to force a confession. They never, *ever* admit to it.

Luke stepped to his father's side. 'She confessed.'

'So what?'

'So don't we let her go?' he spat. 'We don't need to see if she survives the dunking, right?'

His father looked at him with a distasteful sneer, like he smelled something rotten. 'What? You reckon we let her go? Off you pop, love, don't do any more witching? It don't work like that, son. It's not *fishing*, there's no letting them go once they're caught.'

Peter gave a nod to the man operating the pod. He pressed a sturdy green button and, with a mechanical clank, the chair jerkily began its descent into the water. Sheila's eyes widened.

'Luke, my lad, this just saves us time. Make it out in time for last orders.'

Next to Luke, Big Jock almost came in his pants. 'Oh, here we go, here we fuckin' go.'

Water lapped at Sheila's calves as the chair inched downwards. They'd designed it this way, painstakingly slow, to elicit the confession. 'Dad, come on. You can't just kill her.'

'Just watch. She'll try something. Just wait.'

'What if she's not one of the ones who can . . .'

'Luke, shut your fuckin' mouth or I'll shut it for yer. They always try something, believe you me.'

Luke took a step towards the tank, but Peter seized his arm. 'If you do one thing to mess this up, I swear to God, I'll bury you myself. You hear me?' And Luke believed it. He'd killed his first wife after all. Luke glanced up and saw not Sheila, but his mother, in the chair. She was petite, with waist-length coils of chestnut hair. He thought of her wearing the bridle, her big eyes darting around, looking for anyone who might take pity on her.

The device continued to crank Sheila further into the water. She groaned, panicking, as she was submerged to her chest. She struggled against her restraints.

'Most hags can last between thirty seconds to a minute underwater,' Big Jock explained. 'But of course, if what we have on our hands here is a real, live witch, who fuckin' knows what she's gonna do!'

But Sheila squealed as best she could. Dribble ran down her chin. Her eyes rolled wildly. Peter's grip on Luke's arm tightened. He knew nothing about Sheila's powers. Niamh had explained the seven-point scale once, but how only 4 per cent of witches ever were more powerful than a Level 5. Could Sheila survive this? He had no clue what level she was, or what level of witch could theoretically survive drowning.

She struggled against her ties as her face entered the water. She shook her head back and forth. The noise. The noise was the most awful thing Luke had ever heard. 'Dad, please. This is murder.'

His dad looked at him as if he were thick. 'They're not fuckin' human, Luke. It's a *monster*. A *witch*.'

The wailing stopped, but the winch continued once her

head went under. The chair kept going. Through the translucent sides of the tank, they still had a clear view of Sheila as she struggled.

'Start the timer!' Jock cried, hardly able to contain himself. Young John Ackroyd took a selfie of himself next to the tank, making a peace sign with his fingers.

At fifteen seconds in, the longest fifteen seconds, all the air burst out of Sheila's mouth. 'Sixteen, seventeen, eighteen . . .' the crowd chanted. It was like being at a football stadium.

Sheila went limp in the chair, all her fight gone. Her eyes closed.

'Twenty-one, twenty-two, twenty-three . . .'

Luke pulled his arm free. 'Fuck you,' he hissed in his father's face and he strode towards the tank, picking up PC Steve Brent by the collar and tossing him aside. The winch controls were within sight. He could take the guy holding it.

'Stop him!' Peter shouted.

John Ackroyd got in his face. Luke made a fist and thrust it into the pipsqueak's nose. He felt a satisfying crunch and the boy shrieked. Arms wrapped around his throat, but he shrugged off whoever it was attempting to leap on his back. The guy holding the control box saw him coming, took in the determination on Luke's face, and dropped it at once. He fled.

Luke seized the control panel and tried to figure out which button would lift her to safety.

He stopped. On the other side of the screen, Sheila's eyes popped open. They were white hot, blazing through the water. She looked right through him.

Cracks, like spiderwebs, fractured the plastic walls of the pod. Water hissed through at great pressure. Luke stepped aside. Maybe she didn't need a knight in shining armour after all.

'What the fuck?' Jock cried, edging away.

The pair of men trying to drag Luke away from the tank eased off, more focused on what was happening inside the pod. The entire tank vibrated. 'What is she doing?' someone yelled.

'Get back!' Peter ordered. 'Run!'

Too late. The Cucking Pod exploded. Luke threw his arms up to protect his face, but was knocked off his feet as water gushed over the warehouse floor. As he hit the deck, he heard someone else scream; he glanced up and saw Jock's lackey clutching a blooded shard of plastic shrapnel, now jutting out of his midriff. Luke felt a brief headrush of delight.

In the middle of it all was Sheila Henry. Soaking wet, she levitated a metre or so off the floor, free from the chair contraption. She reached for her head and undid the bridle, letting it fall to the floor with a clang. Her eyes continued to burn like ice-fire.

The witchfinders ran, screaming, for the exits. 'Freeze,' Sheila commanded and even Luke found himself unable to move. The witch hovered down to earth. She sought out Big Jock Romaine as their leader. '*You*,' she said vengefully. She reached out and he was dragged across the wet floor on his arse to her waiting hands.

'Stop!' Big Jock whimpered. 'Please.'

Luke found himself able to move a little. He tried to stand.

Sheila held Jock about a foot off the ground before her. His hand flew to his neck as if she had him by the throat. Through gritted teeth, she told him, 'I will live to see the day when men no longer fear powerful women.'

But Sheila didn't see what Luke saw.

Behind her, Peter Ridge stepped forward, a stout crossbow in his hands.

'No!' Luke cried.

There was an efficient pop, and then a cloud of red sprayed through the air. Both Sheila and Jock gracelessly thudded to the ground. 'No, you won't,' Peter Ridge told her dead body. A sleek arrow was wedged in her skull, the tail sticking out of the back of her head. Jock retreated, whimpering.

Peter now turned his attention, and the reloaded crossbow, to his son. 'And what are we gonna do with you, eh?'

Leonie *SURPRISE* 30th
Niamh, Elle, Helena, you

> Hello. Have you guys heard anything from Leonie please?

Elle Pearson
Hey love. Afraid not. How are you doing?

Niamh Kelly
Me either, I'm afraid.

> I'm a little worried. Nothing since yesterday.

Elle Pearson
Keep us posted. I'll call if I hear anything.

> Thank you, ladies.

Chapter Forty-Five

WOMEN'S INTUITION

Chinara – London, UK

With this much nervous energy, the only place to turn was the gym. It was open twenty-four hours. It was bright; it played deep house around the clock; it had air con. This place was a sanctuary to Chinara. Everything made sense here. If you get inside your body, you have to get out of your head. It never failed.

She upped the speed on the treadmill, her calves burning. Sweat poured down her face. She couldn't worry about Leonie when she was pushing herself so hard.

A figure appeared on the neighbouring treadmill. 'Back again?'

Chinara slowed the machine down to a power-walk. 'You're one to talk.'

Samantha Kwan was her trainer. They'd had a punishing circuit session that morning. 'Just finished with my last client.' Her accent was pure Melbourne, but she now lived in Clapham. 'What's up?'

Sam was a witch. A lower-level healer, she was training to be a physio alongside her PT gig. Chinara admitted,

'Leonie hasn't replied to her phone since yesterday evening.'

Sam had made no secret of the fact she was *interested* in Chinara *that* way, but always feigned the appropriate level of polite interest in Leonie. 'Maybe her phone died? I'm sure it's nothing to worry about.'

'Hmm.' Chinara made a neutral noise, unwilling to say how she really felt. What she wanted to do was scream and scream and light the sky with fire. As she always did, she squashed it down, sat on the suitcase until it zipped shut. Chinara understood her role; she was the calm, stoic one. So which was it? Leonie was in trouble, or she was at the bottom of a K-Hole somewhere. For the first time in their relationship, she really hoped it was the latter. Alas, this time she knew Leonie's head was in the game. With Radley's life on the line, she wouldn't be so reckless. So that only left Option A.

'You're really worried?'

Again, Chinara said nothing, her jaw straining.

'You can tell me the truth, Chi.'

Chinara continued to pound the treadmill. She knew Leonie. She'd have found a way to charge her phone. She nurtured the thing like *it* was a baby.

Samantha sighed. 'OK. What would she do if the tables were turned?'

Chinara made a fist and hit the big red button that stopped the treadmill. 'She'd move heaven and earth.'

She hopped off the device, and headed for the changing room without saying another word.

'Chi? What did I say?'

Chinara spoke to the universe and hoped her partner got the message. *Sorry, my love. I'm coming to get you whether you like it or not.*

Chapter Forty-Six

DRESS REHEARSAL

Ciara – Manchester, UK

'Darling, who are you talking to?'

'Gaia. I can hear Gaia. She talks to me. She takes care of me.'

'Ciara, my love, that's a dead spider. Now, come down from there.'

It took everything she had, but Ciara rolled across the ceiling so she was flat on her back. Everything hurt. It felt like her limbs were fused in the wrong sockets. 'Leave me alone.'

Dab idled across the ballroom floor, metres below her. 'You've been up there for two days, Ciara dear.'

Her arms were covered in bruises, where unseen demon hands had held her down. Where Dab had held her down too. She was safer up here, with the dust and cobwebs. Millington Hall, their country retreat, was falling fast into disrepair. Stately homes were notoriously hard to maintain, and Lord and Lady Hale much preferred the ease of their Chelsea townhouse.

Hale walked circles around their altar: a rectangular

marble slab. It was rust-red with dried blood. Hale had killed a child. A human sacrifice to summon Belial.

Ciara hadn't stuck around to see if it worked. She also hadn't asked where they'd got the child. Who he was. The only thing that had made her feel better was eloping with Asmodai, a powerful demon of lust. She'd experienced arousal for days, orgasm after orgasm, her body spasming. Each violent release blasted her out of reality, into some sensual galaxy, light years away from the hard edges of Millington Hall.

She hadn't heard from Jude in months. She'd ticked off all the stages of grief: shock, pain, fury, depression and acceptance. He had gone. She did not know why. They were in love. She was a fucking mind reader, for fuck's sake. You can't fake it around a sentient. He'd left her with a dogsitter – Dabney Hale. She was struggling with things now. Getting washed and dressed, making food. She didn't have much strength if there wasn't a demon inside her to move her body.

It's funny how it creeps up on you. When she wasn't invoked, she felt so rancid, the only way to cope was to seek yet more demon help. And they were always so willing. Even now, she was only too aware of a lesser demon whispering to her from inside the air vent to her left. It was in the air itself. Ciara considered letting it in; the borrowed power could get her down from the ceiling. She could take a bath, maybe eat something, although the thought of solids in her stomach felt painful to even think about.

'Ciara, come down,' Hale now commanded. He raised a hand and she felt him peel her off the cornicing. She floated downwards, crumpling to the floor. Her legs were jelly. There was no way she could stand. Stark December light blared through three tall sash windows. It hurt her

eyes to look up at Dab. He crouched at her side, turning her chin to face him. 'Pull yourself together,' he told her. 'You're a mess.'

'I can't do this.'

'Can't do what?'

'The little boy . . .' A tear ran across her nose and onto the floor.

'And what little boy would that be?'

'Stop. Please stop. Just stop this. I don't want to kill mundanes, Dab.'

'Bit late for that, darling. Can't make an omelette without breaking eggs.'

'They're not eggs.'

'Tell that to hens.'

She half-laughed, half-cried. 'It's too much. We've gone too far. It's not fun any more.'

He crouched beside her, took her by the shoulders and hoisted her into a sitting position. Her head lolled forwards. 'This isn't about fun. It's about claiming our birthright on this planet. We are gods, Ciara, and we're forced to lurk in the shadow of myth. We pretend to be inferior, and for what? To not scare the tadpoles? It's insanity. The mundanes don't have to die. They just need to recognise their place in the natural order.'

Ciara shook her heavy head. 'They'll fight.'

'Let them try.'

She shook her head. 'Not the mundanes; HMRC. They'll fight you.'

Dabney Hale's eyes gleamed like quicksilver, and she suddenly understood. He wasn't alone in there. His voice deepened. 'I certainly hope so.'

✧

Ciara awoke, almost choking. She coughed and sat upright in bed. She was alone because *someone* wasn't checking his WhatsApp messages. She checked her phone and Luke still hadn't even read her last message. Annoying.

It was almost 5:30. There was no point in going back to sleep now, her alarm was set for 6 a.m.. Instead, she took out the notebook she'd started using to keep track of her debris. What a sorry timeline it was:

Born
Revived sparrow
Trip to London???
Mum and Dad dead
Move to Hebden
Hex scummy boy in town with Lee
Uni
Jude
Move to Niamh's
War???
Hotel Carnoustie
Got severed

Ciara rubbed her eyes and added 'Millington Hall with Dab' to the timeline between *Jude* and *Move to Niamh's*. That was when she'd started to think about leaving. Hale's plans were fucking ridiculous. It was embarrassing that she'd gone to him so readily. She'd had no one else to turn to and couldn't cope by herself. She'd never be that weak again. A vow.

She tried to force herself to remember more, but all she could think about was how much she wanted a black coffee.

It would have to wait. Today was a big day.

⛤

The HMRC events team, a department of very stressed young witches fresh from the graduate intern scheme, were already preparing the Great Hall in the House of Hekate. Autumnal floral boughs were suspended at intervals from the upper mezzanine: Opulent golden and red oak leaves, and wheat, and amaranths trailed over the hall.

Now Ciara was here, this all felt very real, and very like being back at school. The room was breathtaking really, even for someone who didn't give two shits about architecture; an arched ceiling soared over them, and a trinity of stained-glass windows loomed over the stage they were now erecting. They abstractly depicted the three ages of Gaia: Maiden, Mother, Crone.

Halloween had really crept up on her. Three days to go, and she'd be High Priestess. If it weren't so fucking absurd, it'd be laughable. Clearly, becoming the poster girl for Good and Nice Witches™ hadn't been on her agenda, but why not? With the resources of HMRC at her fingertips – she could do anything, go anywhere. She could delegate all the boring bits to minions and do the ceremonial stuff she wanted to do. The exact same way Guy Milner seemed to. Elle would keep her mouth shut and, when the time was right, she'd let Leonie in on the secret. Most of it.

No one was more surprised than Ciara, but she was starting to *enjoy* life in Hebden Bridge. Cocktails and yoga with old friends; a strapping man who liked eating her out; a clever young witch to mentor. Niamh had elbowed her away from the trough her whole life. Maybe now it was Ciara's turn. A plan beyond simply locating Hale was starting to take shape in her mind.

What if she kept it up for two years or so, until Theo

was old enough to stand on her own two feet, and then Ciara could retire at forty. In that time, she could even makeover the crusty old coven too. Why not? She was in charge, right? In her eyes, it was fucking wild they were swishing about in capes at vainglorious events like this when – according to the news – the ice caps were melting at a terrifying rate; plagues; wars; actual fucking Nazis were a thing again, and witches like Fay and Hale were trying to introduce eugenics to the coven.

Truly the best playground game: *If you were in charge for the day, what's the first thing you'd do?* Ciara found she quite wanted to play that game for real.

If Elle and Leonie *could* keep schtum, where was the issue? It was funny, Ciara had even selected a much more Helena-ish outfit today; every woman owns a black roll-neck mime jumper, and she'd paired it with a smart skirt and boots. She felt she looked the part; her hair pulled into a neat ponytail.

'The audience sits here,' Sandhya told her, walking her down an imaginary aisle. 'You enter from the main doors, do the whole procession nice and slow, and go on stage via those stairs to the left.'

Ciara was aware of Selina Fay hovering at her side. 'Where will the Prime Minister be?' Fay asked.

Moira Roberts answered that one. 'Ideally two hundred miles south of here.' Ciara hid a smirk behind her hand. She was starting to warm to Roberts.

'He's determined to come,' Fay replied.

'He is, or that shitweasel Harkaway is?' said Ciara.

Selina smiled tersely, again in her signature Ruby Woo lip. 'On the contrary, I think the Prime Minister is rather fascinated by us all. We're a new hobby.'

'Like fox hunting?' Ciara quipped.

'Quite. Given what I've learned about him since the election, I suspect he'll get bored soon and move on to a new whim.'

'Here's hoping,' said Moira.

'The Prime Minister will be on stage,' Sandhya explained wearily. Ciara was starting to think the young woman was singlehandedly running HMRC. 'We're going to have a few seats for dignitaries.'

Selina Fay then added, 'The Prime Minister has requested that he give a brief speech.'

All the women said no in unison. 'Tell him it's forbidden for men to speak in the House of Hekate. He won't know any different,' Moira said. 'Sheila Henry will do the opening address and introduce Niamh.'

Oh, that was her. 'I'm not going to give a great big speech,' she said.

'You have to,' Selina said. 'It's tradition.'

'Fuck tradition,' she said, before remembering to be her sister. 'We're a modern coven now, let it be a sign of things to come. We have far more pressing issues than the coronation.'

Last night, Chinara Okafor had called her. She hadn't been able to get hold of Leonie for over forty-eight hours, and was starting to worry. She'd contacted Moira at once to mobilise Supernormal Security but it had kept Ciara up until the early hours. For one thing, she owed Leonie her life, but if Hale alluded her, Ciara would be back to square one. 'I want Leonie and Radley found, now. Leonie's had enough time to dig him out. I want witches from every coven looking for them, OK? If I'm in charge of HMRC, that's what I want everyone working on. It's, like, an order.'

The other witches nodded agreement. 'She was last in

Ankara,' Moira said. 'There's no formal coven there any more, but I've already asked the Athens sisterhood to get over there.'

'Good. Can't we send a team? Could we put all those scary bitches who tried to kill Theo to better use?'

Someone cleared their throat at the other end of the Great Hall. The young oracle, Emma Benwell, entered the chamber. 'Leonie is in danger.'

Ciara strode to meet her in the middle. 'What have you seen?'

'Bloodshed. The walls run red.'

'What? Where? Where is she?' Ciara was surprised at how panicked her voice sounded.

'They travelled north,' Emma said, staring past her.

'To where?'

'It's cold. Very cold. A sea of white as far as the eye can see.'

Ciara looked to Moira. 'That could be anywhere. Can you be specific?'

Emma shook her head. 'It's dark. She can't see. It's so very dark.'

'Is she alive?' Ciara hissed.

'Yes,' said the oracle. 'For now.'

Chapter Forty-Seven

REUNION

Leonie – Siberia, Russia

She would not eat the rats. Not yet, anyway. At any rate, they were keeping her company. They too were looking for food, warmth. They knew to avoid the stinking grate she'd been using as a toilet. Rats aren't daft.

Leonie understood she was being tortured, and it was torture. They'd given her a cheap jumper and some sweat-pants to wear, but her feet were bare. There was a thin blanket on a thinner mattress in the windowless cell, and she curled into a foetal ball, but between the starvation and the crippling cold, she had to face the fact this might kill her.

She didn't know precisely where she was; she'd been drugged unconscious back on Aeaea. The men who'd dragged her into this dungeon, and the ones who brought her water, spoke Russian, so that was her best guess. She knew only she was underground, deep underground. She couldn't sense a mundane for miles and miles. As she grew weak through hunger, her powers faded too.

There was no way out of this one.

She thought about Chinara. What a fool she'd been to take that woman for granted. Why hadn't she treated every single moment with her like it was pure gold? She couldn't even remember what her final words to her had been; she'd been in such a hurry to get on the road. Leonie cursed her childish recklessness, her arrogance. Chinara would be left with nothing except half a basket of dirty laundry in the bedroom. No tearful departure gate at sunset for them.

With what meagre sentience she had left, Leonie told the universe – the walls, the air – how much she loved Chinara Okafor. Like a message in a bottle, hopefully someday it would come ashore.

She thought about Senait. Where the hell did she go? It troubled her greatly. Her betrayal, yes, but also how much she doubted it. Leonie was a Level 6 sentient. While Senait was powerful, Leonie had seen inside her. She had never once sensed deceit. Lies are cobalt blue and magenta, hard to conceal. Senait was many things: fickle, inquisitive, loyal . . . it didn't add up that she'd willingly sell out the coven for grubby old money. So that left only the consideration that the young witch had tried to double-cross Hale.

So who was really the naïvest? Senait for thinking she could outsmart Dabney Hale, or Leonie for truly thinking Senait wasn't guilty as sin? Why else would she run? Why wouldn't she collect the other half of her reward? Nothing made sense.

Wherever she was, Leonie hoped she was safe, sincerely. There was even an ember of hope in her heart. Maybe Senait could get her out of this somehow. She owed her one.

She thought about Zehra, about how she'd rejected her

on what transpired to be her final night. One minute, eating halloumi and necking Sauvignon, and the next . . . how can a thing as huge as death be so blithe? She couldn't have known, but Leonie couldn't shake the thought that Zehra had gone to bed that night embarrassed about their aborted kiss. There was a pain in her middle. She didn't really know much about the woman beyond her academic excellence. Was she married? Did she have kids? She hadn't taken the time to find out.

Nor had she taken the time to learn about Jason Ellis or Carlo D'Agostino's private lives either. She'd deliberately hidden from whatever foibles made them men, not just killers. She didn't even know the name of the man she'd so casually maimed on the island.

Savages, pure savages, all of us.

Hale had teleported her off Aeaea so fast, Leonie had no idea how they'd left the island. For all she knew, they'd massacred the lot of them. She wouldn't put it past him. She couldn't cry any more, she was too weak.

And, finally, she thought about her brother. She couldn't sense him. For the first time, the doubt crept in. She might well be too late. Her brother – one of two people who'd been in her life always – may be dead. If she'd taken her girlfriend for granted, her treatment of Radley was worse by far. *She* knew how he felt about her, of course – the pride, how he idolised his big sister. In contrast, she'd treated him as a *nuisance* her whole life. She had never ever told him how much she loved him; how they shared a life; how only they knew the journey that had taken them from the Belle Isle estate to being two of the most powerful witches in the country. No one but Leonie and Radley really knew. And she'd never told him.

And now she might not get a chance.

'No regrets' had been the motto of her twenties. No regrets! Saying yes to every invitation; staying out for nights on end; washing her knickers in the sink and drying them on the radiator for the next day; powering through on Excelsior or coke. No regrets! So how come she now had so many with her in this damp cell?

When the door opened suddenly, the light from the corridor almost burned her eyes out of her skull. How long had she been in the dark? Two burly men entered. 'What's happening?' she barely got the last word out before a burlap sack was shoved over her head. Her wrists were already in silver cuffs and she was dragged to her feet by them now. She felt strong hands steer her towards the corridor; the air was at once less rancid. 'Where are we going?'

One of the men spoke in Russian, she guessed it was nothing kind.

Leonie could see about a centimetre of floor if she looked down, and managed to walk in a straight line. She felt acutely nauseous; hungry but beyond wanting food. She felt like she was levitating, even if she could see her feet on the concrete floor. Eventually, they came to a service elevator and she was rammed inside. As the lift went up, some listless sentience returned to her. They must be above ground.

The lift jolted to a stop and she was driven forward by a gun tip between her shoulder blades. Here, she heard more voices. All male, all Russian. Except one. 'There she is!' The sack was yanked off her head. She stood before Dabney Hale in what looked to be an old factory. The air smelled brutish, of engine oil and woodchips. Maybe a timber mill? 'Crikey, Miss Jackson. You've seen better days. You've smelled better days too.'

Leonie, honestly, was too weak for sass. The Russian men, mundanes she sensed, flanked her. She saw now they all had machine guns too.

Hale went on. 'I wonder now if you have some sense of what my poor sister went through in captivity.'

Maybe she did have room for sass after all. 'Your sister was captured during a war you started because you told her to fight. You should . . .' her mind went hazy through starvation, 'put *yourself* in a dungeon.'

Hale raised an eyebrow. 'Good one.' He was still wearing Solomon's crown. 'Anyway, I found I worked out a lot of my resentment on your brother . . .'

Leonie's heart sank. 'What did you do to him?'

He smiled. 'Right this way.'

The factory floor was partitioned by medical screens, the space divided into makeshift cubicles. A stout man in a white lab coat emerged from a bay and, as he stepped aside, Leonie saw a form that once resembled Radley on a gurney. 'Oh my gods!' she cried. 'What the fuck?'

She lunged to his side. Her brother's face was bruised and swollen as he lay unconscious. There were colours of bruise she wouldn't have thought possible – almost canary yellow circles under his eyes. His head was wrapped in blood-stained bandages. 'You motherfucker,' she spat at Hale, throwing her whole body at him.

Hardly raising his hand, he crushed her to the floor like a tin can. She howled, grovelling at his feet. 'Stay there,' he said, pressing her face to the grimy floor.

Leonie grimaced. 'Why don't you just kill us, Dabney?'

She felt his psychic hold loosen and she sat up. Using Radley's bed, she climbed to her feet. 'That would be wasteful,' he said simply. 'I have use for you both.'

Her vision swam. Leonie had to lean on the bed to stay

upright. 'What? What the fuck is all this? Where even are we?'

A smarter man definitely wouldn't do the whole Bond villain exposition thing, reveal his dastardly masterplan, but this was *Dabney Hale* and she was like 98 per cent certain he would. His ego got its own seat on a plane. 'We're in Siberia,' he told her. 'This place was to be my safehouse if I had to leave the UK during the war.'

'I guess you didn't get out in time.'

'Evidently. It's a relief to know I'm still a hero to so many warlocks all over the world. I was welcomed with open arms.'

'I can believe it.'

'Mock if you want, Leonie, but I dared to say what almost every warlock on this sorry planet was thinking. Including your brother, I'd hazard.'

'Fuck off!' Leonie snapped. 'Rad has spent the last eight years trying to pick up the pieces of what you did.'

'Because he wanted to, or because he was scared he'd end up in a cell like me? Every time a warlock spoke out, we were subjugated by HMRC. Men have been silenced for years.'

'Oh cry me a river. Get over it; witches are just more powerful.'

'Not any more, you're not.' Once more she felt blinding pain ripple through her skeleton. It was like he was trying to force her organs out from inside her torso. Her screams echoed off the factory walls as red spots danced across her vision.

'Stop!' she gasped, and he did.

'King Solomon knew to fear you,' he tapped the Seal. 'Oh, he knew. I'm going to finish what he started.'

'Why?' Leonie panted. 'Why can't you just let us *be*?'

'The way *feminism* let men be?'

That's not the same and you know it, she told him directly.

Hale gestured at the men milling about the factory. 'Think about it. The world started to unravel when women rejected their natural place in things. Since our rotten species dragged itself out of the ocean and walked tall, it was woman's duty to rear children, and man's to hunt, to provide for his offspring. When women renounced their birthright; when machine replaced man, the world plummeted into terminal decline. Men and women are not the same. We have different biology, different temperaments, different roles in the world. We must elevate man to his previous dominion.'

Leonie glared at him. 'Then answer me this: why did Gaia make us stronger than you?'

He ignored that. 'This has been in the works for a long time. Most of the time I was in Grierlings, in fact. This compound is a training camp. Here, mundanes learn to fight witches.' He stroked Radley's hair as he slept. 'That's why we need fresh meat for the troops to practise on. Find ways to hurt witches.'

Leonie stared him down, perplexed. 'What? Why would you do that? That's suicide.'

Now he spoke only to her. *Warlocks and mundanes have a common enemy.*

'Witches?'

Hale sat in an office chair and kicked his feet up onto the rim of Radley's bed. 'I hadn't long been in Grierlings when an official from the Shadow Cabinet came to see me. Part of my plea deal to keep me out of the Pipes was my cooperation. I told both HMRC *and* the government how I'd planned my uprising, but I soon saw an opportunity. After your actions during the scuffles, the Shadow Cabinet were suddenly – and rightly, in my opinion – terrified of you. I think they thought of you as a quaint book club with a bit of sage and a few black cats. Now, because of the war, they saw you for what you are – women of mass destruction.' Hale leaned in closer. 'They want you gone.'

Leonie shook her head. 'You had witches in your . . . cult or whatever it was. Ciara, Clarissa . . . loads of women.'

Hale grinned. 'Women who knew their place! I agree; initially my quest was for supernormal supremacy but if the war taught me one thing it's that women cannot be trusted. Not ever. So now I have refined our goals.'

'Male supremacy.'

He grinned again. *Not quite, dearheart.*

She began to speak but he put a finger to her lips. *Warlock supremacy.*

Mundane men really hate women. Even I was quite taken aback. But if they hate women, you should hear how they feel about powerful *women. And if they hate powerful* mundane *women they reserve their most feverish hatred for witches.*

'You're going to use them?' she breathed. '

A limitless army all around the world. A hundred men to every witch. They don't fear powerful men, *after all, and I'm the most powerful one there is. They bow before me as a god. Under my guidance, they will rid the world of witches for me and then . . .*

The truth crept over her like nightfall. In a world with no more witches . . . 'No one can stop you.'

'No one,' Hale said with purpose. *The world will be mine to do with as I please. A new age is upon us, Leonie.*

You might want to consider joining me. Everything will change, and Leviathan will rise.

She shook her head. 'We stopped you before.'

Once more he tapped the new toy on his head. 'I didn't have this. I control every demon in the wind, rain and soil. There isn't a witch on earth who can stop me, Leonie.' He licked his thumb and wiped a mark off her cheek. She flinched from his touch. 'Why don't you join me? I'll spare witches who are willing to kneel before me. You already quit HMRC; you're halfway there.'

Leonie glared at him. 'I'd rather die.'

'I thought you'd say that.'

'So what? You're going to use me as target practice too?'

Now he frowned. 'No! I told you; I have really exciting plans for you.' When she didn't say anything, he went on. 'I can't take credit for this one, the idea came from my friend inside the Shadow Cabinet. Leonie Jackman, you're going to be the most famous witch since Tituba! Your name will be written in the history books.'

'Why?' she said through gritted teeth.

He came close, so close she felt his breath on her cheek. 'You're going to assassinate the Prime Minister.'

Chapter Forty-Eight

UNRAVELLING

Elle – Hebden Bridge, UK

Elle had found great comfort in cleaning long before #cleanstagram was a thing. A few years ago, she started a @myhebdenhome account but had soon got bored with only 19 followers, two of which were Leonie on different accounts. Still, her mother had always said *a tidy home makes for a tidy mind* and she was – on that note at least – right. But today, organising the pantry wasn't helping.

That evening, it had started simply enough – a quest to find an old bottle of White Sorbus she could use to keep Holly out of her mind while she worked out what to do with the Jez problem. Her daughter was getting more confident with every passing day and, while it was possible to occlude her thoughts for much of the day, by night, when she was tired, it was nigh on impossible. Elle just needed a little more time.

Thoughts of Leonie were eating at her too. Ciara had told her things had escalated. Selfishly, Elle had hoped Lee would be on her way to the UK with Hale by now. As much as she hated it, perhaps Ciara was right and he was her best shot. That hope was going south fast. She'd had to mute her phone, checking the group chat for a reply from Leonie was becoming obsessive. Poor Chinara too, she must be going out of her mind.

Digging out the jar of sorbus had escalated to a full-on shelf meltdown. Not even using her label maker was taking the edge off her spiralling anxiety.

As the autumn nights drew in earlier and earlier, it felt too like life was closing in on her. Her options were narrowing. She could go and confess all to HMRC, tell them she'd performed witchcraft against a mundane. She supposed, in a way, Ciara *was* HMRC, or at least she would be in two days' time.

Elle wasn't a total simpleton. Aligning herself with Ciara was a one-way ticket to Grierlings. The Device name *did* have clout though. If she went over Ciara's head to the elders – Moira Roberts or Sheila Henry – they might be able to get the sentients on the case and oust Ciara as an imposter.

Ciara. Even thinking her name was enough to make Elle feel like puking. Reality meant nothing now, not a thing. It kept hitting her from different angles like a wrecking ball: Niamh is dead; Ciara is inside Niamh's body; Ciara is *back*.

She stopped with the label maker. She put her elbows on the table and cradled her head in her hands, pressing her eye sockets with the balls of her palms until she saw glitter.

Niamh was *gone*. Her best friend in the whole world. She loved Leonie, and she had loved Helena, despite everything, but in the last few years it was Niamh who she had come to rely on. Their brunches at the Tea Cosy; mulled wine at the Christmas market; *Strictly* with a

Chinese takeaway. And now she was gone. She had been gone for some time.

Elle realised she wasn't breathing and inhaled sharply.

The door to the kitchen swung open and Theo entered. Elle's eyes darted around guiltily, and she felt the urge to hide the evidence, although there was none. Just her label maker and a load of fridge tubs. 'You all right, Theo, love?'

She smiled shyly. 'Just came to get some more Coke. Is that OK?'

'Of course, help yourself.'

'Do you want the lights on?' Elle truthfully hadn't realised she was sitting in the dark. Theo flicked them on, and crossed to the fridge, eyeing the carnage all over the kitchen table. 'Niamh could use you in her kitchen. She keeps her potions in a tin under the sink.'

Elle somehow managed to feel worse. Poor Theo. Ciara was a very specific kind of dangerous, always had been, and Elle honestly couldn't say if the orphan was safe in Niamh's cottage. When they'd been teenagers, even though Elle was older, she'd never quite trusted Ciara. A night out with her had always ended somewhere it shouldn't; hopping on the last train to Leeds; a sketchy afterparty with some sketchier guys. She'd much preferred the certainty of Helena being in total control or when Niamh had acted as her sister's Jiminy Cricket.

'Where's, um, where's Niamh today?' Elle asked.

'It's the dress rehearsal for the coronation in Manchester,' she said, digging a bottle of Diet Coke out of the fridge.

'Oh yeah.' Elle monitored herself carefully. She knew Ciara was using White Sorbus on her – that was where she'd got the idea from – but she also knew Theo had been a powerful adept. 'Theo, love?'

'Yeah?'

'How are things at home? How's Niamh? High Priestess is a big change, obviously.'

Theo shrugged a moment, clearly eager to get to the sanctuary of Holly's room. No teenager relishes talking to grown-ups. 'I dunno. I . . . things have been a bit weird, I guess.'

'Weird how?'

'Well, she's never really there. When she is, she's meditating a lot, using memory stones and stuff. Since Ciara died . . . she hasn't really been the same.'

I'd fucking well say so, Elle thought and hoped Theo couldn't hear. What to do? Ciara had her over a barrel. If her secret got out, then so would Elle's, and then what?

This year – her own *annus horribilis* – had seen her @myhebdenhome crumble metaphorically. She'd lost so much. She wouldn't lose Milo and Holly too. Absolutely not. But nor did she want to leave poor Theo in harm's way.

'Grief is a funny thing,' she said awkwardly. 'Everyone has to deal with it in their own time. But you know you're welcome here any time right? I mean that. You're a sister. You're family, Theo, and this is your home too.'

Theo looked to her feet. 'Thank you. That means a lot.'

'Come here!' Elle stood and gave Theo a hug, although she wondered if she needed it more than the girl did. A long, dark winter loomed over them, and everything felt hopeless.

Chapter Forty-Nine

MORE QUESTIONS THAN ANSWERS

Theo – Hebden Bridge, UK

While Elle was holding her, Theo saw the bottle marked White Sorbus on the table next to her label maker. She held the thought in her head all the way upstairs and into Holly's room.

'What's White Sorbus?' she asked Holly, who lay on her bed on her tummy, legs kicked up.

'No idea. This book is fucking ridiculous, by the way.' Holly leafed through *The Song of Osiris*. It had taken a fair few pricked fingers, and a scar on her thigh, but the whole book was now full of words. None very enlightening. A vampire book, though? Cool.

'Told you.'

'Like, what is this supposed to mean?' Holly rolled over and swung her legs off the bed. '*The vessel is not the entity and the entity will not assimilate the shape of the vessel.*'

Theo shrugged and dumped the Diet Coke on the desk, before turning to Holly's collection of craft texts. She had a bigger collection at the cottage, but they owned many of the same titles. What book would tell her about White Sorbus? She ran a finger along Holly's bookcase until she found a very seventies-looking hardback called *The Practitioner's Guide to Herbs, Draughts, Tinctures and Potions*. That ought to do it.

Holly went on. '*The entity can exist autonomously of its vessel although not in perpetuity. Sentient integrity will perish in the region of the hundredth day and night.* Like, what?'

'Not a clue,' Theo replied half-heartedly before giving Holly her full attention. They were listening to classic K-Pop from the late 00s/early 10s; the zenith years. Brown Eyed Girls, 2NE1, BigBang. 'I don't know what I thought was going to happen,' Theo admitted. 'I was hoping the words would fill in and it'd be all like *Oh hey, Theo Wells, here's what happened in the woods that night in twelve easy bullet points*. But, I guess not.'

'Do you need to know? I don't spend any time trying to figure out why I'm a girl, I don't see why you should have to.'

She had a point there. 'I would like to.'

Holly chewed her lip. 'So what is it about? The book?'

Theo had struggled through it, for all the good it had done. 'It's very not a page-turner. It's a lot about death, I think. What happens when we die.'

'Wasn't Osiris the god of death?'

'I think so, yes.' Theo had googled, naturally. 'Death and rebirth.'

'You were reborn in the forest.'

'I know, but I can't make head nor tail of it. It's all in riddles.'

Holly flicked through the pages and pages of scarlet words. 'I wonder why it was so secret? And why it was in my granny's house. She always said that death was inevitable and fundamental to nature.'

'The book seems to think otherwise.'

Holly's eyes widened. 'What?'

Theo, meanwhile, scanned the index pages of her own book. 'The last section . . .' She found *White Sorbus* and turned to page 165 while Holly attended to the final chapters of *The Song of Osiris*. From what Theo could tell, they were about necromancy, which HMRC took a very grim view on. That might explain why the text was concealed. It was witch porn.

She found the right part of the textbook.

White Sorbus (*Sorbus Album*)
White Sorbus is derived from the white fruits of the White Wax or Mountain Ash tree. The desiccated fruits, when ground with raw sienna or opium, and dissolved in moon-charged water, can be evaporated to produce a fine, tasteless powder. The powder can be ingested directly or mixed with food or drink.

Uses: White Sorbus is a magical sedative. Popular during Maleficarum era Europe, it was historically used to dampen a witch's gifts that she might avoid detection or persecution. Powerful and habit-forming, usage dwindled over the 20th century, replaced with the less potent Sister's Malady (see page 78).

Theo frowned. Sister's Malady she knew all too well from her time at Grierlings *and* when she'd first arrived at the cottage. It had somewhat kept her powers under control. Surely Niamh wasn't still . . . ?

She had lost nearly all her powers though, and there was no clear reason why . . .

No! No way! When Niamh had introduced Sister's Malady to her at bedtimes it was to stop her from huffing and puffing and blowing the house down, *and* she'd expressly sought her permission to administer the drug. Niamh had all sorts of shitty old bottles lying around the kitchen, and so did Elle. She was being paranoid, there was no way on earth Niamh was drugging her. What would the point be?

Gods, things were so much easier when she could read minds.

'What's up?' Holly asked.

'Nothing,' Theo said, closing the textbook and focusing on her friend.

They were both hiding. Holly was her best friend, and she knew when things weren't quite right. Even like this, Theo could sense it. There was something she wasn't saying. 'What's up with *you*?'

'Nothing,' Holly echoed.

'There is,' Theo said. 'I think a mundane could sense it to be honest, Hols.'

Holly couldn't look her in the eye. 'Did you see Milo?'

'What?'

'I read him. He came to your place.'

Shit. She'd worried this might happen.

'You promised you'd leave him alone,' Holly muttered, sullen.

'Holly, he just came over, I can't control what he does!'

'Yes you can. Hex him.'

Theo laughed, despite everything. 'I actually can't right now, but I *wouldn't* because that's really fucked up.'

Holly rolled her eyes. Sometimes Theo really felt the eleven-month age gap between them and, not to be shady, their wildly different starts in life. When you'd seen the things Theo had, it was pretty hard to give a shit about this PG13 crap, but she also knew Holly was wounded, and that was valid.

'Couldn't you just tell him to fuck off?'

Theo paused, about to tell Holly she didn't want to. 'Why?'

Holly picked up a throw pillow and hid behind it. 'Because I'm jealous,' came out as a muffled sigh.

Again, Theo wished she'd been able to read that in her first so she'd have had time to prepare an intelligent response. 'What?'

'Theo, I liked you when you were a . . . well before, and I . . . I think I like you still.' She didn't emerge from behind the cushion. 'I hate the thought of you being with Milo. I hate the thought of you being with anyone. It makes me want to rip his face off.'

Theo couldn't find the words. 'I . . . I don't know what to say. You're my sister, and I love you, Holly . . . will you look at me? Please?' Holly lowered the cushion, her face bright red. 'But I don't feel that way about girls. I would tell you if I did. I wish I did; I expect life would be more interesting.'

Holly said nothing, but sadness and shame pulsed from her in swamp green waves.

'Are you telling me you're queer?'

'I guess so. Don't tell anyone.'

Theo jumped onto the bed beside her and pulled her into a hug. 'Holly! That's so wonderful, though! Don't you think?' Her friend shrugged. 'It is! I'm so glad you said, it was very brave, and it's not like I can read you any more is it?'

'Right? Could have saved me a job.'

Theo wanted to address her crush somehow. To be

honest, she felt a little prickle of anger. Why would Holly bring something as base as sex into something as pure as friendship? Getting into that now wouldn't help, and it wasn't like Hols could help it. 'I'm very . . . flattered.'

'Great. Thanks.'

'Sorry, that came out wrong. But listen: we are witches. We took an oath. I will love you more than any boy I ever go out with. That's a promise. OK?'

That seemed to break through the cloud cover. 'Promise?'

'I swore, and I meant it.' But – as a part of that oath – she had sworn to let no man tear them asunder. Easier said than done, it turned out.

BUCKINGHAM PALACE

Dr Niamh Kelly,

I wish to send my sincere congratulations and that of my family to you on this most momentous of days.

Like my dear mother, grandfather, and all monarchs before me, I take great comfort in knowing Her Majesty's Royal Coven continues its diligent work to keep our great country, and the Commonwealth, safe from supernormal threat. I thank you personally for accepting the solemn role and responsibilities of High Priestess. I know only too well the honour and duty of the crown.

I extend a warm invitation to a reception at the palace in due course.

CHARLES R

Chapter Fifty

ST NIAMH

Ciara – Hebden Bridge, UK

It took about a thousand pins, but her hair was up, ready for a coronet. Ciara stared at her reflection, Theo behind her head. Ciara didn't look like herself, but what else was new? 'Where did you learn to do makeup like that?' she asked Theo.

'YouTube. And Drag Race.'

Ciara laughed. 'Either way, thanks.' Her eyes were smoky, black and violet, her lips palest rose pink. It had been a long, long time since she'd felt beautiful.

Being groomed by Theo sparked the echo of a memory. Her and Niamh, doing their makeup for a Friday night out. The little ritual: selecting the right music; necking as much corner-shop booze as they could so they wouldn't have to spend money once out; competing for mirror space. Gods, she could almost smell the Mugler Angel drifting all the way from 2002.

As teens, Niamh had hated their unfashionably pale skin, ruining all their towels with fake tan. Vile stuff, reeks of rusks. Ciara had always enjoyed being pale and interesting, the fact they didn't make a foundation white enough. How she'd relished *I'm not like the other girls*. She chuckled at the memory now. You learn the hard way that *every* girl wants to think they're not like other girls, and that's because girls are regarded so poorly by the world.

I think you're the prettier twin.

Niamh, you're an eejit, what are you talking about?

I heard someone say at school.

Someone blind, like? Anyway, we're identical.

No, we aren't.

Too fuckin' right. You're the good twin, and I'm the bad twin. You're Elizabeth and I'm—

No. Not this.

When she thought on Niamh, it no longer felt like a blade slicing between her ribs. It felt more like her chest had been scooped out, leaving an indentation, half a hollow easter egg. It was almost worse. She put it out of her mind. There was a coronation to worry about.

Her dress hung in a garment bag on the back of the door; for now, she wore a white terrycloth robe. She imagined this was what brides felt like on their wedding day. It was almost overwhelmingly feminine, this princess on a lily pad sensation. Ciara doubted she'd ever get married, so she might as well enjoy the moment. Still, she felt sick. She couldn't face food, but her stomach grizzled.

There was a violent gust of wind, and rain lashed against the cottage windows. Alanis was right, it was ironic. An already momentous night felt doubly foreboding, as if Gaia herself were sending bad omens. The letter from the fucking king was bad enough. She'd almost fled when the courier delivered it.

On top of everything, it seemed Luke was giving her the cold shoulder. She texted him three days ago and nothing. What did Theo call it? He was *ghosting* her. During her coma, they'd come up with a whole new word to describe what boys had done to her since she was in her teens. First Jude, and now Luke. Maybe she should be more like Niamh and marry someone like—

The whole room seemed to capsize like a ship and Ciara almost fell off the stool.

'What's wrong?' Theo asked.

For a moment, Ciara couldn't speak. 'I . . . can you open the window? I can't breathe.'

Theo frowned before doing the task. Ciara gripped the rim of the dresser. Even with the makeup she looked really, really pale. Not in a good way. 'Niamh?'

'Give me a minute,' Ciara said quietly. The dizziness passed.

'Do you want some water?'

'No. Fuck.' The ruse wasn't so funny any more. Her prior confidence was bullshit posturing. She was a fucking sham. Trapped then, and trapped still. If they put that crown on her head, there was no way out. She didn't want to be Niamh, she wanted to be Ciara. It felt like she was losing herself, fading away in the act.

You get what you deserve.

Shit. She almost puked again. It felt like there were barbs under her skin, like she was a cactus. She loosened the robe a bit, feeling constricted.

Another thought occurred to her after what the presence in the Vance Mausoleum had told her. What if this choice wasn't her choice at all? Ciara had felt in control, but what if this was Belial's plan all along? She imagined a chessboard, covered in little black pawns. Gaia on one side – or how she liked to imagine Gaia – and Satanis on the other. There they were in the middle: Niamh, Helena,

Ciara, Theo, Hale. What hands moved these pieces around the board?

The legend went that Gaia had gifted humanity with limitless freewill. Ciara sometimes questioned that.

'I can't do this,' she said again, and turned to the clock on the bedside table. Ten thirty. She'd be crowned at midnight. 'It's not too late, I can pull out.'

Theo shook her head. She'd already done her own makeup, changed into her new outfit. 'It's just cold feet or whatever. Can you remember what you told me on my first day of school?' No, clearly not. 'You said it'd be more weird if I *wasn't* nervous.'

Ciara said nothing. That sounded like a sentiment her sister would say. Niamh would have made a great mother. Ciara found herself speechless, and if she couldn't talk now, how bad would it be in that great fucking hall?

Theo perched on the foot of the bed, behind her. 'Niamh, is something going on?' There was a note of suspicion in her voice.

'What? No,' she swiftly shut that down. 'I just think this is a mistake. I'm no High Priestess. I'm not.'

Theo met her gaze in the mirror. 'I can't think of anyone who'd be better.'

From nowhere, Ciara felt tears burn her eyes. It took her by surprise.

'I meant it,' Theo went on. 'HMRC is problematic for sure – at least, it was when Helena was High Priestess.'

'Understatement.'

Theo shrugged. 'I dunno. I think it could be good again with someone like you in charge.'

Ciara smiled wryly. 'Someone *like* me?'

'Maybe the first question they ask potential High Priestesses should be *do you want to be High Priestess* and if you say yes, you're disqualified. You don't *want* the power, and that's why you should have it.'

Ciara swivelled on the stool to face Theo. 'Fuck me, you're wise for one so young.'

Theo laughed. 'It's true though. You should become High Priestess if you think you can do some good . . .'

'Girl, Helena *thought* she was "doing good", remember?'

'You are a good person, though.'

Ciara repressed an urge to cackle. 'Am I?'

'You're the best person I ever met.'

Oh fuck off, Hannah Montana. 'Then maybe you don't know Niamh Kelly the way you think you do,' Ciara said, flirting with risk. Saint Niamh rearing her head again. Ciara didn't have all the pieces, but her sister was no angel.

But Theo went on. 'Niamh; I was a crazy feral Sullied Child floating around in a cage and you let me into your home on a whim. You gave up half your life to train me, and Holly, and Snow. You gave up your career.'

Ciara longed to say her sister was addicted to praise, a dog rolling over and giving paw like a slut for Scooby Snacks. Instead, she said grudgingly, 'It was the right thing to do.'

'Exactly! Your instincts are good instincts. Like, it was kind. You're a kind person.'

Ciara looked away from her before she said something she'd very much regret.

Once, a very long time ago, she and Niamh had been at the Year 4 school disco. This was still back in Galway. 'Saturday Night' by Whigfield came on and Niamh immediately started the familiar routine. She knew it off by heart. Ciara didn't because she wasn't a massive loser. As such, Niamh *showed* her how to do each move using her sentience. As some other kids joined in, Ciara showed them too. They wouldn't have known it was witchcraft, they just picked up the vibes. Soon every single adult and child was performing the dance perfectly. The euphoria in that hall. The unity was joyous.

Only then their mother picked up on what was happening. She clapped along, smiling tersely, until the song was finished and then steered Ciara to a quiet spot at the side of the school hall. *Niamh started it*, she'd whined.

I felt what you were doing Ciara, do not lie.

Niamh just watched from the end of the corridor, drinking a Panda Pop cherryade through a straw. Did she admit to starting the dance? No she did not.

It had been in her sister's interest to maintain that status quo. Everything that had happened, Niamh had allowed to happen. 'Can you leave me alone for a second, please?' she said.

Theo said sure and headed out. Ciara looked deep into her eyes in the mirror. They would pay for putting their faith at the altar of St Niamh of Kelly. *Fuck it, let's do this.*

Chapter Fifty-One

CAPTIVITY

Luke – Wakefield, UK

The cellar reeked. The Ackroyds, when they weren't hunting women, were keen fishermen, and their basement stank of their tackle: sawdust, damp and stagnant water. In the feeble light that dribbled down the stone steps, Luke saw pearly white maggots writhing in crates. Who, honestly, would keep live bait in their cellar?

That's precisely what he was: bait. At least that's what he assumed; that they were hoping Niamh would come looking for him. He couldn't think of any other reason why he was still alive.

He wriggled his hands behind his butt again. The duct tape seemed to be loosening a little, but – with his circulation cut off – his hands were now swollen and numb. His ankles were strapped to a white garden chair. He probably could hop up the stairs with it attached to his body, but he didn't see much point; he couldn't battering-ram the basement door open with his head.

If only he could convince them to release his hands,

then he might be able to fight them. He had his contingency plan. But why would they do that?

Muffled voices from the kitchen distracted him, and he shuffled the chair to the bottom of the stairs to move within earshot. At once he recognised the nasal whining of John Ackroyd, 'No, I wanna come with you!'

'We need someone to watch him,' replied Mick. 'And I want you safe, son.' That piqued Luke's interest. *What might not be safe?*

'He dunt need a babysitter,' John replied.

'Yer stayin'.' This more authoritative voice was Peter's. His father had returned. Maybe it was time to finish him off after all. Luke suspected it would be his dad who'd do the deed. He'd always suspected.

Luke heard the bolt on the cellar door open and at once moved his chair into the corner. Footsteps thudded down and the dim overhead lightbulb buzzed on. His father wearily stood over him. 'Well?' he said.

'Well what?'

'You still under her spell?'

Luke glowered up at him. There was no point in playing along any more. A woman, an innocent woman, was dead and he wouldn't go through that again. 'I was never under any spell, Dad.' And then, he added, 'Unless you count love as magic.'

Peter's face contorted. 'Don't make me sick . . .'

'That's what this is about, isn't it?' Luke went on. 'Mum left you, and you didn't like it. All this because she dented your pride.'

Peter punched him hard in the face. Luke turned his head just in time to feel the impact on his cheekbone. 'You think yer so fuckin' clever, don't you? After everythin' I've done for you. Ungrateful little shit.'

'Tell me it isn't true.'

'No, it bloody isn't,' his father said, but anyone could tell he was lying. Luke had it right, maybe for the first time ever. He had glimpsed a taster of the sisterhood Niamh had with the other witches. The men in their lives were supporting characters, and that was OK. That wasn't wholly fair; the witches did love, they loved fiercely; but the coven came first. And it wasn't like his dad's deranged little cult, which bred only hatred; the coven was a glorious thing from what he could tell. And that was why his mother had died; she had chosen the coven over him, and he didn't like it.

'Why didn't you let her take me?' Luke said. A tear crept out of the inside corner of his eye. 'You never even *liked* me, Dad. Why didn't you just *let us go*?'

Peter Ridge said nothing a moment. 'I wanted you more than anything in the world,' he muttered.

Luke wasn't sure what to say to that.

'I wanted a son.' Luke swore he heard a crumb of emotion in Peter's voice, a tremble. 'I wanted a son to carry on the Ridge name. We had two miscarriages before you so, well, when Angela said she was 'avin a boy, I was the happiest I've ever been in my whole life. So don't you lecture me about love. And I did love your mum. She lied to me. Time and time again, she lied to my face. She promised me her friends were harmless. She told me she'd never leave . . .'

'So you fucking killed her?'

'To keep you safe!'

Luke saw that Peter believed this edit. He was less certain. 'I don't buy it. All my life, you've treated me like shite, Dad.'

Peter sat on the last step opposite him. 'I was tough on

you to make you tough. I treated you the way my dad treated me. I didn't always thank him for it at the time, but I do now. I raised you to be a fighter.' Luke said nothing. 'But you've got her eyes,' he said quietly. 'You're the spit of her.'

It was like dark clouds rolling over him. He turned and started up the stairs, only to mutter over his shoulder, 'It'll all be over soon.'

'What? What will?' Luke shouted after him.

Peter ignored him, and continued upstairs. Luke heard the cellar door close. What? What would be over soon? Luke manoeuvred himself to his listening post. He caught the tail end of a sentence: '. . . how are we gonna find it then?' Mick Ackroyd said.

'Ralphie says he can find the way in usin' his powers. He knows where it is. Not far from Victoria station,' his father told Ackroyd.

Luke frowned. There were Victoria stations in London and Manchester.

'Near Strangeways?'

'Aye.'

Right, that was Manchester then. What was happening there? Luke ran some numbers in his head. How many days had he been down here? They were bringing him water, tea and toast, mostly. Lorraine Ackroyd had taken pity on him and brought him some leftover shepherd's pie too, but he had no notion of day and night in the cellar.

The coronation. He knew Niamh's coronation was taking place in the city. That would mean he'd been stuck here for four days. He half-hoped and half *didn't* hope that Niamh would be searching for him by now. On a separate note, he also fucking dreaded to think what was going on with his business. He assumed young Danny – an employee he'd been training up to take over the day-to-day running of Green & Good – was keeping them afloat.

The coronation felt like too much of a coincidence for it to be anything else. Although, surely the witchfinders weren't thinking they could take on that many witches at once? Even if several cells came together, it'd be suicide. Unless . . . unless they had something planned. Something planned for Niamh.

His mind conjured a showreel of worst-case scenarios. He envisaged an ambush on her way to the ceremony, or a single sniper taking her out as she took to the stage.

He had to get out of here.

Luke waited for what felt like an hour or so, until he was sure. From down here, he could more or less count how many people were in the house from the footfalls overhead on the kitchen floor. The booming male voices had gone, and he'd heard the front door slam.

He wasn't alone, however. 'John!' he called over and over until he heard the bolt slide up above.

'What?' the younger Ackroyd shouted down. 'Shut the fuck up.'

'I need a shit,' Luke called.

There was a pause. 'You can shit your pants for all I care, hagfucker.'

'Seriously? You want me to shit with maggots down here? What's your mother gonna do with a house full of flies?' He tilted his head. 'Your dad's been letting me use the downstairs loo.'

Luke wasn't entirely sure of the science behind maggots, shit and flies, but John seemed to be running the numbers in his head as he descended the stone stairs. Luke was satisfied to see a pair of black eyes and a plaster across his nose. 'Fine,' he said at last. He reached for a Stanley knife and cut the tape around Luke's ankles. 'Right. Don't try owt.' John held the knife at arm's length and prodded Luke towards the stairs. 'You first. Don't think I won't stab you, you fuckin' cuck.'

Luke, Gender Traitor, made his way up the stairs, the air becoming sweeter with every step. The cellar opened onto a narrow galley kitchen, which led to a hallway, off which there was a water closet under the stairs. John was behind him every step of the way. 'Well?' Luke said.

'What?'

'You'll have to untie my hands.'

'Fuck off.'

'Are you gonna wipe my ass?' John seemed to consider it for a second. 'C'mon, you have a knife, what am I gonna do, John, you dick? I'm not the Rock, am I?'

While talking, Luke managed to slip his hand into his rear jeans pocket.

Ready. Set . . .

John turned him around by the shoulder and sliced through the tape around his wrists.

Go.

Without wasting another second, Luke raised his hand and emptied the baggy of Sandman directly into John's face. He coughed and spluttered, getting a mouthful of the powder. The boy's eyes widened for a moment before fluttering shut. He slumped against the staircase and awkwardly slid down the wall to the floor, fast asleep.

Luke wiped his palms on his jeans, mindful of inhaling any of the powder himself. Of course he'd taken the Sandman to the execution, as a precaution, but had known it wasn't nearly enough to stop them all. He'd been watching witches a *long* time. He knew how the dust worked, what it did.

After all, Luke Ridge was half-witch.

Chapter Fifty-Two

CONFESSION

Ciara – Hebden Bridge, UK

Sandhya had outdone herself. The dress was gorgeous, and Niamh would have loved it. Ciara loved it too. A fitted corset bodice with lace sleeves, collar and layers of skirt. She wore old-school heeled lace-up boots, a nod to *The Craft*, like she'd asked. Ciara admired herself in front of her bedroom mirror and smiled. This would have been much more fun twenty years ago with the others.

At least Elle was still here to see it.

That reminded her. She took a final look at herself and hurried downstairs, where Elle, Theo, and Holly waited in the living room. 'Oh wow!' Holly said. 'You look beautiful.'

Ciara couldn't pretend she didn't enjoy the involuntary gasp Elle made. 'Thank you!' Sandhya must have arrived while she was finishing up too; she now waited with the others. 'Sandhya, you did *good*.' Her assistant blushed a little. 'Have we heard anything from the Greek coven about Leonie?' It was hard to focus on a glorified party when Leonie was so on her mind.

She hesitated, and Ciara urged her to speak. 'I didn't want to tell you until after the coronation.'

'Tell me what?'

Sandhya squirmed, looking around the room. 'It's Protected Information.'

'Sandhya! I'm the fricking High Priestess!'

She answered sheepishly. 'There's an island, off the coast of Greece . . .'

'And? Gods, spit it out.'

'It's a sanctuary, top secret – for witches. They found a massacre.'

Ciara hoped she'd misheard that last part. 'What?' Elle beat her to it. 'Was Leonie . . . ?'

'No.' Thank fuck for that. Sandhya went on. 'The survivors said Hale took her.'

Ciara couldn't take this today on top of everything. She perched on the arm of the settee to steady herself. 'Took her where?'

'We don't know,' Sandhya admitted. 'Every coven in the world is now looking for her. We've got everyone searching. Chinara's AWOL too. We don't know where she is.'

Ciara looked to Elle. 'Message her. Call her. She might answer if it's just us.' Elle nodded and went to find her phone.

Oh God, Leonie. Come home. Ciara sent the blast as far as she could into the ether. Hale was making moves; she was certain of it. When this was over, her first duty as High Priestess was finding him – personally, if necessary. Somewhere out there did he have another house like Millington Hall, stacked high with demons and dead bodies?

Briefly Ciara remembered a summoning ceremony from her time at the hall: lightning strobing outside the windows; her scarlet arms pulling the intestines out of a horse carcass; her demon eyes wide and wild. She heard now the scream that tore at her throat.

And she pushed the memory away. Not now. Only a fool would want to remember every sordid detail. Some things are best forgotten. She focused her mind on the rain drumming on the patio outside. Somewhere, a gutter was leaking and a little waterfall spattered noisily onto the drive.

'Chinara's going straight to voicemail,' Elle said. 'There's something else too.'

How much had she missed while she was getting ready upstairs? 'Goddess, what now?'

'Sheila Henry has gone missing,' Sandhya told her.

'What? Isn't she meant to be carrying out the whole freaking coronation?'

Sandhya looked sheepish. 'Yes. I know.'

'Well, where is she? Is she OK?'

'We don't know. Her wife got home from a walking holiday yesterday, and found the dogs alone in the house. The mundane police are involved.'

'I hope she's OK, it's not like her,' Elle said to no one in particular. Ciara hadn't seen the reverend since the burial. She didn't know the woman well enough to know if this was out of character or not.

'Moira is going to perform the ceremony,' said Sandhya.

Ciara threw her hands up. 'This is fucking ridiculous! Three witches have vanished! We have to call off the coronation.' She looked around the room. 'Right? It's an emergency.'

Sandhya raised a timid hand. 'Once you're High Priestess, you can call an official State of Emergency, and gather with the Priestesses of One Coven Alliance. But you don't have the authority until you're crowned.'

Ciara drew a deep breath in through her nostrils. 'Are you kidding me? *Bureaucracy* is going to fucking kill us all?' Ciara replied, the nerves kicking in anew. 'Whatever, let's get on with it then. Sandhya, can I just say this coven would be fucking lost without you.'

Her assistant looked bashful. 'We should be going,' Sandhya said. 'It's time.'

Ciara hardly heard her, listening instead to the wind howling through the eaves like a banshee. Elle answered for her. 'Do you want to arrange the teleport? Are you sure it's OK for us all to come?'

Sandhya assured her it was, and duly contacted the teleportation division. Sandhya went first, dissolving into gold dust, followed by Elle and Holly.

'You ready?' Theo asked her sincerely.

'Honestly, no,' Ciara replied. Really, this was deranged. Even she was ready to admit Niamh would probably be a great High Priestess, but not her. Not ever. Theo took her hand, and she felt a little bit of reassuring radiance pass into her skin.

They were both distracted by a commotion, a clatter, at the back door. A tall, broad, silhouette filled the glass panel. 'Is that Luke?' Theo asked, and Ciara went to let him in.

She gave Theo an arch look. 'I thought I'd been ghosted . . .' The door was only half opened when she let out a gasp. 'Oh my gods! Your face!'

He lurched into the kitchen. One eye was so swollen he could hardly open it and he had a fat lip. 'Come here.' Ciara pulled him over to the dining table and sat him down. She placed a palm – gingerly – on the side of his cheek. His skin glowed like his veins were full of honey and the damage healed before her eyes. It had been *years* since she'd flexed her healer muscles, but it was like riding a bike.

'What happened?' Theo came to her side, pale and anxious.

Niamh, is there a problem? Sandhya's voice filled her mind.

'We need to talk,' Luke said, feeling his own face with his fingers.

Men really pick their moment. 'I have to go.' Ciara motioned at her dress. 'It's the coronation.'

It was like he saw her for the first time. 'You look so beautiful.' But he still looked like he might cry. 'But I really have to talk to you. There's no time. They'll be on their way here.'

'Who will?' Theo asked.

Ciara turned to her. 'Theo. Go to Hekate. Tell them I'm . . . running late.' When Theo protested, she said, 'They're not gonna start my coronation without me, are they?'

Theo nodded, and Ciara instructed Sandhya to proceed. If Luke was shocked to see her swirl away like a cloud of dust, his face didn't register it.

She sat beside him at the table. She almost didn't want the answer to this question, but she asked regardless. 'What the fuck happened, Luke?'

He stared, hard, at the oak, like he was searching for his lines of dialogue in the grain of the wood. 'I, um, don't know how to tell you this . . .'

In that case, Ciara read him. Luke's head, normally, was granite; guarded but sturdy. An old, benevolent fortress on a hillside. Now it was a mess. She saw men beating, kicking him; a dark cellar; and a woman . . . no, not just a woman, Sheila Henry. And she was drowning. 'What the fuck?' she said aloud.

'Please. Let me tell you. I'd rather tell you myself.'

'Then start talking,' she said, her patience thinning.

'I haven't been honest with you,' he began, and looked straight into her eyes. 'Niamh, I'm not who you think I am.'

Well, that made two of them. 'What do you mean?'

'My father . . . he's not dead. He's a witchfinder. I was . . . I was a witchfinder.'

Ciara felt the whole planet plummet a few inches south. 'What?'

He took a deep breath. 'I was sent here four years ago to weed out witches in Hebden Bridge.' His blue eyes drilled into her. 'But you have to believe me, Niamh, as soon as we met, I knew I could never, ever let anything happen to you.'

'Luke,' she spoke slowly, softly, like she was in a lion's den. 'Where is Sheila Henry?'

A tear plopped onto the table with an audible splat. 'She's dead.' His voice cracked. 'They killed her . . . my dad . . . but I . . . I led them to her.' The last part was barely a whisper.

Ciara pushed herself away from the table, her chair toppling over. So it was true, after all, every last man was a waste of oxygen. It was official. 'You have got to be kidding me! For fuck's sake! All you had to be was a fuck buddy, Jesus!'

'Niamh, I'm so sorry. I wanted to tell you a thousand times.'

'Oh shut up!' A spark of fury in her, too. How, how the hell had none of them seen this in him? The lies a woman will believe coming from a strong jawline. She paced the length of the cottage. 'Is your name even Luke?'

'Yes. Luke Ridge. My mother was a witch. My father

killed her. I grew up thinking . . . that you were evil. I . . . had to see for myself.'

'You had to *see for yourself* that killing women is wrong?' Ciara whipped around to face him, and lifted him out of his chair.

He tried to wriggle free. 'Niamh, stop!'

She floated him to her position in the cottage lounge. 'One day I'll meet a man who doesn't have a piece of dry shit where his heart should be.'

She held him aloft and pictured squeezing his thick neck. And then she squeezed harder. His eyes bulged. 'Niamh, I love you.'

She let him go and he hit the floor painfully. He folded in a heap at her feet. 'No, you don't.'

He looked up at her, his face clammy with sweat. 'I do. I fell in love with you the first time we met.'

'Shut the fuck up. I'm done.'

'It's true.'

Ciara shook her head, chuckling under her breath. 'What is it she does?' she said aloud. 'Is it actually witchcraft?'

He went on. 'In the cinema that time, I told you you're the best woman I know. I meant it. I want to be with you, Niamh. More than anything else. If I have to kill every last witchfinder to prove it to you, I will. I'll kill my father. I love you.'

Ciara looked down at him. 'Get up off the floor, it's embarrassing.'

He wearily climbed onto his feet. 'I'll do whatever it takes.'

'Save your breath, lover boy. You're wasting your time, and so am I.'

He looked at her, brow furrowed with confusion. 'Niamh—'

She sidled close to him. 'I'm not Niamh . . .' she purred in his ear. The truth didn't matter now.

'What?'

She got a kick out of watching the seed of doubt germinate in his eyes. 'Saint Niamh is recently martyred, I'm afraid. You're not the only one that's been telling fibs.'

His brow crumpled. 'I don't get it . . .'

'And you never will.' With a swipe of her right hand, she threw him up against the cottage wall. The whole house shook, a crack appearing in the plaster. She'd fix it later, and didn't care. He crashed down onto the sideboard and then the floor.

He wasn't quite unconscious, but very nearly. He rolled onto his back with a groan, dust raining down on his body.

Ciara strode to him. 'It's game over, Luke.' She clamped her hand over his mouth and nose like a face-hugger. This wasn't even personal, it was a matter of coven security now. 'My dear old sister is gonna be a wet dream you once had, and then forgot come the morning . . .'

Ciara began to wipe Niamh Kelly out of his head forever.

Chapter Fifty-Three

CORONATION I

Ciara – Manchester, UK

And suddenly, Luke was gone. The *cottage* was gone.

For a moment, it felt like she was being sucked down a plughole, and the next thing she knew there was a threadbare rug under her fingertips. It smelled old, musty, like libraries. 'What the fuck?' she breathed, unable to stand for head-spin. She got her bearings and saw she was in one of the cloister rooms at the House of Hekate.

The first voice she heard was Moira Roberts's. 'Sorry, Niamh, but there's really no more time to waste. I ordered the teleport.'

'Is everything OK?' Sandhya asked, offering to help her up.

'Yes. A personal matter arose.' They'd interrupted her. She prayed to Gaia that little bit of jiggery-pokery on Luke had worked, and worked how it was supposed to. Fuck, what if she'd severed him and a dribbling zombie now lumbered around Heptonstall village?

'Dr Kelly, how lovely to see you again.'

It took her a moment to place the voice. She lifted her

head to find the Prime Minister staring down at her. She took Sandhya's hand and rose unsteadily to her feet. Dignified. 'How embarrassing,' she said, trying to muster as much decorum as she could, smoothing down her pretty dress. 'Have you ever been teleported, Prime Minister?'

'I can't say I have,' he smiled. Next to him was his horrid little Gollum-in-a-suit. What was his name? Harkaway. 'Anyway, I just wanted, on behalf of the government, to wish you the very best of luck.'

He offered her a hand and she shook it. He had manners if nothing else going for him.

'All this pomp and circumstance! All eyes on you! I remember meeting the queen, God rest her soul, for the first time after I won the election. I know exactly how you're feeling!'

Ciara smiled. 'Exactly.' She turned to her assistant. 'Sandhya? Do you have the rat?'

'Yes, ma'am.' Sandhya reached into the cage that rested on a desk and handed her a lithe black rat.

'Did they hand you a rat when you met the queen?' Ciara asked sweetly.

Eight hundred years ago, this ceremony would have taken place on a beach, or in a forest, or high on a clifftop. She'd have preferred that. She was a witch, not a princess. It would have seen the coven ritually pleasure themselves with dildos – where else did the notion of *flying broomsticks* come from – communing through raw sexual energy with nature. The crown would have been floral, or of real ivy.

With the formation of HMRC in Victorian times, and the truce, came the dawn of 'respectable witchcraft', which came to explain why Ciara now hovered at the threshold of what may as well have been a cathedral. Thuribles – Ciara had had to ask what the *incense swingers* were called – swooped across the space above the audience like pendulums, the air thick with myrrh. Candelabras lined the walls and filled the alcoves. Enchanting, certainly, but it all felt oppressively formal.

The harpist, a woman so pale her skin was almost translucent, started to play. The piece was by Bantock, 'The Witch of Atlas'. A violinist joined the harpist, and that was their cue.

As was traditional, the youngest witch in the coven led the procession through the banquet hall. Right now, that was Holly Pearson. In her hand, she held a hyacinth bulb. Dressed all in green, she represented the future, potential, what was to come. Some corners of wicca would refer to her as 'the maiden'.

Ciara counted Holly's five paces and then followed. On her back was the bow of a huntress, but in her hands, held aloft, was the rat. This showed her deference to Gaia; demonstrated her understanding of her place in the hierarchy. Even as High Priestess, she was of no greater importance than the lowly creature in her hands.

In theory, it should have been a retired or ousted Helena Vance bringing up the rear, ready to pass the coronet to her successor. In practice, the only living former High Priestess, Zelda Crane, carried the ancient Chalice of Wisdom in front of her chest. The elderly woman was ninety-two years old now, and a little hunched, but still spry enough. She'd held the post in the seventies. Now, she was smaller than Holly, drowning inside the midnight blue cloak.

The dais loomed up ahead and the procession felt endless. Ciara couldn't shake the wedding analogy. It did feel like she was giving herself away, to some new state of being. On the stage, she saw Guy Milner seated next to the HMRC board. In Radley Jackman's absence, an elderly warlock represented the cabal. Ciara felt like an adolescent, like she was stomping down the aisle in her mother's stilettos and pearls, little red circles of blusher on her cheeks.

Never had she felt so many eyes on her body. The audience craned around to watch her strange catwalk. To her left, in the pews close to the stage, Theo was next to Elle. Elle filmed the whole thing on her phone, dressed in her Sunday best, while Theo looked almost as nervous as Ciara felt. Ciara gave her a subtle nod. *I must be insane*, she told her.

It felt like she was strapped in to the rollercoaster now and there was no getting off. At least not yet.

The school assembly terror was very real. She remembered, suddenly, trying to get Niamh to switch places to do her reading from *Charlotte's Web* one time, so afraid she was of taking to the stage. Niamh had refused, of course, because the teachers would be cross if they found out. Imagine if Niamh Kelly got a demerit card.

Languishing in the memory of it, Ciara arrived at the stairs before she knew it. She was back in the room. She climbed the three shallow steps and followed Holly to where Moira waited in her indigo cloak. Sandhya stepped forward to take the rat and bow from her. Ciara wondered where the rodent was going now its big moment was over. She'd worry about that later. Now her hands were free, she adjusted the brand-new claret cape an aide slipped over her shoulders. Only the High Priestess wore this colour.

Zelda made it onto the stage, Selina Fay guiding her by the elbow. Moira accepted the chalice from her, and the old woman was steered to a waiting chair next to the Prime Minister.

A hush fell over the room as the music came to a close.

'Who here knocks upon the night?' Moira asked the same question Julia Collins had asked of her all those years ago.

'Niamh Maryanne Kelly.' Her voice was pathetically shy now that it came to it. It somehow felt like sealing the deal. She had completed the transformation and was truly Good Kind Niamh.

Moira turned to the audience, her voice booming off the high walls and arches. 'We are gathered here this evening to bestow our trust in a sister, a sister to lead sisters. Our revered friend embodies our collective heart, mind and will. She is the best of us, sacrificing herself to the coven above all else, freed from earthly desires or personal agenda. She gives of her body and self. She stands before her sisters and our eternal Mother in equal strength and surrender.'

Ciara felt a shiver down her spine, as Moira turned to face her once more. 'Repeat after me: I, Niamh Maryanne . . .'

'I, Niamh Maryanne.'

'Servant of Gaia . . .' Ciara repeated the lines. 'Pledge my life and service to Her Majesty's Royal Coven, forsaking all else.' It left a bad taste in her mouth, but Ciara said the words.

Moira continued. 'I renounce the three faces of Satan.'

'I renounce the three faces of Satan.'

'And swear to honour the wonder, grace and infinity of nature above all else.'

Ciara finished the oath, feeling some of the weight take flight from her shoulders. Her part was over.

Sandhya stepped forward with the ivy coronet – which Ciara had recently learned was actually called Morgana's Wreath after the first witch to wear it – on a plush cushion. Up close, it looked so delicate, so *snappable*, that Ciara couldn't imagine how it had survived so many skulls.

Don't worry, it's a replica, Sandhya told only her and Ciara almost laughed aloud.

Moira once more faced the audience of witches. 'For our part, we exalt our High Priestess in recognition of her devotion to the coven. Our servitude is in thanks of her great sacrifice. Niamh Kelly joins a legacy of powerful witches who will lead the coven to greatness.'

Considering what happened to the last High Priestess, maybe they ought to have edited that line out of the vows, thought Ciara.

Moira now handed her the Chalice of Wisdom. 'Do you come before us of your own free will?'

'I do,' Ciara said.

'Then drink,' Moira told her.

Ciara raised the goblet to her lips. The wine was bitter, laced with Rhapsody, as had always been the way, even if it was fifteen times more addictive than heroin. Tradition!

Moira took the cup from her. At once, Ciara felt the Rhapsody wash over her like a tide of caramel. She felt warm, woozy from her toes to her hair follicles. She felt quite, quite drunk. Would this sensation pass?

Addressing the audience one last time, Moira said, 'We enter into this covenant as sisters. Is there any daughter of Gaia present here today who knows of any reason as to why Niamh Kelly should not be crowned as High Priestess?'

Ciara looked to Moira and the audience. Many witches smiled politely at this archaic formality.

Only then, a kerfuffle. On the third row, Theo stood, a frown creasing her young face. Next to her, Elle pulled on her wrist, urging her to be seated.

'Theo?' Moira said, perplexed and a little annoyed. 'What's wrong?'

Theo shook her head, her eyes narrowing. She raised an accusatory finger in her direction. 'That's not Niamh.'

Chapter Fifty-Four

CORONATION II

Ciara – Manchester, UK

Ciara's hand flew to her collarbone, suddenly coy. *Who me?* The drink, the drug, whatever it was. She'd let go, just for a second. But how? Theo was supposed to be fucking powerless.

'What?' Moira said, unsure of whether this was a joke or not.

Ciara took a step away from her. 'I don't know,' she said, scarcely convincing herself.

'Read her!' Theo shouted from the congregation. 'Read. Her.'

Whereas before she'd felt all eyes on her, Ciara now acutely felt all eyes *in* her. There were what, twenty-five sentients in the room? All of them probed her mind at the same time. It could well be psychosomatic, but Ciara swore she could physically feel them.

Moira winced at her. Now that she was rumbled, how could Ciara *not* think about the truth? It was like saying *don't think of a red car*, the first thing that springs to mind is a red car.

'Ciara?' Moira breathed; her face ashen.

'No!' Ciara lied.

'How . . . ?'

Elle clung to Theo's wrist. 'Sit down, love.'

Theo now whirled to face Elle. 'And you knew . . .'

Fuck. Theo wasn't here to play. The little cunt must have figured it out and stopped eating her food. Ciara coiled. Which was it going to be: fight or flight? She could probably make it out of one of the huge windows in seconds. She was a powerful sentient – perhaps the most powerful in the hall. No one would hold her down.

As the congregation started to mutter, realising this wasn't part of the plan, the proud double doors at the rear of the room creaked open. Reinforcements? Fuck. Moira must have signalled to security outside the hall. Ciara backed away further from Moira, ready to take flight.

'Don't you move another inch,' Moira demanded. 'Where's Niamh?'

Instead, Ciara focused on the lone witch who crossed the threshold into the banqueting hall. She wore the cowl over her face, but Ciara recognised the braids trailing out from under the hood. 'Leonie?'

Moira scowled. 'I beg your pardon?'

'That's Lee.'

Leonie pulled down her hood as she stormed the aisle. Her eyes were jet black. She held out a hand. Fucking hell, if there was one witch that could take Ciara out, it was Leonie.

Moira's eyes widened. 'What on earth . . .'

As Leonie strode ever closer, Ciara saw how tightly her jaw was clenched; saw the pearls of sweat on her forehead. Leonie bit her lip so hard, blood trickled down her chin.

Ciara knew a hex when she saw one. This wasn't Leonie Jackman at the wheel. 'Oh fuck . . .'

Leonie held out a gnarled hand. Ciara braced herself for whatever Leonie was about the hurl at her. This was gonna hurt.

Only it didn't. She opened her eyes, and wondered why she hadn't struck. Only then she heard a ghastly hissing sound behind her right shoulder. She saw Guy Milner, on his feet, red-faced and clutching at his throat like he was choking.

What the fuck? Some members of the audience got to their feet, deliberating about whether to try to stop their returned sister. This was all happening so fast.

'Leonie?' Ciara called. 'Stop!' She tried to force her way into Leonie's mind, rid her of the hex, but whoever was pulling the strings had her in a vicelike grip. And she had a fairly good idea of who'd do such a thing.

He was trying to assassinate the fucking Prime Minister. Bold move, but why? There was no time to figure it out now. If no one else was gonna act . . .

With one hand, she shoved Leonie down the aisle, and with the other tossed Milner to the side of the stage. This, hopefully, would break the hold Leonie had on *him*. She saw Milner gasp, finally able to breathe. It had worked.

She stepped forward, and glided off the stage into the aisle. Hopefully she'd be able to hold Leonie at bay long enough for Milner to get away—

Only, as she raised her arm to pin Leonie to the floor, she saw it dissolve into a cloud of amber dust. *Not now* . . .

Everything went very dark, and she once more felt the gut-twisting lurch of teleportation. For an instant, all she could hear was the unbearable plinky-plonk of piano jazz. A moment later, light returned to her eyes.

She gasped, steadying herself. She was in a sleek restaurant, windows on all sides. The view of the inky night sky and the metropolis beyond suggested they were very, very high above Manchester. There was a single diner tonight, seated alone with a half-eaten meal of sirloin steak and frites before him.

Dabney Hale raised a glass of red to her. 'Cheers,' he said.

Chapter Fifty-Five

HEX

Leonie – Manchester, UK

Her teeth hurt. Her molars were clamped together as she fought to regain control of her body. She couldn't stop. The horrific procession continued, one foot in front of the other.

When she was a little girl, in their terrace house on the Belle Isle, if she'd been bad, her mother would send her to her room – sometimes with no tea. The duration of the exile would depend on the misdemeanour she'd committed. This was the same, only she hadn't been sent to her room, she'd been sent to her mind. The real Leonie sat hunched in a dark corner of her awareness, sulking, unable to affect anything else in her body.

She was *aware* though. She was aware of what Hale was doing to her. She was some sort of sentient Barbie doll, fully poseable. And it was excruciating. The more she pushed back against him, the more it hurt.

At present, she could only watch as she continued towards the altar, where Niamh was poised to fight. Her friend levitated down from the stage, and Leonie prayed

Niamh would stop her. Her target, Milner, was now in a heap to the left of the stage. *Forward*, Hale commanded and she pressed ahead. *Don't worry about her.*

And just like that, Niamh vanished in a shimmer of gold dust. Teleported out. Leonie wanted to scream. Every fucking witch in HMRC was in this room. Why weren't they stopping her? Together, they could.

And then she learned why they weren't. She heard them coming; the men.

Hale had made her put to sleep the security detail guarding each of the entrances to the House of Hekate. Now, the witchfinders, about fifty men in total, stormed the banquet hall, a war cry in their throats. It was a scene from the darkest days, the days of the trials, of King James. Nothing had changed, only instead of pitchforks and torches, in their hands they held machetes, hunting rifles or Molotov cocktails.

Don't concern yourself with them. Kill Milner.

Leonie marched on. A tear ran down her face. She took hold of Milner's ragdoll body and levitated him in her direction.

Ensure they all see.

The screams. The screaming. Unable to turn her head, Leonie could only dimly see the flaming projectile land in the audience from her peripheral vision. There was a bright light, and a terrible *woof*, as a woman was set alight.

Fuck. FUCK. There had to be an elemental to save her, right? Someone save her, Leonie begged silently. Uselessly. She kept walking.

Moira Roberts ran to the front of the stage and took control. 'Witches! Kill these men!'

Ignore her. Finish your job.

Guy Milner, his legs flailing, floated to where Leonie

waited amid the carnage. Now, she heard some men screaming as the witches retaliated. Good. Kill those fuckers. To her right, a young elemental seized a man's wrist before freezing him solid: his lips, his skin turning deathly blue. Glistening with frost, the witchfinder fell to the floor, stiff as a log.

Someone tugged hard on Leonie's arm, and she whipped around to come face-to-face with Elle. 'Lee, what are you doing? Stop!' Elle's eyes widened as she no doubt recognised that she was under a hex. Her lips forming a resolved line, she raised her fingers to Leonie's temples. She was going to release her. *Please, Elle, please get me out.*

Kill her.

NO. Leonie fought harder than she'd ever fought before. She would NOT harm Elle. Milner crashed to the floor and started to make his escape. Leonie felt her powers swelling out of her control. Her arm jerked upwards and Elle was thrown high across the hall, thudding into the wall, before flopping down like roadkill.

Once more, she turned her attention to the Prime Minister. He was within her reach now. He cowered; a cornered animal. 'Please stop,' he whimpered. 'Please . . . just let me go.'

Kill him. Tear off his head.

She was interrupted by a shower of glass. The stained-glass window to her left exploded, a gale blowing in. More screams.

Kill him NOW.

But she couldn't. The wind was too strong. She was pummelled away from Milner, fighting to even stand. She shielded her eyes to see.

Overhead, Chinara descended.

She was poised as ever, surveying the carnage in the

hall, weighing up her options. Her favourite Burberry trenchcoat billowed, and lightning flickered in her eyes. From her inner prison, Leonie's heart soared, but the jubilation of seeing her love was soon tempered.

Uh-oh. Well, this should be interesting.

No. Please, not this.

Kill her.

Chapter Fifty-Six

CORONATION III

Elle – Manchester, UK

Elle woke to the sound of screaming, and the odour of burning flesh. Nothing else smells like it, and you never forget. She must have been knocked unconscious, albeit briefly.

Where was her daughter? In the midst of all this horror, Holly was Elle's only concern. There was nothing else she could do. She crawled forward, feeling her shoulder snap into joint. Her shoes had dropped off somewhere, and there were tears in her stockings. She felt a cut on her forehead heal itself, and a warmth in her ribcage suggested they were mending too.

Elle froze. A ruddy-faced ginger man saw her, stopped, and then charged towards her, brandishing some sort of hunting knife.

She couldn't leave her kids alone in this world. 'Please . . .' she begged.

Only then her would-be attacker stopped dead in his tracks. Eyes wide, he lifted the blade to his neck and slit his own throat. For a second, a mist of red sprayed from the wound and then his body plunged to the ground like a felled oak. Behind him, Sandhya Kaur gave Elle a nod and moved on to the next.

Daring to look around the hall, it seemed the witches had quickly gained the upper hand. Well of course they had. Just what on earth did these idiots think would happen?

'Mum!' Holly had made it off the stage and found Theo in the crowd. They were pressed into one of the alcoves, taking cover.

Elle launched herself across the battlefield, and grabbed hold of them both. 'Oh thank the gods! Are you OK?' Both girls said they were. 'I want you out of here right now.'

'But, Mum—'

'No. I need to stop Leonie . . .'

A gale tore through the hall. Oh, what *now*? But as she saw Chinara fly in, Elle felt a palpable relief shudder through her skeleton. There was no witch more powerful than her, she'd have this under control in seconds. 'I'll get you out and then—'

'Mum, Guy Milner!' Holly pointed at where the Prime Minister was unconscious and bleeding on the floor. The glass; he must have been hit by falling glass.

'For crying out loud!' Elle hadn't even voted at the last election, unable to bring herself to support either unpalatable party. She scanned the area for anyone else who could attend to him while she got the girls out. She couldn't identify another healer. *For crying out loud.* Her conscience kicked in. 'I better help him. But I want you girls to go. There's a way out through the back.'

'Wait,' said Theo. 'That was Ciara! Where's Niamh?'

Elle inhaled sharply, choking on acrid smoke. A body on fire lumbered across the chapel. She had no idea if it was a witch or a mundane but it was far beyond her reach as a healer. 'Niamh is dead,' she said simply, there was no time to sugar the pill now.

Theo said nothing, but her face fell. Elle could see her piecing it together. 'Ciara drugged me . . . that's why I lost my power.'

'Where's Niamh?' Holly's voice was shrill.

'In Bluebell Meadow.'

'And where did Ciara go? She vanished!'

'Holly, I don't have time—'

A bolt of lightning missed her by inches. Elle felt her hair singe. She pressed herself into the recess, shielding the kids with her body.

'What is she doing?' Theo shrieked.

In the centre of the hall, Leonie now seemed to hold Chinara afloat, her arms raised over her head. Lightning poured through the empty window and through Chinara like she was a conductor. The woman's eyes were the same inky black as her girlfriend's. Chinara angled her arms downwards and channelled the electricity, hurling bolt after bolt towards *witches*, not the men.

'Oh no . . .' she breathed as she realised just what was unfolding.

Leonie was hexed, and had, in turn, hexed Chinara. She had total control of her *and* her powers. Who was doing this? Elle looked around the smoky hall, searching for the person puppeteering Leonie. You have to be in range of someone to control them that way. If she could take them out, she'd break the hold.

A woman screamed as she took a hit from Chinara. Blinding forks of lightning licked the walls and floor like the tentacles of a jellyfish. That smell again; burned flesh. Everyone, witches and hunters alike, ran for cover.

'What do we do?' Holly shrieked.

Across the hall, Moira Roberts stepped forward; her face grimy, sweaty. She lifted both hands, levitating three wooden pews as she did so. She swirled them around her head in a circle, building momentum. She threw her arms forward and launched the projectiles directly at Chinara.

Chinara didn't flinch, directing all the energy at the benches. They exploded like kindling and she turned her attention to Moira.

'No . . .' Elle felt her stomach drop. She grabbed the girls and sought better cover behind an upturned table. She peeked over the top. 'Moira! Run!'

Chinara turned her palms upwards, her emotionless shark eyes focused on the older woman. Moira stood her ground but she *knew*. She was outmatched. Elle saw it on her face in the split second before Chinara discharged the fullest extent of her power.

Elle covered her eyes. The light was searing. When she dared open them again, Moira was a blackened, charred husk on a scorched floor.

Leonie now turned her human weapon around, in the direction of the Prime Minister.

'Elle!' She could hardly hear Theo over the ringing in her ears. The girl shoved a little brown bottle in her face. White Sorbus. 'What would happen if they inhaled a load of this?'

'Where did you get that?'

'I stole it from Ni— Ciara.'

Tears streamed down Elle's face, the smoke stinging her eyes. 'I . . . I don't know. Normally you eat it . . . but in very small doses. It's poisonous.'

Theo floated the bottle in front of her. 'Holly; can you steer it between them? They might not see it until it's too late. I'll blow it.'

'Are your powers OK?'

Theo nodded. 'I can feel them again.'

Elle wasn't at all sure about this. Holly's telekinesis wasn't *great*. If Chinara turned on them, it'd be game over, but Theo's plan was better than anything she had. 'It's worth a try. They'll kill us all.'

The girls pressed themselves close together. Holly took control of the vial, and off it went, floating across the great banquet hall. It was a delicate job; witches and men were still tearing about the room, seeking refuge from Chinara's firepower. If someone crashed into the bottle, that was the plan finished before it started.

'Careful . . .' Elle whispered as some bloke charged past, his face bloodied.

Leonie remained underneath her girlfriend, controlling her actions. 'Get it between them,' Theo urged, helping Holly control the levitation. 'Right in the middle . . .'

Leonie seemed so focused on turning Chinara around, she didn't see the tiny vial. 'Aim for Leonie, she's controlling her . . .' Elle said. 'Do it!'

Theo grimaced and the bottle shattered. A thick cloud of milky white powder filled the air between the two women. Theo's eyes narrowed, blowing the dust directly into both of their faces.

Leonie spluttered, taking the brunt of it. Right away, Chinara plummeted to the floor. Elle didn't wait a second more. She dove out of their hiding place and raced towards Guy Milner. If a witch assassinated the Prime Minister, they'd all be burned at the stake. All of them. Was that what all this was about?

She threw a final glance at Leonie, who seemed confused, trying to wipe the sorbus off her tongue with her hand.

Her pupils were still hugely dilated, but she was focused only on getting the poison out of her mouth.

Out of nowhere, Chinara closed the gap and punched Leonie in the face, really hard. Without decorum, Leonie went down like a sack of spuds, as Elle's gran used to say. Well, that's one way to do it. With Leonie out cold, the hex was broken. Chinara knelt over her, and made sure she was truly down. 'I'm so sorry, my love,' she told her sleeping partner. 'Sleep it off.' She kissed her forehead.

Elle passed Chinara. 'Are you OK?' Elle asked, ready to heal her.

'I'm fine. I'm needed.'

How much of the Sorbus had she inhaled? 'Can you fight?'

Chinara's fists caught fire. 'Looks that way.' She turned her attention to the remaining intruders, who knew enough to run for their lives.

Elle leaned over the Prime Minister. This was surreal. The man on the telly was *real*. He was starting to come around, although there was a nasty gash in his cheek. 'She's trying . . . she's trying to kill me,' he muttered.

Elle placed her fingers gingerly on his temple and let her radiance flow into his body. 'It's OK,' she said. 'I'm going to help you.'

Chapter Fifty-Seven

MEANWHILE . . .

Luke – Manchester, UK

As he hit the outskirts of the city, the traffic got worse, as did his impatience. He honked his horn at a car taking too long to emerge onto a roundabout. Pointless, and petty, but this was killing him. He drummed the steering wheel irritably.

The tracker app on his phone showed the whereabouts of his father's car. For most of the drive over, it had appeared stationary in Manchester city centre, but now he was on the move. Why? The map showed his car now heading towards Deansgate through Spinningfields.

Luke wasn't sure exactly what was happening, but his instinct was telling him that Niamh was in danger.

He had awoken on the living room floor, his neck and his head sore, and with no clue how he got there, or what had happened. He remembered making his escape from the Ackroyds' home, but nothing past that point. Had some of the Working Men beaten him to the cottage? There was an almighty crack in the living room wall.

By the time he came to in the empty home, he could

only hope Niamh had already left for her coronation. He'd jumped straight in the car and hit the road. He had to stop Peter Ridge, whatever he was planning.

He didn't know the precise location of the coronation – Niamh had spoken of a coven safehouse hidden from mundanes – but he assumed, if shit was going down, that's where his father would be.

He finally got across the roundabout and traffic started to move again. He pressed his foot to the accelerator and moved into the right lane to overtake. He let his eyes flick to the map.

The car icon came to a halt again. Luke waited to see if it was stopping for lights. After a minute, the car was still. One eye on the road, he reached over and expanded the map on his location. What the fuck is Cloud 23?

And then Luke realised where they were. The Beetham Tower. He looked ahead and, through the rain on the windscreen, he saw the skyscraper on the horizon.

Hold on, Niamh, I'm coming.

Chapter Fifty-Eight

TABLE FOR TWO

Ciara – Manchester, UK

I can make you sit down, or you can do it yourself, Dab had told her. He was wearing a crown of his own, she noted.

'Ciara Louise Kelly is High Priestess! I thought we ought to celebrate!'

Ciara sat opposite him. The view up here was astonishing; the neon veins of the city pumping far below. 'Where are we?'

'The restaurant in the Beetham Tower. Best vista of the city by far. It's where all the footballers live, so I'm told.'

A waitress silently brought a bottle of champagne to the table and left. 'Is she hexed?'

'Not exactly. But my will is strong, look at it that way.' A bearded pianist, clad in a velvet jacket and bowtie, was forced to remain at the baby grand too; beads of sweat on his forehead as he struggled to resist.

'Where's everyone else?'

'I willed them to go home. I wanted the establishment

to myself.' No change there then. He took a flute and held it aloft. 'To the new High Priestess!'

Ciara took the other glass and downed it in one, the Rhapsody wooziness felt like a lifetime ago. She now felt sober as a nun. 'Bit premature, darl. Do you see a crown on my head?'

He held a fey hand to his mouth. 'Oh no! I so wanted you to have your little moment! Not that it matters. You becoming High Priestess was never part of the masterplan.'

'There's a masterplan?'

'Of course.'

Now Ciara was listening. *Finally*, she might come to learn the *why* of all this. Why she was resurrected, why Niamh and Irina had to perish, why, why, why? She craved clarity more than she'd ever wanted anything, but nor would she lap from Hale's cupped hands like his other minions did. 'Care to let me in on the secret?' she said, trying to maintain her cool.

'Ciara, my love, you can't hide your thoughts from me. I'm the most powerful being on earth. I can feel the spiders in the basement twitch their legs.'

Her lips curled into a smirk. 'That'll come in handy.'

'Enough,' he said calmly, and she found she was no longer able to speak. She couldn't even move her mouth. 'I can explain everything. If I could have, I'd have come to you as soon as I got out of Grierlings, but you can understand why I had to get as far away as possible.' He considered her. 'Oh my poor sweet girl. You've had a rough few weeks, haven't you. I had no idea you'd have amnesia. What do you remember? About us?'

He released her from his grip, but she got the message. No more games. 'Nothing. I don't remember anything.'

Hale sipped his champagne, saying no more.

'Why did you bring me back?'

Dabney Hale looked genuinely confused. 'Why? What do you mean?'

She shook her head. He was right; these last weeks had ground her into the earth. She was *tired*. 'You could have just left me in that hospital. Niamh didn't pose a threat to you.'

'Ciara, you silly sausage.' He smiled broadly. 'I brought you back because I love you.'

And now it was her turn to be confused. 'What?'

He took her hands over the table. 'I had a lot of time to think while I was held captive. I thought about you a lot. About us.'

Ciara scanned his face, looking for clues that this was some sort of a skit. 'Is this a joke?'

'Of course not.'

She exhaled, incredulous. 'Dab, you left me in that hotel to rot while you fled. You *used* me in rituals; let demons . . . hurt me.'

He stopped her from talking again. He took a sip of water, choosing his words carefully. 'I'm not proud of that time. We were young; I was ambitious, and blinded by that sometimes. But I always loved you, Ciara. I loved you in Durham; I loved you when you were with Jude and I was with Helena. It was always you. You are my equal.'

Ciara felt tears sting her eyes. She fought it, fought it so hard. She didn't want him, want anyone, to see her cry. Not ever. She sounded like a little girl as she said, 'So why did you let them do that to me?'

'Because I needed *them* too. I needed the demons. I needed them to be who I am now. I am the Demon King, my love, and you shall be my queen.'

She shook her head. Not again. She couldn't go back to being the way she used to be. That pain, that constant pain or the hollowness that came with it. 'So that's the plan?' She didn't know whether to laugh or cry. Either way, she felt borderline hysterical. 'All of this, everything I did, was because you wanted to fuck me?'

He raised a brow. 'I won't deny that, gorgeous, but it's so much more than that. We are part of a greater tapestry. So much bigger than mundanes or witches, men or women. This is about gods and demons. It's about Him. You've all been so helpful, you witches. You were the most powerful coven in the world and, with only a little tinkering, you self-destructed. You ate yourself. Your most powerful women: Annie, Helena, Niamh, Irina, all gone, all dead, and He barely had to lift a finger.' Ciara felt seasick. She might vomit. 'Ciara, it was me all along. I'm the one the oracles saw.'

'The Sullied Child?'

He nodded slowly. 'Leviathan will rise, and Satanis will be as one. This is the end of things. Gaia's creation is coming to an end. It has already begun.'

'So we all die? Just like that?'

'No. Not the gods and monsters. We evolve. We are pioneers of the new universe. A universe made to their design.'

Ciara rested her head in her hands on the table. 'Dab, you got what you wanted. You're the most powerful man on earth. Well done. You can retire now. Buy a beach house. Get a Tesla. Trade some crypto.'

If she was riling him, he didn't show it, remaining infuriatingly earnest. The deluded certainty of a cult leader. 'This is the deal I made. Belial, Leviathan and Lucifer; they want their turn. They are the architects of a new reality. The Age of Gaia is over, but you and I will live forever amongst the new gods.'

'For fuck's sake, no,' Ciara said, feeling every second of the last few weeks suddenly crush her. Even on this vacation in Niamh's flesh, she'd brought her baggage with her, and she was *done*. She'd . . . she'd *killed* for this vision. 'I don't fuckin' want to live forever. Just let me go, Dab.'

He took hold of her wrist. She never thought she'd see Dabney Hale desperate. She couldn't read him with the crown on, but she realised *he* really believed it. He *believed* he was in love with her, and isn't that more or less love itself? 'I won't let you go again. It won't be like before.' He touched the crown on his head. It was simple, stylish really. It looked old, but timeless somehow. 'It's the Seal of Solomon, Ciara. Now I control the demons, not the other way around.'

Ciara couldn't help but laugh at his naïvety. 'That's what they all say.'

'Ciara, please. You're the most powerful witch I've ever known. Your sister was a pussy, Helena was a narcissist, Chinara lacks imagination, and Leonie is an impulsive little brat. You stand above them all. They are wet with human weakness. You have never hungered for love like they do, and that makes you invincible.'

Ciara took a deep breath. She would *not* cry. *I'm not like the other girls.* How she'd bent backwards to distance herself from girlhood to appease men like Hale.

How could it be that no one, not one person, truly saw her? It was telling he described her as a witch, not a woman. It would be so lovely if she didn't have to be alone, just for a day. If, on that day, she could recline in the lap of a lover, and watch the clouds sail by. She had always believed it was mortal weakness to let a man take control from her, but if someone else would take the wheel, she could be a passenger. What would *that* be like? Watch a sunset; read a book; paint her nails. She'd be able to see, hear, smell, feel the world around her for once. She could stop, she could rest, she could heal. Is that not strength too?

Dab wiped away a tear from her cheek. Shit, one got out. 'Don't cry, Ciara. This was always your destiny. From the day you were born, this is where you were headed. You and I are world eaters. Together, my love, we will bring ruination and rebirth.'

She hoped he was listening to those spiders in the basement. 'Dabney?'

'Yes?'

'Your crown?'

'Yes?'

'Does it do anything for your neck?'

He frowned. 'What?'

With a twist of her wrist, she snapped his neck. It made for a deeply satisfying crunch, and he slumped over the table, the Seal flopping off. What a fucking cunt, honestly.

The waitresses were released from his control. They looked around, confused as newborn Bambis. 'Just go,' Ciara told them. 'Now. Just fuck off.' The girls, not much older than Theo, didn't need to be asked twice. The poor pianist took his leave too, slipping out of the door behind them.

Ciara picked up the crown where it had landed. It was warm, but more than that, the metal seemed to pulse somehow, like it was a living thing with a heartbeat of its own. It almost buzzed in her hands and she felt a gentle euphoria, simply holding it. For a moment, everything was totally silent, and she felt more centred than she had in weeks.

This crown was powerful. No doubt about it. It was *flirting*. It *wanted* her and the desire was mutual.

Fuck it. It was her coronation day. She should get to wear a crown.

It felt correct. She was meant for this. She could fix things. She could fix herself.

Ciara climbed out of the velvet booth and stood in the centre of the empty restaurant. Her heart beating giddily, she lifted the Seal of Solomon and placed it on her head.

Chapter Fifty-Nine

WHAT CIARA DID

Ciara – Manchester, UK

For a second, she felt only the smooth metal against the skin of her forehead. She couldn't help but feel that was an anticl—

And then, gripped by a white-hot pain in her head, she folded to her knees and howled in agony. She didn't recognise her own voice, it was animal. She screamed and screamed, clutching her head. She tried to remove the crown, but it wouldn't budge. It felt like her brain was swelling, cracking her skull like an egg.

Glass shattered. One by one, the ceiling-length windows blew out. Shards rained down onto the Manchester streets far below.

This high up, wind sliced through the now exposed restaurant. The lights flickered and then went out altogether. Ciara continued trying to yank the Seal from her head. This was going to kill her. What a fucking stupid way to go.

Only then the pain subsided. Instead, it felt like there was electricity skittering through her body. She pulsed with a sort of static.

Next came the voices . . . little minnows first.
Mistress
She hath returned to us
We knew she would
Our sister, our blessed maiden
We love you, Ciara, we always loved you the most
But they were followed by some bigger ones, deep, red molten like the core of hell. *We yield to you, your majesty. We serve only you.*
Ciara, exalted mistress.
Let us in, witch, we serve.

No, she told them. Entities, some visible, some not, swarmed around the restaurant. It was as if she was a black hole, drawing demonkind to her vortex. She saw them out of the corner of her eye. Some of the shapes were vaguely humanoid; some were animal, some were like nothing that belonged on earth. Things from nightmares. These spectres circled her hungrily.

'Stop,' she said aloud. They obeyed at once. They cowered, submissive. 'There's a new sheriff in town.'

They were hers. She allowed them to come one step closer before stopping them again. At last, these demons were *her* servants, *her* little puppets.

She rose to her feet and opened her arms wide. She closed her eyes and absorbed the entities. This wasn't like before, they flowed through her and she felt them in her fingers and toes. Her skin blazed and her veins filled with fire. Ciara was knocked off her feet, dimly aware of falling flat on her back. She lay still, and let her body adapt to this intoxicating new energy supply.

And everything started to make sense.

She could heal herself. *At last.*

All those fragments, those little scraps of her past started to stitch themselves together. Little things returned to her: her first concert (the Spice Girls minus Geri at Don Valley Stadium); her first kiss (some random in a park, to get it over with, the taste of cider on his tongue); their tenth birthday party in Galway. All these things, these treasured Polaroids, she'd feared gone forever.

Niamh hadn't erased them; she'd torn them up and scattered the shreds.

Ciara harnessed dozens of demons, squeezed them to fit her. They didn't like it, they pushed against her, but she was stronger. She felt like a giant, breaking boulders in her palms.

Ciara smiled as memory lane grew longer and longer, as she became whole once more.

Her eyes snapped open. It *all* came back. Everything. And that didn't feel so good.

Just what do you think you're doing? Her mother's voice was low, serious, as she dragged her across the lawn towards the house.

Nothing, Ciara said, knowing it must be plainly obvious.

Her mother swung for her, slapping her across her bare legs. It stung. Niamh watched, framed by the patio doors. What is the matter with you, Ciara Kelly? Miranda clamped her hands on Ciara's arms, squeezed them tight. Why can't you just be good like your sister?

It was not long after that afternoon in the garden that they went to London. Ciara was enormously excited because, as a twin, it's exceedingly rare to get a parent to yourself for even a minute, let alone a whole day. 'Why isn't Niamh coming?' she'd asked.

'Because this is just for us,' her mother had told her.

'But remember, it *has* to be a secret, OK? You can't tell Daddy or Niamh, or it won't work.'

It being forbidden and clandestine appealed greatly to eight-year-old Ciara. She was a morbid little girl, far more into Christina Ricci's Wednesday Addams than she was Tinkerbell. It was exciting. They drove to Shannon airport and her mum bought her a Fanta and a giant chocolate chip cookie before they boarded the Aer Lingus flight to Heathrow. On the plane, she read *Goosebumps*, but it felt almost like as soon as they took off, her ears went deaf from coming in to land. She remembered her mum giving her a lemon sherbet to suck on until her ears popped.

Her mum had it all planned out. From the airport, they first got on the blue line, which took ages, and then the brown one. Ciara was massively disappointed that Elephant & Castle contained neither of those things. It was noisy and dirty and nothing like Galway. The roads were so wide you could get four cars down them at once. England was *nothing* like Ireland.

Suddenly tower blocks loomed over them and Ciara felt worried because if she got lost here, no one would ever find her. 'Mummy, where are we going?'

'Not far now. Come on, Ciara, pick your feet up.' She heard an edge in her mother's voice too, and that scared her even more, because if her mammy was scared, she definitely should be.

They came to a block of flats, square and hard. The lift was out of order, so they had to take the stairs. They smelled of wee and her mum dragged her up. Their special girls' trip didn't seem so nice any more. Ciara had thought London was all Mary Poppins and museums. 'Mum?'

'Hush, now. Everything will be OK. Just do as the lady tells you and you'll be fine.'

They came to a flat, and her mum knocked on the door. There were flowers outside, and a basket full of tins and fruit. Eventually, a Black boy not much older than her answered the door and let them in. The flat was dark, and smelled of smoke, it made Ciara's eyes itchy. It was a weird place. There were shelves, and they were filled with skulls and strange things in jars. Ciara didn't like spooky things so much now she was in them herself. 'Where are we? Mum?'

'Ciara, just hush, *please*,' her mum snapped.

Long scarlet nails snaked through a beaded curtain, followed by a very tall woman. She had bright red lips and a sort of turban on her head. She had great big boobs, all squashed up under a corset. Ciara was scared of her. She pressed herself up against her mother's leg. 'Greetings. Welcome to my humble home, Mrs Kelly.'

'Thank you. Thank you for seeing us.'

The woman bowed her head. 'Not at all. I sensed your plight.'

Ciara looked up at her mum, so confused. Was she crying? Why was she crying? 'Can you help her?'

'Let me see the child.' The woman crouched to her level. Her mother pushed Ciara towards her. 'No!' she whined.

'Here, child. Come here to me. Don't be scared, now. My name is Madame Celestine, and I'm not going to hurt you.'

'Don't make a scene, Ciara,' her mum said, and pushed her forwards.

'Well, aren't you a pretty little thing?' Celestine stroked her hair. 'And that red hair. So beautiful.'

Ciara relaxed. Madame Celestine rose and offered her a hand. Ciara took it. It was soft and warm.

'Come with me. Trust in me, and everything will be fine . . .'

In the rear room, a sea of candles illuminated a single wooden chair in an otherwise bare space. The window was boarded over with planks. There were symbols on the floor and walls, Ciara knew them to be sigils; she'd seen them in the books she wasn't supposed to look in.

Ciara didn't like this room one bit, but her mother pushed her further inside.

'We're going to play a game,' Madame Celestine told her. 'You sit in the chair. It's like Hide and Seek. Here, put on this blindfold.'

Ciara wasn't at all sure, but her mother nodded encouragement. Celestine tied a black silk around her eyes and then she felt her wrists and ankles being tied to the arms and legs of the chair too. 'Mammy?'

'It's all right, Ciara. This will all be over soon. You'll be fine.' Her mother then spoke to Madame Celestine, but she heard well enough. 'What do you see?'

'Oh she's a powerful one . . .'

'But is it true? What the oracle saw? Is there *darkness* inside of her?'

Ciara tried to pull her hand free, but the scarves around her wrists were too tight. What was this? Why would her mother do this to her? She hadn't done anything wrong. She'd been sent to her room after the bird incident, but that was the last they'd spoken of it. 'Mammy?'

The other woman spoke again. 'Mrs Kelly, there be a darkness inside every one of us. Not a soul out there free from sin.'

'You know what I mean. Is it *demons*?' she hissed the last word.

Behind the blindfold, Ciara sensed Celestine move closer,

holding her hands over her face. The woman made a curious *hmm* noise but said no more.

'What?' her mother said.

'Oh I see demons. There will be many demons in this girl. Not now but later.'

She heard her mother sigh. 'I knew it. I *knew* it,' she breathed.

'Can we please stop?' Ciara asked Celestine. She was scared now. She wanted to go home. She wanted Niamh. 'I don't like it.'

'Can you help her?'

'Lady, there is nothing to exorcise. She is a child.'

'You just said!'

'The future is for Gaia alone to understand.'

Her mother's voice grew more frantic. 'Please. There must be something you can do.'

Madame Celestine seemed to muse on this a moment. 'I can. For a price I can protect the child. Like I told you, this is dark spells, and it don't come cheap.'

'Money doesn't matter!' her mother said. 'Just do it. I'll pay whatever you want, I just want my daughter to be OK.'

'Be sure, Mrs Kelly. The ritual won't be pleasant . . . for either of you.'

'I don't care. Just do it.'

Ciara wriggled in the chair. 'Mammy, I want to go home!'

She felt someone smooth down her hair, and her mam's voice. 'Ciara, my love, it's for your own good. It's not your fault, but there's evil inside you, my girl.'

'No! Mammy, no! I'm not evil! Please let me go!'

Her mother stepped aside to allow Celestine to work. She started by flicking water at her. It was cold. It smelled funny, like vinegar. 'Be gone, vile, writhing creatures! Return to the hell you slithered out from. Back! Get back to the sea and stones. Leave the child! Leave her be!'

But it got worse. After the water, came foul-smelling smog. It choked her, made her sick. 'Please! Stop!'

'Leave this child! Leave her in peace!'

It was two hours before Celestine was satisfied all the demons had got the message.

Home in Ireland, and terrified to tell Niamh or her father in case the demons did come for her, Ciara said nothing. For a while, her mother doted on her the way she did Niamh. For six months or so, Ciara was the happiest she had been all her life.

But it was around this time the twins had their first major spurt; their powers markedly increased. Ciara and Niamh could communicate fully by telepathy and their telekinesis knew no limits. And, once more, her mother started to regard her with suspicion.

'Ciara,' she asked one winter night as they were getting the Christmas decorations down from the attic. 'Do you ever hear voices?'

'I hear Niamh. I sometimes hear you or Daddy.'

'Anything else? Do insects talk to you? Does the wind? You can tell me, Ciara. You can tell me anything.' Her eyes were wide and white, with little red veins. Her mother's fingernails dug into her arms. And that was when Ciara knew Celestine had done nothing to free her of her mother.

When their mother hid charms and crystals under Ciara's bed, and not Niamh's, Niamh asked why. They were told it was because Ciara was poorly and needed help. Niamh never questioned it further. Sometimes Ciara would be given a potion to 'rid her system'. It would make her very sick *for her own good*. Niamh would hold her hair sometimes, hold the bucket, but never said a word to their dad.

Only then they died. The car crash. Both her mother and father were decapitated.

The day her mother had caught her with that bird, Ciara had wished she'd die. She had prayed to Gaia. All this time, her mother was right after all. She was The Evil Twin. To manifest her parents' demise, she must be something terrible indeed.

The move to Yorkshire was hard. When your parents have died, no one tells you how to be. Are you allowed to watch *Friends* on the day of their funeral? No? Even if it's the one after Ross said 'Rachel' instead of 'Emily'? The only other thing to do was cry, and Ciara had done all her crying. She had to do some pretending so people didn't think she was monstrous.

It wasn't all bad. The memories immediately after they came to England were unexpectedly fond. Meeting other witches her own age was nice. Getting to know Leonie, Elle and Helena. Being tutored by Annie.

She remembered how excited she was that night in Helena's treehouse, the night before they took the oath. The thrill of joining this incredible girl gang! Anne Boleyn; Marie Curie; Oprah; and now Ciara Kelly, the sad little orphan from Galway. Once she drank from the chalice, she was cured in a second. It was correct. She was a powerful witch, and would be forever. No one could take that away from her.

Until they did.

Maybe a woman, any woman, just can't be powerful in this world. It's not even a *glass* ceiling, we can all fucking see it.

First Julia Collins. When she was fifteen, she and Leonie were loitering around Hebden Bridge Market Square. They bought disgusting milkshakes piled high with candy, syrup and marshmallows. They were truly foul, but looked cool. There were some boys, some mundane boys, from the other school.

They started on her first, calling her Firecrotch and Orangutan, before they moved on to Leonie, touching her hair and calling her Scary Spice. There were more of the boys than there were of them, and when one of them grabbed Leonie's breast, Ciara hexed him.

Why would any girl with the firepower she had not use it? It was perverse. The natural order dictates females wilt under dominant men, but Ciara felt the 'natural order' was a myth because she felt Gaia in her veins, and Gaia was telling her that females are very, very powerful.

She watched, transfixed, as the boy writhed on the floor. He fought it, and she'd never done it before, but she could control him. She jerked his arms and legs around. He was like an upturned beetle, flailing helplessly while his friends shat themselves. One ran off, one called 999. She and Leonie laughed and laughed.

Until Collins appeared. What fucking bad luck that she was out for dinner on the square. Ciara didn't even see her until the High Priestess seized her by the wrist and dragged her away over the bridge. The little townie picked himself up, and got away with it, albeit with wet pants.

For a minute, she thought she might get off scot-free too. Her grandmother grounded her for two weeks, and she almost forgot the whole encounter, but then they were summoned to HMRC in Manchester. It transpired that what she did that evening on the square was technically in breach of the 1869 treaty. She had used witchcraft on a mundane in peacetime, thus threatening to expose the coven.

She recalled the big conference room. It smelled of coffee and Malted Milk biscuits. It was a 'Case Review', not a trial, but Ciara knew she was in trouble. Big trouble. She was brought in only after the adults had discussed her fate. Julia Collins, her features stony, addressed her as she sat, feeling very small, beside her grandmother and Annie Device. 'What you did constitutes a serious incident. You were impetuous, inconsiderate and disproportionate.' She took a breath. 'But you are a minor, and we must take into consideration your lack of formal training.'

Ciara looked to her grandmother for reassurance, but her pale face was fixed on Collins. Even her own nana was scared of her.

'However, we can't let this go unpunished, Ciara. As such you'll attend compulsory sessions with Edna Heseltine . . . and we have chosen to revoke your offer of a place at the Bethesda School of Dance.'

'No!' Ciara blurted out until her grandma squeezed her hand so tight she cried out. They couldn't do that! She'd only just passed the audition, and she'd never worked harder on anything her whole life. Seren Williams, the headmistress, sat across from them in the conference room and couldn't look her in the eye.

'I'm afraid so, Ciara. You have to learn your actions have consequences . . .'

And they would.

She went to Durham, coincidentally alongside Helena, and fate matched her with both Jude and Dabney. The irony! If they'd only let her attend the single-sex dance college, things would have gone very differently.

Seeing the whole picture for the first time it was crystal

clear how each fork in the road had led her to the Beetham Tower on this night, her body twitching with demons.

She recalled the first time she had invoked with Jude. They both lay naked, at the centre of a salt circle in a derelict church hall. Harnessing the power of a lesser demon, she saw out of a hole in the roof and the entity's eyes allowed her to see far, far beyond the earth's atmosphere. She saw the stars up close, saw the sun burn and bubble, a ball of tomato soup.

All the while she felt Jude's hand in hers, an anchor to his love. They shared the moment and they were bigger than human. They were *supernormal*.

Only then Jude vanished. No note, no texts, no emails. It wasn't that she'd forgotten where he went, it was that he just went. He really did just go, and she didn't know if he was dead or alive.

Ciara did not take it well. But by then she knew how to lessen the pain.

With nowhere else to go – she never actually graduated after spending most of her third year possessed – she'd joined Dab at Millington Hall. She might well be a failed dancer *and* an academic dropout, but she was still a fucking powerful witch. And now she had a cause – his cause.

I mean, he had a point, right? Like, Magneto definitely has the right idea in *X-Men* too. It felt like mundanes had got the better deal in 1869. *OK, we won't burn you at the stake, but could you only use your powers in private, or to serve the national interest?* How about no?

It looked like this might be as good as her memories of those years were going to get. She was under the influence for much of her time at the manor. That might not be a bad thing.

She almost died a couple of times: once of starvation, and the next after falling from a window while trying to fly. It was then she fled to her grandmother's house in Hebden.

Ciara had missed her nana's death and funeral, but Niamh and Conrad welcomed her home. It had been much easier than she'd expected; no begging or pleading necessary, and she was back in their old bedroom. Nothing illustrates failure like an adult in their childhood bed.

It wasn't painless. Without demons inside her, she felt her body again and it hurt. Demons kept coming to her, offering to take the edge off, and sometimes she let them. A demon came to her as an earwig and, in a moment of acute, breathless panic, she let it in.

Niamh had found her three days later, wandering in the woods, naked and covered in mud. Some children had told the police there was a 'Bigfoot' in Hardcastle Crags.

She was at Elle's wedding! How had she forgotten that? They all had matching bridesmaids' dresses: ghastly toga-like things in midnight blue. Ciara knew she was a pity invite, only being added to the roster at the last minute, but it was nonetheless sweet of Ellie to include her.

The ceremony was at Todmorden Unitarian Church (only Elle would think a witch getting married in a church was normal), followed by the reception at Harmsworth Hall Hotel.

Elle was so happy, and looked so beautiful, her hair piled on her head in ringlets. Jez was drunk, dancing up a storm to 'Oops Upside Your Head'. Ciara, seeking a moment of quiet, went outside for a cigarette. They reminded her of Jude.

It was a warm July night. Under the lamplight, midges swarmed, and the view over the valley was stunning under a moon just shy of full. Ciara sucked on her cigarette and wondered if she'd ever find this sort of love. She had with Jude – her equal in so many ways – and she thought she'd be highly unlikely to strike gold twice.

Inside, '2 Become 1' started to play and she smiled. The Erection Section. She turned to go inside and find the girls, but walked straight into Conrad. 'Oh shit, sorry.'

'Can I have this dance?' he asked.

'It's Ciara!' she said. With Elle's very strict policy, they did look identical that day.

'I know!' Conrad smiled. 'You looked a little lonely out here. And also, I can feel 'Come On Eileen' about to drop any second now and I wanted to get clear.'

Ciara laughed. 'God the *worst*.' He offered his hand again, and she took it timidly. 'OK. I'm no good, though.'

They started to dance. 'Weren't you meant to go to dance school?'

'I specialised in ballet and contemporary. Not slow-dancing to the Spice Girls.'

'Well, you're better than me.'

He held her close, his hand on the base of her spine. He smelled good, like cypress and . . . something zesty. It took all she had not to place her head on his shoulder, to rest a moment.

'Are you OK?' he asked.

She shook her head.

'Hey, don't be so hard on yourself. You're doing so well,' he told her, his breath tickling her ear. He looked into her eyes, and she felt that singular magnetism that came in the seconds before a . . . She couldn't not.

She went to kiss him. Her lips only grazed his when he pulled away. Never one for learning, she tried a second time.

'I don't think that's helpful, do you?' he said kindly.

'Oh God, I'm sorry.' She winced.

'It's OK.'

A tantrum voice at her core was screaming that she was in love with him, but it was a lie. She was lost and he was nice. He was a rubber ring and she was drowning. 'No, I . . . I, um, fuck, that's embarrassing.'

'There you are!' Niamh's silhouette filled the terrace entrance. 'You're missing the Spice Girls!' she said. Only then she saw their closeness, perhaps a centimetre short of appropriate. 'What's going on?'

'Nothing,' Conrad said. 'We were just dancing.'

Niamh stepped out into the night and stared only at her. 'Did you try it with Con?'

'No . . .' Ciara said, which both was and wasn't a lie. She had kissed him; she wasn't *trying* anything.

'Oh, for crying out loud.' Niamh shook her head. Not angry, *disappointed*. 'What are you doing, Ciara?'

'Don't,' Conrad defended her. 'It was my bad, I asked her to dance. It doesn't mean anything.'

The way he said that, as if such a thought was preposterous, stung as much as Niamh's judgement. Niamh just rolled her eyes, gently exasperated. 'Girl, I get he's really hot, but we'll find you a nice fella of your own, OK?'

Ciara returned to Millington Hall the next day. She was no one's charity project. She would rather be dead than be the version of Ciara they thought she was. How dare they pity her? The seed rotted in her, turning foul and noxious. Now, when Dabney Hale spoke, she listened. She relinquished herself to him in every way a woman can. Yes, mundanes should bow down to them and yes, they should destroy the pious, conservative, HMRC or any witch that got in their way.

Hale summoned ever more powerful demons. For the first time, she believed he could do it. Although, that said, she was very, very out of it a lot of the time.

The next time she returned to Pendle it was under Dab's instruction. A simple glamour and she really did look *exactly* like Niamh. It was almost too easy to attend the oathtaking at summer solstice and hex Julia Collins. From across the bonfire, and peering out from under her hood, she focused on the High Priestess, and it was all done in a matter of seconds; a quick in-and-out. The dagger was right there on the altar. She entered Julia's mind, forced her to seize the blade, and then slice it across her own neck. Maybe the old bitch should have let her go to dance school.

Blood sprayed across the forest and, a second later, the screams began as Collins toppled forwards over the Great Sleeper. Ciara slipped away before anyone clocked that there were two Niamhs at solstice that June.

That night, Ciara Kelly started a war. Cool.

And then, like the most awful night out cutting through a hangover fog, her final trip to Hebden Bridge returned to her, wholesale.

'You'll need to kill your sister,' Dabney told her one night at Millington Hall. She was on their bed, naked and covered in chicken scratches. She wasn't quite sure how they'd got there.

'Why?' she asked, too weak to argue.

'Because she's a key target, and she'll let you get close enough. If we're lucky, you could kill Jackman and Vance too. They're three of the most powerful witches in England and you could merely ask them out for a coffee.'

She strongly doubted they'd reply to that text message any more. She did not want to kill her sister. 'Get Smythe to do it,' she slurred.

'It has to be you,' Dab breathed in her ear. 'Don't you see? It's the only way you'll finally be free of her. With her around, you're a half, Ciara. I need you whole. Don't you want to? After everything she's done to you.'

As she travelled to Hebden Bridge, she dwelled on that. What had Niamh done, really? Bathed in the sun of their mother's love? Yes. What child wouldn't? Had she lived joyfully in Dublin while Ciara's own life unravelled? Also, yes. But had she ever *meant* to hurt her? Ciara could not say. She knew Niamh had, at times, been a bystander. She hadn't *stopped* their mother, but what an impossible ask of an eight-year-old.

She knew it wasn't fair. To look so identical but have such clashing fortunes. It was almost cruel. Life was cruel. Gaia was cruel. Gaia was a mother like her mother was a mother.

And when she eventually got to the cottage in Heptonstall, Ciara was every bit as cruel. She didn't find her sister in the living room that afternoon, she found Conrad.

He put down his novel, surprised. 'Ciara. Oh my God. Are you OK?'

But at that point, she probably didn't look OK. He looked very scared. She was scary. 'I came to kill Niamh,' she said, black-eyed, listless.

Conrad stood and shook his head. He came closer. 'You don't want to do that.'

'When did what I want matter? I wanted a lot of things.'

'Please, don't do this.'

But this made sense to her. She wanted Niamh to feel *bad* for the first time in her whole charmed life. How blessed her sister's parallel life had been. Now, she would know pain.

Ciara rose off the cottage floor, arms wide. From nowhere the words came to her tongue. It wasn't English, Irish or any other mundane language. It was demonaic. How long had these words been hiding under her teeth. The lights flickered and went out. The sky outside grew dark, night falling early over Hebden Bridge.

'Ciara, please!' Conrad cried.

He thought she was going to kill him. Silly little man. She was going to do something so much worse.

Every shadow in the cottage trickled down the walls like oil and pooled on the flagstones before slithering towards Ciara. The puddle bubbled like the floor was scorching hot, and the foul, festering gas rose into her body, creeping into her nostrils, mouth and eyes.

Satanis.

Briefly, she was healed. Her body felt strong, her mind sharp. She was more powerful than she'd ever, ever been. Her mind became blades, liquid steel scalpels, and she sliced into Conrad, into Niamh, into everyone she had ever known and ever would know. This was *incredible.* She was a creator goddess, making the truth whatever she wanted it to be.

First she wiped Conrad. He'd never met, never known, Niamh Kelly. She took it all. He wouldn't remember his fucking *name*, much less hers. He slumped onto the sofa, blinking vacantly.

Next Niamh. Oh dear. She would *believe* she'd found Conrad dead in the kitchen. Why not? *Boom!* Niamh, you're a widow. She made the false memory nice and gory too, blood running down the cabinets, his eyes all dead and empty. Her sister would know loss as intimately as she did, and finally they would be equals in this world.

And not just Niamh; everyone else too. *Everyone* would

believe Conrad Chen had died. She made it so. It was that easy. Reality was hers to write.

Satisfied with her morbid tapestry, she hauled Conrad off the settee, folding him in her embrace, and – with her limitless new powers – teleported them together. They went far, as far as she could go.

When they materialised, they were on a long, curving stretch of beach. Where, she wasn't sure. It was cold, remote, the sky grey and low. On one side, a burly tide surged, and on the other there were sprawling sand dunes. Silver marram grass shimmered in the wind. There was no one else around for miles and miles.

With a wave of her hand, his clothes disintegrated, scattered like dust on the breeze. He stood before her, naked, confused. 'Who are you?' he said.

'Who are *you*?' Ciara said with a grin.

He frowned. 'I don't know.'

'Nor will anyone else.' She made sure of it. 'Good luck, darl.'

She teleported away, leaving him all alone.

Chapter Sixty

WHAT CIARA DID NEXT

Ciara – Manchester, UK

She was complete. But it didn't feel good. It didn't feel good at all.

She rolled over, curling into a foetal C-shape. She was crying, like when you wake up from a really sad dream and realise you're crying in real life.

It was supposed to be a joke.

OK, not a joke, a trick.

She had no intention of killing Niamh, or Conrad, and never had. Niamh was her sister, and Conrad had never been anything but kind. Nor was she Dab's puppet. She just wanted to mess with her, nothing else.

That day, that last day at the Hotel Carnoustie, she'd known it was all over. She just didn't want to end up in the Pipes. She was going to wait until the right moment and use Conrad to bargain for her life: *let me live, and I'll tell you where the cutie-pie is.*

She felt it, still. In the attic of her mind was the knot she'd tied to remind herself of reality. Only *she* knew the truth about Conrad Chen.

What a fucking dick move. She'd left him cold and naked on a beach in South Wales. The Gower Peninsula, to be exact. Eleven years ago. Where he was *now*, she had no idea.

She couldn't stop crying. She held a hand over her mouth to stuff the sobs in.

If Niamh hadn't severed her, she'd have told her the truth. She would have! It was never meant to be forever; it was just supposed to hurt her. Eleven years. *Eleven years* her dark spell had endured.

And then she'd killed Niamh anyway.

She *did* kill Niamh, and she *was* Dabney Hale's puppet. She *was* a murderer. She'd slain Julia Collins in cold blood. Irina Konvalinka. And now Hale. A killer. She was a killer. A monster.

What a dreadful mess she'd made. She couldn't blame her mother; or Niamh; or Collins or HMRC or anyone. Ciara Kelly was a fucking natural disaster. Every word her mother had said was true. She was evil.

The pain. The pain of it. It stabbed her guts over and over. Guilt was not nearly adequate a word for this. It fucking *hurt*.

A freezing wind cut across the restaurant floor. She was cold. She tried to pull the Seal of Solomon from her head, but it was seemingly welded on. It didn't want to leave her skull. She and the crown were one now.

Ciara's shoulders shook. She was a fucking idiot. She'd wanted so badly to be whole, but what a gift amnesia had been.

Over her sobs and shaking breaths, she heard a sound. *Ciara, child.*

She sat up. The voice was warm, rich as chocolate cake. Ciara looked around the darkened bar and she was still alone, save for the entities inside her body. The wind died down and she felt a certain comforting pressure around her body, a closeness, like she was being held.

To forgive is divine, sweet daughter, and you must forgive yourself.

Ciara crossed her legs, Buddha-style. She knew this voice. She had always known she was there. The presence was all around her. It felt kind, good and compassionate. She felt soothed. 'I fucked up,' Ciara wept. 'I'm sorry. I'm so sorry.'

Your story is not finished yet, child. I have seen it all, and you are far from done. You, like your fallen sister, are great of purpose.

The thought of even moving was too much. 'No, please. I can't . . . I can't do this any more.'

There isn't long left now. This is the end of one era and the dawn of a new day. You are to be the morning sun. Come, daughter, follow me . . .

The warming entity blew out of the restaurant, and she felt bereft at once. *Don't go,* she told her. Ciara wiped her cheeks, stood, and walked to a smashed window. She was twenty-three storeys over Manchester, but stepped off the ledge without pause. Dab wasn't lying about the crown, she felt invincible.

She followed the presence upwards, flying all the way up the side of the Beetham Tower, all forty-seven storeys, to the roof. She soared past apartments, getting glimpses of the mundane lives within.

There were stories in the newspapers about how the tower 'whistled' in high winds, due to the distinctive metal grille on the roof. She landed next to it, amid a network of pipes and airducts. It was filthy, and even birds didn't seem to roost this high. She was really, really high over the city now. She saw car lights move through the streets, an ant farm.

Once more, Ciara became aware of the sympathetic being folding its great wings around her. *Can you hear it?*

'What do you mean?'

Listen, child. Be one with me. See as I see.

She listened. Ciara's sentience was greater than it had ever been. Her mind cast a net over the entire city, and much further beyond. There was no limit to her reach. She could see everything. Everywhere there were demons, she had eyes.

She first checked in on the House of Hekate.

The aftermath. The fight was finished, and the witches had made short work of the witchfinders. She was like a ghost in the hall, darting around the scene in staccato blasts. Elle tended to the wounded. Holly and Theo helped. With Dab dead, Leonie was free. She and Chinara spoke heatedly with the Prime Minister. Who was in charge? Where was Moira? Ciara felt her essence at once, but realised it was only the remnants of her dwindling in a burned corpse under a sheet.

All around, women cried. Some privately, some wracked with noisy sobs. There was no sense of victory here, only horror, shock and bewilderment. What did this all mean for them, as witches? Ciara searched for that turd Harkaway, whom she strongly suspected was Hale's man on the inside.

Soaring high over Hekate House, she located him at once. He was in a sleek hotel room not far from the hall. The lights low, he hunched over his laptop at the desk, tie loose around his neck. Ciara read him and his saw his threadbare machinations: a plot, a doomed plot, to out witchkind by staging an assassination; to turn the world of mundanes against them. Hale had used them all.

Harkaway was watching footage of the ambush. He must have scarpered before the ceremony got underway. The image bounced around as whoever was filming sprinted into the banquet hall, but she caught a glimpse of herself on stage before she was teleported out. This was his proof, his proof of witchcraft.

Not today, honey. Ciara reached into his chest and stopped his heart beating. The heartstopper was a favourite in the olden days because it's that much easier to make mundanes believe the victim died of natural causes. Men and their weak hearts.

Eric Harkaway gasped, clutching his arm. He rocked in his seat before slumping forward onto his laptop keys. She turned her attention to his laptop. The device gave off a sad alarm before that too died, accompanied by the slightly fishy odour of melting plastic. Ciara wondered who else had copies of that video. There were bound to be more.

Ciara, child. Every road led you here. This is what I made you for.

Ciara returned to her earthly body on the roof.

Listen.

She pushed harder, connecting with every demonic presence she could. Eyes and ears everywhere.

See.

The massacre in Hekate House was the tip of a tip of an iceberg. She saw – no, felt – such misery. The city ached. Everyone was pretending all the time. Every smile was a grimace, masking the ache of what it is to be human. Ciara tasted every sour flavour: grief, envy, desperation. She felt the panic, the despair and the hatred. She heard their darkest desires; their dreadful appetites. She went much further afield than Manchester, but the picture didn't improve.

Being human wasn't a pleasant business. Humanity was not sweet in the slightest, it was rotten.

Their time is done.

What?

I'm reclaiming my creation before it's too late.

Ciara felt what she meant. Underneath the maudlin lament of the human race, was the scream of the earth, of Gaia herself. We have our foot on her throat. Ciara's eyes widened. She took flight some feet over the hotel, trying to hear better.

Everything was wrong. The air was acrid, burned; the sea was bleached with chemicals; the landfills reeked of decay. There wasn't enough air, and what air there was was filthy.

I'm dying, daughter. I beg of you.

Ciara felt tears run down her face. They, as witches, had failed their mother – their true mother. Humans were a plague.

She was the cure.

She spread her arms wide. She felt change within her, the chemistry of her body shifting somehow. Her whole body buzzed. She felt herself physically expand and elongate, creating space for ever more demons.

Lightning crackled across the night sky, thunder following at once. Blinding white rods lashed at her body, but she felt nothing. Was this what it was like to be an elemental? She'd always wondered; she'd always secretly been jealous of Helena.

A new dawn, Ciara. A reset. A chance to begin again. A chance to heal.

All of them?

It's the only way.

Ciara wasn't sure how to control these strange new gifts. She used the lightning the way she would her telekinesis, steering it. Sure enough, lightning split the sky, bolts whipping into the city below. A café, closed, bore the brunt of it and it burst into flames. She laughed. It was so easy. She unleashed another bolt onto a parked BMW. *Boom!* At first, the insect people on the streets were stunned stiff, but soon screamed, ran for cover.

Ciara did it again, and again, raining destruction onto Manchester. She ignored the screams. They had to be cleansed if Gaia was to live. She would mourn them no more than she would a virus. She had failed at everything she'd ever done. She would not falter now.

She summoned the winds, drawing forth mighty storm fronts from the seas to the north.

Cars swerved to avoid the onslaught, smashing into other cars. Horns blared. Pedestrians raced indoors to avoid her squall.

More. Faster.

Ciara summoned more brute force from her mother's arsenal. This was just the start. She'd hoist the waves over the shores; pelt hailstones the size of boulders; erupt the sleeping volcanoes. Nothing was beyond her, and Gaia would get her much-deserved revenge.

She felt her skeleton rattle as the fire flowed through her. She clenched her teeth together. Her skin felt freezing cold, taut like it might split. Her teeth rattled in her skull. She realised the truth: this was going to kill her too.

Oh well. It was time.

Ciara screamed as she unleashed a maelstrom of lightning.

Only then it all stopped. Something hurt. She looked

down, and saw an angry-looking little man looking up at her. 'Who the fuck are you?'

'That's for my son, bitch.'

And then she saw his crossbow, and the silver bolt sticking out of her chest.

Chapter Sixty-One

THE END OF THE WORLD
(AS WE KNOW IT)

Luke – Manchester, UK

It was a fucking disaster movie. The streets outside the Beetham Tower were carnage: people abandoning cars; screaming; running for cover, so it hadn't been a surprise to find the plush reception area of the tower block unattended. If there was someone to operate the lift, they'd legged it.

The lift only went up as high as the 46th floor, but Luke quickly located the service door which led to the roof. He found it ajar, almost kicked off its hinges. He took the final stairwell two steps at a time, his shoes clanging off metal.

Luke emerged onto the roof just in time to see his dad fire a bolt at the woman who used to be Niamh Kelly.

Fuck. He was too late. It was all for nothing.

The woman, now a giantess, examined the arrow protruding from her chest for a second and then fell to the roof with a thud. She knelt, confused.

The lightning, the thunder, the gales, abated at once. She didn't look a thing like Niamh any more: much of her hair had turned pure white, but she was also inhumanly tall; her flesh mottled, purples and pinks like she was bruised all over. She clutched at the arrow jutting from her breast for another second, before folding face-first.

As his father loaded another bolt into the crossbow, Luke ambushed him. He threw himself onto Peter's back and they both stacked it, the weapon skidding out of reach. Peter twisted himself over and reached for Luke's face, trying to gouge at his eyes. Luke was taller, his arms longer, and pinned his father to the grimy rooftop. 'You saw her,' Peter snarled, spittle flying from his lips. 'You saw what a real witch looks like.'

To his left, he saw Niamh lying in a tangled heap of legs and cape and dress. She wasn't moving. 'You bastard.' He wrapped his hands around his dad's throat, something he should have done a long time ago. This man murdered women. He didn't know how many. A serial killer with a cause is still a serial killer.

His father's eyes bulged, his face turning beetroot red. 'Please . . .' he rasped.

No. Whatever happened to Luke didn't matter now. This man had to be removed to stop this happening ever again. He'd take his sentence. Without Niamh, what was the point anyway? He'd known it was her or nothing for years. He'd made peace with nothing.

Out of the corner of his eye, he was too late to see whatever his father had in his hand. He just felt a sharp scratch drag through his cheek. He yelped, pain flashing through his face and Peter took advantage of the distraction, kneeing him in the groin and pushing him over. Luke was winded, doubled up in agony. He felt hot blood gush down his chin and into his mouth. His father held a Stanley knife in his right hand.

Before he could get up, he felt the steel toe of his dad's boot drive into his torso. Again and again, Peter kicked him while he was down. 'You piece of shit, pussy-whipped cuck,' his father spat. 'I should have bashed your skull in when you were a baby. Half-witch bastard.'

This time the foot came to his skull. Luke rolled over, silver glitter swirling over the night sky.

Tasting blood, he waited for the final blow. His head rolled to the side.

His vision fuzzy, he watched Niamh's pretzel body unfurl beyond Peter. Like a marionette, she rose from the roof, hovering a few inches off the surface. Her eyes burned like ice, the white hair swimming about her face. With one pale hand, she tugged the arrow bolt out of her chest and the hole sealed itself up.

He looked past his father and laughed, quite hysterically. 'What's so funny?'

'You're so fucked.' Luke spat out a mouthful of blood.

'Is that right? What makes you think that when you can't even fuckin' stand up?'

Luke propped himself up onto one elbow. 'Because you think women are weak.'

With an outstretched hand, Niamh hoisted Peter off his feet. His eyes widened. 'Luke!' he shouted against the wind.

Niamh spoke to Luke, her voice much deeper than it should be. 'Any final words?' she asked.

Luke looked up at his father, dangling helplessly as a fish on a hook. 'Not especially.'

'Son!' he cried again.

Too late. Niamh swiped left, and tossed the man off the side of the Beetham Tower. He would fall long after they couldn't hear him scream any more. Luke just hoped there was no one on the street below.

The witch floated towards him, and landed at his side. She held a hand over his face and healed the gash in his cheek and his smashed eye socket in a matter of seconds. 'Go,' she said.

'Niamh . . .'

She considered him. 'This is not Niamh.'

And then, all at once, he remembered what had happened at the cottage. It was like some magician's blanket had been pulled off to reveal his own memories with a flourish. The rabbit in the hat. The witch restored his memory.

'You're her *sister* . . .' He remembered: Niamh was dead.

Ciara regarded him coolly before walking to the furthest edge of the skyscraper. She levitated onto the rim to overlook Manchester. 'Go. This is the end.'

Luke found he was able to stand. He followed her, carefully, to the edge. He'd never loved heights. 'What are you doing?'

'This is the end of man.' She lifted her arms aloft. A whirlpool of cloud started to form above them. 'Our time draws near.'

This wasn't her. If she'd been Ciara for a while . . . oh God. The reality of everything dawned on him. He'd fucked her. He should have known. He *had* known, but had been scared to question it in case he lost her. 'Why?'

'Humanity is a pox on Gaia's creation. I hear her dying. She needs me. It begins again.'

Luke and Niamh had spoken at length about her belief system, about the role of Gaia. Niamh had always called her *Mother*.

Was it how high they were, or was he finding it hard to breathe . . . ? He went to inhale and found he could not, at least not fully. It wasn't his imagination; the air was getting thinner. 'Ciara, are you doing this?'

'It is the kindest way.'

'You're going to *suffocate* the whole world?'

'Only the humans. It's what she wants. She talks to me.'

'Gaia is telling you to kill us? I thought she *made* us.'

The amazon woman turned and looked down at him. 'Silence.'

'You don't want to do this! And neither does Gaia!'

'Don't even say her name.' Ciara raised a hand and he was shoved across the rooftop, crashing into an air-con pipe. He gasped for air. It felt like being underwater, however hard he tried, he couldn't breathe enough in. He got to his feet and tried again. Already, he was lightheaded, drunk-feeling.

'How do you know it's Gaia?' he said, struggling to get the words out. Thick purple cloud now spiralled over Ciara, a deep, mauve vortex, crackling with lightning.

I know my mother's voice.

He knew she'd hear him, even without words. *How? I don't know anything about demons, but this sounds like what demons would do. I thought Gaia loved all her children? You said it yourself: Gaia gave us free will.*

He fell to his knees, his head spinning. *This isn't Gaia. It can't be. A mother couldn't do this to her children.*

You might be surprised what a mother could do to her children.

You're being used. Now he felt *really* drunk. The rooftop was spinning. It felt like the night was closing in on him. *Please, Ciara, stop. This isn't you.*

'How the fuck would you know?' she hollered aloud, her voice slightly more like her own. She flew down from the precipice and tugged him off the roof with her hands, grasping his shirt. His legs dangled uselessly. 'You don't know me!'

You do a really good impression of your sister. He felt sleep nip at his edges. But it wasn't sleep, of course, and he mustn't give in to it. *Maybe you're more alike than you think.*

'I am *not* Niamh.'

You looked after Theo. You could have hurt her, but you didn't. You tried to help Leonie, and Elle. You healed me. You could have killed me, but you didn't.

'I AM NOT NIAMH.'

'So . . . who . . . are . . . you?'

Lightning snapped and thunder growled. She let go of him, and he crashed down to the roof surface. Ciara gripped the sides of her head and let out a pitiful howl. The woman folded to her knees. 'I am *bad*.' He said nothing, just looked up at her. 'I'm bad, I'm bad, I'm bad.' Tears rolled down her face and she hid her eyes with her hands.

Luke found he could breathe once more. It was like the best water he'd ever sipped. 'You aren't bad.'

Ciara shook her head. 'I am, I *am*.' A pause. 'I killed people. I *killed people*.' Her shoulders hunched. Almost imperceptibly, the woman was reverting to her normal height.

'Me too,' Luke admitted, feeling sick every time he thought of Sheila Henry. Still woozy, he lumbered to his feet. He tentatively put his arms around her. 'Come here.' Drawing her upright, he folded her into an embrace. Tears soon soaked his shirt. Her body shook.

'I want to die.'

'Do you?'

'I want it to go away, this feeling.' She sobbed. 'I killed my sister.'

Luke said nothing a moment and then, 'Maybe we don't deserve to feel better. There has to be consequences. What we did, what we've done, shouldn't . . . it can't be easy. So now we suffer.'

She shook her head. 'There's no way back for me.'

'No. There's *always* a way back,' he said, trying to convince them both. 'You just . . . turn around and go the way you came.'

She half-laughed, half-cried. 'That's a really fucking long way to go.'

He stroked her hair, now *mostly* red again. 'Then we better make a start. We'll go together. We take whatever's coming our way.'

The abyss in the sky above them was now dissipating. Far below, Luke heard alarms and sirens start.

Ciara looked up at him. Her eyes were green; her skin its usual creamy shade; only a compelling streak of white hair remained at the crown of her head. 'I can't make it right. How can I, when I've done so much?'

Luke shrugged. 'I don't know. But I know you'll never make amends, *ever*, if you wipe us all out. *Show us.* Show us who you really are.'

Ciara looked out over the city. She was her regular size now, but looked smaller, dwarfed by the universe. 'Maybe I can be Niamh after all,' she said.

'Can you bring her back?'

She looked to consider it a moment, but then shook her head. 'No. I *could* but I mustn't. It's forbidden.' She looked to Luke. 'Did you love her?'

'Yes.'

'She wasn't perfect, you know?'

He shrugged. 'I know. Who the fuck is?'

Ciara said nothing for a second. She seemed to feel the

cold now, and wrapped her arms around her body. 'I loved her too. And she loved me, and that made me hate her more. I thought it made her stupid, and weak.' She looked like she might cry again. 'I miss her.'

Luke went to hold her, but she pushed him away. Instead, she took the crown off her head. 'Is that your High Priestess crown?'

'This is . . . something else.' She considered it. 'I thought it would make me powerful.'

'Did it?'

'No. I was the power.'

She floated the bronze ring before her, between her hands. Her eyes glazed over as she watched it spin. She spoke almost to herself: 'No one should have this. This . . . this was too powerful for even the mighty King Solomon.' Luke was confused. *The* King Solomon? What had he missed? Ciara went on. 'It scared him, and so he gave it to a more powerful witch, his consort. She knew it must be concealed, but she didn't destroy it, because how else could she wield that kind of power as a woman? Well now it ends.'

Ciara raised a hand, and the crown disintegrated like it was a sandcastle in the tide.

'So there we go,' she said sadly.

'What now?' Luke asked.

Ciara paused a moment, turned and started for the stairs. 'We go back the way we came.'

Chapter Sixty-Two

THE LEFTOVERS

Leonie – Manchester, UK

Five Days Later

He would be OK. At least physically. With each passing day, her brother looked more and more like her brother. For now, Leonie was staying in a different room at the coven safehouse – the one which had formerly housed Ciara. She wanted to be close to him, to be there when he woke. Pungent Virgo Vitalis made Leonie's eyes gluey, or at least she *told* herself it was the incense, and not her exhaustion.

When she wasn't sleeping, Leonie kept vigil at his bedside. Radley still looked very thin, but the bruises around his eyes were fading and yesterday he'd been able to hold a short conversation, sip some water. Healers came in morning and evening to get him through the nights. Now, it was all about patience – a trait Leonie lacked.

It had been the Kremlin witches who'd found him. The Russians had been closing in on Hale's little outpost for weeks. They'd reached the remote location mere hours after Leonie had been teleported to her fateful date at Hekate House. Hale's mundane army hadn't stood a chance against the might of the Russian coven, and the imprisoned witches and warlocks, the test subjects, were soon rescued.

That said, it had been a mess of mixed messages. At one point, HMRC – also in disarray – had heard there were no survivors. In that brief moment, Leonie understood what *rock bottom* meant. She already felt entirely steamrolled into the earth, only to learn there was further to fall.

And then they received a hasty clarification – none of *Hale's acolytes* survived – and Radley was flown home (the mundane way) as soon as he was fit enough to do so.

Leonie didn't even realise she'd nodded off, her head resting on Radley's bed, until the healer woke her. She was a young, curvy witch called Nadja, and she was fast becoming a friend. 'Leonie, babe? Chinara's here.'

She said nothing, leaving Nadja to perform her healing rituals. Leonie headed downstairs. The safehouse was just that, a Victorian townhouse, converted into a cottage hospital for witches and warlocks in the absence of a dedicated infirmary for the community. There was one near Whitstable too, mostly for elderly witches. Witches don't let old witches be lonely witches.

There was a salon and dining room on the ground floor, and Leonie found Chinara leaning over a steaming mug of lemon and ginger tea at the dining table. She waited in tranquil quiet, a grandfather clock tick-tocking from the hall. A warlock asked Leonie if she wanted a cup too, but she told him no, and he excused himself.

Leonie sat opposite her girlfriend. 'So?'

Chinara looked tired; more tired than she'd ever seen

her. She hadn't properly slept since . . . 'HMRC is taking no further action.'

Leonie felt some twisted knot click under her right shoulder blade, the tension ebbing out of her. 'Against either of us?'

Chinara nodded, and Leonie felt a long, shaky breath leave her body. She felt lighter. 'Oh thank the goddess.' But Chinara didn't seem so relieved. 'Babe? We didn't do anything wrong.'

'The coven agrees. Or at least what's left of it.' Chinara bit her bottom lip. 'It was chaos. They forgot I was scheduled. We could have been in Aruba for all they cared.'

'Have they found them?' It'd be fucking laughable if it weren't true. Ciara was Niamh, and Niamh was dead. Ciara was on the run with the mundane greengrocer. Sure, why not? Made about as much sense as anything else right now.

'No.' Chinara took a sip of her tea. 'Seren Williams is Interim High Priestess.'

'Oh shit,' Leonie muttered. She wouldn't trust the Bethesda headmistress to organise a bouncy castle party. A wet weekend if ever she'd met one. 'Fuck. Is this it? Is this what finishes HMRC?'

Her girlfriend shrugged, face slack. Her eyes glistened. Leonie walked around to her end of the table and crouched at her side, taking her hands. 'It wasn't our fault.'

'I killed Moira Roberts.' Her voice *almost* cracked.

Leonie shook her head. 'No, you didn't. And neither did I. *Dabney Hale* killed Moira Roberts.' Leonie shuddered. Having that man inside her body had left a grubbiness in her marrow. She felt cold, all the time. She wanted to take out all her bones and put them through the dishwasher. Even that might not do the trick.

To have no control over her body was . . . well, she didn't have a word for it. *Disgust* wasn't strong enough. At night, although she was struggling to sleep at *all* in case someone else got in, she'd sometimes wriggle her toes or fingers, just to make sure.

'I don't know how I get over this. I don't know if I can, or will,' Chinara said, a rare admission of weakness for her.

'It helps that Hale got his neck snapped.'

'I agree.'

They owed Ciara for that one, if nothing else. *Fucking Ciara.* As if there wasn't enough going on.

And Niamh. When would she find the time to mourn Niamh? It hadn't hit yet, and that was scary. Sometime soon, an avalanche was going to bury her. Fuck. Leonie had so many questions. But she had to get Radley back on his feet first. Nothing else mattered. She hadn't thought about Diaspora all week. She wasn't Supergirl, and family had to come first.

'Did HMRC say anything about Senait?' she asked while she remembered.

Chinara shook her head. 'No. She isn't registered with any global coven. You're going to have to let that one go, my love.'

'No,' Leonie said. 'She's a good witch, I know it. I need to know she's safe, and then I need to find Aeaea and—'

'No!' Chinara raised her voice, and the flames in the open fireplace leapt angrily from the hearth. 'I mean it, Leonie. No more quests or missions or adventures. No more. *I* need you. I need you here.'

Embarrassed by her outburst, Chinara shrunk, and took a sip of her tea.

Leonie pressed her forehead to Chinara's hoping she

could feel what she felt. 'Hey. I'm not going anywhere. Look at me.' She kissed her lips. 'When I was being held in that cellar, you were all I thought about. I'm not running away any more. I'm not scared any more. I'm right here.'

'You are scared of *us*?'

Leonie nodded. 'Maybe. Yes. I was.'

'What do you mean? Tell me.'

Oh, she was very tired to be having *this* conversation. 'You and me are endgame. Endgame means I'm fucking getting old. Everything I was before you, that world, is over. That's scary. When we met, I wasn't an adult. I thought I was, but I wasn't. Now I am. The only place I want to be is home.'

'Where's that?'

'Wherever you are is home.'

Chinara kissed her again, slow and tender. She felt her affection wash through her, all candy colours. 'I understand, and I love you. But can we go back to London? The poor cat is going to punish us so badly.'

Leonie laughed. 'Sure. I'll ask HMRC if they'll teleport us . . .' she trailed off.

'Lee?'

'Wait.' Leonie strained, sensing another witch teasing at the edge of her sentience.

An Irish voice filled her reverie. *Leonie. It's me. We're gonna need your help. I promised Ellie. Please come to Hebden Bridge.*

Chapter Sixty-Three

THEY COME AT NIGHT

Milner – London, UK

Wake.

When Fabian 'Guy' Milner was a little boy, he'd had a recurring nightmare. He would believe he was awake until he'd enter a room and, with a creeping dread, become *aware* of a tall, thin presence looming in a dark corner. When he'd go to switch on the light, nothing would happen, and the figure would edge towards him from the shadows. A bedwetter, he'd had to see a child psychologist about it all.

Now, he woke with a start, mid-snore. Milner squinted into the coaly darkness of their bedroom. For the first time since he was a child, he felt the familiar creeping dread.

At the foot of his bed, stood an impossibly tall human silhouette.

The dream.

He reached for the bedside lamp. He flicked the switch on and off, and nothing happened. The shape moved closer, and he recoiled, pressing himself against the headboard. 'Tiggy,' he said to his wife, 'wake up . . .'

'Don't bother,' a voice said as she floated into view. It was the Kelly woman, levitating at the bottom of his bed. She looked down at him with emotionless, hooded eyes. 'She won't wake.'

'Please don't hurt her; she's pregnant.' It hadn't been announced yet, but it was true. A baby would play well for the tabloids, it was thought, his polls were down.

'That very much depends on you . . .' Feeble grey light from the street filtered through an inch-wide gap in the curtains, and he now saw the High Priestess had a new, striking white stripe in her hair, framing her face.

'What do you want?'

'I thought we should talk. About witches.'

Milner had only that day had his formal Return to Work meeting. The pretty blond witch had worked miracles in Manchester, but his nerves were shot. He'd spent the last few days at Chequers, recuperating. Officially, he was 'undergoing tests as a precaution', whatever that meant. 'Don't you think you've done enough?'

'It wasn't witches who wanted you dead, Mr Milner. It was your own staff. You must be a terrible boss. Harkaway planned the hit.'

'We don't know that . . .'

'We do.'

'He had a heart attack.'

'No, he didn't.'

'What?'

The woman cut him off. 'Listen, we need to talk about our alliance. If any footage from that night leaks to the mundane press, we're both in a lot of trouble. You're in the video, so the whole country will know you lied to them about our existence. Your career will be over.'

Milner sat up in bed, propping himself up with pillows.

Every muscle still ached. 'I had nothing to do with it, I swear.'

'I believe you. But given you were installed as Prime Minister *by* the media, you control all the newspapers and TV stations. I think *if* that footage turns up, you can bury it.' She considered him with a tilt of her head. 'The way you buried the story about the cute ski instructor in Chamonix . . .'

How did she know? He felt sick. 'I think you overestimate my reach.'

Her expression hardened. 'For your sake and mine, I hope not, Prime Minister. I don't think either of us wants a war between mundanes and witches. After all, I just walked into 10 Downing Street in the middle of the night, and strolled into your bedroom while you slept. No one lifted a finger to stop me. They *let me in*. Who do you think's going to win that war?'

She had him by the balls. He knew it, and he knew she knew it. He slumped into the mattress. He honestly thought being the most powerful man in the country would feel more powerful. He actually rather hated it. 'Is this what you want, Dr Kelly?' he asked. 'You want us to be scared of you?'

The witch crossed to his window and drew the curtain aside. All by itself, the sash window slid up with a wooden scrape. 'Witches have been scared for centuries,' she told him. 'Now it's your turn.'

She stepped onto the windowsill, and took flight.

Chapter Sixty-Four

THE ORPHAN

Theo – Hebden Bridge, UK

A swelled full moon hung over the cul-de-sac, perilously low. Theo wheeled her sad little suitcase up the drive to Holly's house. Luke had once called her *The Littlest Hobo* and she had no idea what he meant to be honest, but if the cap fits. This didn't feel like home. None of the others had except for the cottage. *That* had felt like home. To make matters worse, poor Tiger had gone to stay with Niamh's vet friend Mike, because Elle didn't want a dog in the house. This all really sucked so hard.

'Come on,' Elle said, waiting on the front steps, and trying to remain upbeat. 'Let's get you unpacked.'

They entered the hallway and Theo's face almost melted off. Elle always had the thermostat set to twenty-four degrees regardless of the weather. Theo was resigned to whatever happened next. Elle, sensing her despair, stroked her hair off her face. 'Love. We'll figure it out. I promise you don't have to go anywhere you don't want to. You can stay here as long as you like.'

Theo nodded, tears pricking her eyes. She just wanted

Niamh back. Hell, she'd even take *Ciara* if it helped to get to the bottom of things.

'Theo!' Holly called. 'Come on!'

Theo pushed the handle in, and carried the case upstairs. She'd been here since the coronation, but she'd run out of clean clothes and had made a last pilgrimage to the cottage with Elle for supplies.

'I made you some room in the wardrobe,' Holly said. With the camp bed set up in her already narrow bedroom, they were both suffering bruised shins from continually walking into the frame. Holly read her. 'I know it's not ideal, but it'll be like having a really, really long sleepover.'

Theo smiled. Holly was more than a friend; she was a sister. If she couldn't be with Niamh, she was in the right place with her. 'I wonder what'll happen to the cottage?'

'Mum says it's technically half Ciara's, wherever she is.'

'Hiding.' Theo's powers were pretty much where they were over the summer now. She could cast her sentience wide enough, but she couldn't sense Ciara anywhere, and a witch that powerful would stand out. She was shielding herself, or was somewhere very far away.

No one had seen her since the night of the coronation, or – as mundanes called it – *The Night of the Storm*. Not since 1987 had the weather people on TV had to apologise for failing to predict a freak weather occurrence. Theo and Holly were getting all the tea third hand through Elle, but apparently some HMRC sentients had read the waiters who worked in that tower in Manchester. They'd confirmed that Ciara was there, and had killed Dabney Hale.

That didn't explain the splattered corpse at the foot of the skyscraper – Luke's dad, it turns out – or where Luke was. HMRC just kept saying 'wait for the inquest', although Theo suspected they'd be waiting years. The security division at the coven was seriously investigating if Luke had killed Ciara, but Theo knew with her whole heart that that wasn't true, even if he *was* a witchfinder. It didn't add up. He'd had a million chances to kill all three of them – Niamh, Ciara *and* Theo – and he hadn't. *If* he was a witchfinder, he was really, really bad at it. He'd literally lived under a roof with them.

Theo's guess was that he was hiding too. Twenty-four witchfinders had died in Hekate House, their families since receiving visits from sentients to inform that their loved ones had perished in the storm. But others had survived and fled, and there'd be more besides. Of that, Theo had no doubt, and HMRC was going after them. Luke was probably pretty high on their Most Wanted list.

And so, Theo was orphaned. Again.

Elle appeared in the doorway, her coat still on. 'Right, I'm going to meet Leonie. I might be late. Will you lot be OK?' They said they would. 'You may use Deliveroo, but use it wisely. Theo, make sure she doesn't just order waffles and ice cream.'

Theo managed a thin smile. 'I promise.'

Holly ran downstairs to get the iPad so they could order waffles and ice cream, and Theo made a start on unpacking. She knelt on the floor and unzipped her case. It was pitiful, how little stuff she had. That said, it sure made it easier to keep moving around all the time.

'Hey,' a voice said. Theo looked up and saw Milo hovering in the doorframe. He wore his football kit, socks slouched around his ankles.

Neither said anything for a moment. Theo went first. 'So I live here now.'

He considered this. 'Is that weird?'

'It would have been,' Theo said, 'if we'd . . .'

Milo looked at her through his floppy, sandy hair. There was a faint, knowing smile on his lips.

Theo smiled too. 'What? What is it?'

'Do you trust me?'

'I guess.'

He said, 'Will you come with me? I wanna show you something.'

Theo stood and closed the wardrobe. 'What?'

There was a certain mischief in his eyes. 'It's a secret.' From behind his back, he produced her book, *The Song of Osiris*.

Chapter Sixty-Five

REUNION

Elle – Hebden Bridge, UK

Elle found Chinara and Leonie already waiting outside the garage. 'Sorry!' she said, running across the car park. 'You must be freezing. Come in.'

She unlocked the door and hurried the girls inside.

'Elle, what's this all about?' Leonie said, unravelling her scarf.

Elle didn't need to explain, because Ciara stepped out of the shadows as soon as they entered.

There was a split second of shocked silence and then Leonie said, 'Girl, what the fuck is up with your hair?'

Ciara smiled. 'Elle can't fix it. I guess I'm stuck with it. Ginger Spice, right?'

'You've been here the whole time?' Leonie looked to her. 'Elle?'

'I let her stay here. I didn't know what else to do.'

Leonie circled Ciara on the workshop floor. She looked her up and down. 'Did you kill Niamh?'

'Yes,' Ciara said at once.

Chinara silently slipped a hand around Leonie's wrist.

Elle stepped between them because she really thought Leonie might kill her.

'And I am sorry.' Ciara sank to her knees before Lee.

Elle faced her. Was she going to cry? Ciara had told Elle the truth immediately following the events at Hekate, although, as with Jez, she'd long suspected. Elle wasn't nearly as dumb as she liked to look. Leonie said nothing.

Ciara went on. 'I wish I hadn't. More than anything in the world, I wish she was here. I wish I could say I was possessed when I did it, but I don't know if that's true.'

'Ciara,' Leonie started, but she cut her off.

She wiped a tear off her cheek. 'All I ever wanted was to be Niamh. Careful what you wish for.' She took a breath. 'I *am* sorry. I can't make you believe me, and I deserve whatever it is you'll do to me, but I made a promise to Elle and I'm gonna keep it.'

Elle wished Niamh was here too. But Ciara was here, *now. You have to play the hand you're dealt* was what her gran would have said in times like this. After everything, she found she no longer wanted Ciara locked away in prison, even knowing what she did. She knew it wasn't to be, but she wanted her *friend*. Here. Was that so selfish?

In the gloom of the garage, Elle saw Leonie weighing all this up. She said nothing for a moment, and then, 'Bitch, I can't believe you're here. Get off the floor, you dickhead.' She pulled Ciara up into a hug, cautious at first, and then tight, a proper bear hug.

With her chin resting on Leonie's shoulder, Elle saw Ciara's eyes glisten. 'I missed you.'

Leonie couldn't say what Elle also felt, and that was *I missed you too*. Too much tragedy had happened for them to be able to admit it. 'You can't stay here, Ciara. Everyone knows.'

'I know,' Ciara said sadly. 'I have to go.'

Leonie let go of her and got a good look. 'You look better than the last time I saw you, even with the Rogue do.'

'I feel better.' Ciara looked tired, Elle thought, and hiding out in a garage probably hadn't helped. 'I don't know if you heard, but I saved the world. Technically from myself, but . . . it's a step in the right direction?'

'Where's the Seal of Solomon?'

'Dust.'

Leonie looked like she was about to argue, but Chinara stepped in. 'It's for the best.'

Leonie nodded. 'What about Luke? You didn't . . . ?'

'No! He's gone. If the witchfinders get to him, *they'll* kill him. I shielded him for twenty-four hours, but now he's on his own. I don't know where he is.'

Elle was confused. 'I thought the government promised to help HMRC get rid of the witchfinders? Don't tell me I saved that smarmy git for nothing?'

Ciara grinned. 'I paid said smarmy git a visit last night. I think he'll behave.'

Chinara was rather more serious. 'We don't know if Eric Harkaway was the only witchfinder hiding in government. There might be more.'

'And HMRC is falling to fucking pieces,' added Leonie. 'The last priestess was executed; the new one was an imposter – no offence.'

'None taken.'

'This could be it, for real. This could be the part when HMRC is done, like finito, done. Fuckin' hell; is Diaspora now the biggest coven in the country?'

Elle thought Leonie didn't seem thrilled at that notion. None of them belonged to HMRC any more, but it had been a solid fact, a monolith, at the centre of their lives since the day they'd learned they were witches. Being a witch without the matronly, watchful eye of the coven was an unsettling prospect. Elle didn't like it one bit. Maybe she'd subconsciously got used to it being there, taken comfort in it from afar. Then again, she used to say that about the police until Leonie had taught her better.

'You said you needed our help?' Chinara asked softly.

Ciara looked to her. 'Elle does. I need to get the fuck out of town before HMRC get their shit together, but I – we – owe Elle this much.'

'What is it?' Leonie asked.

Together, they surveyed the statue of Jez, still stuck in his dingy office. After the initial shock had worn off, Leonie read him, verifying her tall tale. 'Elle, what the fuck?'

'I don't know!' she said. 'We had a big fight and then . . . boom!'

Chinara regarded the statue, and then Elle, with suspicion. 'Aren't you a Level 4?'

Elle nodded.

'I doubt that, somehow.'

Leonie added, 'Elle, did you try at *all* when you took the Eriksdottir Test?'

Elle shrugged. 'I don't know. I think I was on my period, and it was hard.'

Even with everything, her friends laughed. This would be the last time they were together; Elle knew it. Ciara had to go far, far away. 'Can you help?' she asked. 'People are starting to ask questions, so either we fix him or we start wiping people who knew Jez.'

'Elle . . .' Leonie said.

Nope, those were the options, pick one. 'I can't go to Grierlings, Lee. What about the kids?'

Ciara stepped up. 'I think we can do this. We have a Level 6 sentient; an adept; the most powerful elemental in the UK, and – apparently – a Level fucking 19 healer.'

Chinara pursed her lips, still examining what was left of Elle's husband. 'In theory, it'd be like a teleport. We take him apart, heal him, and put him back together. But that's a *theory*.'

'Have you performed a teleport before?' Leonie asked.

Chinara hadn't, but Elle and Ciara had. 'We had to learn pretty fast when it was just us during the war,' Ciara explained. 'It's not easy though.'

Elle too had been drafted in to help HMRC teleports during the conflict, but that was ten years ago. She hoped it was like riding a bike.

Ciara went on. 'If we work together, we can do it.'

'Thanks, *Sesame Street*. Very empowering,' Leonie grumbled.

'You've taken things apart and put them back together,' Chinara reminded her.

'Like Ikea furniture, not *people*!'

'Please?' Elle said. 'I can't leave him like this. I . . . I can't imagine what he's going through.' A tear rolled down her cheek until she caught it with the end of her sleeve. 'Please?'

Leonie and Ciara must have spoken telepathically because they both gave a subtle nod. Leonie exhaled deeply, giving in. 'Form a circle,' she said.

'Thank you,' Elle said.

'Thank us if it works,' said Chinara. 'We need some candles. And salt.'

The women worked diligently, preparing the room for

the ritual. The salt circle would – hopefully – keep Jez's essence within its confines. All set up, they took their positions. This wasn't a quick fix. They joined hands around the rock formation and began, settling in for the long haul. There was no telling how long this would take.

Elle focused on her breathing, and the warmth of Ciara and Leonie's palms in hers. She felt herself slipping away into a trance state. Gradually, she became aware of their energies running through her. *Connection*. They were one stream, one current. She'd never felt Chinara's fire spirit before. It was remarkable, blinding yellow, like looking up at the sun in an eclipse. And it had been a long time since she'd felt Ciara up close, mercurial lilacs, cool lavender.

The current whipped around the circle, like an engine starting up. Colours danced in her vision and Elle felt her own gifts amplify, her skin getting hotter. Her feet left the floor as the sheer power running through them lifted her up. A warm breeze blew her hair off her face.

Hold steady, Leonie's voice told them all.

They each levitated about a foot off the ground. Elle gripped their hands tight, and her friends gripped right back.

The candlelight erupted suddenly, each candle blazing, and the room smelled sulphurous. Elle felt sweat beads on her lip.

I sense him. I have him, Ciara told them.

Gently does it, Leonie urged.

Elle too sensed Jez's presence. If he was in the mix, she could lift him out, heal him. That was what she did. She opened her eyes and, in the middle of their circle, the statue had dissolved into a tornado of particles. It looked like a dirt devil, but, in amongst rocks and soil, there were gold embers. They were *him*.

Elle reminded herself of her husband in better times. His white teeth (paid for in Bodrum in 2018); the freckles on his arms; his excellent bum; his freaky left little toe that never grew a nail for some reason.

And the happier times: his crow's feet when he smiled. His hands as he slipped the wedding band on her finger. The arms that spooned her in bed.

One cell at a time, Elle flipped them into their human form. The spell spread and the swirling particles caught fire. Soon, the witches contained a spiralling gold mass.

Hold him, Leonie commanded. Elle saw her and Ciara focus, their eyes narrowing, as if they were forcing his cells into a solid mass. Elle closed her eyes, hoping her memories of Jez would transmit to Leonie and Ciara and they would get it right.

She also trusted in nature. This was Jez's original state, the way he was supposed to be. Gaia didn't make mistakes. What was it they called it? A factory reset?

From very far away, Elle heard him scream. The howl grew closer and closer until it filled her ears. The room was bright, very bright, but if she squinted, she could see the shape of a man hunched over where the statue had been.

With everything she had, Elle scanned the form, looking for red patches, parts that didn't seem normal. She pumped him full of her radiance, and she both felt and heard things click into place within his body.

Stop! Ciara called. *That's enough.*

But Elle didn't stop. She dropped Leonie and Ciara's hands and instead fell to her knees next to Jez. She cradled him in her arms and pressed as hard as she could. She felt lightheaded, drained, but she had to make this right. She continued to channel her radiance into his body. She felt him breathing, felt the sweat on his skin, but she had to be sure.

She hardly felt Leonie's hand loop under her arms. 'Elle, we did it, stop.'

Elle was so busy weeping; she hardly heard his voice. It sounded so normal; it was abnormal. 'Elle? What's going on? Babe?'

He wore an oily overall because they hadn't been able to rematerialise what he'd been wearing. He sipped from a cup of sweet, milky tea she'd prepared for him, because those cure everything.

They'd come outside to talk because the office cabin still smelled sulphuric. However, on stepping outside, Elle remembered that tonight was bonfire night, and the air already had that gunpowder tinge. The pair perched on some stacked tyres outside the garage and watched the fireworks display finish over Hebden Bridge.

It was a cold evening, but she was just glad to be out of that office. Inside, her friends waited in the workshop. Elle could hear them chatting.

She explained – or tried to at least – what had happened, but Jez seemed confused. 'What do you remember?' she said.

Jez frowned. 'It was like . . . nothing. I was asleep. You know how you know you're asleep? Sorta like that, I suppose. I dreamt about food. A lot. You know when you want to wake up, but you can't?'

Elle felt tears push behind her nose. 'Jez, I'm so sorry.'

'And I was gone for that long?'

She nodded. She inhaled sharply, unable to hold in the sob.

'Elle, babe, don't cry. Please. I'm sorry too.'

They could go into whether or not he'd deserved it, but Elle knew he hadn't. They were husband and wife, there were other ways to torture each other than with magic.

Elle wondered how much of their final conversation he recalled. 'She came looking for you. Jessica.' Elle sipped her own tea. Jez said nothing. 'What do we do now?'

'I dunno. We don't have to decide anything here, do we? We go home I suppose.'

This all felt very final, but – after what she'd done – it no longer felt like the end of her world. Just the end of her marriage, perhaps, and that felt like a feat she could weather. 'Is it *our* home any more?' He didn't have a reply to that. 'Jez, what about the kids? They'll be so gutted.'

'We've got time. We need to talk things through. And you have a choice as well, never mind what Holly wants. What about you, Elle? What do *you* want? I wouldn't be surprised if you threw me out. I would in your shoes.'

'Would you? Are you saying you want to go?'

He looked up at the gods, exasperated. 'Elle, love, I don't know. I'm tired, and hungry and I want a shower. I can't rush this.'

Elle shook her head, frustrated. When she'd been eight, her mother threw her dad out, telling her all the gory details about his sordid affairs. Eight years old. She was determined that she wouldn't treat her children as pawns in some big divorce game. 'But what do we tell the kids, Jez? They think you left.'

Jez frowned. 'Elle, what do you mean by *kids*?'

And now Elle was the confused one. 'Milo and Holly.'

His forehead creased. He took her hand in his, stroked it. He spoke softly, in a way he hadn't for many years, and it unlocked the most awful ache buried in her heart. 'Elle, darlin', we've only got our Hols. Milo was stillborn; do you remember?'

And Elle *did*.

Chapter Sixty-Six

BLUEBELL WOODS

Ciara – Hebden Bridge, UK

A little ahead of the others, Ciara began her descent into the forest. Autumn was turning to winter and the air was starting to bite, even for witches. The canopy of Hardcastle Crags was mottled gold and russet, the forest floor thick with leaf litter. Ciara landed and sniffed the air.

Leonie landed alongside her. 'Do you feel it?' she asked.

'What is that?' Leonie said.

'Nothing good.' The night felt sly and knowing. The forest was too silent, like it was holding its breath so it wouldn't be found. No foxes, no owls, no badgers. Silence. The full moon waited expectantly.

Chinara, Elle's arms wrapped around her neck, landed effortlessly in the dell. Elle, stricken, hopped to her feet. 'I don't understand. How can this be happening? How could I . . . how could I forget my baby . . . ?' She was pale, fraught.

'Elle, it's gonna be OK,' Leonie said, convincing no one. Ciara wouldn't lie. This was bad.

They'd gone directly to Elle's home in Todmorden, only

to find a very confused Holly home alone. It hadn't taken any effort to figure out where Theo was, she was a very noisy young witch. She and Leonie had sensed her at once.

She was in the woods.

'Wait!' Ciara snapped. 'There.'

On foot, she darted uphill to the clearing where they'd buried her former body. The others followed close behind. Ciara had no idea what she was running towards, but she was fuelled by adrenaline, by Gaia. She felt nocturnal, animal, her senses heightened and attuned to the forest.

The trees thinned out as they reached the meadow. She saw a figure walking towards them, a young man, his hair flopping over his face. Elle ran alongside her.

'Milo!' Elle cried. 'What on earth are you doing?'

'Stop!' Ciara put out an arm to stop Elle. This wasn't her son. It wasn't anyone's son. That evening, days ago, in the cottage kitchen – she *knew* something was off about the boy. If she'd spent any significant time with him before now, she might have sensed it sooner, but it was much, much too late for that.

'Oh my goddess,' Leonie breathed, just behind her.

The boy passed behind a tree, and emerged a different man: taller, older. A man Ciara recognised. '*Jude?*' she breathed, her throat dry. 'I know him,' she told the others.

They said nothing, and she realised time had stopped still. Elle, Leonie, Chinara . . . their faces and bodies were totally frozen.

Ciara whipped around to face the man who'd left her high and dry over a decade ago. He hadn't aged a day. He looked exactly the same as he had all those years ago: the same shy, asymmetrical mouth, the incredible ocean eyes. 'How are you doing this?' she demanded. Jude only smiled as he came closer, ambling through the undergrowth, hands in pockets, kicking up dry leaves. 'Jude, stop!'

He reached her position and gave her a kiss. She swerved her head, so his lips only grazed her cheek.

'It's been a while, Ciara. I thought you'd have figured it out by now. You had long enough. Come on! The clue was right there! St Jude? The Patron Saint of lost causes and desperation. It seemed fitting for you.'

She dared to look into those incredible eyes. She'd often imagined what it'd feel like if she ever saw him again, but she had grossly underestimated how much her chest would hurt. 'Who are you?' her voice was a girlish whisper. Pitiful.

He whispered in her ear. 'You already know my name . . .'

She looked at him and he smiled broadly. 'No . . .'

'Yep.' *Demons can appear as anything they want; within reason, within nature.*

What a fucking fool she'd been. 'What did you do to Theo?'

Lucifer grinned again. 'The same thing I did to you. I found the thing she wanted the most.' He took hold of her chin and kissed her hard this time. 'I'll be seeing you soon, beautiful. We have unfinished business, don't you think?'

And, for a moment, Ciara saw his real face, and his real wings. He spread them wide and with one mighty flap took flight. The wind beat her backwards into a frozen Elle, and time resumed as normal.

'Where did he go?' Elle cried, catching her. Ciara clutched her head, trying to stop it exploding. 'Ciara! Where did he go? Ciara?'

'What's wrong?' Leonie added.

'It was Lucifer,' Ciara breathed, talking to no one in particular. She couldn't seem to blink. 'It was *always* Lucifer.'

'Are you fucking kidding?' Leonie snapped.

'My Milo?' Elle asked, eyes wide as the moon.

'He's been right here, among us, the whole time?' Chinara added. 'Why? For what purpose?'

'No, it's longer than that,' Ciara said, her brain desperately trying to make sense of things. 'He's been in our lives for *years*. Milo, Jude, fuck knows who else . . .'

'But why?' Leonie insisted.

They were distracted by the sound of footsteps crunching through the forest. Ciara whirled around to see Theo emerge from the thicket. Her face and clothes were blood-soaked, her raven hair plastered to her forehead and cheeks.

She was alive. Ciara ran to her. 'Oh my goddess, Theo. Are you OK? Did he hurt you?' Only then, as she gripped her hands, did she see that they were caked in thick, wet mud. Theo looked at her, unblinking. She was shaking.

'Theo?' Ciara said, suddenly seeing herself in this girl. 'What have you *done*?'

She heard a twig snap. Ciara looked up just in time to see a pale foot step into the moonlit clearing.

ACKNOWLEDGMENTS

Heartfelt thanks to the following people:

Nathan Asher
Natasha Bardon
Charlotte Brown
Ignacio Gómez Calvo
LeBria Casher
Emilie Chambeyron
Fleur Clarke
Nicola Coughlan
Marie Cummings
Russell T. Davies
Katelyn Dougherty
Fairyloot
Max Gallant
Darren Garrett
Helen Gould
Samar Hammam
HarperVoyager UK
Lana Harper
Joanne Harris

Maureen Johnson
David Levithan
Lindsay Kelk
Holly Macdonald
Aoife McMahon
Kiran Milwood Hargrave
Rebecca Marsh
Ivan Mulcahy
Left Bank Pictures
Anne O'Brien
Louise O'Neill
Roisin O'Shea
Penguin Random House USA
Lisa Marie Pompilio
Sam Powick
Nidhi Pugalia
Sian Richefond
Katie Roberts
Kat Sarfas Coviello
Marc Simonsson
Samantha Shannon
Mary Stone
Sallyanne Sweeney
Elizabeth Vaziri
Robyn Watts
Maria Weber
Constanze Wehnes
Margaux Weisman
Jaime Witcomb
Kim Young

And all of the booksellers, librarians, reviewers and fans who have brought the coven to life around the world. You have changed my life, and I love you.